BASED ON THE *NEW YORK TIMES* BESTSELLING SERIES

Five Nights at Freddy's™

FAZBEAR FRIGHTS

THE FOURTH CLOSET

The Graphic Novel

BY SCOTT CAWTHON AND
KIRA BREED-WRISLEY

ADAPTED BY CHRISTOPHER HASTINGS

ILLUSTRATED BY DIANA CAMERO
COLORS BY EVA DE LA CRUZ
LETTERS BY MIKE FIORENTINO

graphix
An Imprint of
■SCHOLASTIC

All rights reserved. Published by Scholastic Inc., *Publishers since 1920.* SCHOLASTIC and associated logos are trademarks and/or registered trademarks of Scholastic Inc.

The publisher does not have any control over and does not assume any responsibility for author or third-party websites or their content.

No part of this publication may be reproduced, stored in a retrieval system, or transmitted in any form or by any means, electronic, mechanical, photocopying, recording, or otherwise, without written permission of the publisher. For information regarding permission, write to Scholastic Inc., Attention: Permissions Department, 557 Broadway, New York, NY 10012.

This book is a work of fiction. Names, characters, places, and incidents are either the product of the author's imagination or are used fictitiously, and any resemblance to actual persons, living or dead, business establishments, events, or locales is entirely coincidental.

ISBN 978-1-338-74116-2

10 9 8 7 6 5 4 3 2 1   22 23 24 25 26

Printed in the U.S.A.   40

First printing 2022

Edited by Michael Petranek

Book design by Jeff Shake

Inks by Diana Camero

Colors by Eva de la Cruz

Letters by Mike Fiorentino

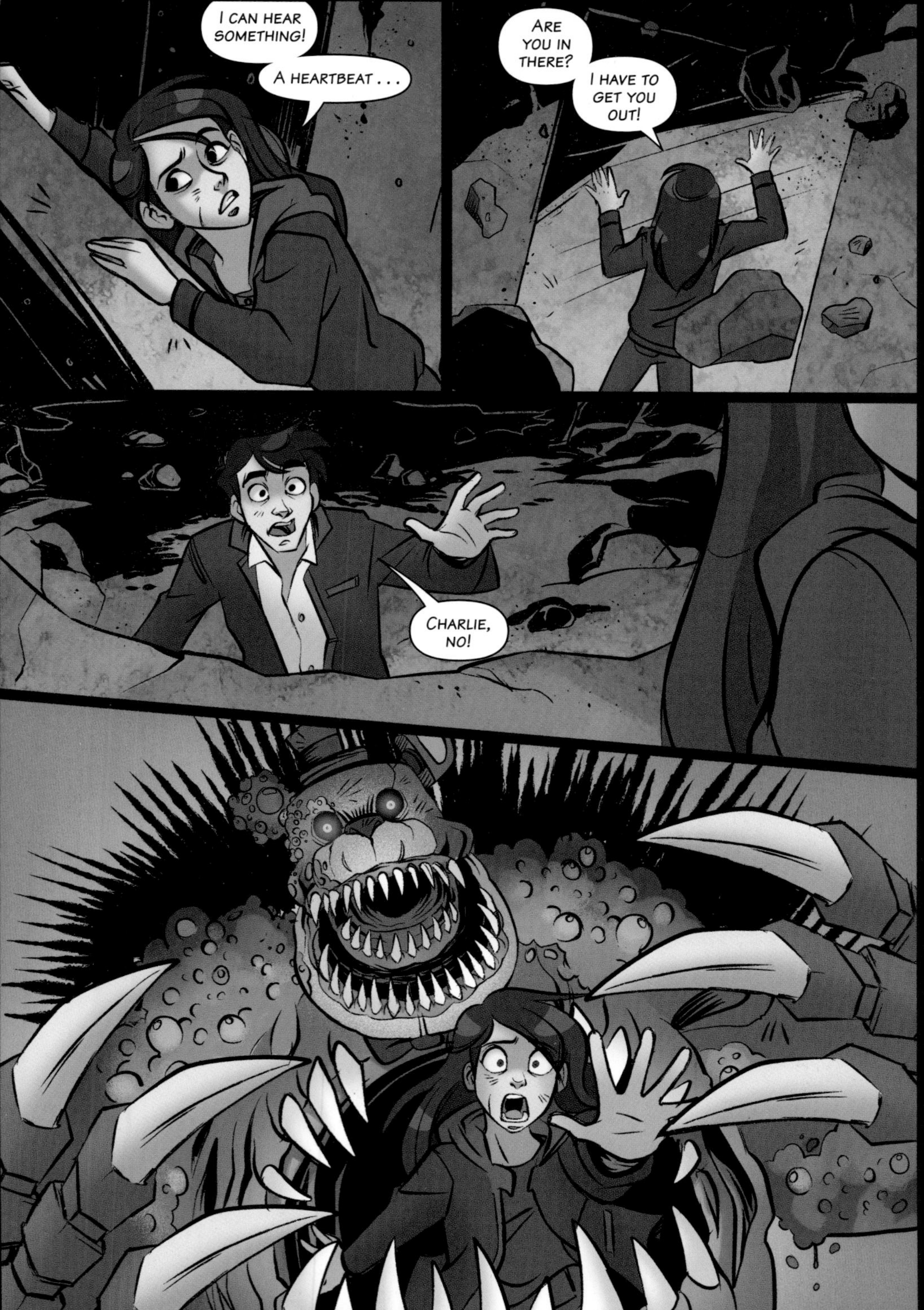
I CAN HEAR SOMETHING!
A HEARTBEAT . . .
ARE YOU IN THERE?
I HAVE TO GET YOU OUT!
CHARLIE, NO!

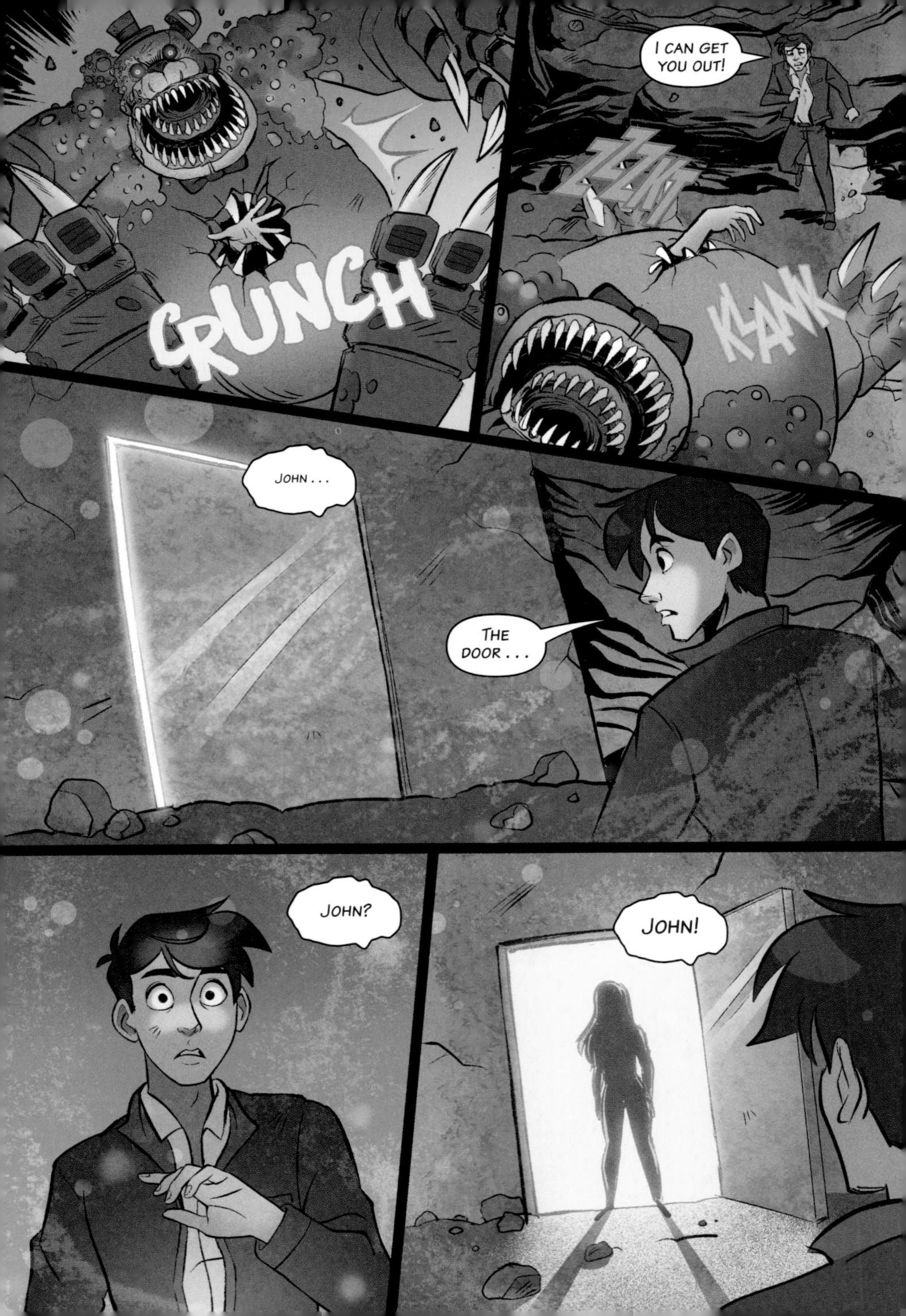
CRUNCH
I CAN GET YOU OUT!
ZZZKT
KLANK
JOHN . . .
THE DOOR . . .
JOHN?
JOHN!

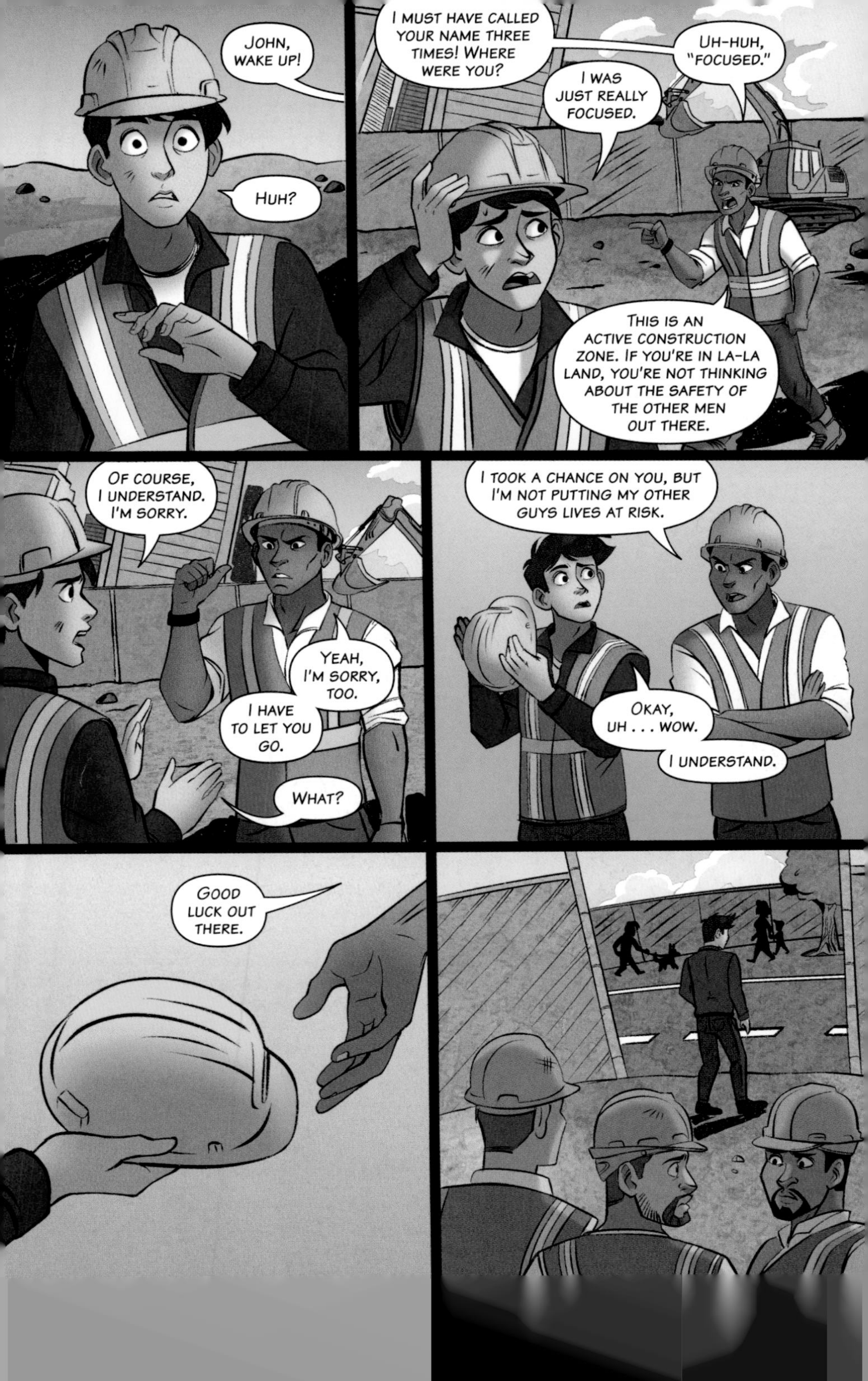
JOHN, WAKE UP!
HUH?
I MUST HAVE CALLED YOUR NAME THREE TIMES! WHERE WERE YOU?
I WAS JUST REALLY FOCUSED.
UH-HUH, "FOCUSED."
THIS IS AN ACTIVE CONSTRUCTION ZONE. IF YOU'RE IN LA-LA LAND, YOU'RE NOT THINKING ABOUT THE SAFETY OF THE OTHER MEN OUT THERE.
OF COURSE, I UNDERSTAND. I'M SORRY.
YEAH, I'M SORRY, TOO.
I HAVE TO LET YOU GO.
WHAT?
I TOOK A CHANCE ON YOU, BUT I'M NOT PUTTING MY OTHER GUYS LIVES AT RISK.
OKAY, UH . . . WOW.
I UNDERSTAND.
GOOD LUCK OUT THERE.

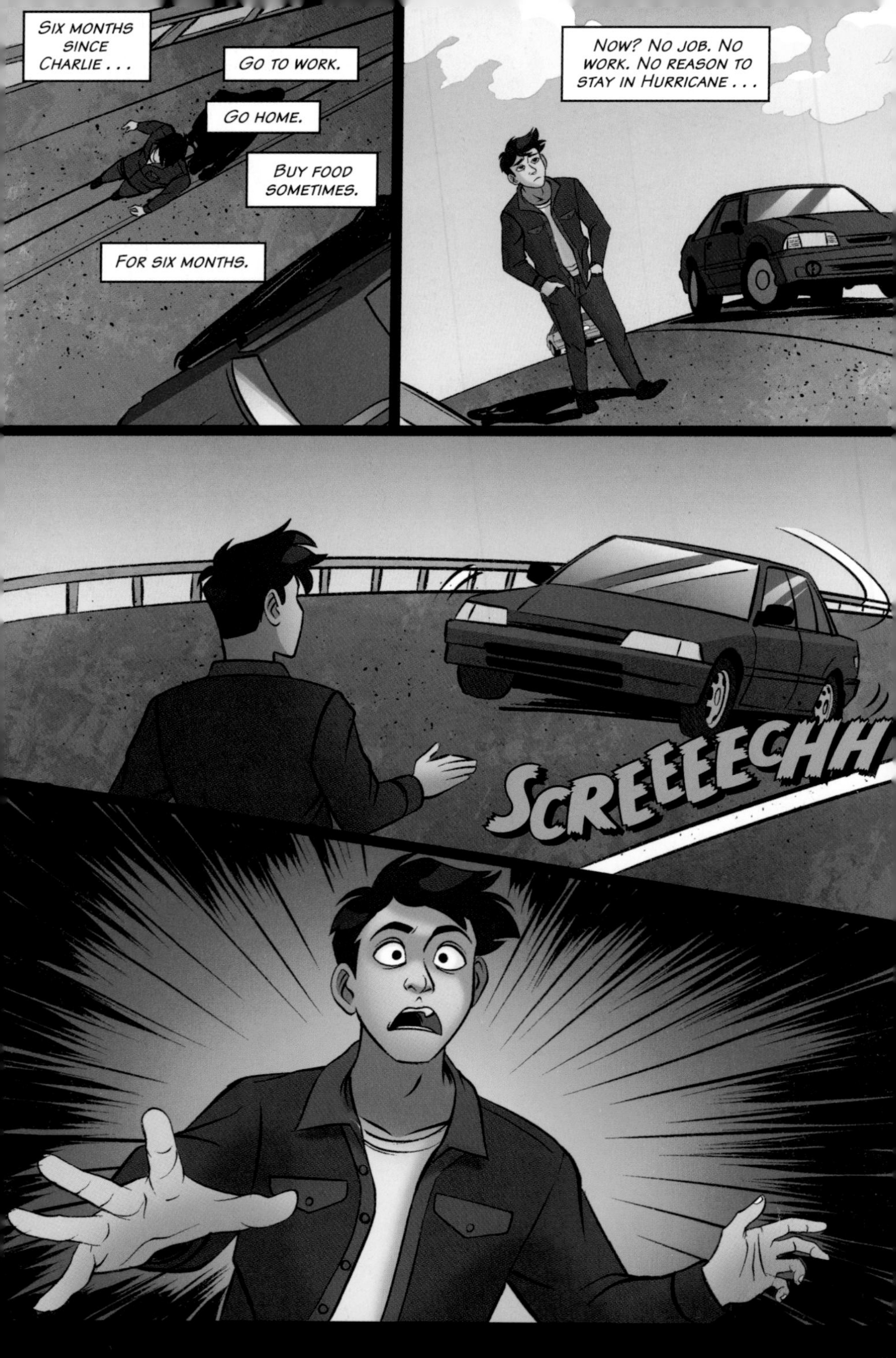
SIX MONTHS SINCE CHARLIE . . .
GO TO WORK.
GO HOME.
BUY FOOD SOMETIMES.
FOR SIX MONTHS.
NOW? NO JOB. NO WORK. NO REASON TO STAY IN HURRICANE . . .
SCREEEECHH

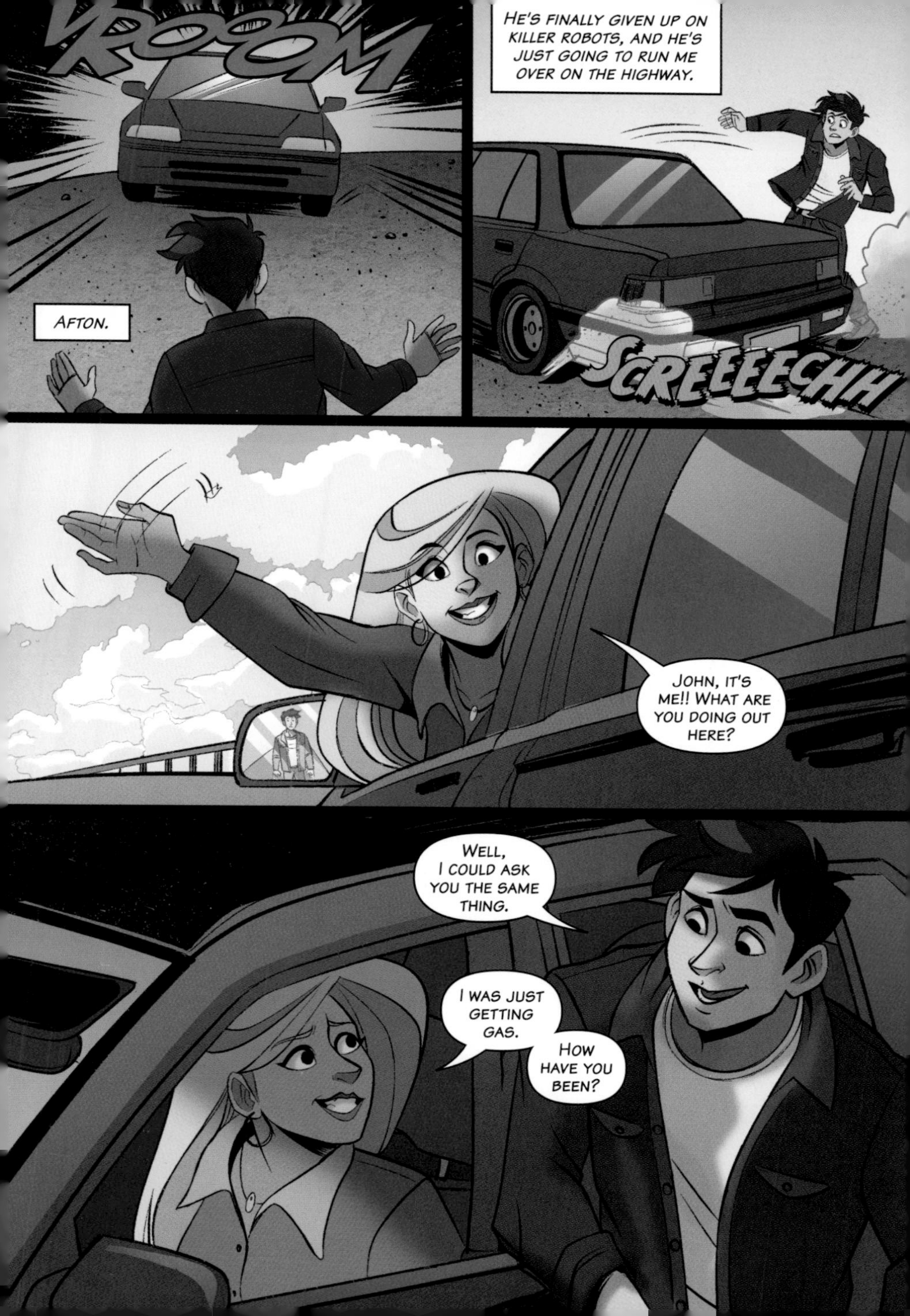
VROOOM
AFTON.
HE'S FINALLY GIVEN UP ON KILLER ROBOTS, AND HE'S JUST GOING TO RUN ME OVER ON THE HIGHWAY.
SCREEEECHH
JOHN, IT'S ME!! WHAT ARE YOU DOING OUT HERE?
WELL, I COULD ASK YOU THE SAME THING.
I WAS JUST GETTING GAS.
HOW HAVE YOU BEEN?

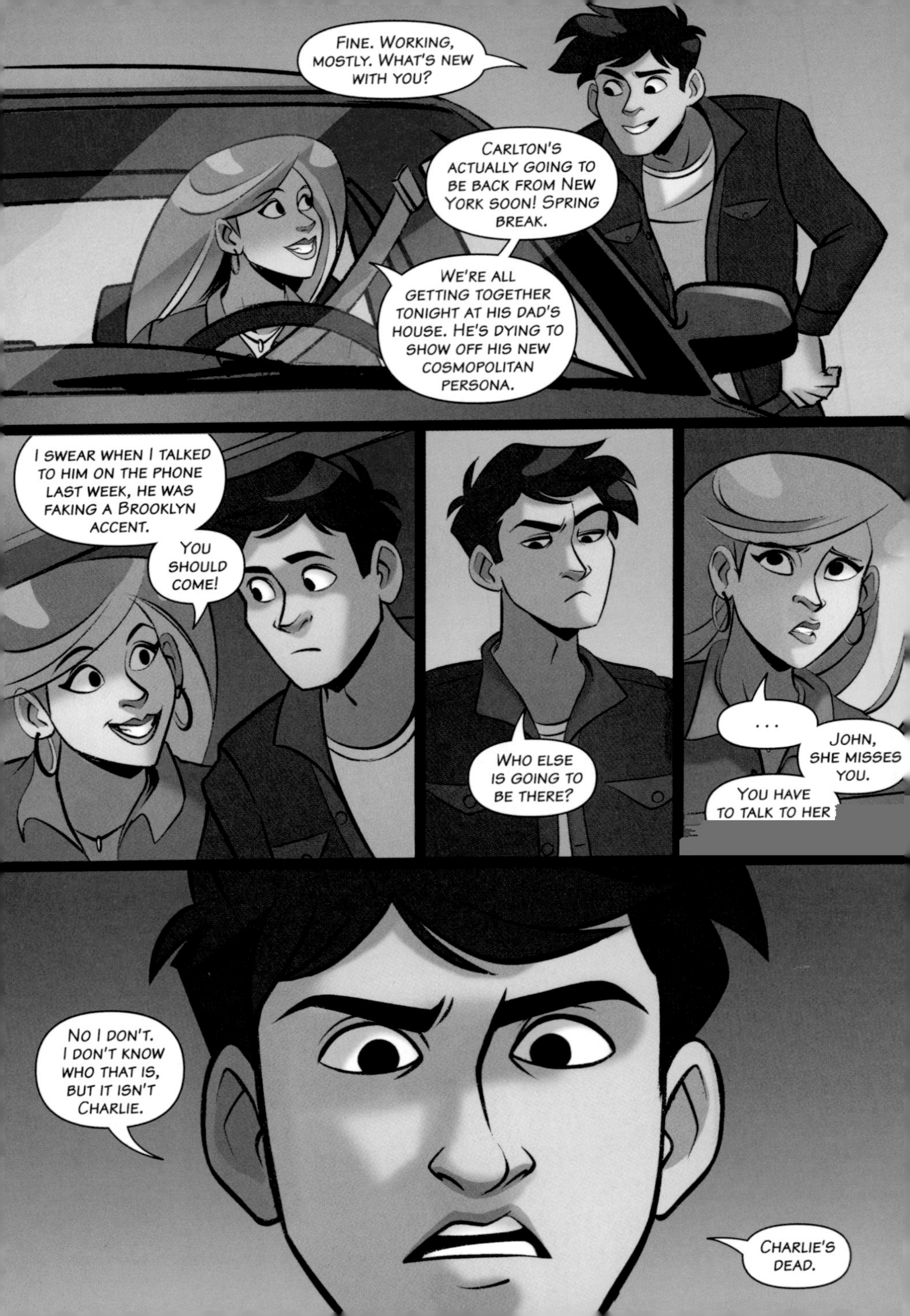
FINE. WORKING, MOSTLY. WHAT'S NEW WITH YOU?
CARLTON'S ACTUALLY GOING TO BE BACK FROM NEW YORK SOON! SPRING BREAK.
WE'RE ALL GETTING TOGETHER TONIGHT AT HIS DAD'S HOUSE. HE'S DYING TO SHOW OFF HIS NEW COSMOPOLITAN PERSONA.
I SWEAR WHEN I TALKED TO HIM ON THE PHONE LAST WEEK, HE WAS FAKING A BROOKLYN ACCENT.
YOU SHOULD COME!
WHO ELSE IS GOING TO BE THERE?
...
JOHN, SHE MISSES YOU.
YOU HAVE TO TALK TO HER
NO I DON'T. I DON'T KNOW WHO THAT IS, BUT IT ISN'T CHARLIE.
CHARLIE'S DEAD.

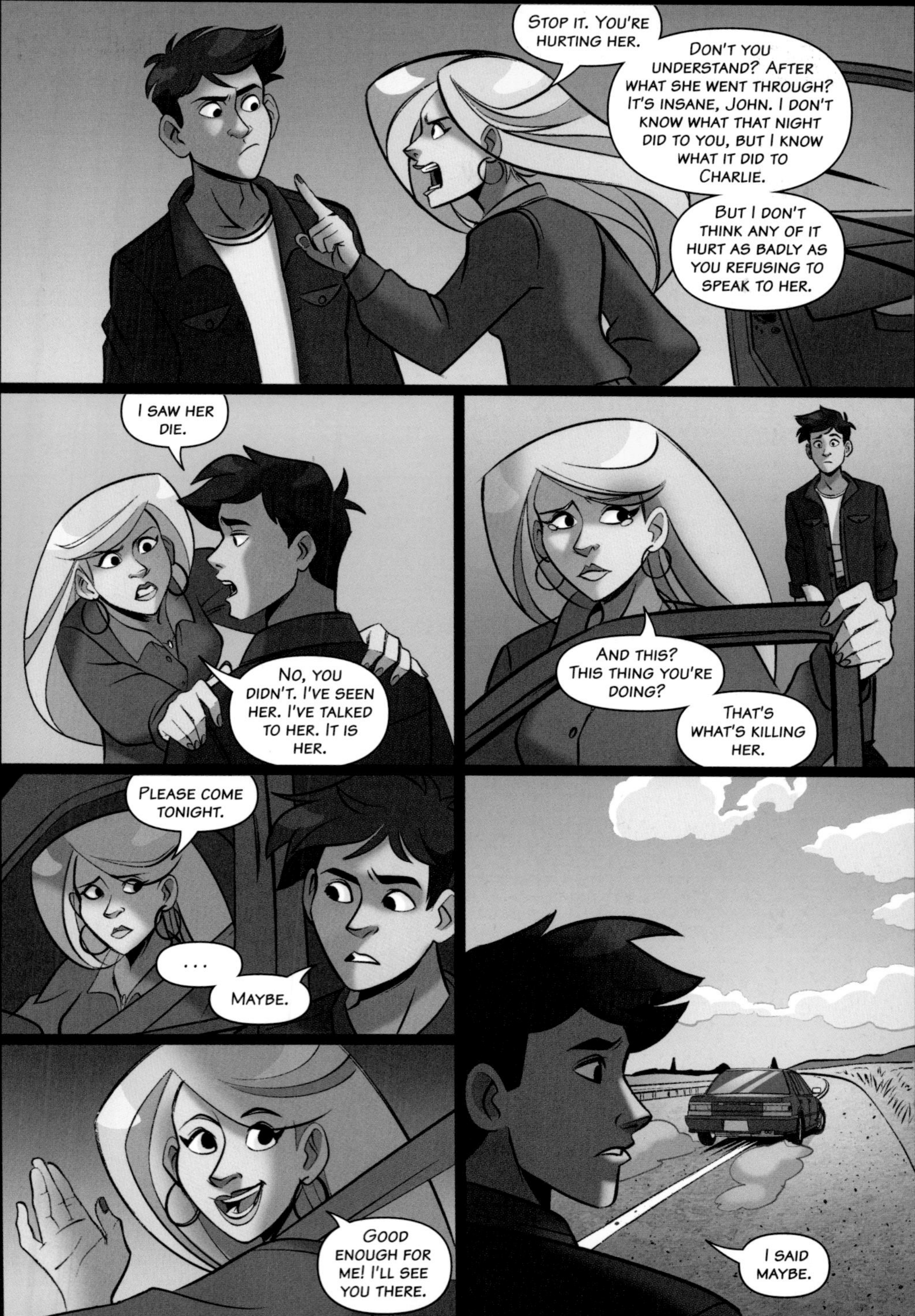
STOP IT. YOU'RE HURTING HER.
DON'T YOU UNDERSTAND? AFTER WHAT SHE WENT THROUGH? IT'S INSANE, JOHN. I DON'T KNOW WHAT THAT NIGHT DID TO YOU, BUT I KNOW WHAT IT DID TO CHARLIE.
BUT I DON'T THINK ANY OF IT HURT AS BADLY AS YOU REFUSING TO SPEAK TO HER.
I SAW HER DIE.
NO, YOU DIDN'T. I'VE SEEN HER. I'VE TALKED TO HER. IT IS HER.
AND THIS? THIS THING YOU'RE DOING?
THAT'S WHAT'S KILLING HER.
PLEASE COME TONIGHT.
...
MAYBE.
GOOD ENOUGH FOR ME! I'LL SEE YOU THERE.
I SAID MAYBE.

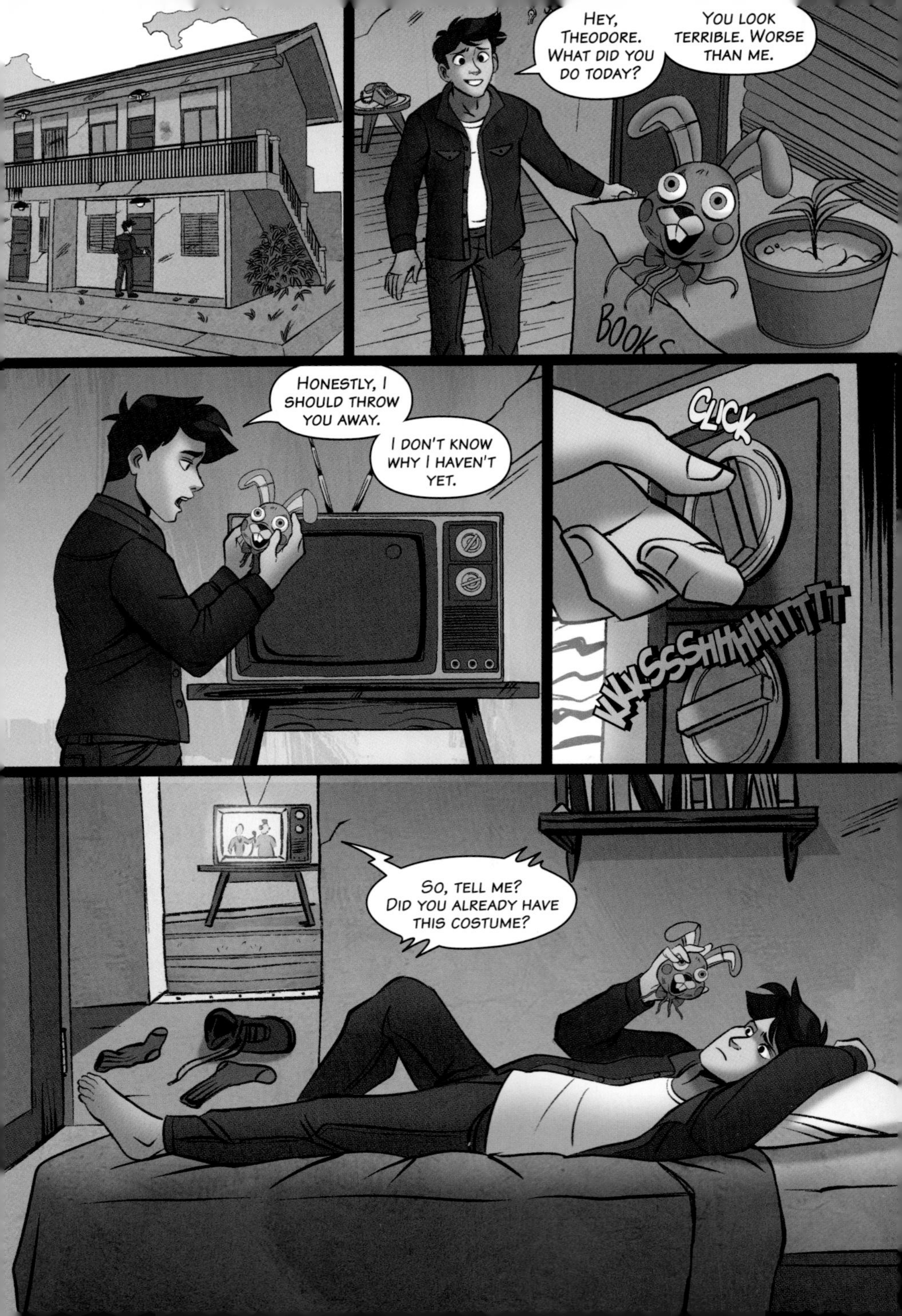
Hey, Theodore. What did you do today?
You look terrible. Worse than me.
BOOKS
Honestly, I should throw you away.
I don't know why I haven't yet.
CLICK
KKKSSSHHHHTTTT
So, tell me? Did you already have this costume?

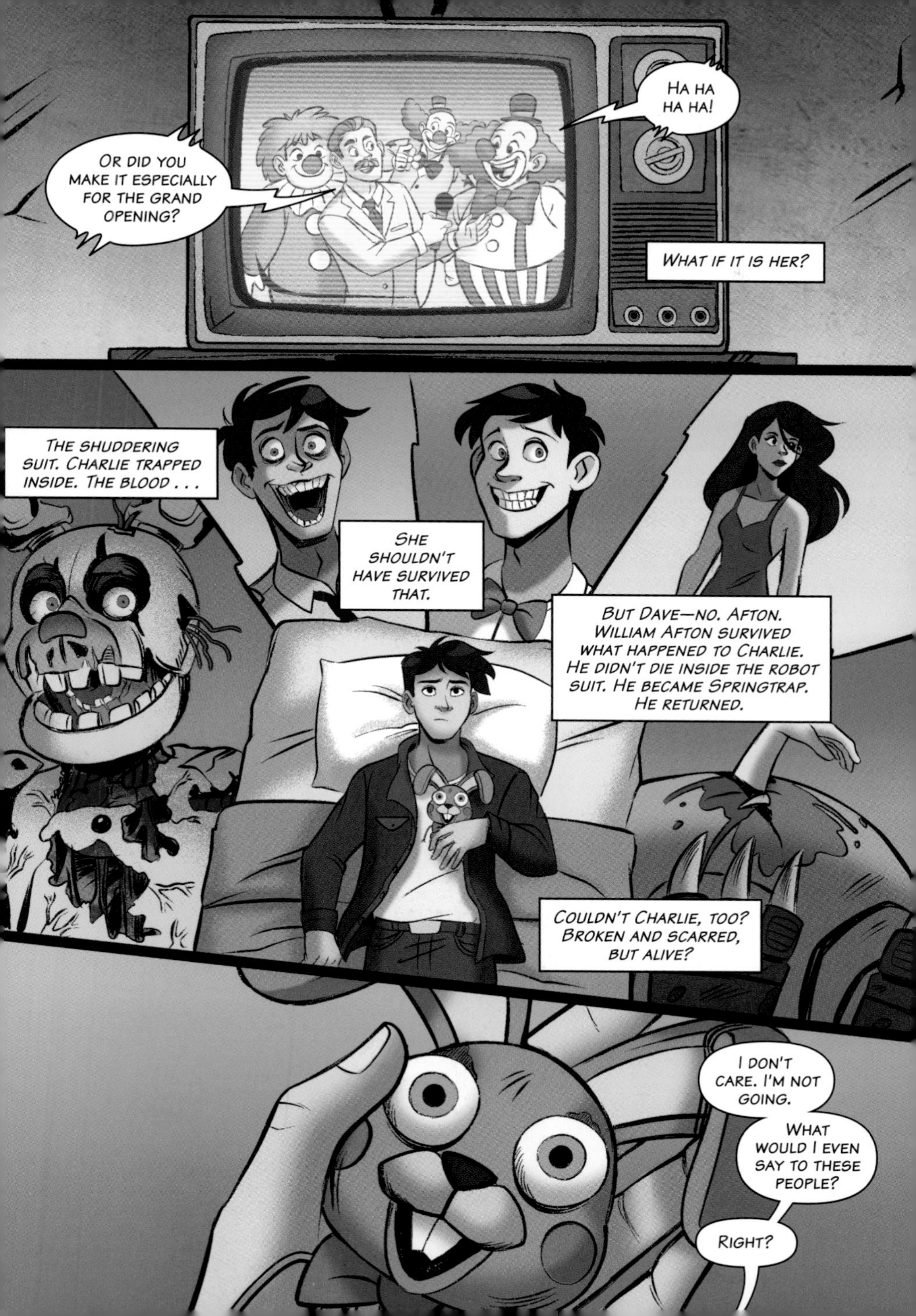
Or did you make it especially for the grand opening?
Ha ha ha ha!
What if it is her?
The shuddering suit. Charlie trapped inside. The blood . . .
She shouldn't have survived that.
But Dave—no. Afton. William Afton survived what happened to Charlie. He didn't die inside the robot suit. He became Springtrap. He returned.
Couldn't Charlie, too? Broken and scarred, but alive?
I don't care. I'm not going.
What would I even say to these people?
Right?

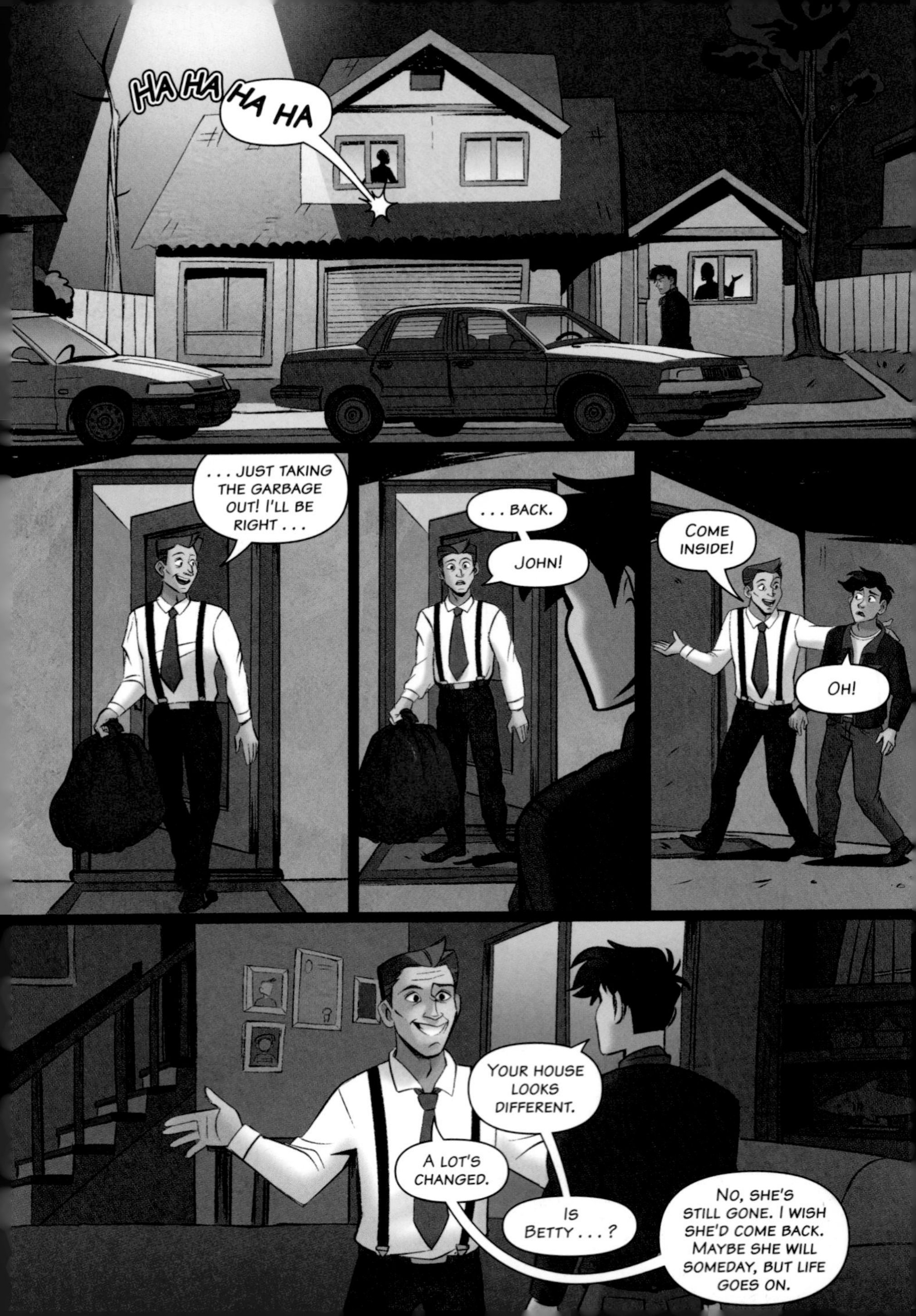
HA HA HA HA
. . . JUST TAKING THE GARBAGE OUT! I'LL BE RIGHT . . .
. . . BACK.
JOHN!
COME INSIDE!
OH!
YOUR HOUSE LOOKS DIFFERENT.
A LOT'S CHANGED.
IS BETTY . . . ?
NO, SHE'S STILL GONE. I WISH SHE'D COME BACK. MAYBE SHE WILL SOMEDAY, BUT LIFE GOES ON.

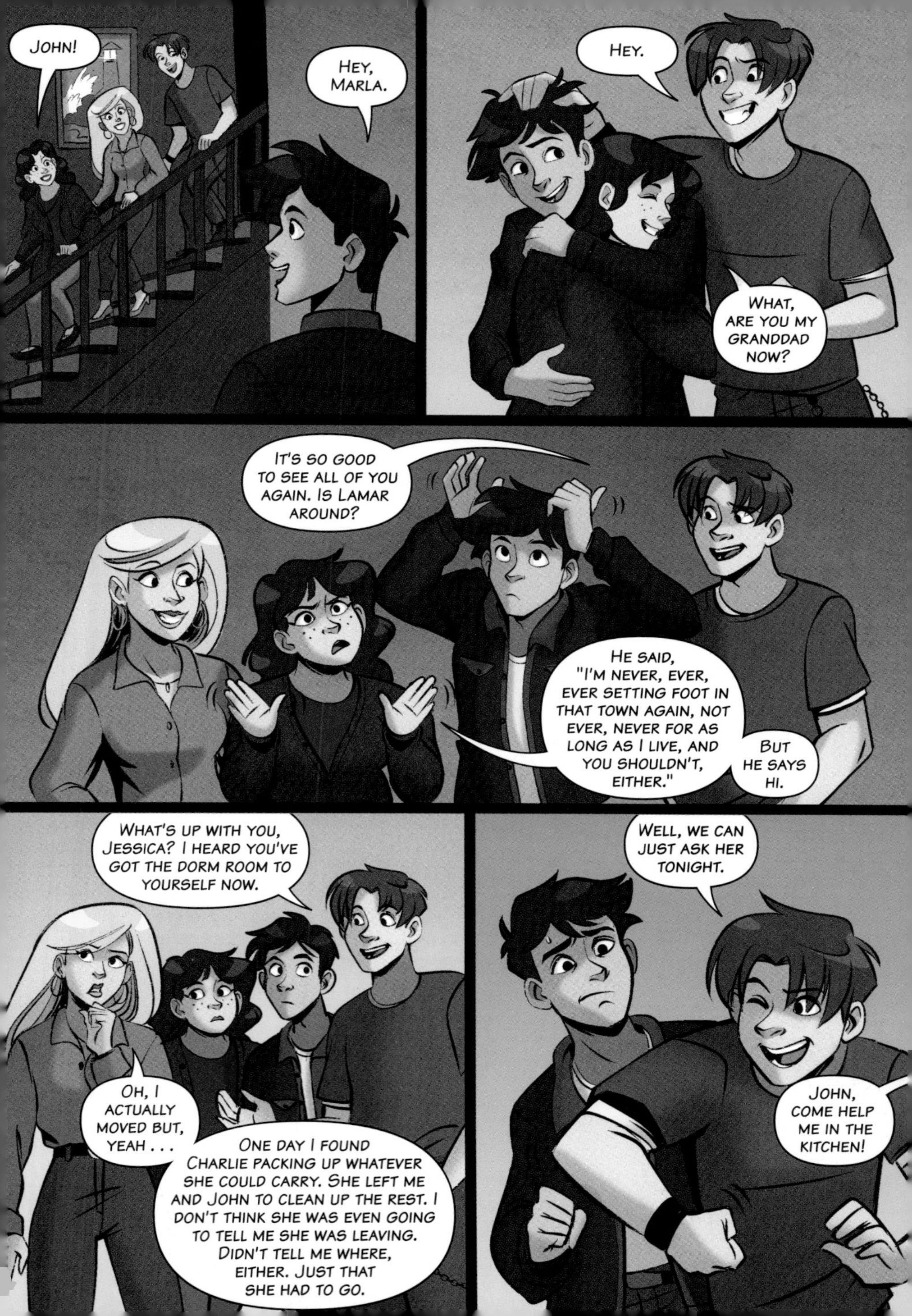
JOHN!
HEY, MARLA.
HEY.
WHAT, ARE YOU MY GRANDDAD NOW?
IT'S SO GOOD TO SEE ALL OF YOU AGAIN. IS LAMAR AROUND?
HE SAID, "I'M NEVER, EVER, EVER SETTING FOOT IN THAT TOWN AGAIN, NOT EVER, NEVER FOR AS LONG AS I LIVE, AND YOU SHOULDN'T, EITHER."
BUT HE SAYS HI.
WHAT'S UP WITH YOU, JESSICA? I HEARD YOU'VE GOT THE DORM ROOM TO YOURSELF NOW.
OH, I ACTUALLY MOVED BUT, YEAH . . .
ONE DAY I FOUND CHARLIE PACKING UP WHATEVER SHE COULD CARRY. SHE LEFT ME AND JOHN TO CLEAN UP THE REST. I DON'T THINK SHE WAS EVEN GOING TO TELL ME SHE WAS LEAVING. DIDN'T TELL ME WHERE, EITHER. JUST THAT SHE HAD TO GO.
WELL, WE CAN JUST ASK HER TONIGHT.
JOHN, COME HELP ME IN THE KITCHEN!

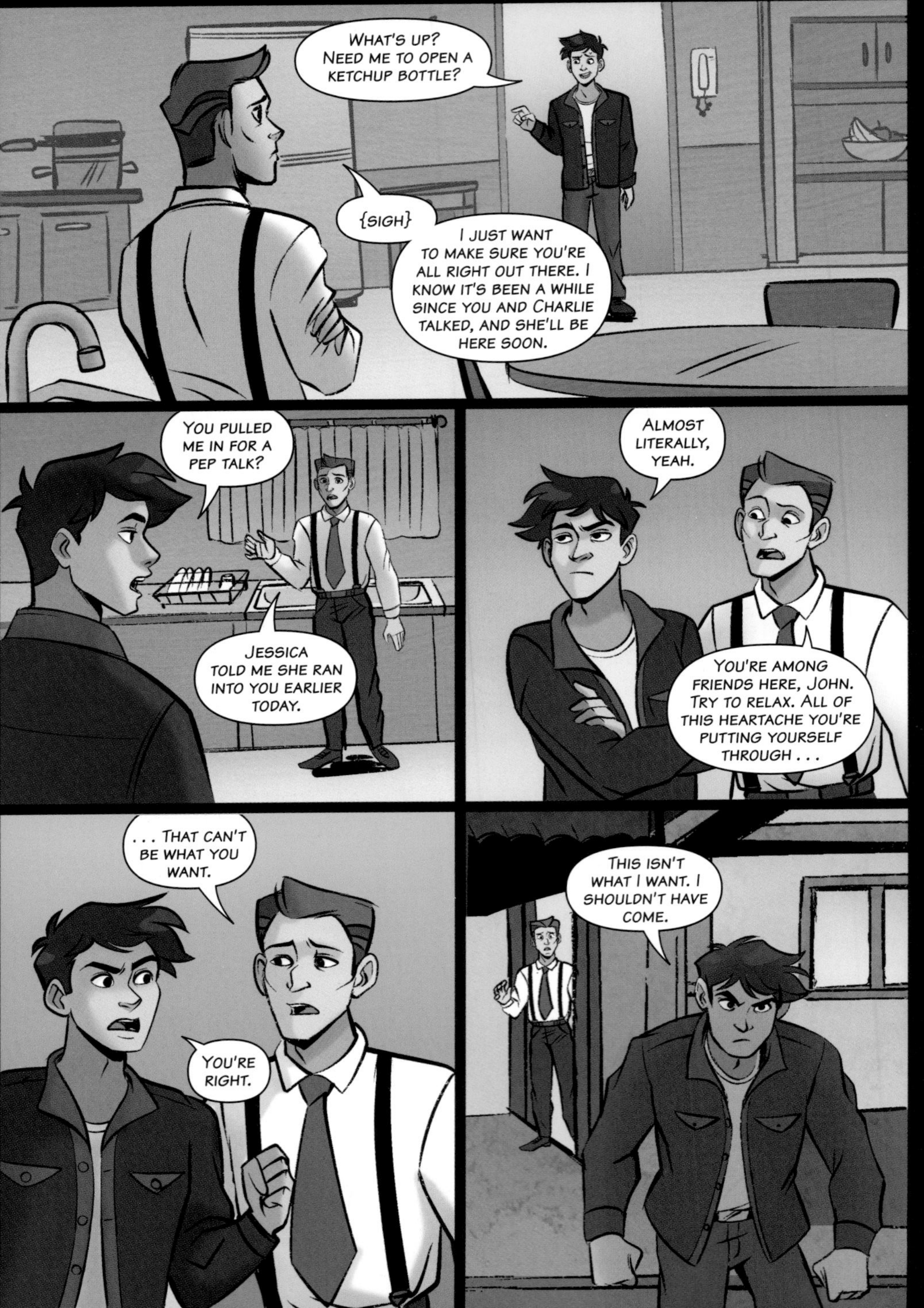
WHAT'S UP? NEED ME TO OPEN A KETCHUP BOTTLE?
{SIGH}
I JUST WANT TO MAKE SURE YOU'RE ALL RIGHT OUT THERE. I KNOW IT'S BEEN A WHILE SINCE YOU AND CHARLIE TALKED, AND SHE'LL BE HERE SOON.
YOU PULLED ME IN FOR A PEP TALK?
JESSICA TOLD ME SHE RAN INTO YOU EARLIER TODAY.
ALMOST LITERALLY, YEAH.
YOU'RE AMONG FRIENDS HERE, JOHN. TRY TO RELAX. ALL OF THIS HEARTACHE YOU'RE PUTTING YOURSELF THROUGH . . .
. . . THAT CAN'T BE WHAT YOU WANT.
YOU'RE RIGHT.
THIS ISN'T WHAT I WANT. I SHOULDN'T HAVE COME.

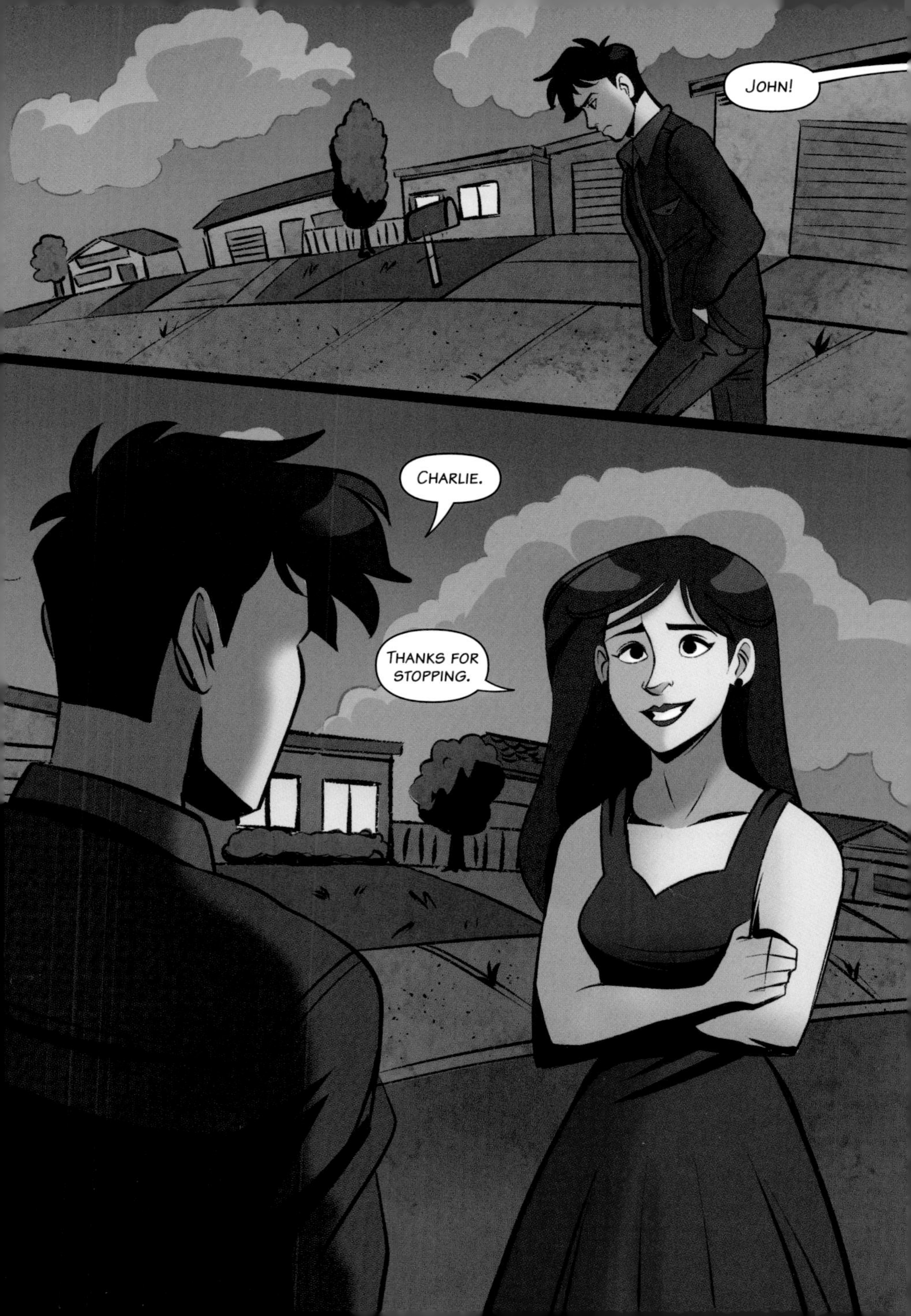
JOHN!
CHARLIE.
THANKS FOR STOPPING.

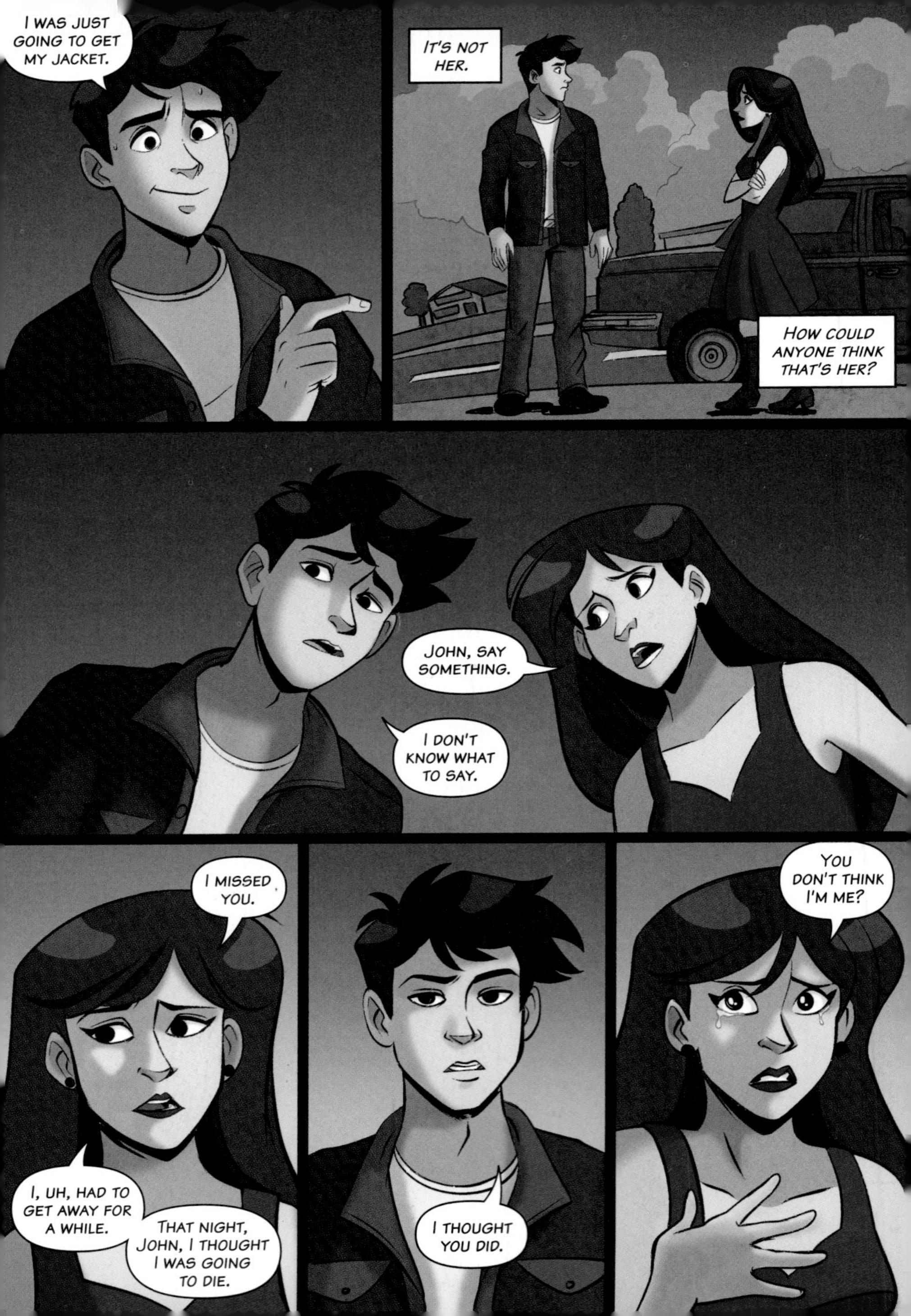
I WAS JUST GOING TO GET MY JACKET.
IT'S NOT HER.
HOW COULD ANYONE THINK THAT'S HER?
JOHN, SAY SOMETHING.
I DON'T KNOW WHAT TO SAY.
I MISSED YOU.
I, UH, HAD TO GET AWAY FOR A WHILE.
THAT NIGHT, JOHN, I THOUGHT I WAS GOING TO DIE.
I THOUGHT YOU DID.
YOU DON'T THINK I'M ME?

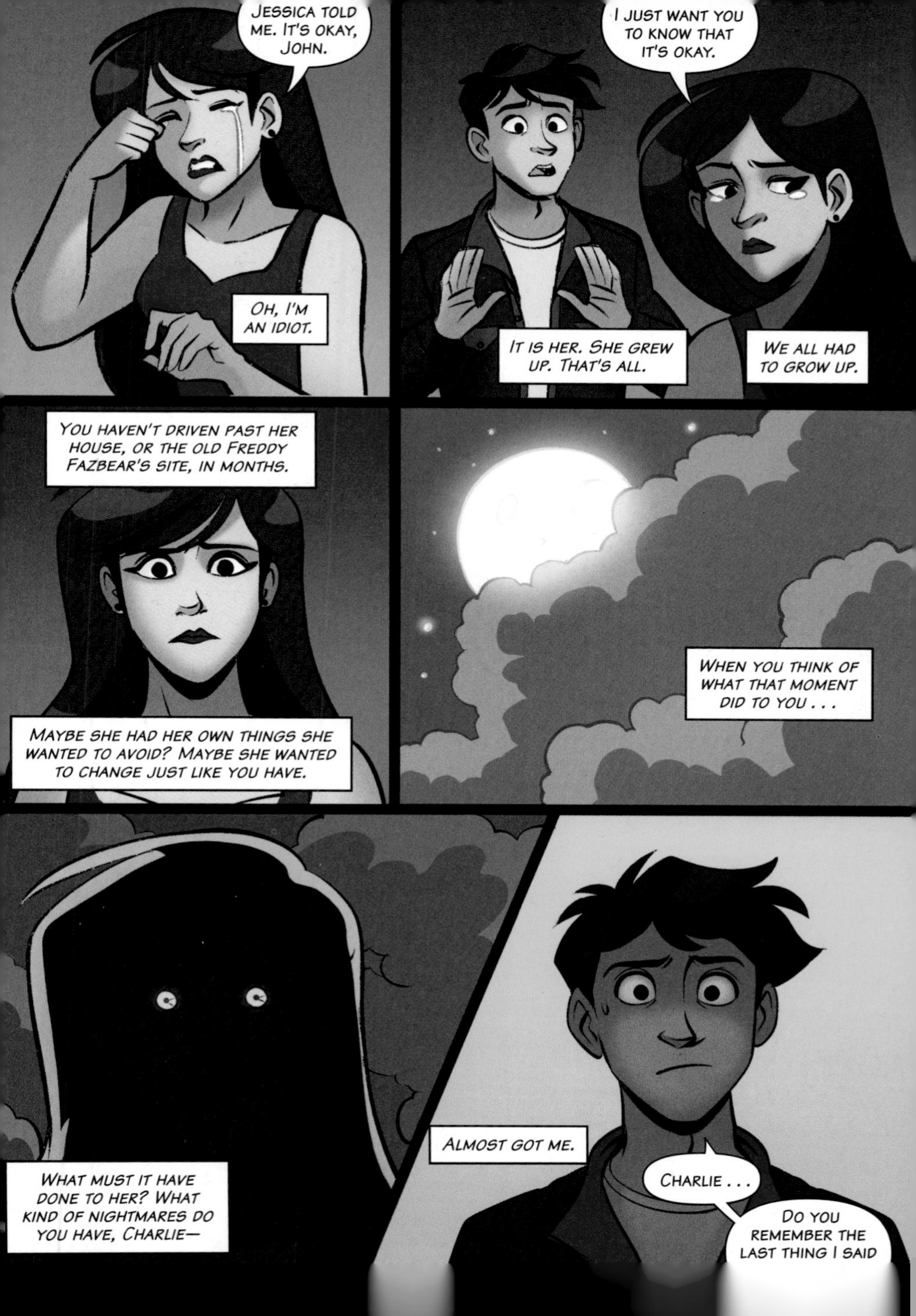
JESSICA TOLD ME. IT'S OKAY, JOHN.
OH, I'M AN IDIOT.
I JUST WANT YOU TO KNOW THAT IT'S OKAY.
IT IS HER. SHE GREW UP. THAT'S ALL.
WE ALL HAD TO GROW UP.
YOU HAVEN'T DRIVEN PAST HER HOUSE, OR THE OLD FREDDY FAZBEAR'S SITE, IN MONTHS.
MAYBE SHE HAD HER OWN THINGS SHE WANTED TO AVOID? MAYBE SHE WANTED TO CHANGE JUST LIKE YOU HAVE.
WHEN YOU THINK OF WHAT THAT MOMENT DID TO YOU . . .
WHAT MUST IT HAVE DONE TO HER? WHAT KIND OF NIGHTMARES DO YOU HAVE, CHARLIE—
ALMOST GOT ME.
CHARLIE . . .
DO YOU REMEMBER THE LAST THING I SAID

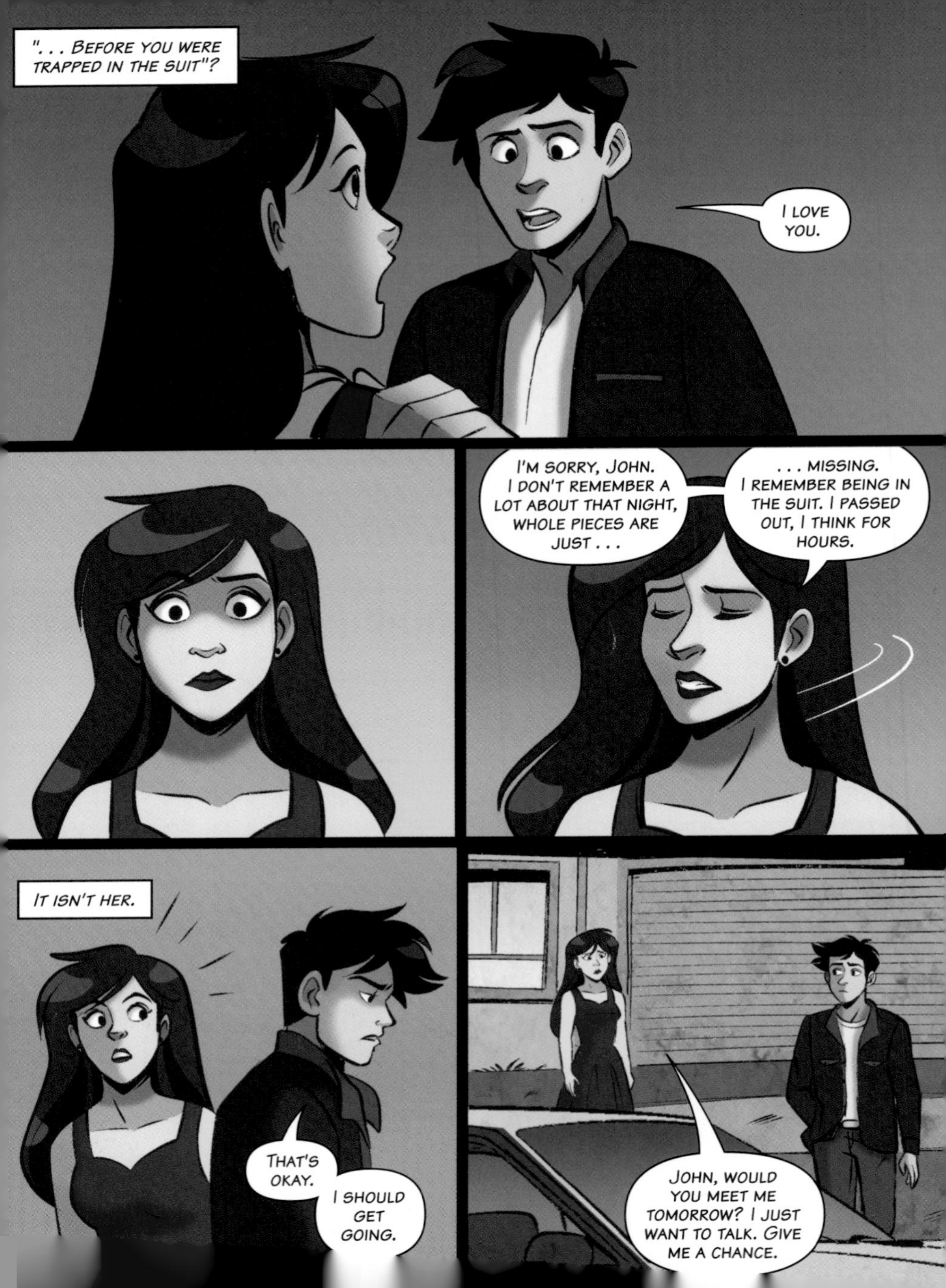
". . . BEFORE YOU WERE TRAPPED IN THE SUIT"?
I LOVE YOU.
I'M SORRY, JOHN. I DON'T REMEMBER A LOT ABOUT THAT NIGHT, WHOLE PIECES ARE JUST . . .
. . . MISSING. I REMEMBER BEING IN THE SUIT. I PASSED OUT, I THINK FOR HOURS.
IT ISN'T HER.
THAT'S OKAY.
I SHOULD GET GOING.
JOHN, WOULD YOU MEET ME TOMORROW? I JUST WANT TO TALK. GIVE ME A CHANCE.

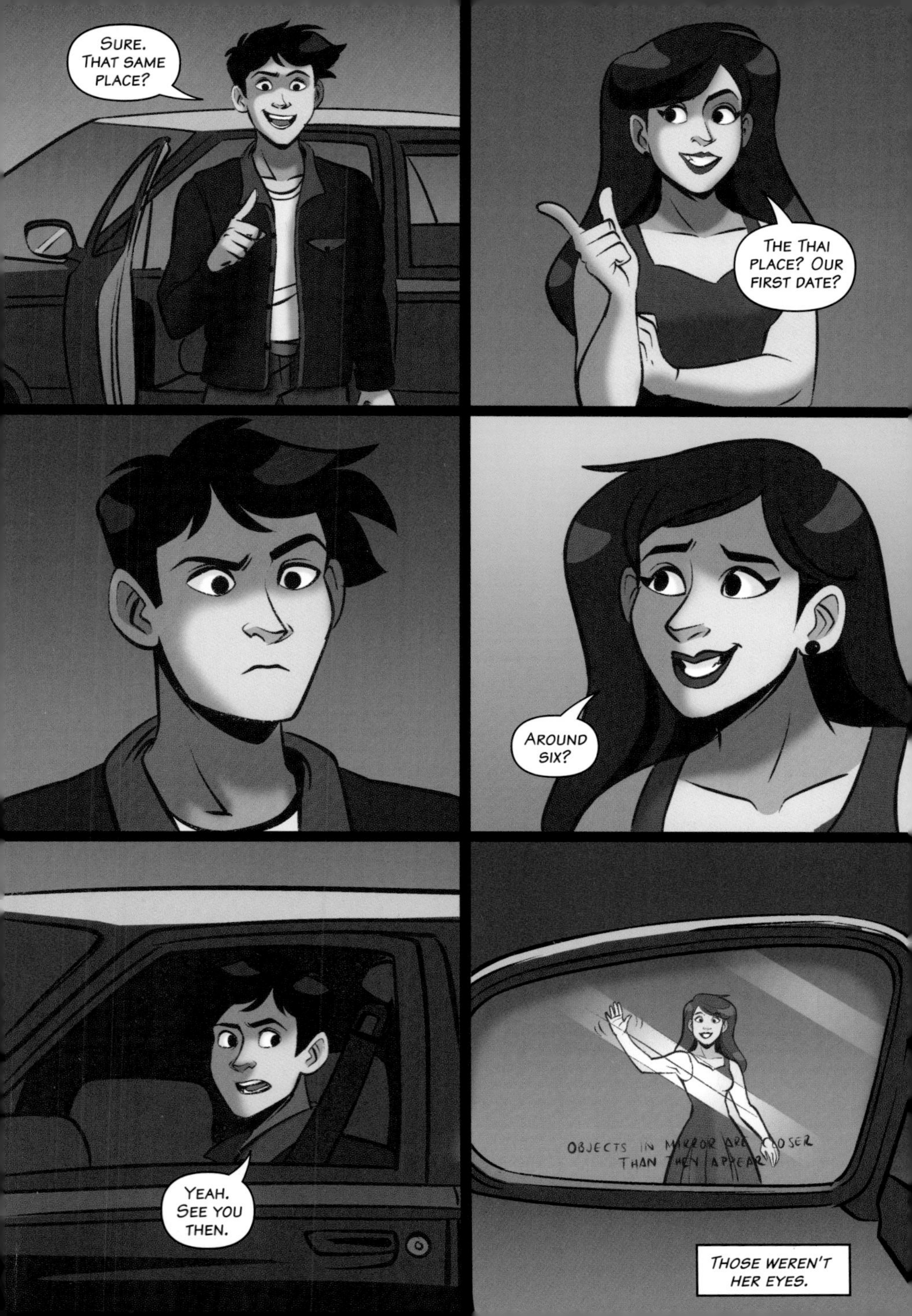
SURE. THAT SAME PLACE?
THE THAI PLACE? OUR FIRST DATE?
AROUND SIX?
YEAH. SEE YOU THEN.
OBJECTS IN MIRROR ARE CLOSER THAN THEY APPEAR
THOSE WEREN'T HER EYES.

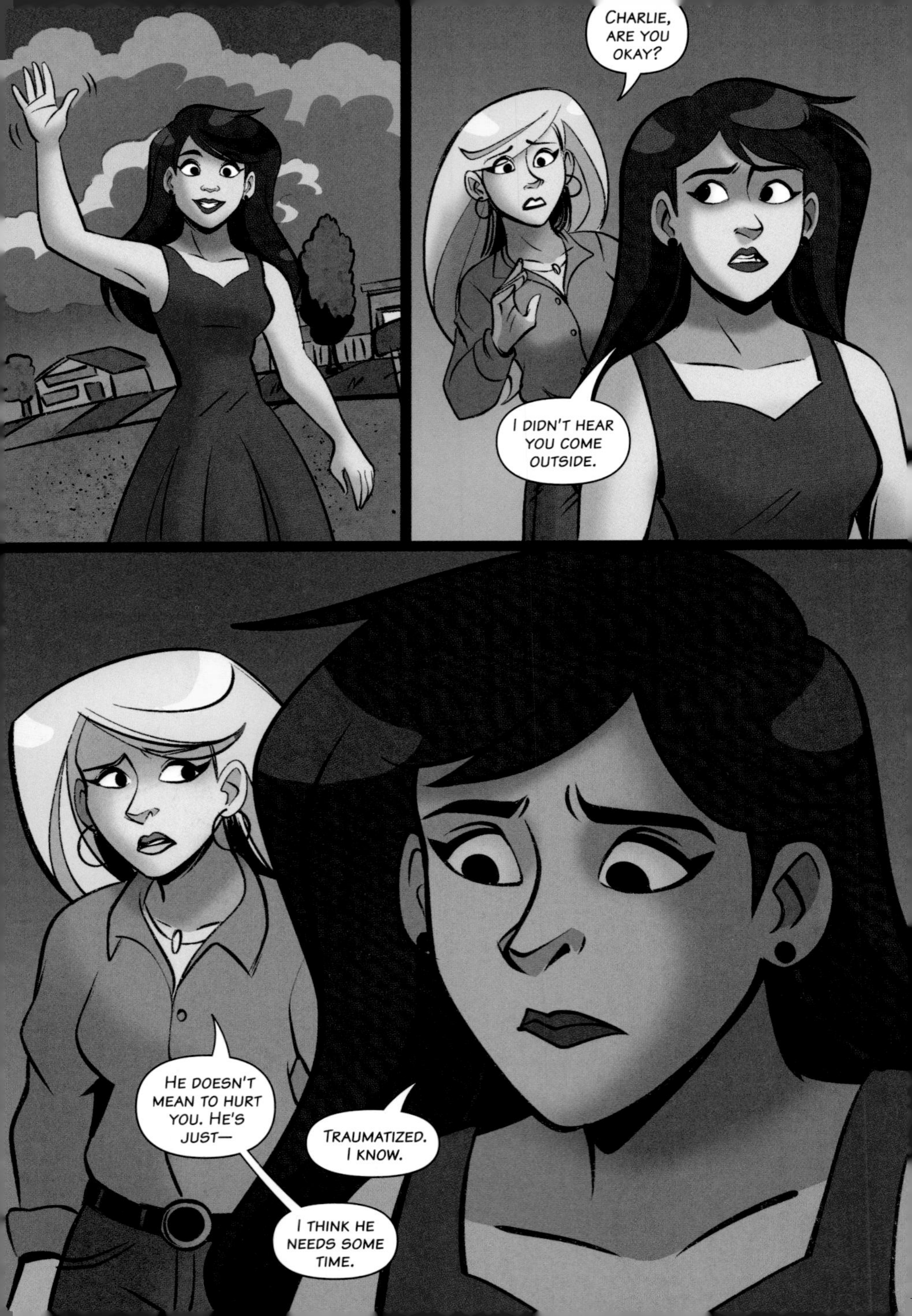
CHARLIE, ARE YOU OKAY?
I DIDN'T HEAR YOU COME OUTSIDE.
HE DOESN'T MEAN TO HURT YOU. HE'S JUST—
TRAUMATIZED. I KNOW.
I THINK HE NEEDS SOME TIME.

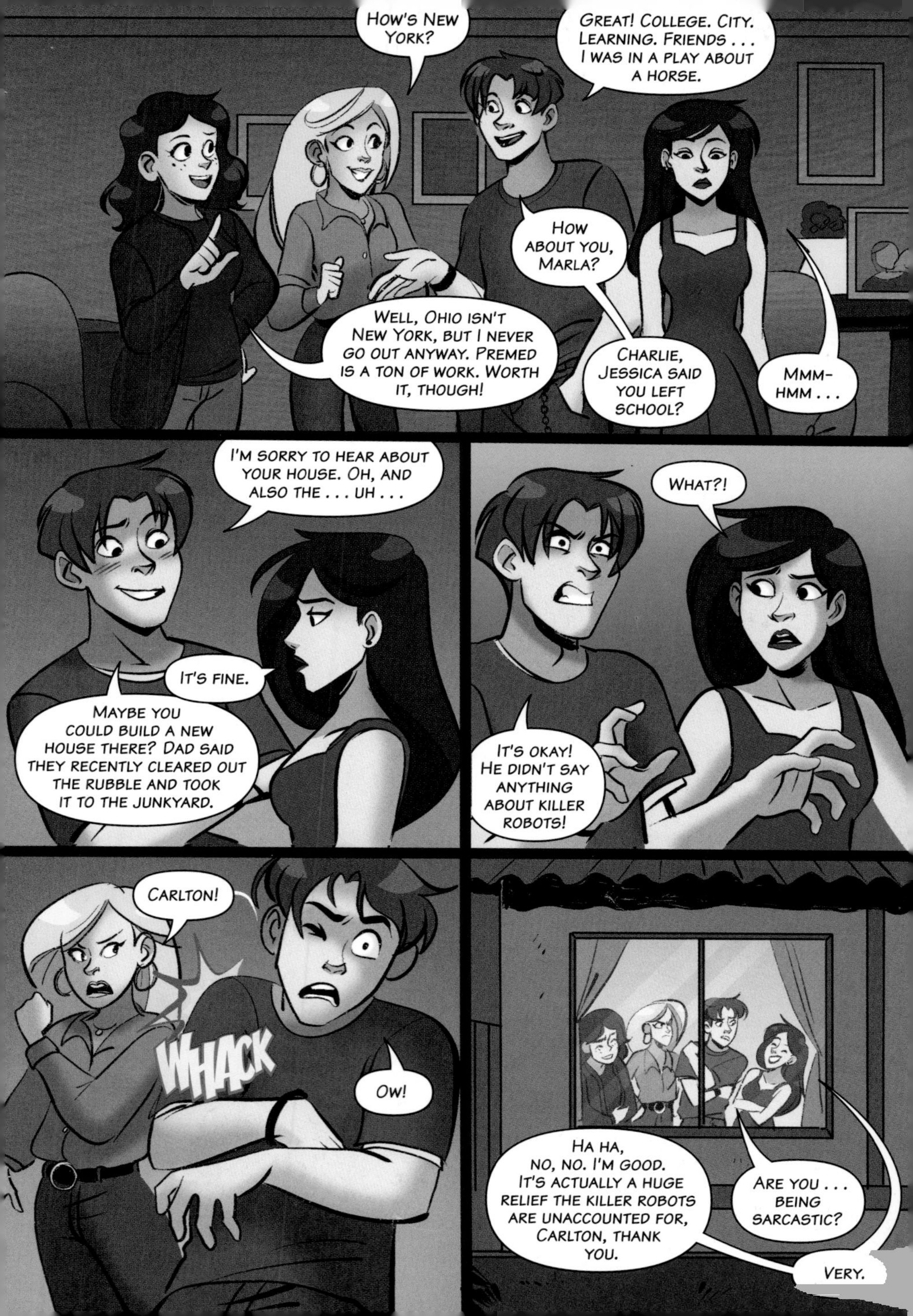
HOW'S NEW YORK?
GREAT! COLLEGE. CITY. LEARNING. FRIENDS . . . I WAS IN A PLAY ABOUT A HORSE.
HOW ABOUT YOU, MARLA?
WELL, OHIO ISN'T NEW YORK, BUT I NEVER GO OUT ANYWAY. PREMED IS A TON OF WORK. WORTH IT, THOUGH!
CHARLIE, JESSICA SAID YOU LEFT SCHOOL?
MMM-HMM . . .
I'M SORRY TO HEAR ABOUT YOUR HOUSE. OH, AND ALSO THE . . . UH . . .
IT'S FINE.
MAYBE YOU COULD BUILD A NEW HOUSE THERE? DAD SAID THEY RECENTLY CLEARED OUT THE RUBBLE AND TOOK IT TO THE JUNKYARD.
WHAT?!
IT'S OKAY! HE DIDN'T SAY ANYTHING ABOUT KILLER ROBOTS!
CARLTON!
WHACK
OW!
HA HA, NO, NO. I'M GOOD. IT'S ACTUALLY A HUGE RELIEF THE KILLER ROBOTS ARE UNACCOUNTED FOR, CARLTON, THANK YOU.
ARE YOU . . . BEING SARCASTIC?
VERY.

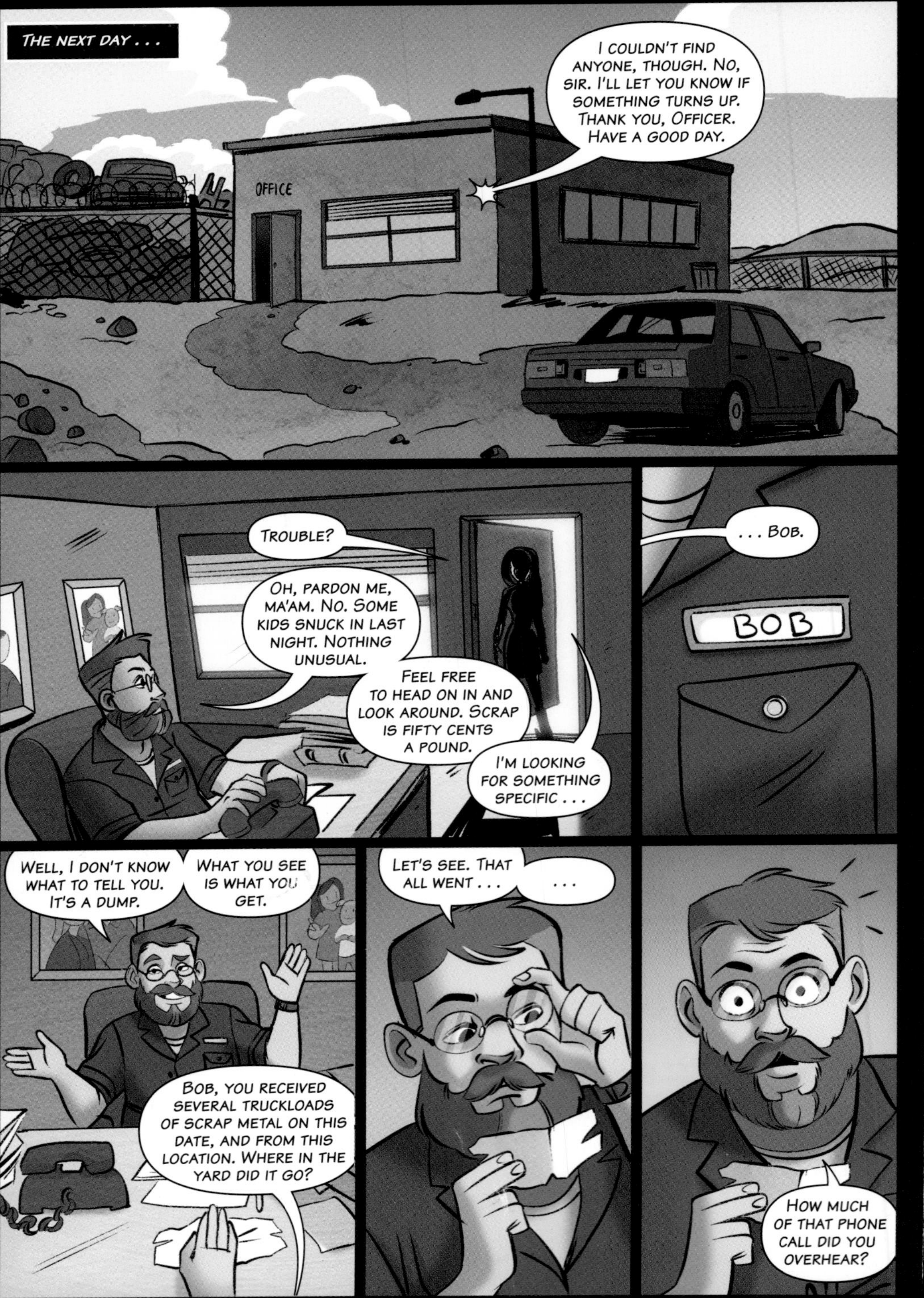
THE NEXT DAY . . .
I COULDN'T FIND ANYONE, THOUGH. NO, SIR. I'LL LET YOU KNOW IF SOMETHING TURNS UP. THANK YOU, OFFICER. HAVE A GOOD DAY.
OFFICE
TROUBLE?
OH, PARDON ME, MA'AM. NO. SOME KIDS SNUCK IN LAST NIGHT. NOTHING UNUSUAL.
FEEL FREE TO HEAD ON IN AND LOOK AROUND. SCRAP IS FIFTY CENTS A POUND.
I'M LOOKING FOR SOMETHING SPECIFIC . . .
. . . BOB.
BOB
WELL, I DON'T KNOW WHAT TO TELL YOU. IT'S A DUMP.
WHAT YOU SEE IS WHAT YOU GET.
BOB, YOU RECEIVED SEVERAL TRUCKLOADS OF SCRAP METAL ON THIS DATE, AND FROM THIS LOCATION. WHERE IN THE YARD DID IT GO?
LET'S SEE. THAT ALL WENT . . .
. . .
HOW MUCH OF THAT PHONE CALL DID YOU OVERHEAR?

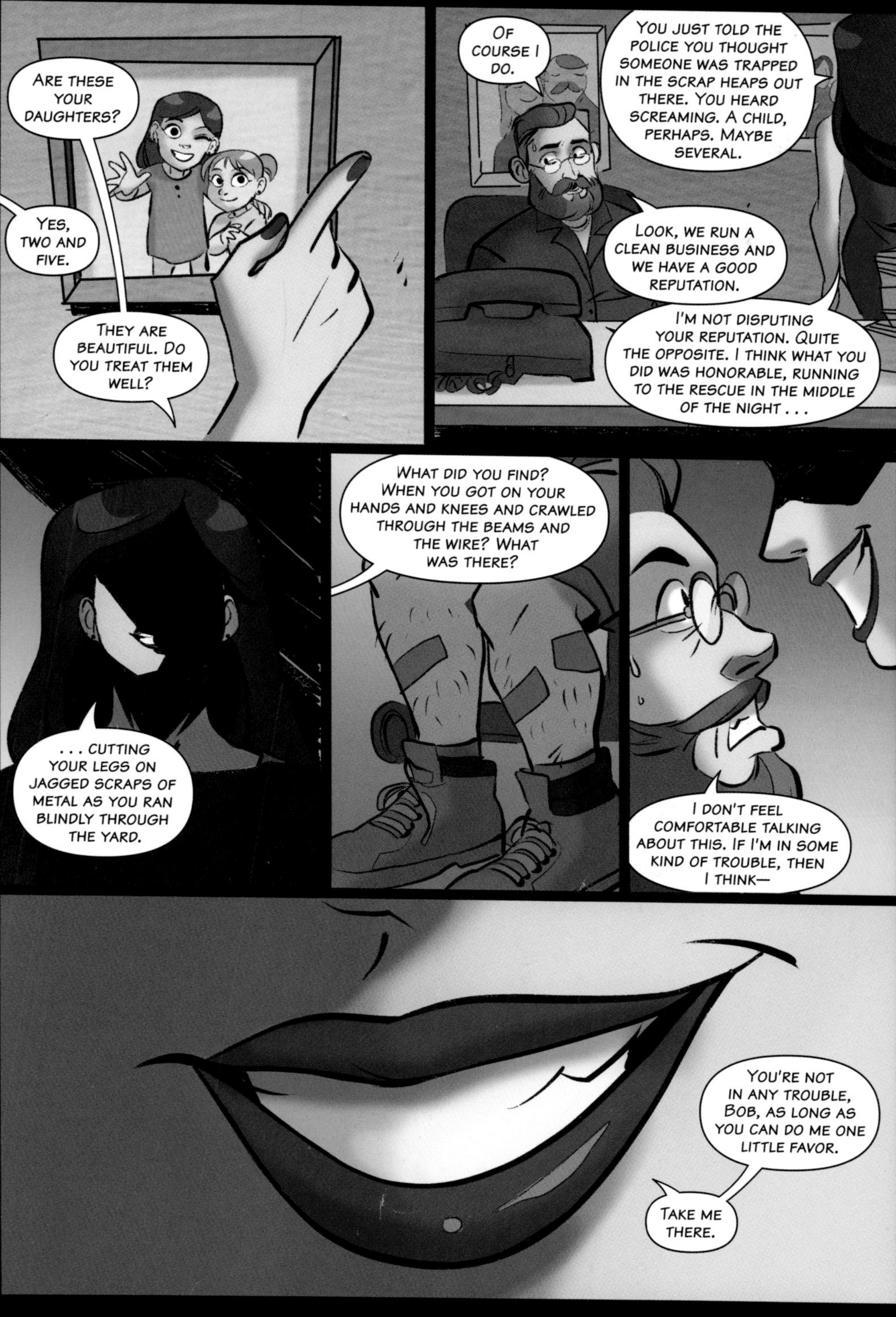
Are these your daughters?
Yes, two and five.
They are beautiful. Do you treat them well?
Of course I do.
You just told the police you thought someone was trapped in the scrap heaps out there. You heard screaming. A child, perhaps. Maybe several.
Look, we run a clean business and we have a good reputation.
I'm not disputing your reputation. Quite the opposite. I think what you did was honorable, running to the rescue in the middle of the night . . .
. . . cutting your legs on jagged scraps of metal as you ran blindly through the yard.
What did you find? When you got on your hands and knees and crawled through the beams and the wire? What was there?
I don't feel comfortable talking about this. If I'm in some kind of trouble, then I think—
You're not in any trouble, Bob, as long as you can do me one little favor.
Take me there.

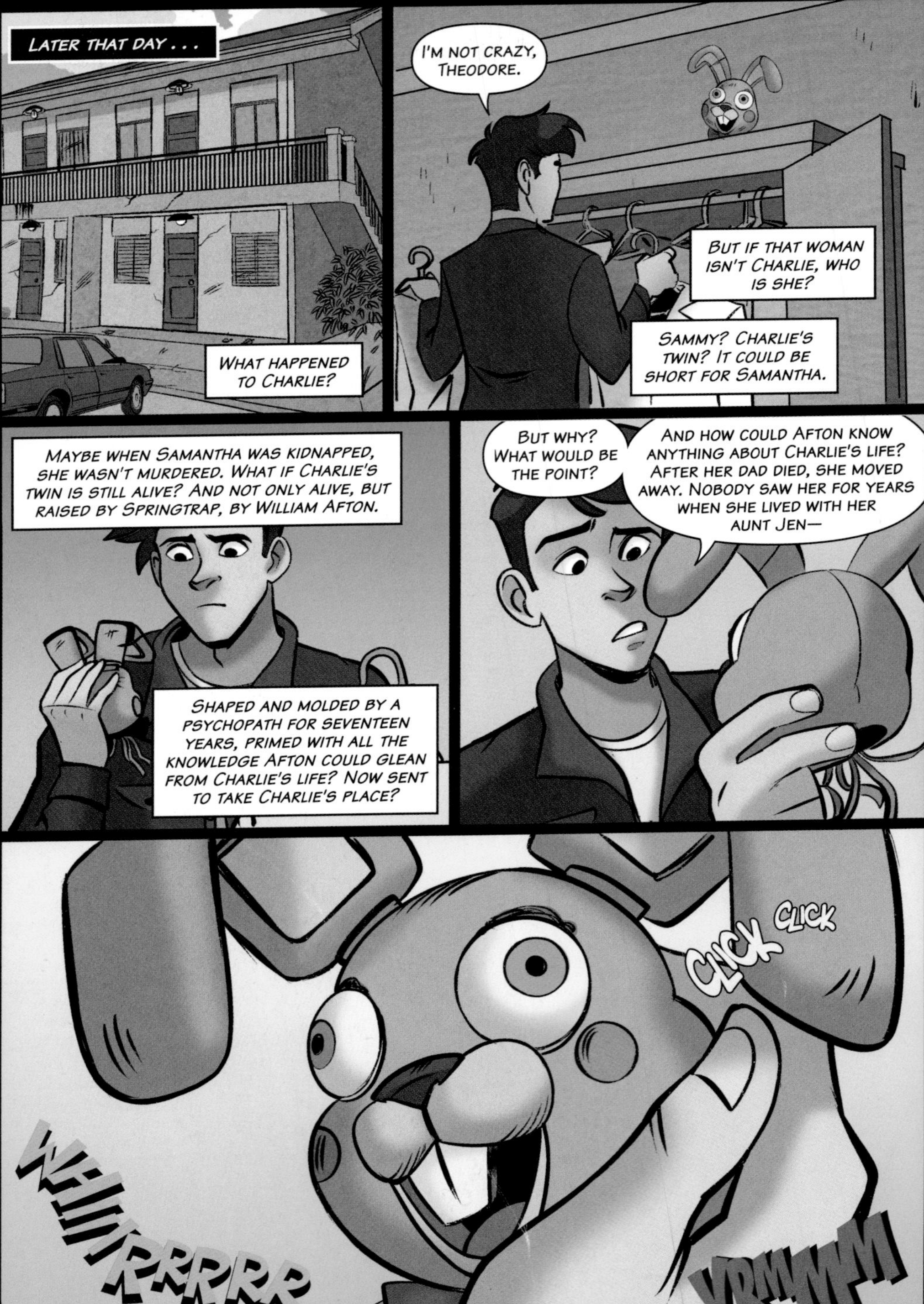
LATER THAT DAY . . .
WHAT HAPPENED TO CHARLIE?
I'M NOT CRAZY, THEODORE.
BUT IF THAT WOMAN ISN'T CHARLIE, WHO IS SHE?
SAMMY? CHARLIE'S TWIN? IT COULD BE SHORT FOR SAMANTHA.
MAYBE WHEN SAMANTHA WAS KIDNAPPED, SHE WASN'T MURDERED. WHAT IF CHARLIE'S TWIN IS STILL ALIVE? AND NOT ONLY ALIVE, BUT RAISED BY SPRINGTRAP, BY WILLIAM AFTON.
SHAPED AND MOLDED BY A PSYCHOPATH FOR SEVENTEEN YEARS, PRIMED WITH ALL THE KNOWLEDGE AFTON COULD GLEAN FROM CHARLIE'S LIFE? NOW SENT TO TAKE CHARLIE'S PLACE?
BUT WHY? WHAT WOULD BE THE POINT?
AND HOW COULD AFTON KNOW ANYTHING ABOUT CHARLIE'S LIFE? AFTER HER DAD DIED, SHE MOVED AWAY. NOBODY SAW HER FOR YEARS WHEN SHE LIVED WITH HER AUNT JEN—
CLICK
CLICK
WHIIIRRRRR
VRMMMM

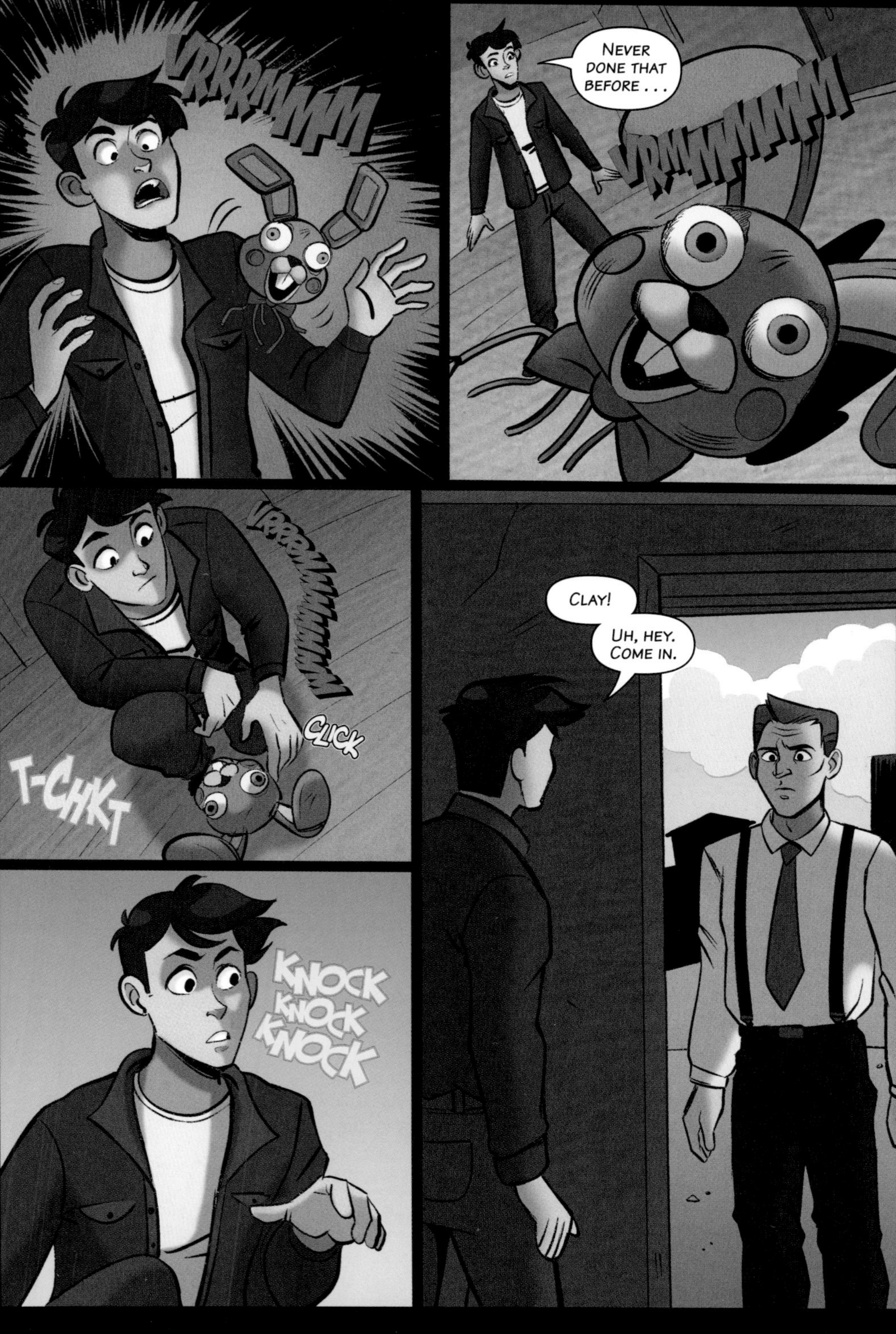
VRRRMMMM
NEVER DONE THAT BEFORE . . .
VRMMMMMM
VRRRMMMMMM
CLICK
T-CHKT
KNOCK KNOCK KNOCK
CLAY!
UH, HEY. COME IN.

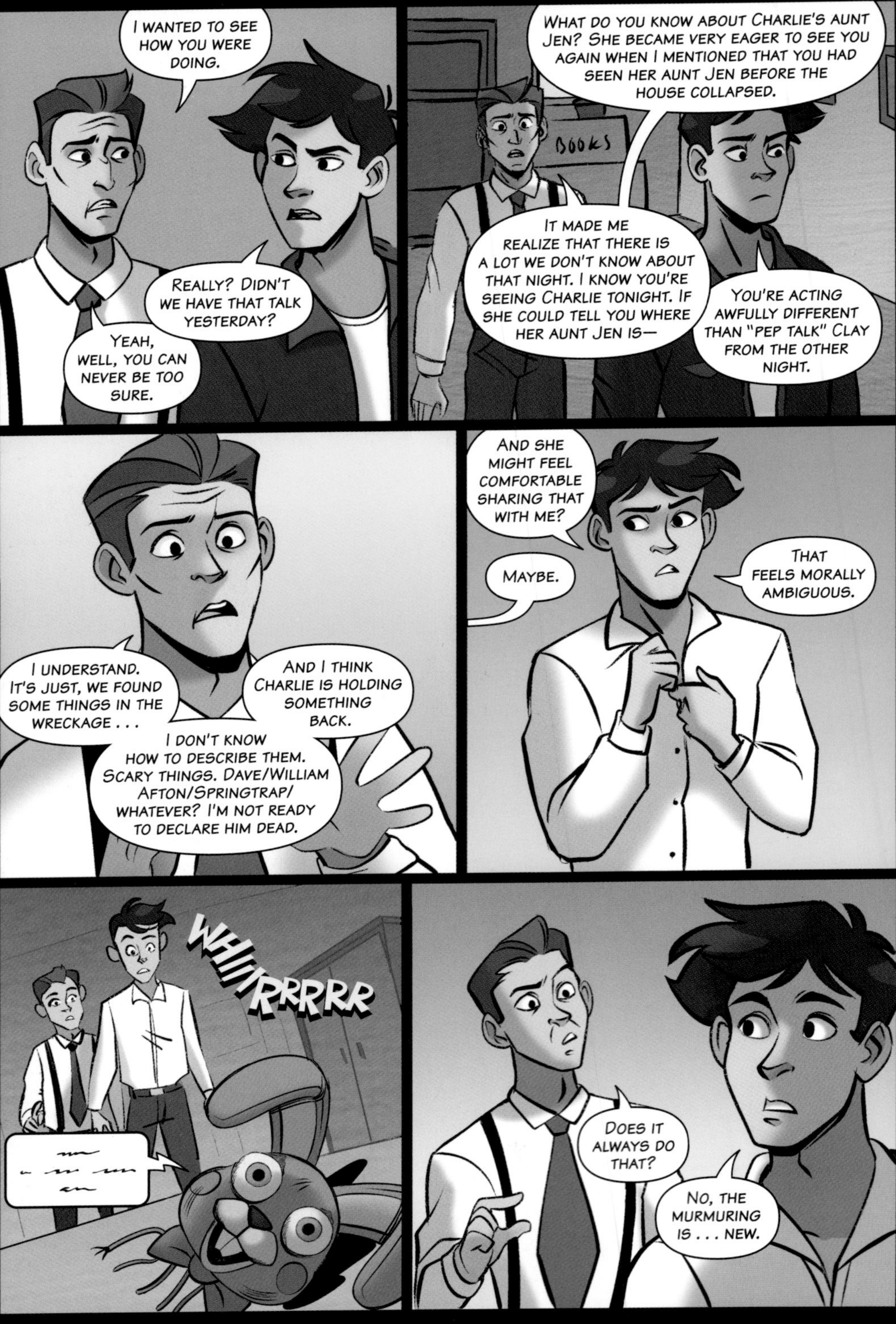
I WANTED TO SEE HOW YOU WERE DOING.
REALLY? DIDN'T WE HAVE THAT TALK YESTERDAY?
YEAH, WELL, YOU CAN NEVER BE TOO SURE.
WHAT DO YOU KNOW ABOUT CHARLIE'S AUNT JEN? SHE BECAME VERY EAGER TO SEE YOU AGAIN WHEN I MENTIONED THAT YOU HAD SEEN HER AUNT JEN BEFORE THE HOUSE COLLAPSED.
BOOKS
IT MADE ME REALIZE THAT THERE IS A LOT WE DON'T KNOW ABOUT THAT NIGHT. I KNOW YOU'RE SEEING CHARLIE TONIGHT. IF SHE COULD TELL YOU WHERE HER AUNT JEN IS—
YOU'RE ACTING AWFULLY DIFFERENT THAN "PEP TALK" CLAY FROM THE OTHER NIGHT.
I UNDERSTAND. IT'S JUST, WE FOUND SOME THINGS IN THE WRECKAGE . . .
AND I THINK CHARLIE IS HOLDING SOMETHING BACK.
I DON'T KNOW HOW TO DESCRIBE THEM. SCARY THINGS. DAVE/WILLIAM AFTON/SPRINGTRAP/ WHATEVER? I'M NOT READY TO DECLARE HIM DEAD.
AND SHE MIGHT FEEL COMFORTABLE SHARING THAT WITH ME?
MAYBE.
THAT FEELS MORALLY AMBIGUOUS.
WHIIIRRRRR
DOES IT ALWAYS DO THAT?
NO, THE MURMURING IS . . . NEW.

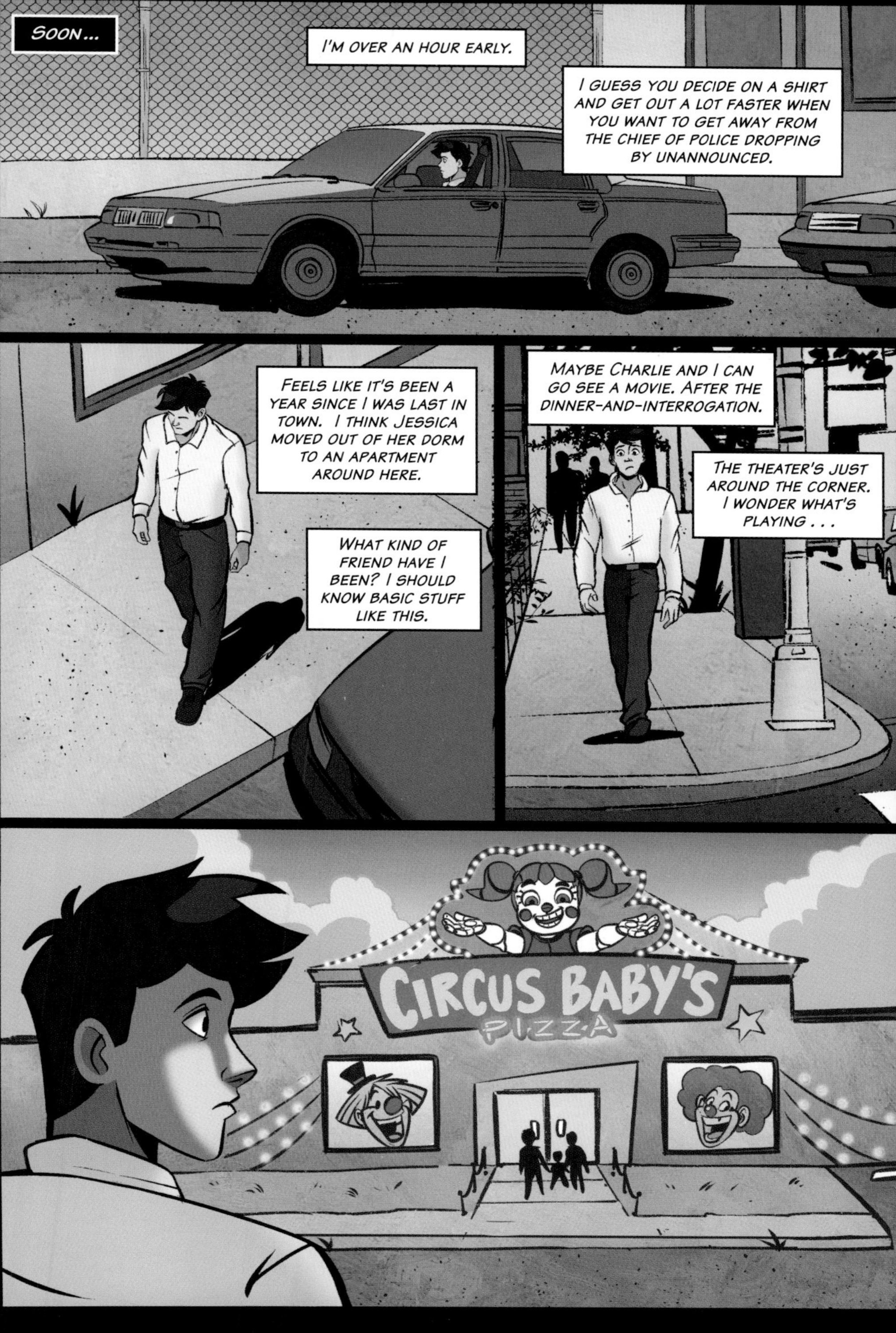
SOON...
I'M OVER AN HOUR EARLY.
I GUESS YOU DECIDE ON A SHIRT AND GET OUT A LOT FASTER WHEN YOU WANT TO GET AWAY FROM THE CHIEF OF POLICE DROPPING BY UNANNOUNCED.
FEELS LIKE IT'S BEEN A YEAR SINCE I WAS LAST IN TOWN. I THINK JESSICA MOVED OUT OF HER DORM TO AN APARTMENT AROUND HERE.
WHAT KIND OF FRIEND HAVE I BEEN? I SHOULD KNOW BASIC STUFF LIKE THIS.
MAYBE CHARLIE AND I CAN GO SEE A MOVIE. AFTER THE DINNER-AND-INTERROGATION.
THE THEATER'S JUST AROUND THE CORNER. I WONDER WHAT'S PLAYING . . .
CIRCUS BABY'S
PIZZA

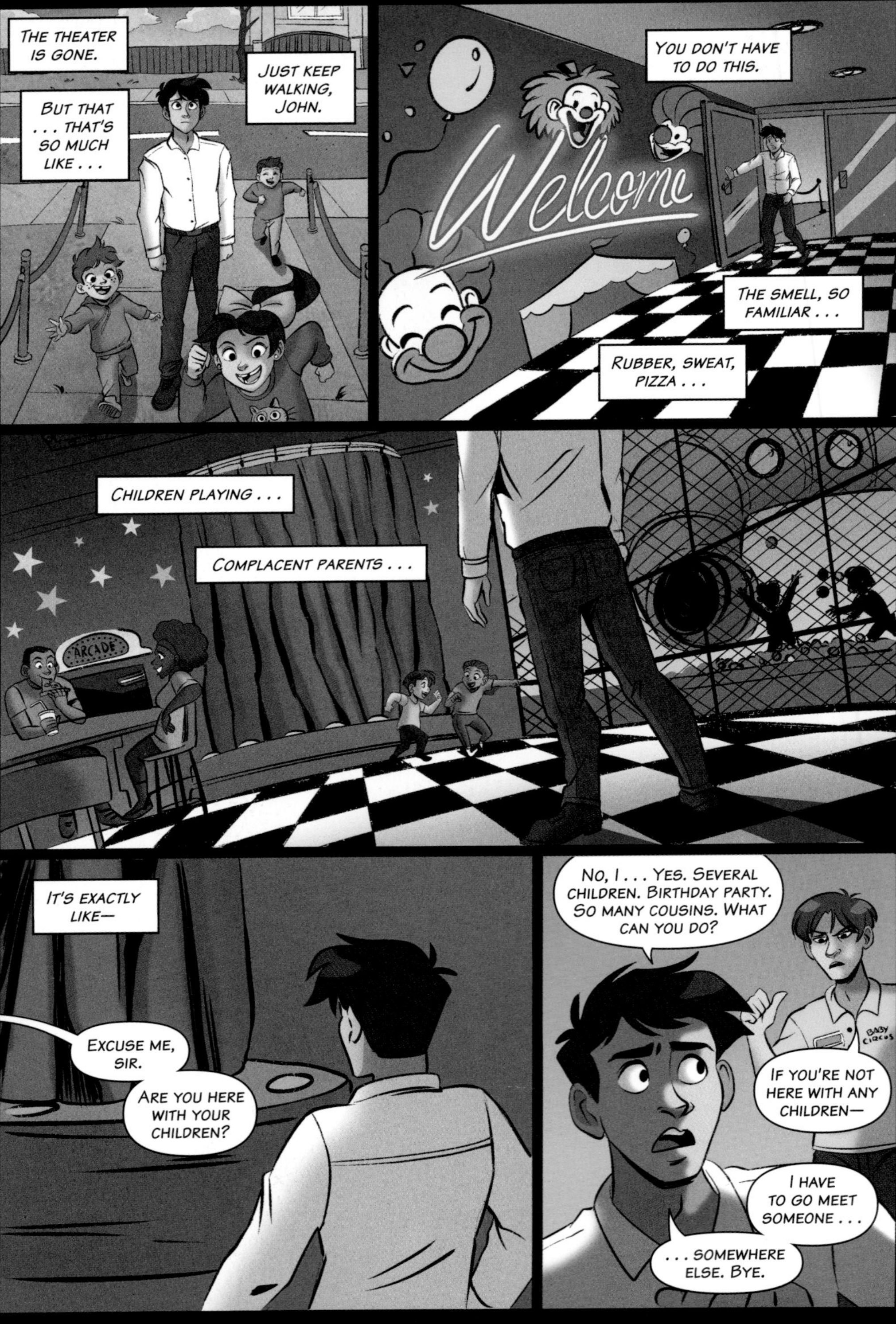

THE THEATER IS GONE.
BUT THAT . . . THAT'S SO MUCH LIKE . . .
JUST KEEP WALKING, JOHN.
Welcome
YOU DON'T HAVE TO DO THIS.
THE SMELL, SO FAMILIAR . . .
RUBBER, SWEAT, PIZZA . . .
CHILDREN PLAYING . . .
COMPLACENT PARENTS . . .
ARCADE
IT'S EXACTLY LIKE—
EXCUSE ME, SIR.
ARE YOU HERE WITH YOUR CHILDREN?
NO, I . . . YES. SEVERAL CHILDREN. BIRTHDAY PARTY. SO MANY COUSINS. WHAT CAN YOU DO?
BABY CIRCUS
IF YOU'RE NOT HERE WITH ANY CHILDREN—
I HAVE TO GO MEET SOMEONE . . .
. . . SOMEWHERE ELSE. BYE.

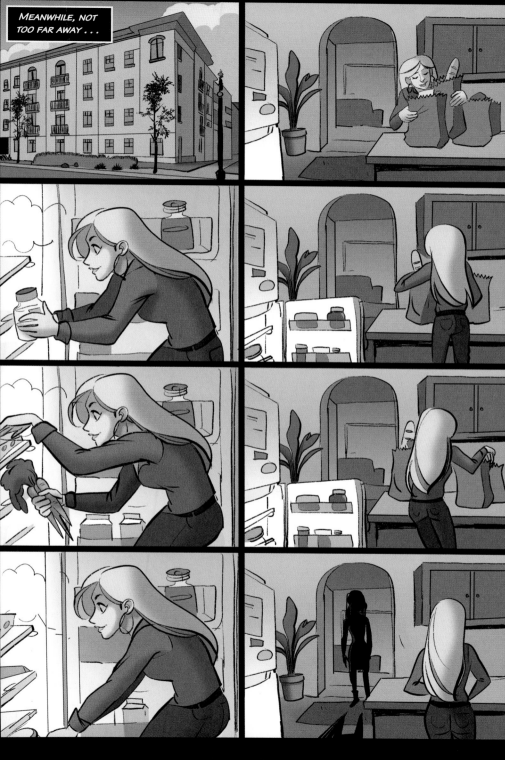

MEANWHILE, NOT TOO FAR AWAY . . .

29

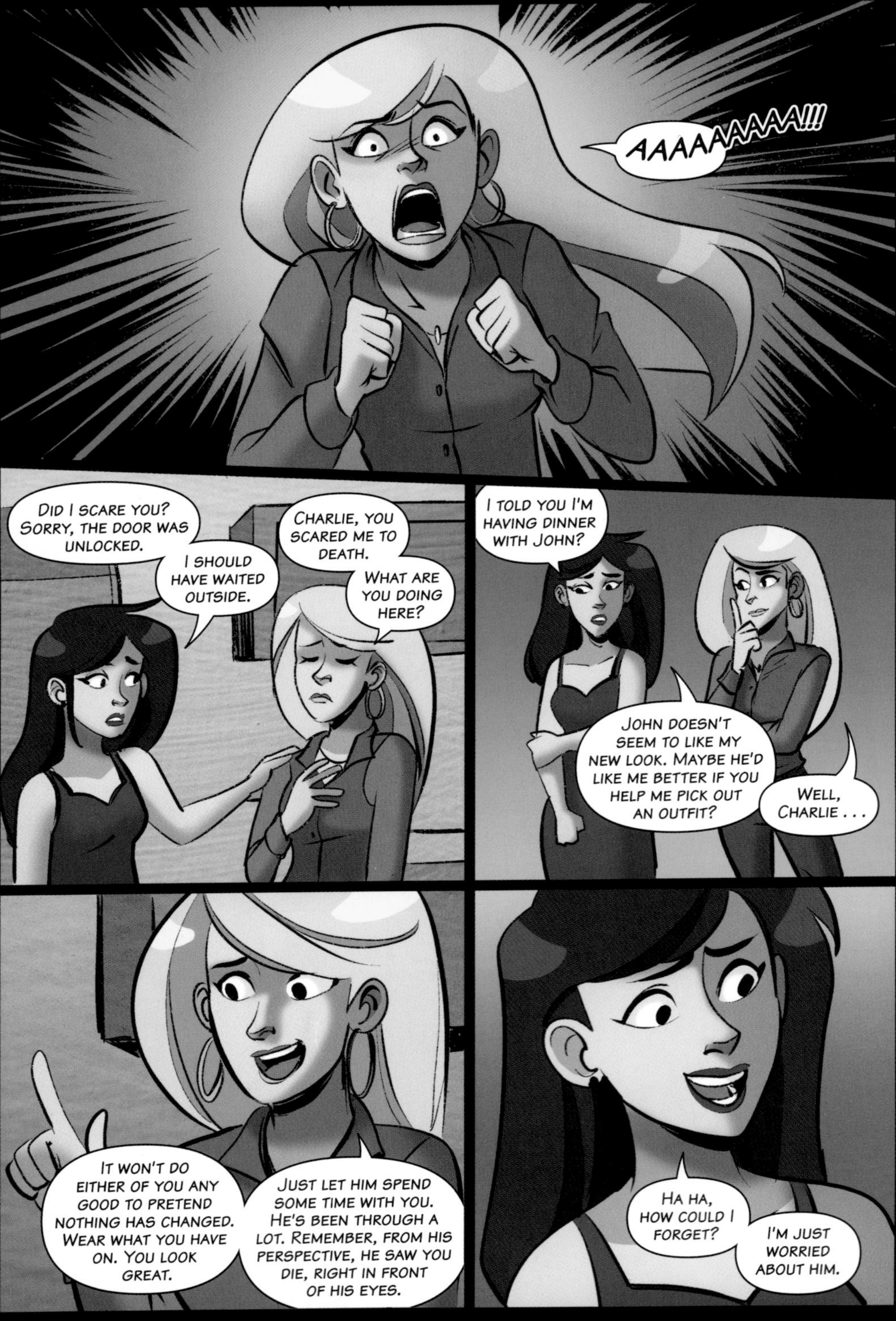
AAAAAAAAA!!!
DID I SCARE YOU? SORRY, THE DOOR WAS UNLOCKED.
I SHOULD HAVE WAITED OUTSIDE.
CHARLIE, YOU SCARED ME TO DEATH.
WHAT ARE YOU DOING HERE?
I TOLD YOU I'M HAVING DINNER WITH JOHN?
JOHN DOESN'T SEEM TO LIKE MY NEW LOOK. MAYBE HE'D LIKE ME BETTER IF YOU HELP ME PICK OUT AN OUTFIT?
WELL, CHARLIE . . .
IT WON'T DO EITHER OF YOU ANY GOOD TO PRETEND NOTHING HAS CHANGED. WEAR WHAT YOU HAVE ON. YOU LOOK GREAT.
JUST LET HIM SPEND SOME TIME WITH YOU. HE'S BEEN THROUGH A LOT. REMEMBER, FROM HIS PERSPECTIVE, HE SAW YOU DIE, RIGHT IN FRONT OF HIS EYES.
HA HA, HOW COULD I FORGET?
I'M JUST WORRIED ABOUT HIM.

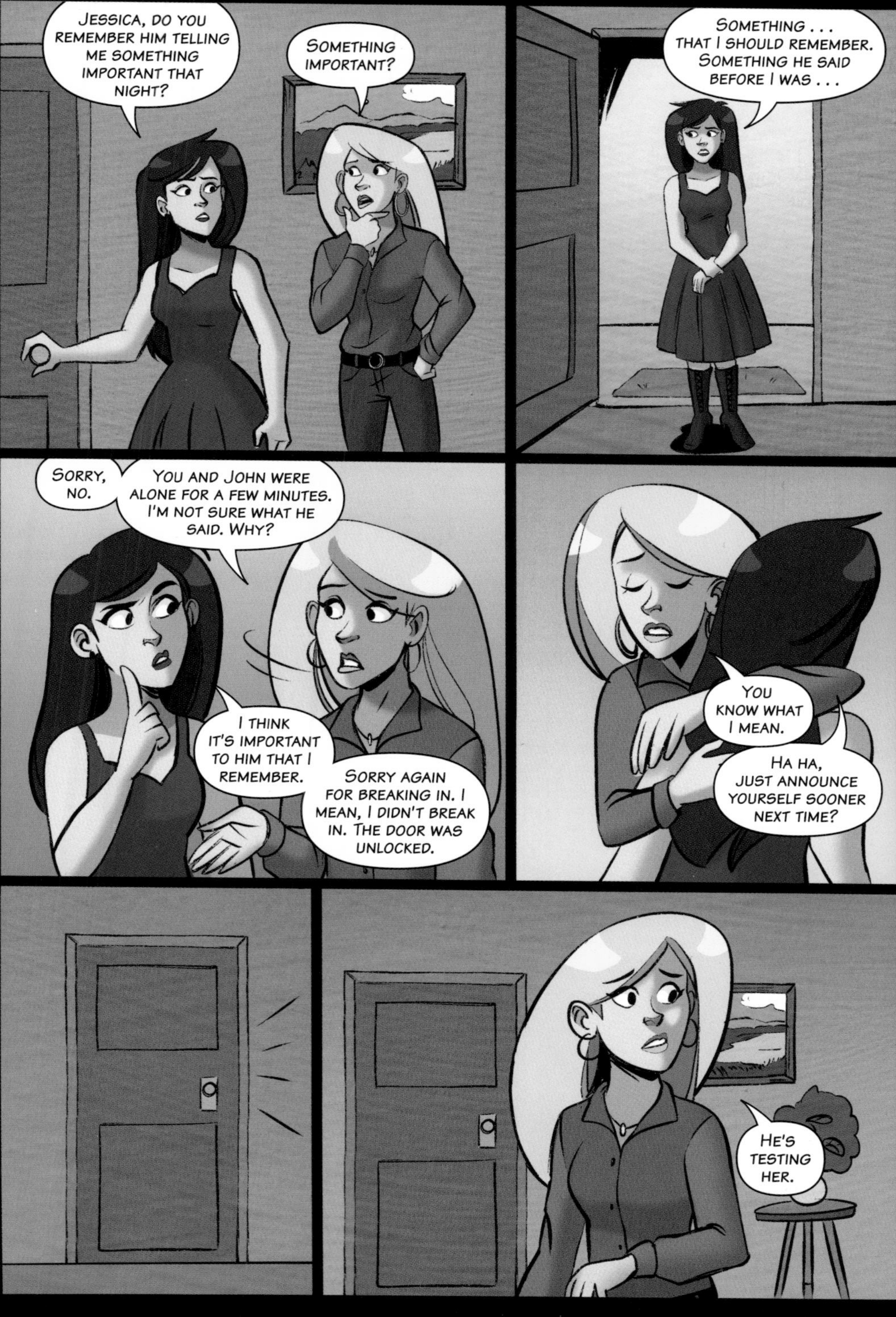

JESSICA, DO YOU REMEMBER HIM TELLING ME SOMETHING IMPORTANT THAT NIGHT?
SOMETHING IMPORTANT?
SOMETHING . . . THAT I SHOULD REMEMBER. SOMETHING HE SAID BEFORE I WAS . . .
SORRY, NO.
YOU AND JOHN WERE ALONE FOR A FEW MINUTES. I'M NOT SURE WHAT HE SAID. WHY?
I THINK IT'S IMPORTANT TO HIM THAT I REMEMBER.
SORRY AGAIN FOR BREAKING IN. I MEAN, I DIDN'T BREAK IN. THE DOOR WAS UNLOCKED.
YOU KNOW WHAT I MEAN.
HA HA, JUST ANNOUNCE YOURSELF SOONER NEXT TIME?
HE'S TESTING HER.

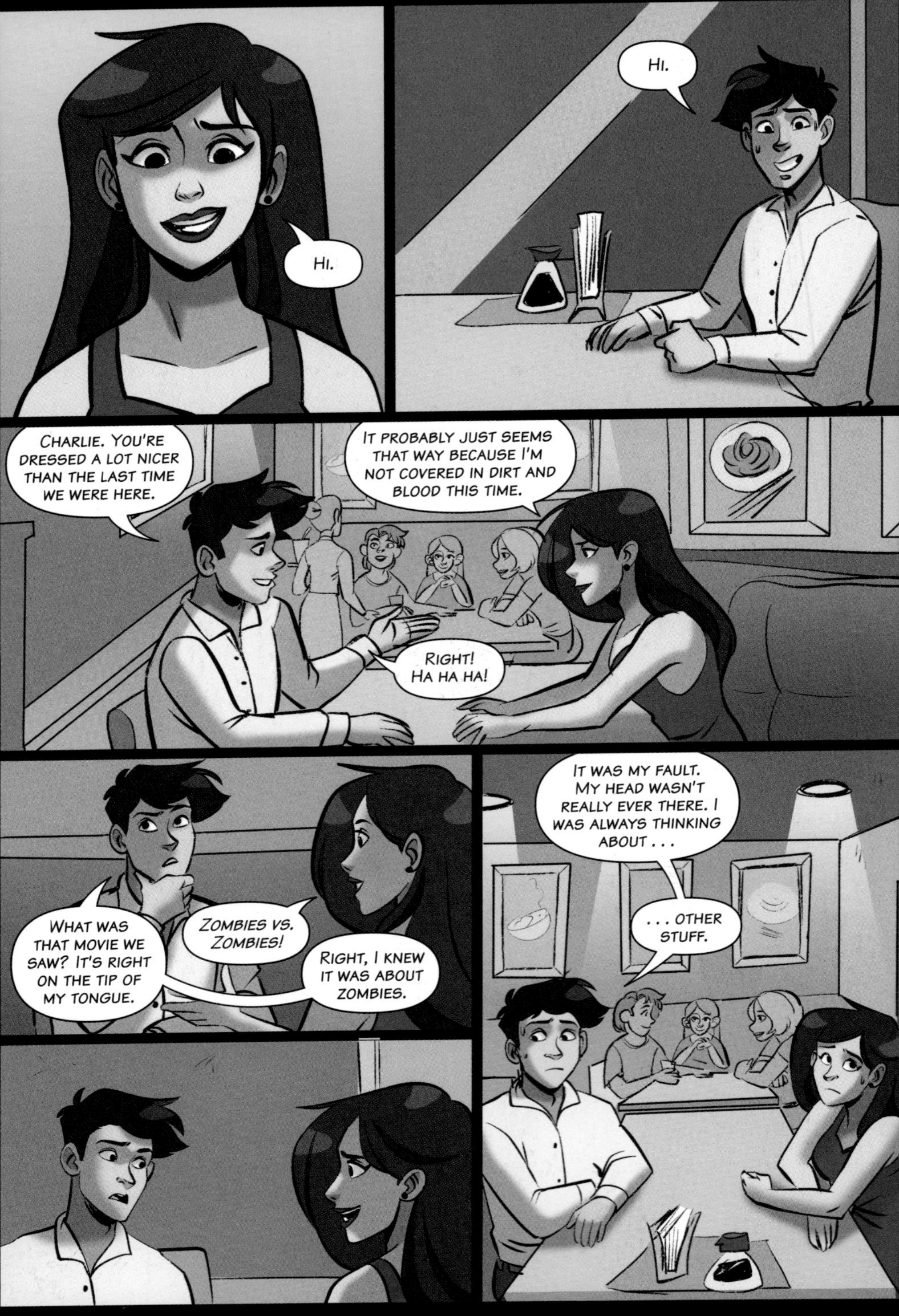
Hi.
Hi.
Charlie. You're dressed a lot nicer than the last time we were here.
It probably just seems that way because I'm not covered in dirt and blood this time.
Right! Ha ha ha!
What was that movie we saw? It's right on the tip of my tongue.
Zombies vs. Zombies!
Right, I knew it was about zombies.
It was my fault. My head wasn't really ever there. I was always thinking about . . .
. . . other stuff.

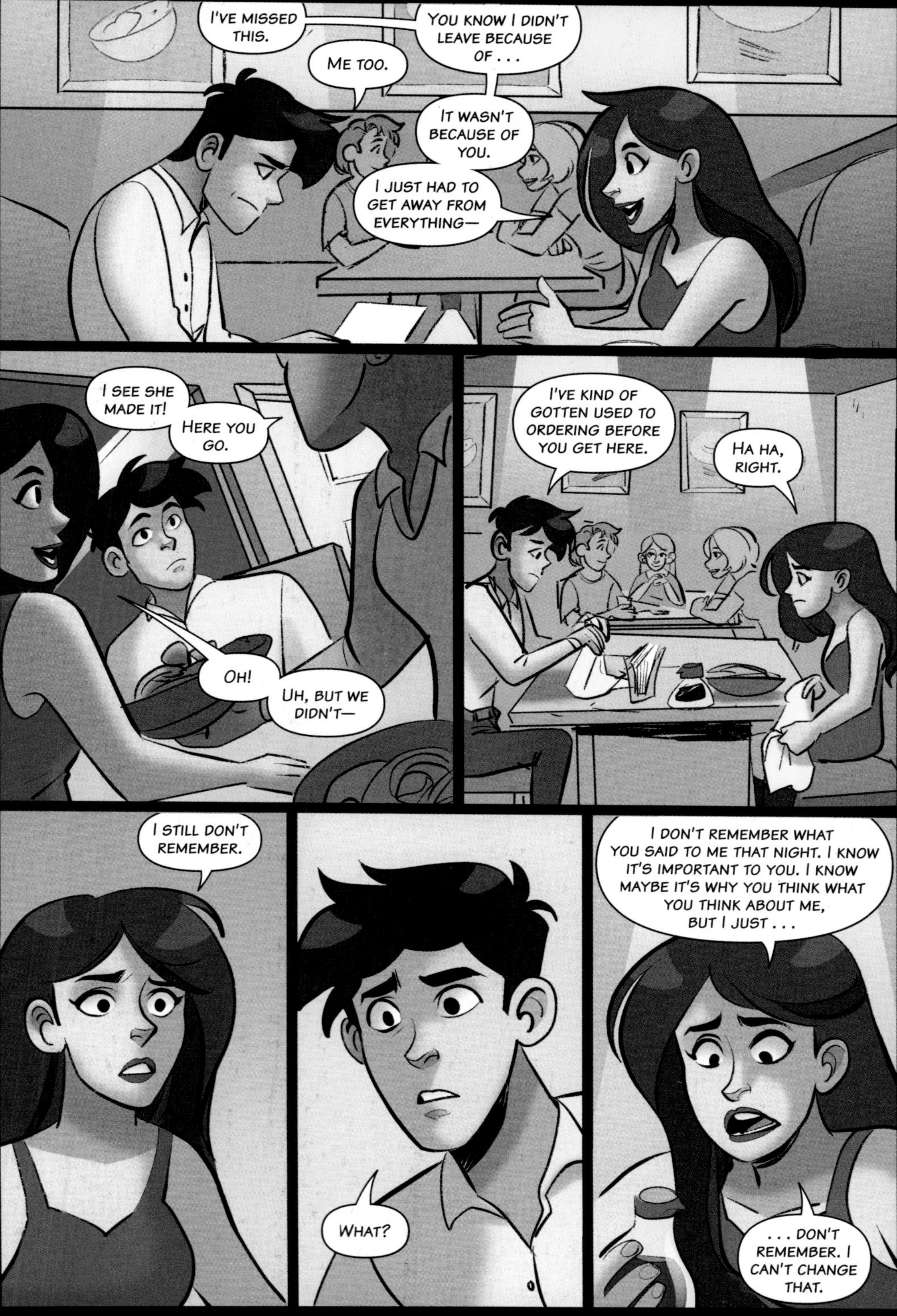

I'VE MISSED THIS.
ME TOO.
YOU KNOW I DIDN'T LEAVE BECAUSE OF . . .
IT WASN'T BECAUSE OF YOU.
I JUST HAD TO GET AWAY FROM EVERYTHING—
I SEE SHE MADE IT!
HERE YOU GO.
OH!
UH, BUT WE DIDN'T—
I'VE KIND OF GOTTEN USED TO ORDERING BEFORE YOU GET HERE.
HA HA, RIGHT.
I STILL DON'T REMEMBER.
WHAT?
I DON'T REMEMBER WHAT YOU SAID TO ME THAT NIGHT. I KNOW IT'S IMPORTANT TO YOU. I KNOW MAYBE IT'S WHY YOU THINK WHAT YOU THINK ABOUT ME, BUT I JUST . . .
. . . DON'T REMEMBER. I CAN'T CHANGE THAT.

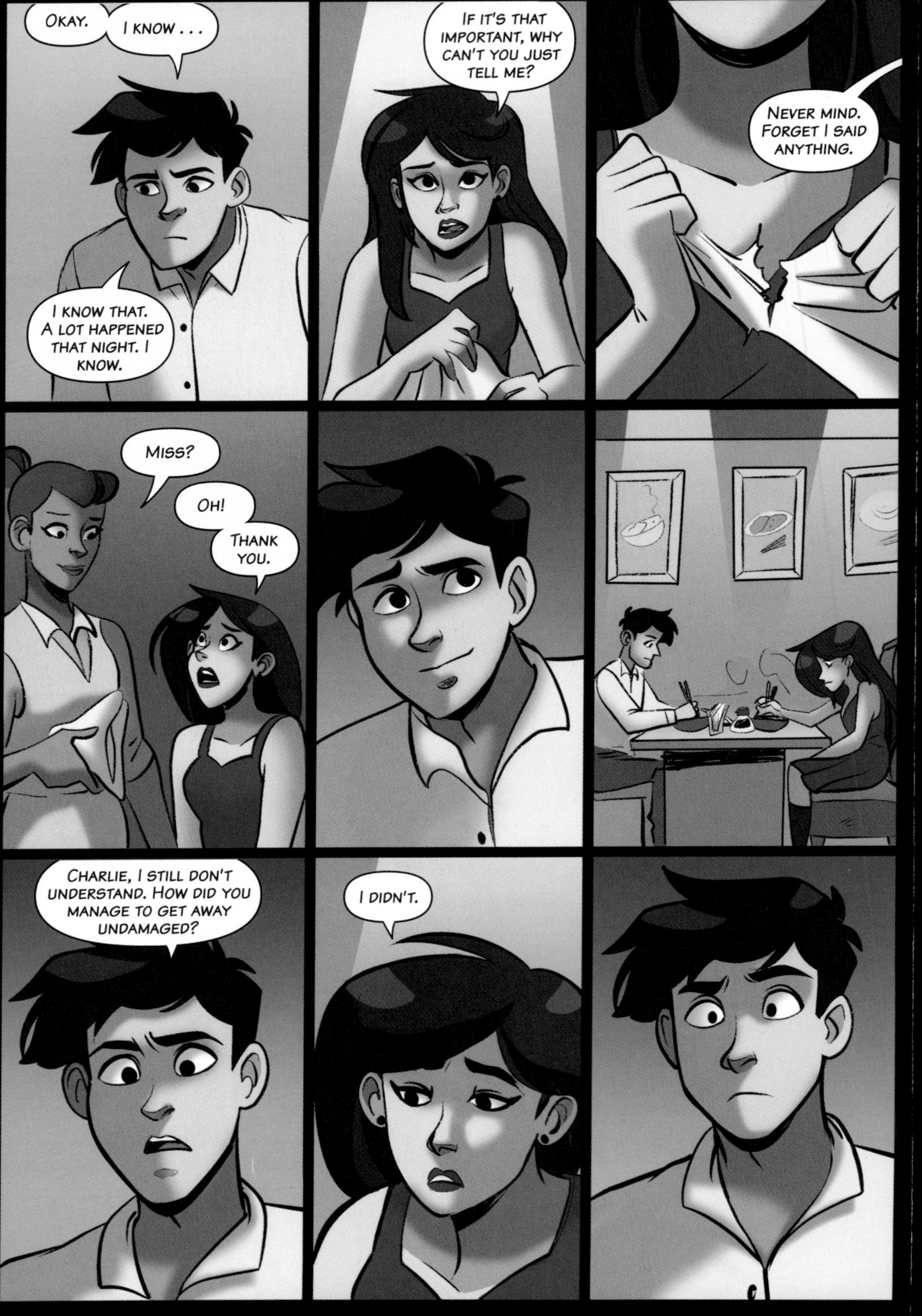
OKAY.
I KNOW . . .
I KNOW THAT. A LOT HAPPENED THAT NIGHT. I KNOW.
IF IT'S THAT IMPORTANT, WHY CAN'T YOU JUST TELL ME?
NEVER MIND. FORGET I SAID ANYTHING.
MISS?
OH!
THANK YOU.
CHARLIE, I STILL DON'T UNDERSTAND. HOW DID YOU MANAGE TO GET AWAY UNDAMAGED?
I DIDN'T.

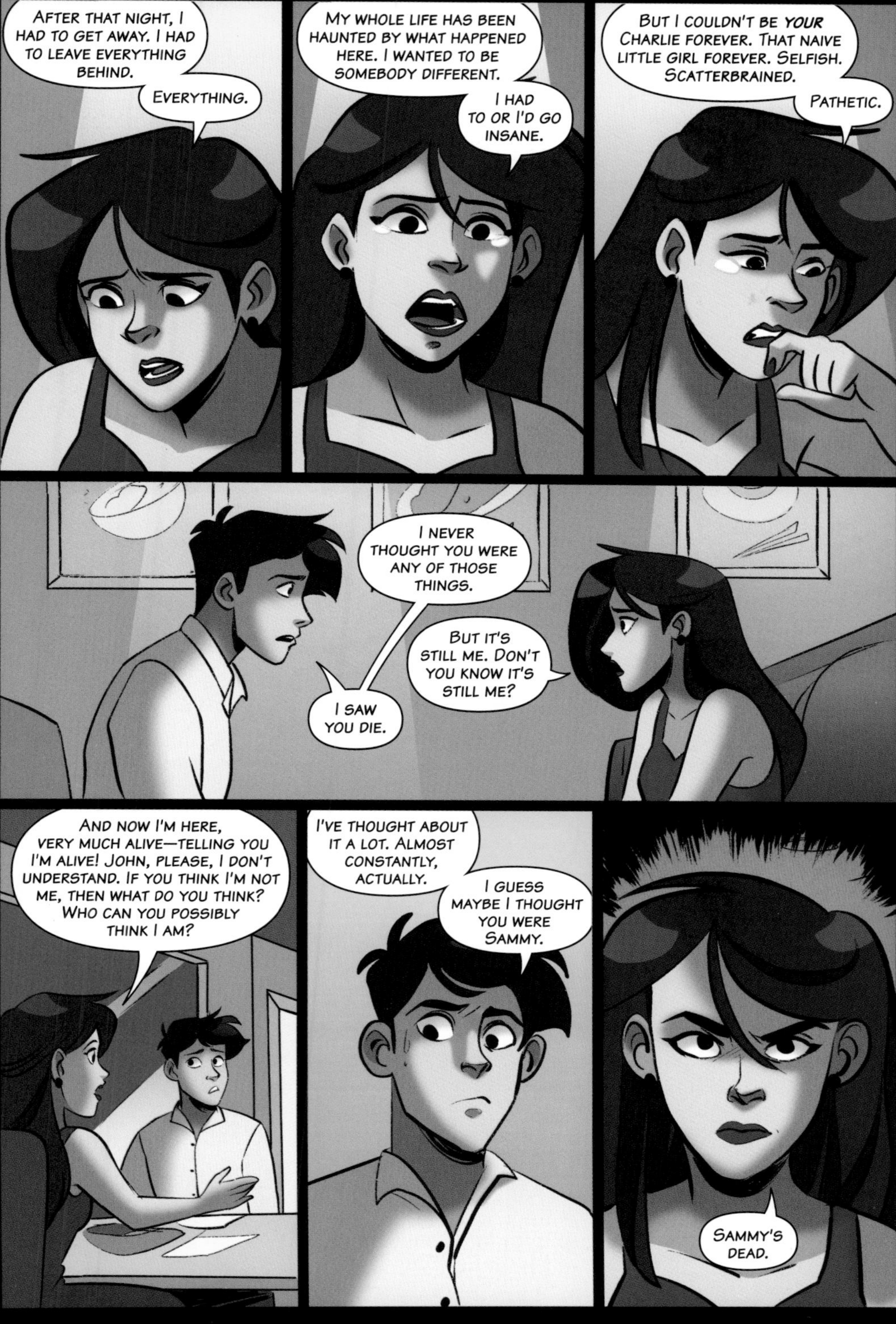
AFTER THAT NIGHT, I HAD TO GET AWAY. I HAD TO LEAVE EVERYTHING BEHIND.
EVERYTHING.
MY WHOLE LIFE HAS BEEN HAUNTED BY WHAT HAPPENED HERE. I WANTED TO BE SOMEBODY DIFFERENT.
I HAD TO OR I'D GO INSANE.
BUT I COULDN'T BE *YOUR* CHARLIE FOREVER. THAT NAIVE LITTLE GIRL FOREVER. SELFISH. SCATTERBRAINED.
PATHETIC.
I NEVER THOUGHT YOU WERE ANY OF THOSE THINGS.
I SAW YOU DIE.
BUT IT'S STILL ME. DON'T YOU KNOW IT'S STILL ME?
AND NOW I'M HERE, VERY MUCH ALIVE—TELLING YOU I'M ALIVE! JOHN, PLEASE, I DON'T UNDERSTAND. IF YOU THINK I'M NOT ME, THEN WHAT DO YOU THINK? WHO CAN YOU POSSIBLY THINK I AM?
I'VE THOUGHT ABOUT IT A LOT. ALMOST CONSTANTLY, ACTUALLY.
I GUESS MAYBE I THOUGHT YOU WERE SAMMY.
SAMMY'S DEAD.

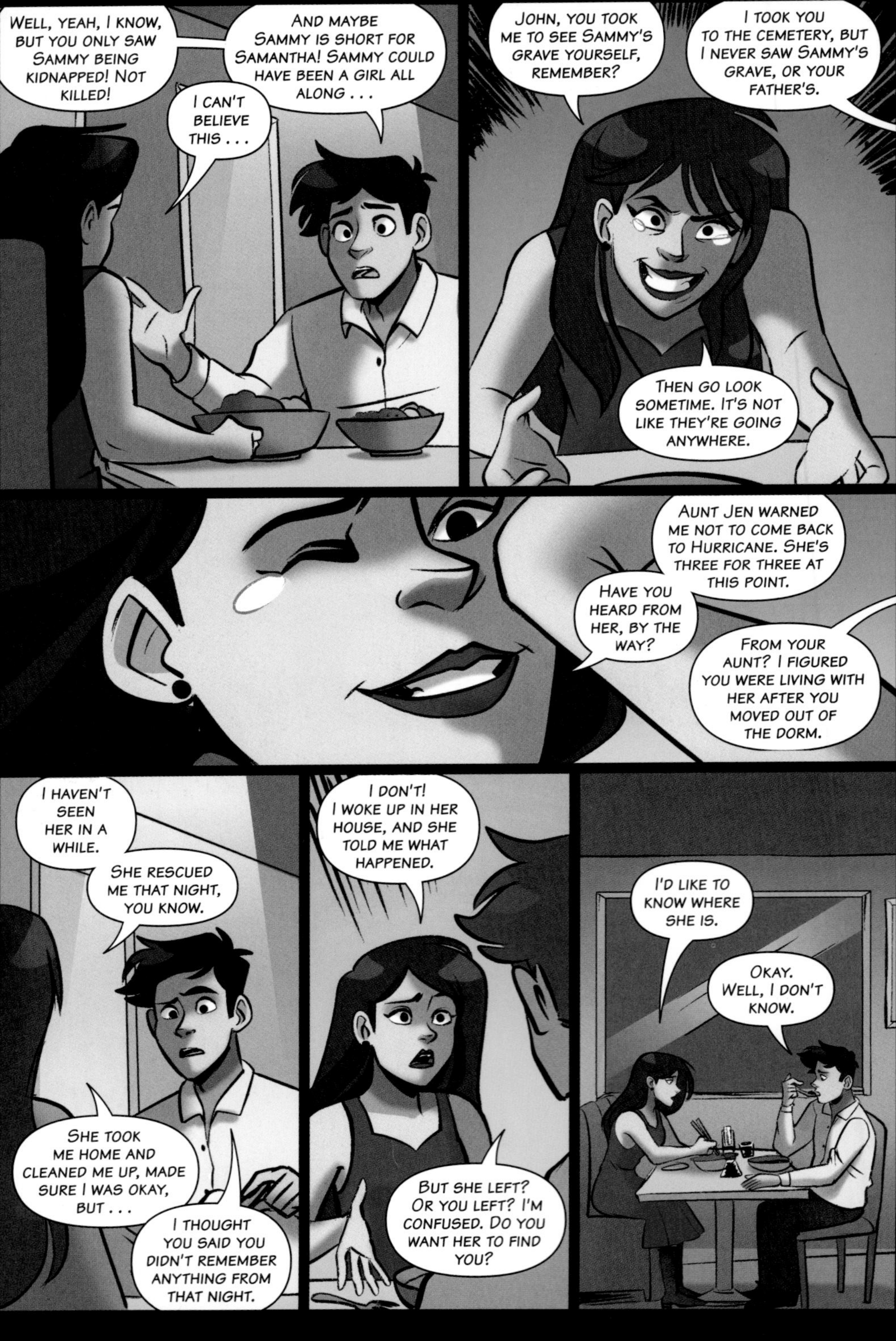
WELL, YEAH, I KNOW, BUT YOU ONLY SAW SAMMY BEING KIDNAPPED! NOT KILLED!
AND MAYBE SAMMY IS SHORT FOR SAMANTHA! SAMMY COULD HAVE BEEN A GIRL ALL ALONG . . .
I CAN'T BELIEVE THIS . . .
JOHN, YOU TOOK ME TO SEE SAMMY'S GRAVE YOURSELF, REMEMBER?
I TOOK YOU TO THE CEMETERY, BUT I NEVER SAW SAMMY'S GRAVE, OR YOUR FATHER'S.
THEN GO LOOK SOMETIME. IT'S NOT LIKE THEY'RE GOING ANYWHERE.
AUNT JEN WARNED ME NOT TO COME BACK TO HURRICANE. SHE'S THREE FOR THREE AT THIS POINT.
HAVE YOU HEARD FROM HER, BY THE WAY?
FROM YOUR AUNT? I FIGURED YOU WERE LIVING WITH HER AFTER YOU MOVED OUT OF THE DORM.
I HAVEN'T SEEN HER IN A WHILE.
SHE RESCUED ME THAT NIGHT, YOU KNOW.
SHE TOOK ME HOME AND CLEANED ME UP, MADE SURE I WAS OKAY, BUT . . .
I THOUGHT YOU SAID YOU DIDN'T REMEMBER ANYTHING FROM THAT NIGHT.
I DON'T! I WOKE UP IN HER HOUSE, AND SHE TOLD ME WHAT HAPPENED.
BUT SHE LEFT? OR YOU LEFT? I'M CONFUSED. DO YOU WANT HER TO FIND YOU?
I'D LIKE TO KNOW WHERE SHE IS.
OKAY. WELL, I DON'T KNOW.

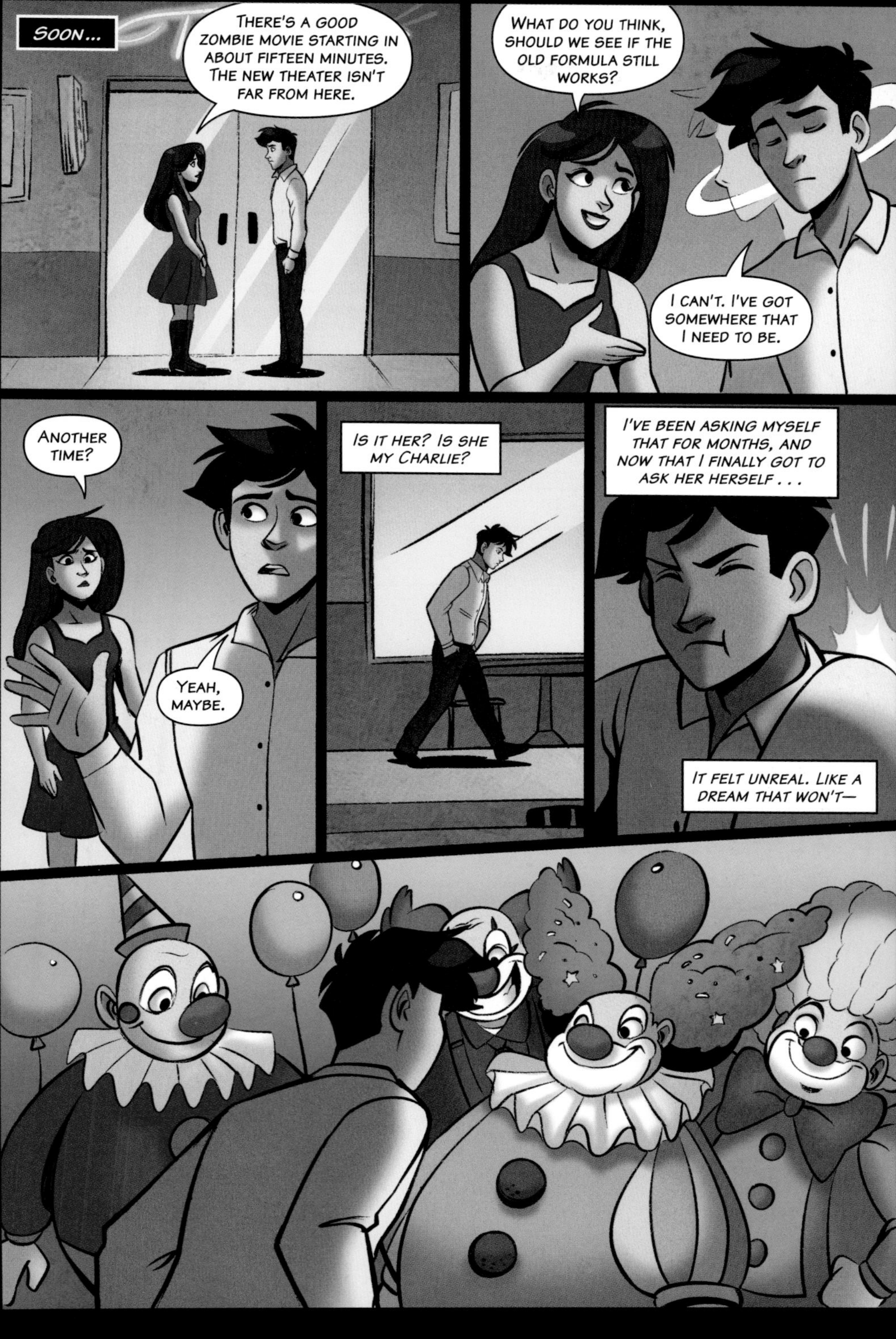
SOON...
THERE'S A GOOD ZOMBIE MOVIE STARTING IN ABOUT FIFTEEN MINUTES. THE NEW THEATER ISN'T FAR FROM HERE.
WHAT DO YOU THINK, SHOULD WE SEE IF THE OLD FORMULA STILL WORKS?
I CAN'T. I'VE GOT SOMEWHERE THAT I NEED TO BE.
ANOTHER TIME?
YEAH, MAYBE.
IS IT HER? IS SHE MY CHARLIE?
I'VE BEEN ASKING MYSELF THAT FOR MONTHS, AND NOW THAT I FINALLY GOT TO ASK HER HERSELF . . .
IT FELT UNREAL. LIKE A DREAM THAT WON'T—

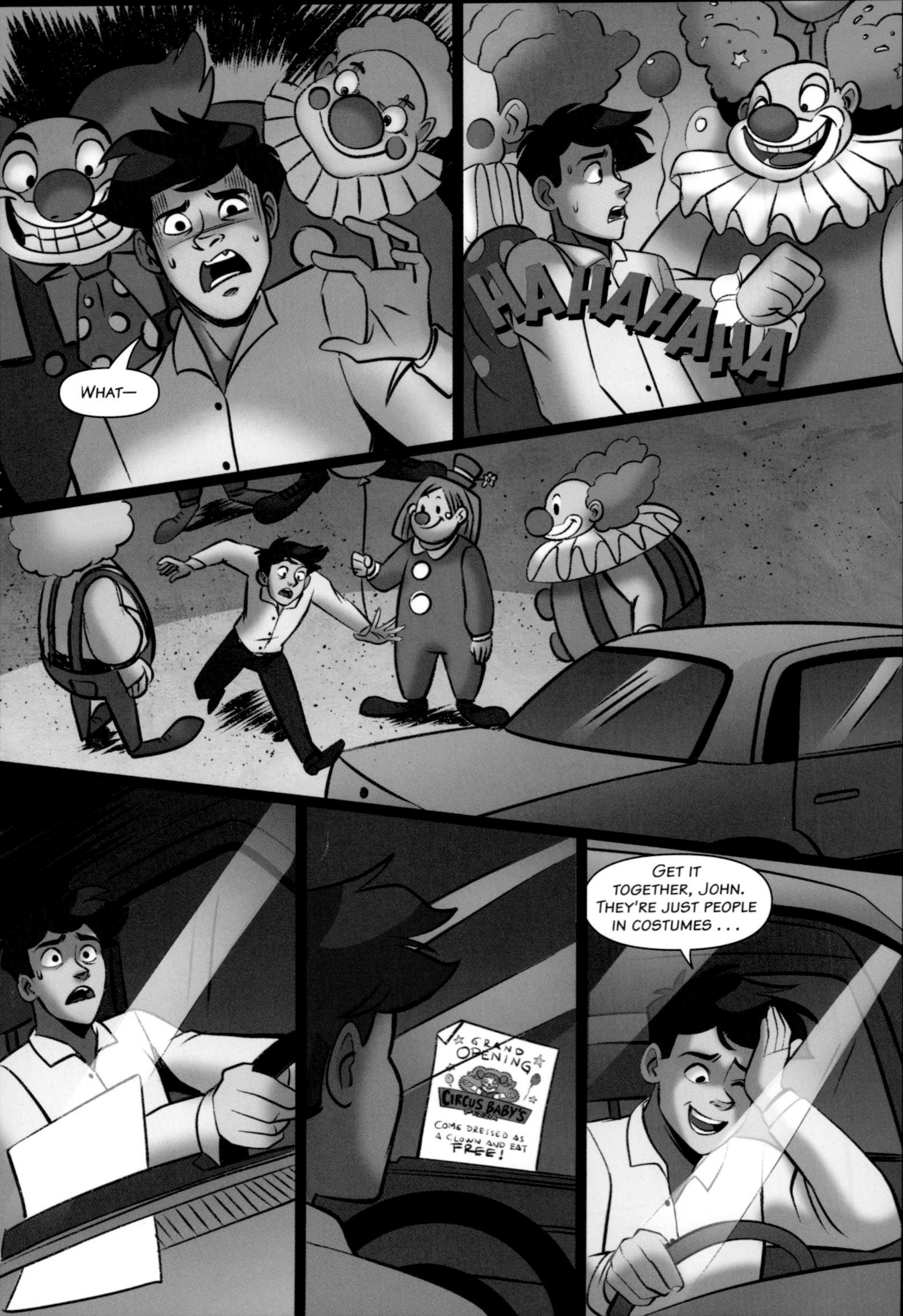
WHAT—
HAHAHAHAHA
GRAND OPENING
CIRCUS BABY'S
PIZZA
COME DRESSED AS A CLOWN AND EAT FREE!
GET IT TOGETHER, JOHN. THEY'RE JUST PEOPLE IN COSTUMES . . .

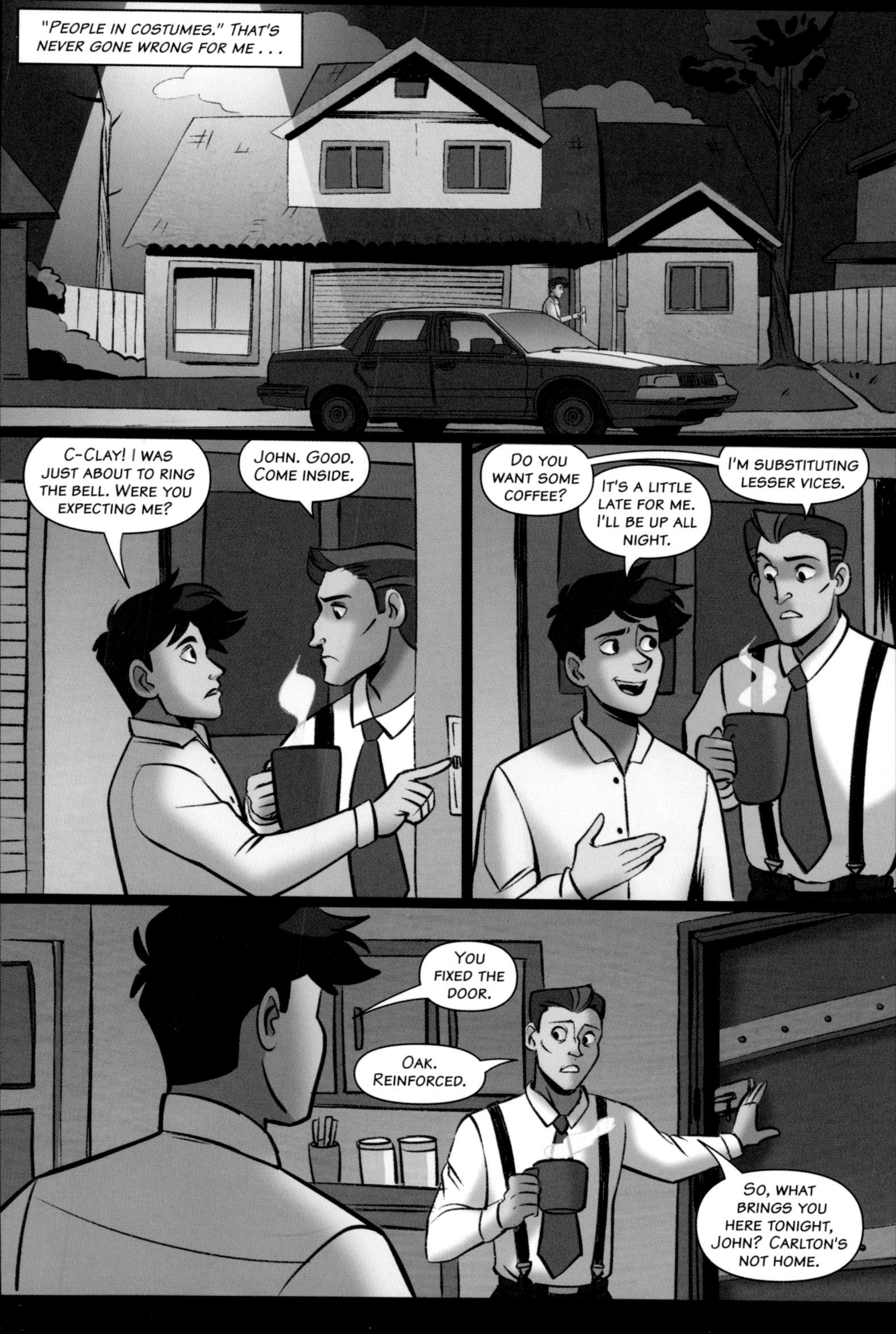
"PEOPLE IN COSTUMES." THAT'S NEVER GONE WRONG FOR ME . . .
C-CLAY! I WAS JUST ABOUT TO RING THE BELL. WERE YOU EXPECTING ME?
JOHN. GOOD. COME INSIDE.
DO YOU WANT SOME COFFEE?
IT'S A LITTLE LATE FOR ME. I'LL BE UP ALL NIGHT.
I'M SUBSTITUTING LESSER VICES.
YOU FIXED THE DOOR.
OAK. REINFORCED.
SO, WHAT BRINGS YOU HERE TONIGHT, JOHN? CARLTON'S NOT HOME.

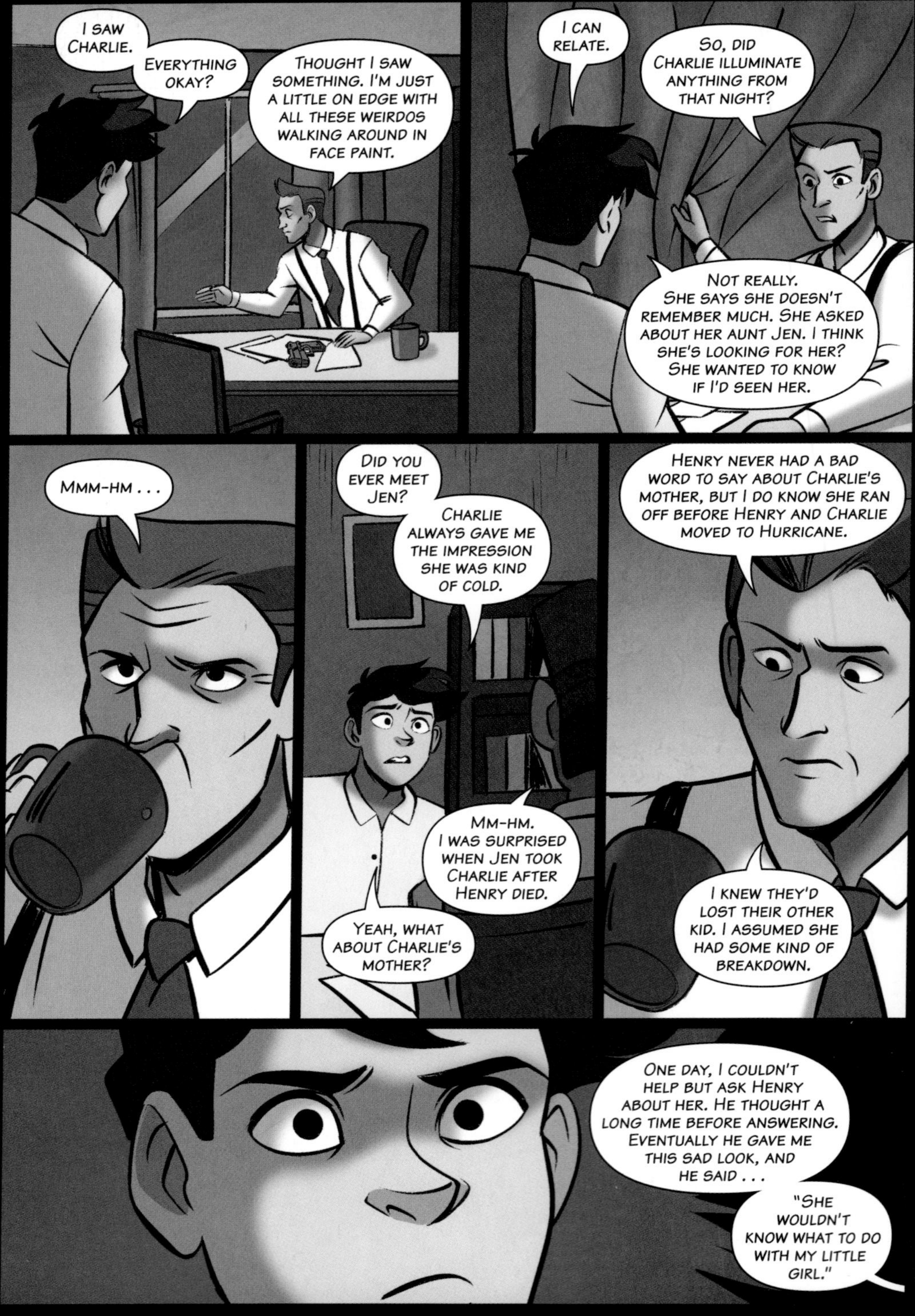

I SAW CHARLIE.
EVERYTHING OKAY?
THOUGHT I SAW SOMETHING. I'M JUST A LITTLE ON EDGE WITH ALL THESE WEIRDOS WALKING AROUND IN FACE PAINT.
I CAN RELATE.
SO, DID CHARLIE ILLUMINATE ANYTHING FROM THAT NIGHT?
NOT REALLY. SHE SAYS SHE DOESN'T REMEMBER MUCH. SHE ASKED ABOUT HER AUNT JEN. I THINK SHE'S LOOKING FOR HER? SHE WANTED TO KNOW IF I'D SEEN HER.
MMM-HM . . .
DID YOU EVER MEET JEN?
CHARLIE ALWAYS GAVE ME THE IMPRESSION SHE WAS KIND OF COLD.
MM-HM. I WAS SURPRISED WHEN JEN TOOK CHARLIE AFTER HENRY DIED.
YEAH, WHAT ABOUT CHARLIE'S MOTHER?
HENRY NEVER HAD A BAD WORD TO SAY ABOUT CHARLIE'S MOTHER, BUT I DO KNOW SHE RAN OFF BEFORE HENRY AND CHARLIE MOVED TO HURRICANE.
I KNEW THEY'D LOST THEIR OTHER KID. I ASSUMED SHE HAD SOME KIND OF BREAKDOWN.
ONE DAY, I COULDN'T HELP BUT ASK HENRY ABOUT HER. HE THOUGHT A LONG TIME BEFORE ANSWERING. EVENTUALLY HE GAVE ME THIS SAD LOOK, AND HE SAID . . .
"SHE WOULDN'T KNOW WHAT TO DO WITH MY LITTLE GIRL."

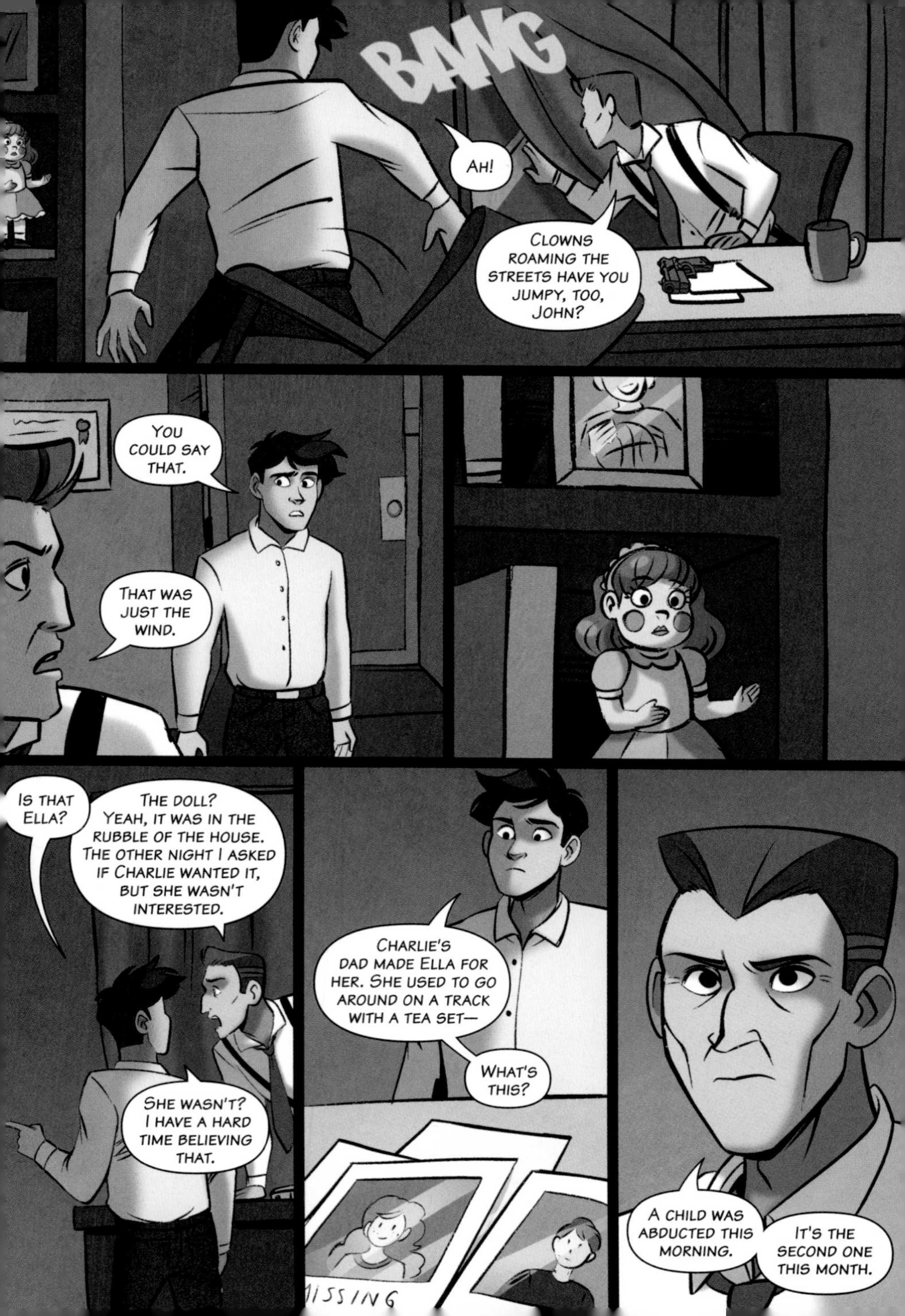
BANG
AH!
CLOWNS ROAMING THE STREETS HAVE YOU JUMPY, TOO, JOHN?
YOU COULD SAY THAT.
THAT WAS JUST THE WIND.
IS THAT ELLA?
THE DOLL? YEAH, IT WAS IN THE RUBBLE OF THE HOUSE. THE OTHER NIGHT I ASKED IF CHARLIE WANTED IT, BUT SHE WASN'T INTERESTED.
SHE WASN'T? I HAVE A HARD TIME BELIEVING THAT.
CHARLIE'S DAD MADE ELLA FOR HER. SHE USED TO GO AROUND ON A TRACK WITH A TEA SET—
WHAT'S THIS?
MISSING
A CHILD WAS ABDUCTED THIS MORNING.
IT'S THE SECOND ONE THIS MONTH.

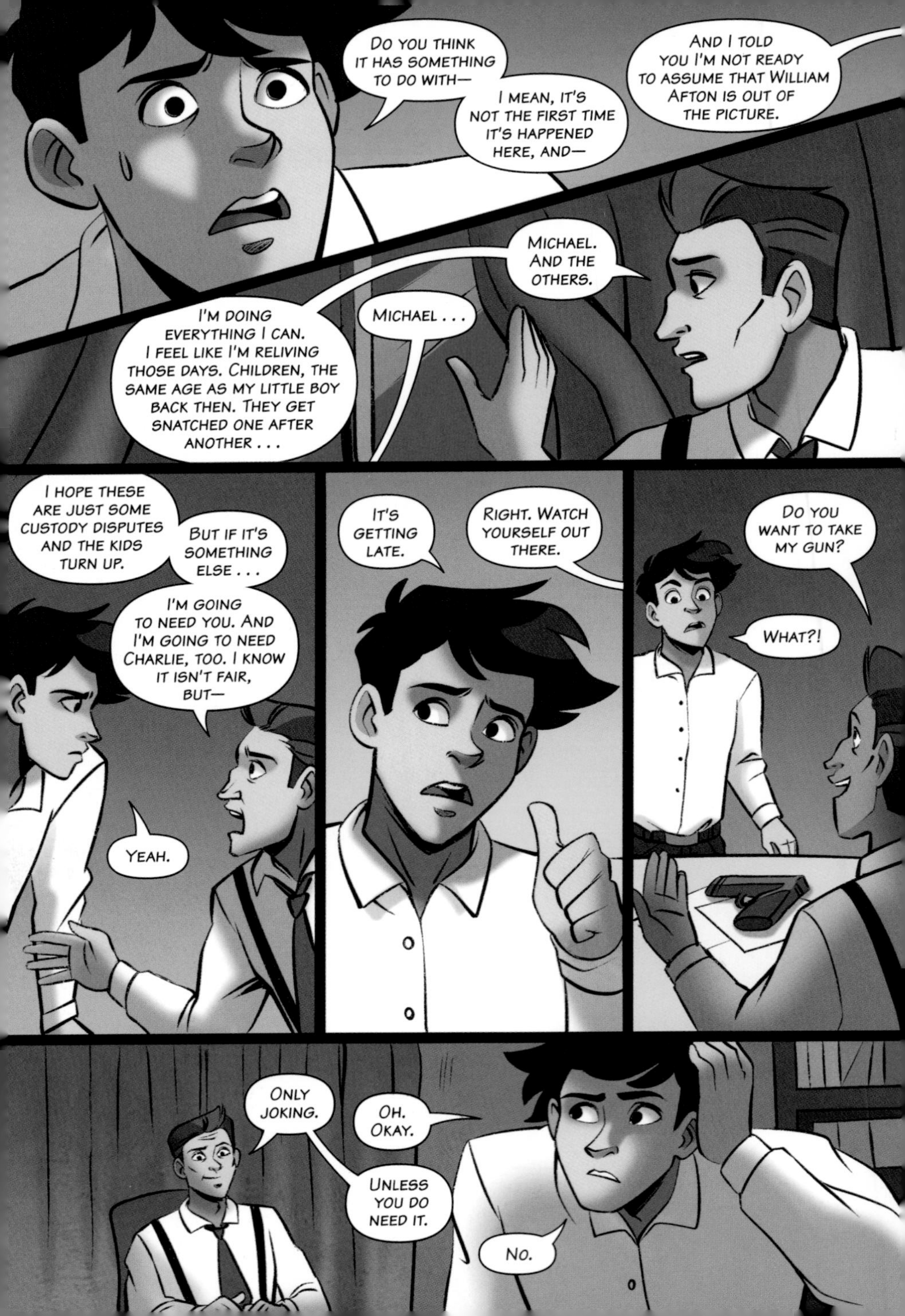
DO YOU THINK IT HAS SOMETHING TO DO WITH—
I MEAN, IT'S NOT THE FIRST TIME IT'S HAPPENED HERE, AND—
AND I TOLD YOU I'M NOT READY TO ASSUME THAT WILLIAM AFTON IS OUT OF THE PICTURE.
MICHAEL. AND THE OTHERS.
MICHAEL . . .
I'M DOING EVERYTHING I CAN. I FEEL LIKE I'M RELIVING THOSE DAYS. CHILDREN, THE SAME AGE AS MY LITTLE BOY BACK THEN. THEY GET SNATCHED ONE AFTER ANOTHER . . .
I HOPE THESE ARE JUST SOME CUSTODY DISPUTES AND THE KIDS TURN UP.
BUT IF IT'S SOMETHING ELSE . . .
I'M GOING TO NEED YOU. AND I'M GOING TO NEED CHARLIE, TOO. I KNOW IT ISN'T FAIR, BUT—
YEAH.
IT'S GETTING LATE.
RIGHT. WATCH YOURSELF OUT THERE.
DO YOU WANT TO TAKE MY GUN?
WHAT?!
ONLY JOKING.
OH. OKAY.
UNLESS YOU DO NEED IT.
NO.

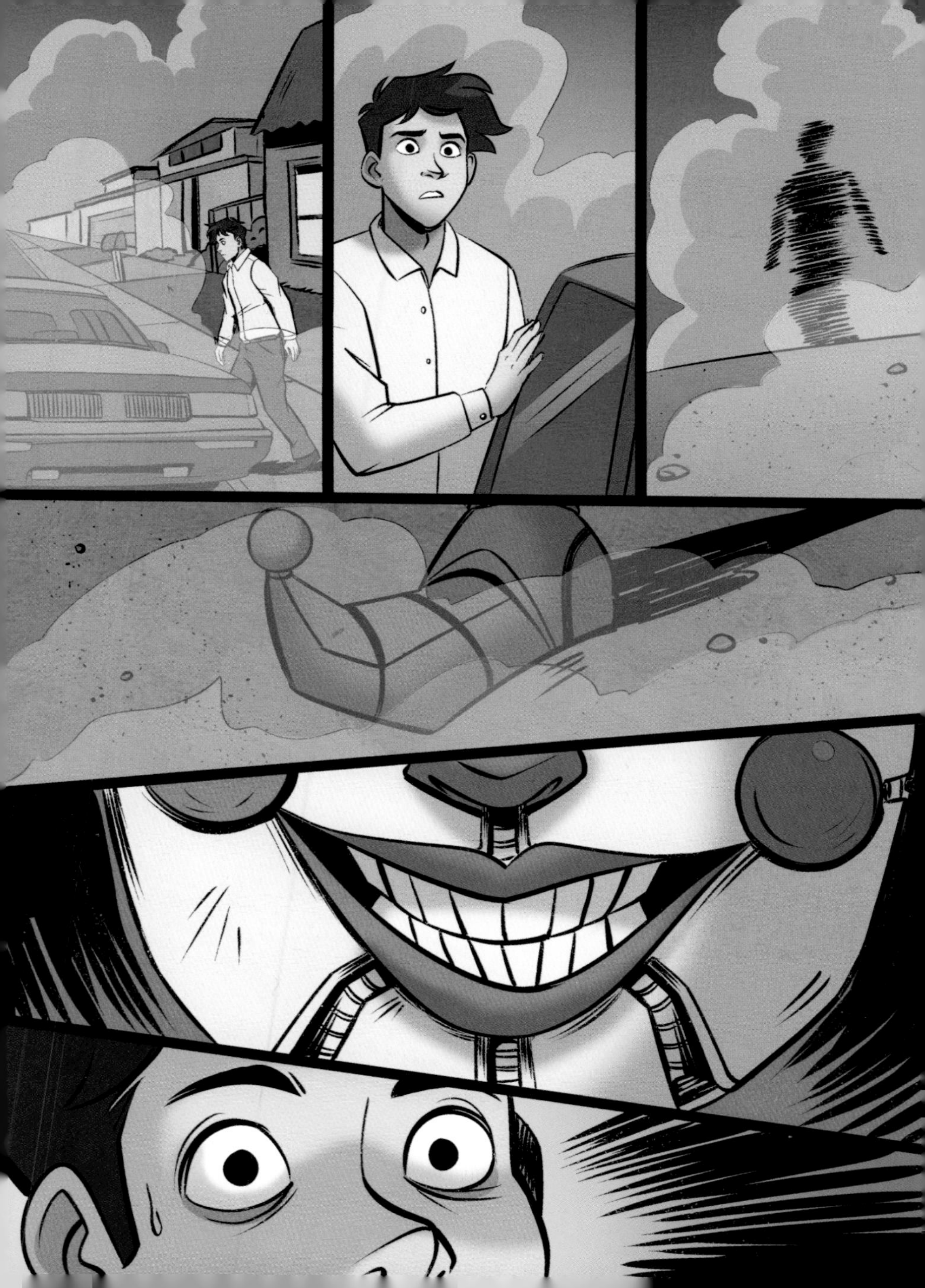

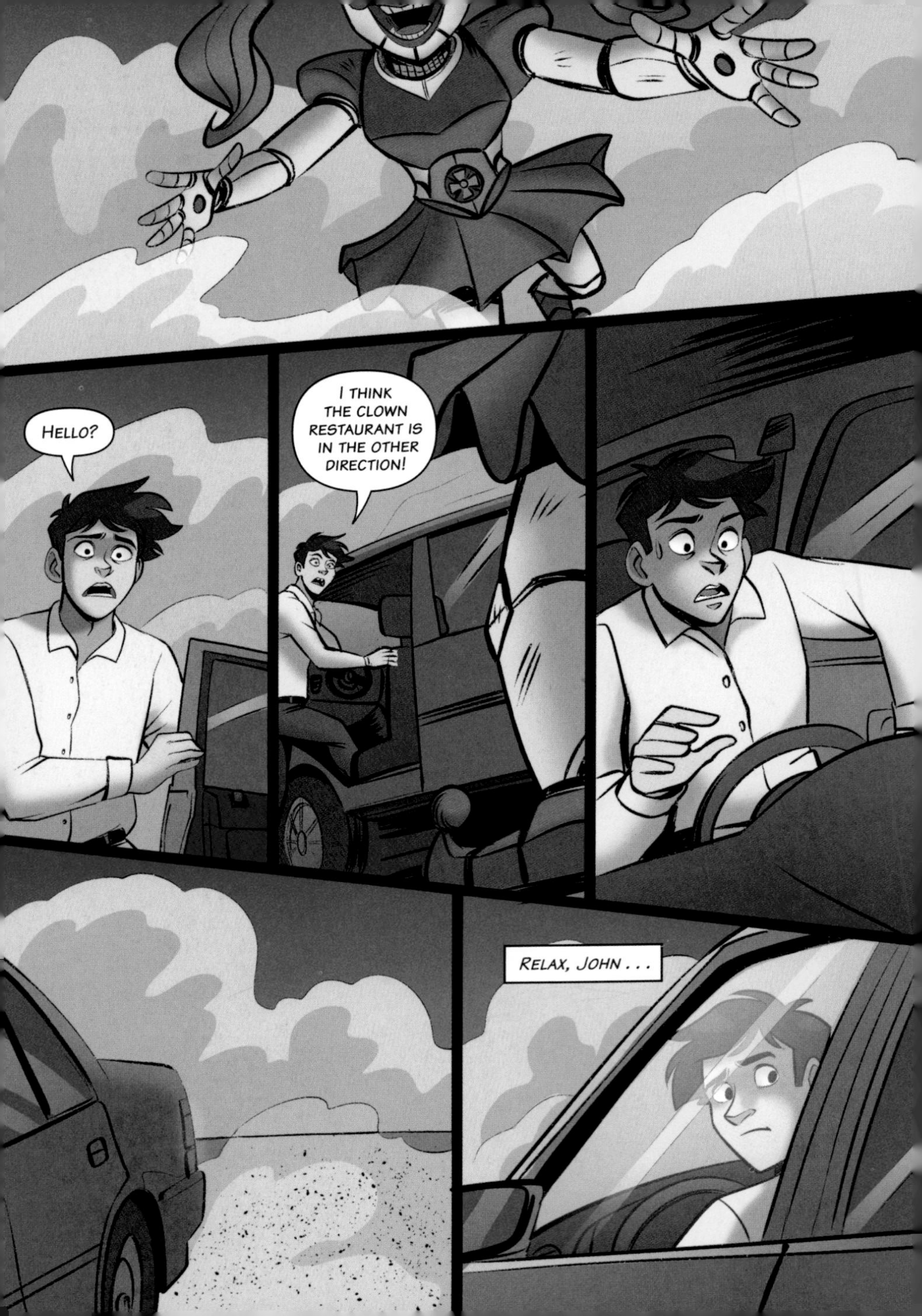
HELLO?
I THINK THE CLOWN RESTAURANT IS IN THE OTHER DIRECTION!
RELAX, JOHN . . .

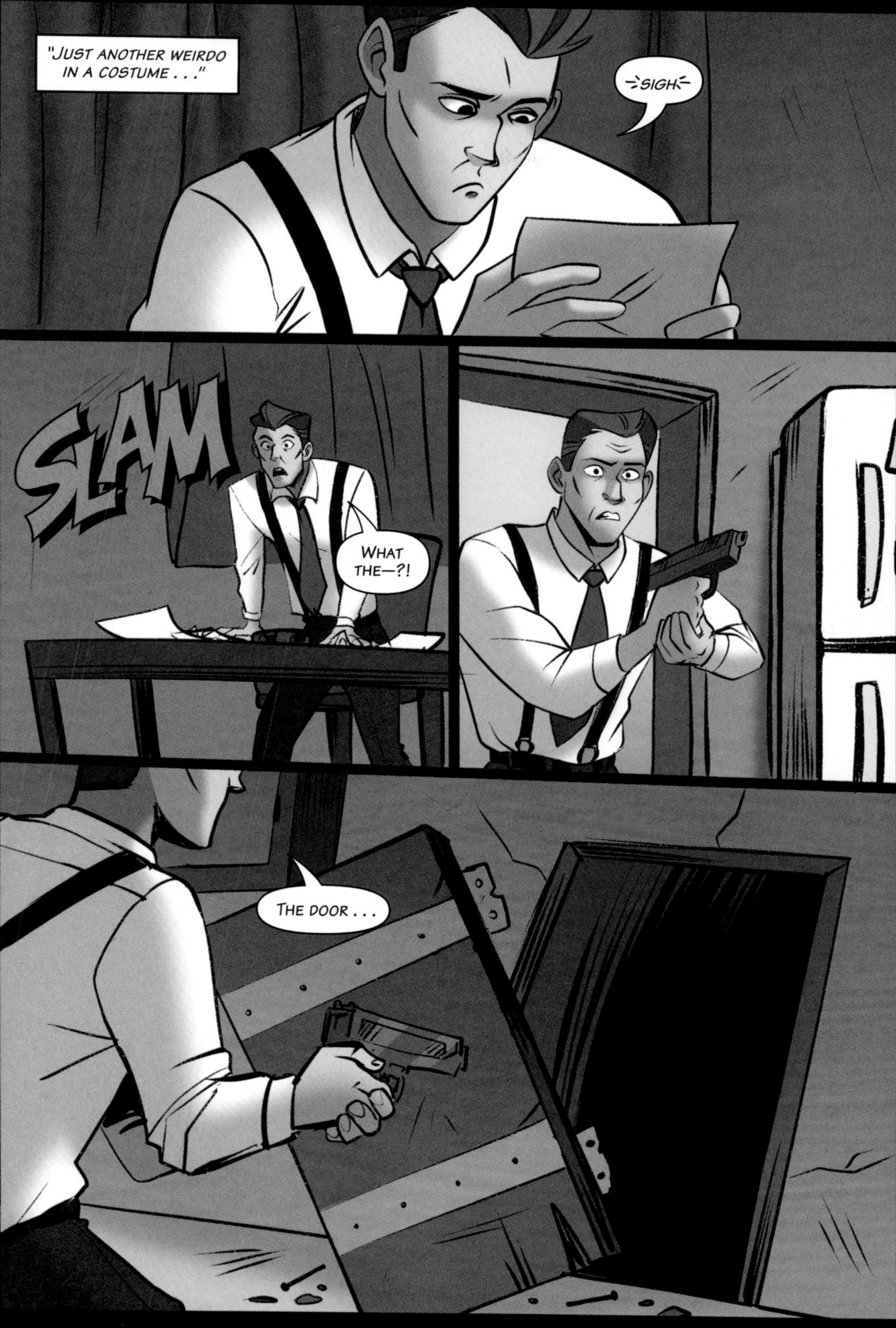
"JUST ANOTHER WEIRDO IN A COSTUME . . ."
-SIGH-
SLAM
WHAT THE—?!
THE DOOR . . .

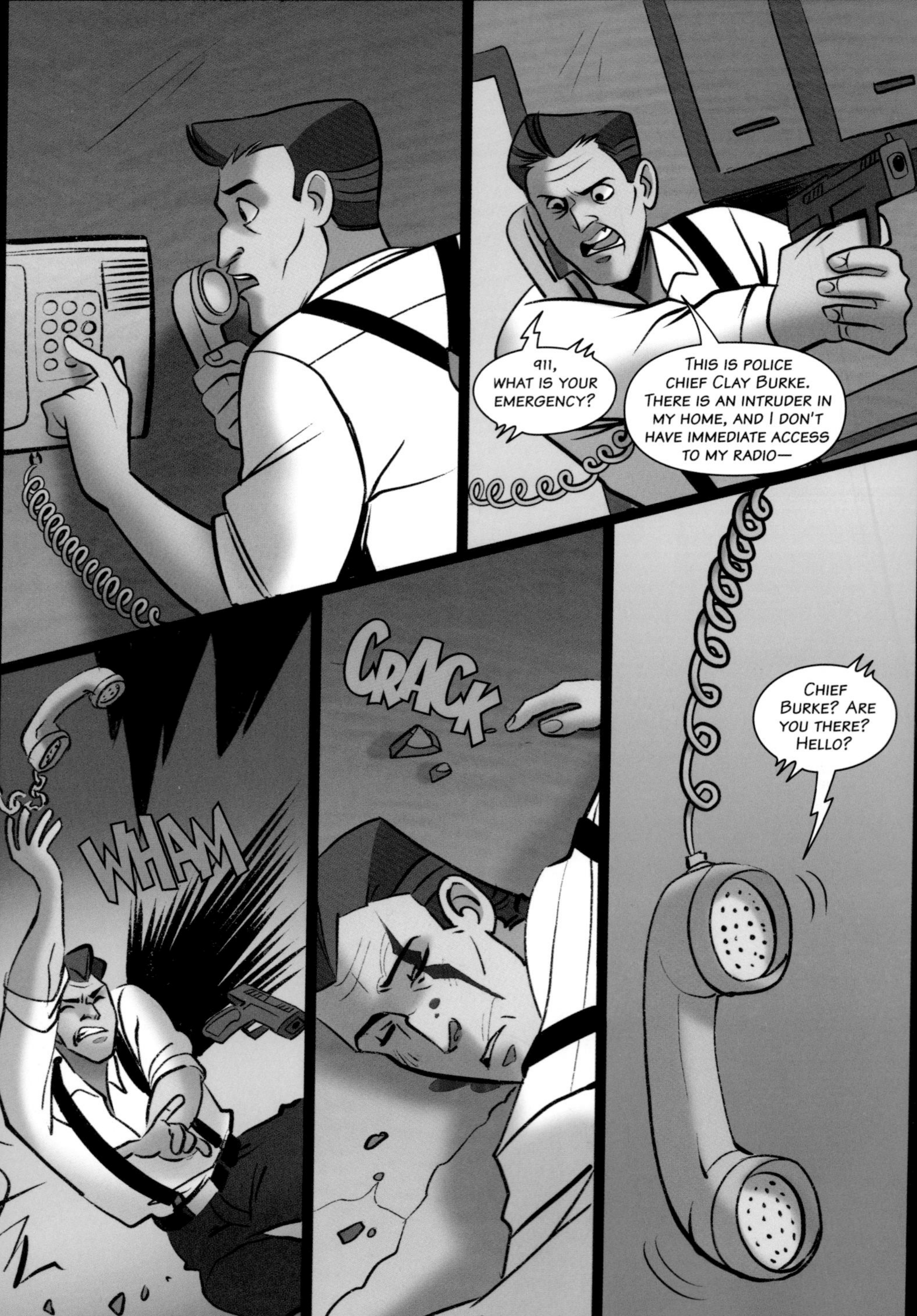
911,
WHAT IS YOUR EMERGENCY?
THIS IS POLICE CHIEF CLAY BURKE. THERE IS AN INTRUDER IN MY HOME, AND I DON'T HAVE IMMEDIATE ACCESS TO MY RADIO—
WHAM
CRACK
CHIEF BURKE? ARE YOU THERE? HELLO?

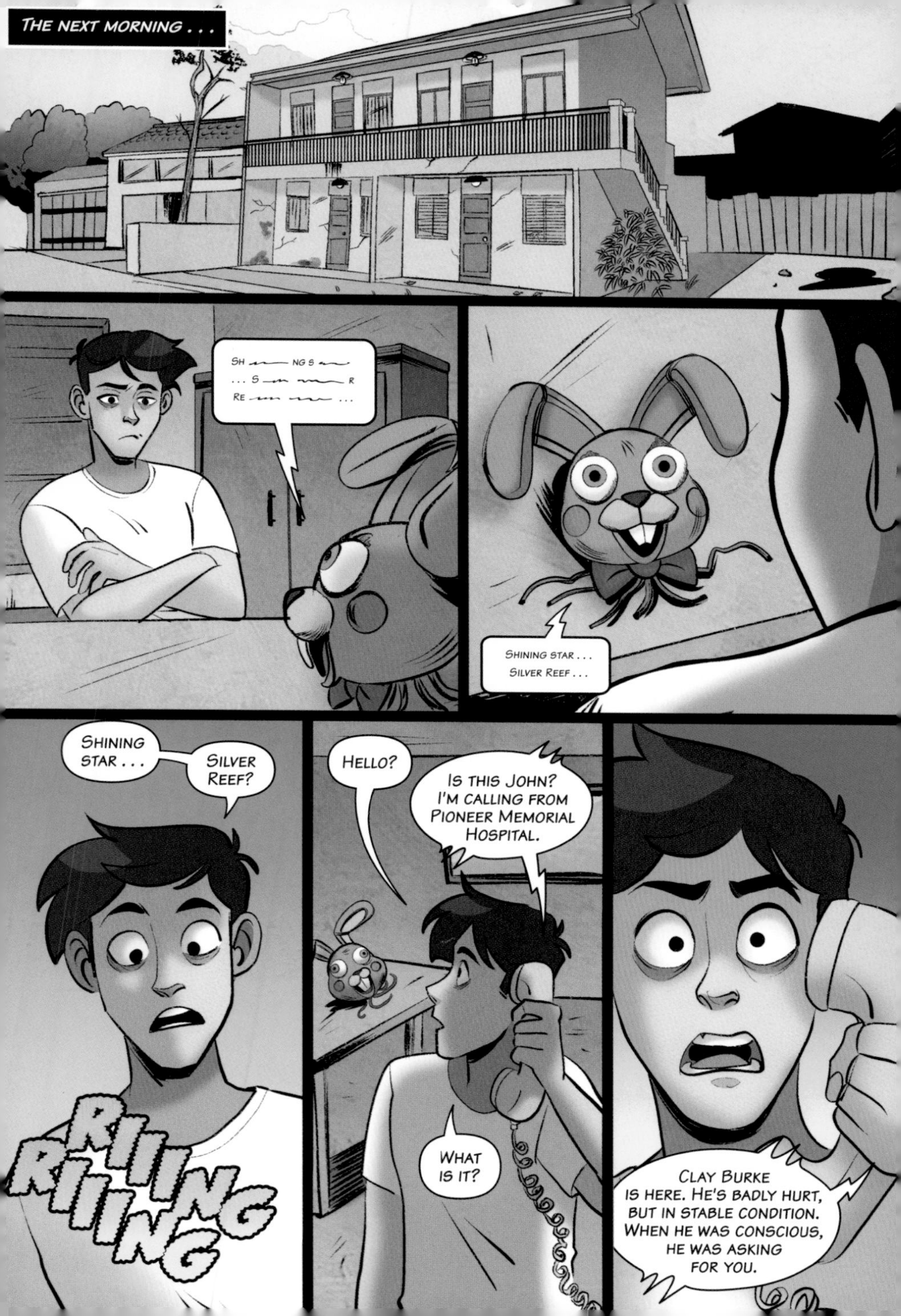

THE NEXT MORNING . . .
SHINING STAR . . . SILVER REEF . . .
SHINING STAR . . .
SILVER REEF?
RIIING RIIING
HELLO?
IS THIS JOHN? I'M CALLING FROM PIONEER MEMORIAL HOSPITAL.
WHAT IS IT?
CLAY BURKE IS HERE. HE'S BADLY HURT, BUT IN STABLE CONDITION. WHEN HE WAS CONSCIOUS, HE WAS ASKING FOR YOU.

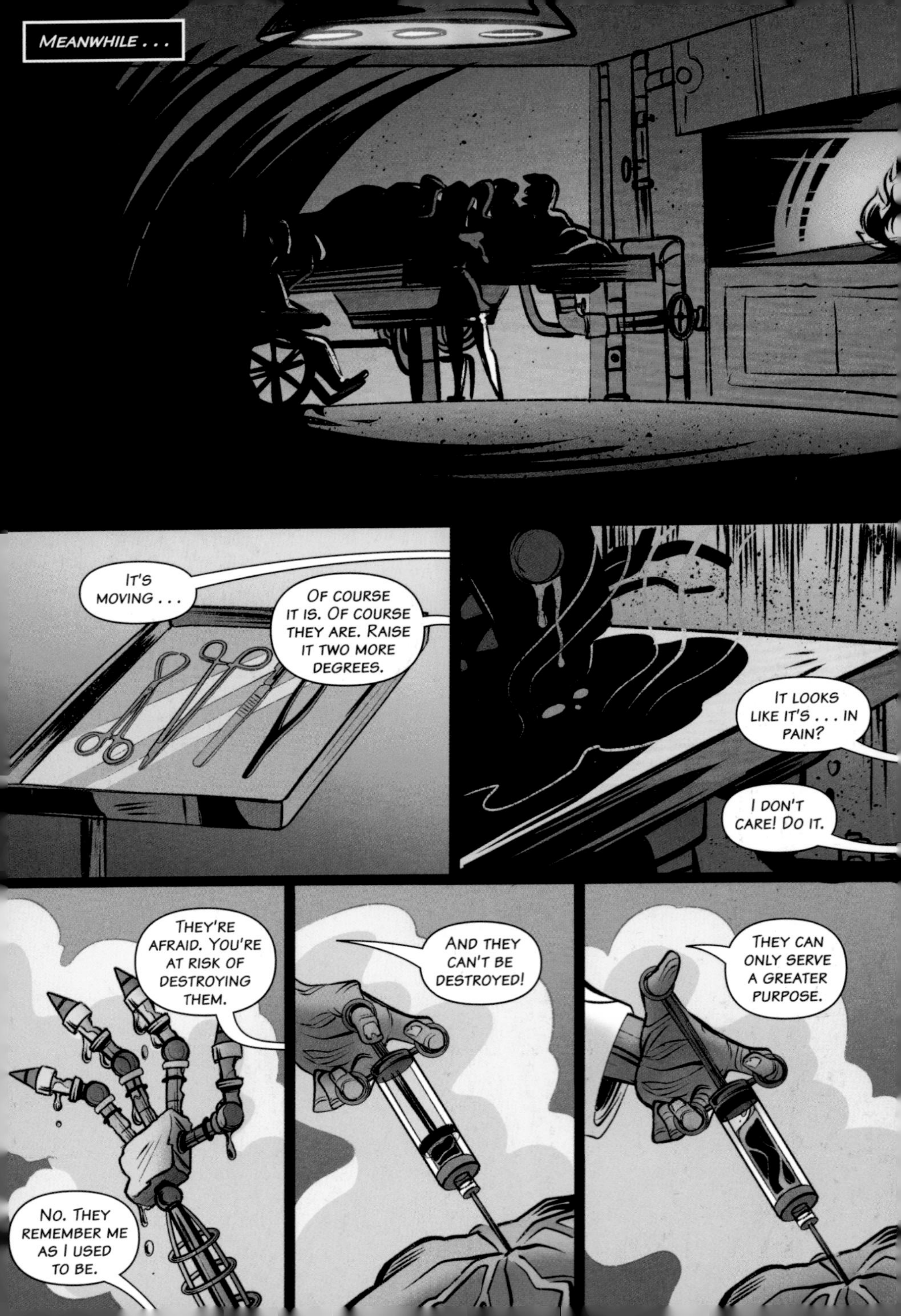
MEANWHILE . . .
IT'S MOVING . . .
OF COURSE IT IS. OF COURSE THEY ARE. RAISE IT TWO MORE DEGREES.
IT LOOKS LIKE IT'S . . . IN PAIN?
I DON'T CARE! DO IT.
THEY'RE AFRAID. YOU'RE AT RISK OF DESTROYING THEM.
NO. THEY REMEMBER ME AS I USED TO BE.
AND THEY CAN'T BE DESTROYED!
THEY CAN ONLY SERVE A GREATER PURPOSE.

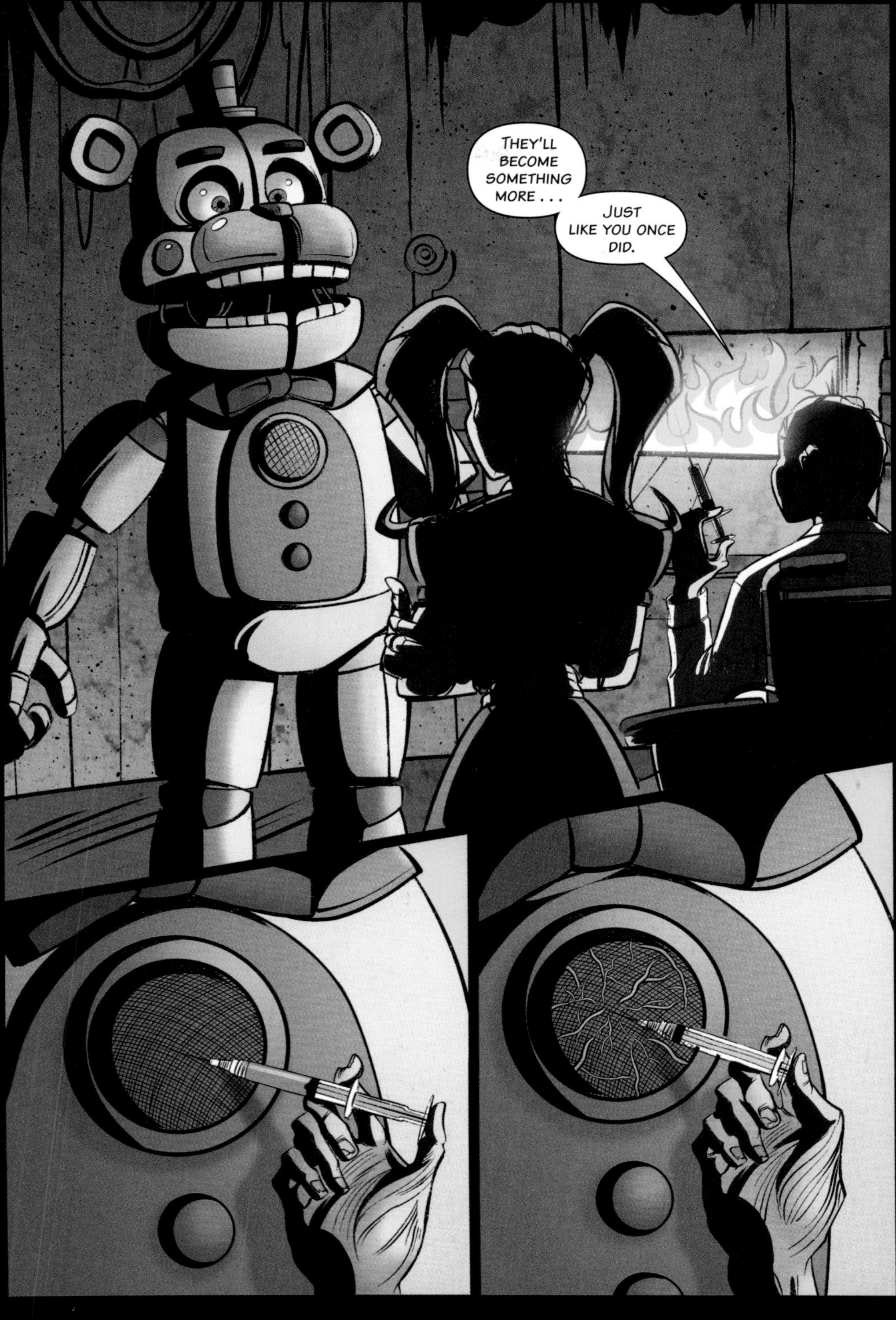
THEY'LL BECOME SOMETHING MORE . . .
JUST LIKE YOU ONCE DID.

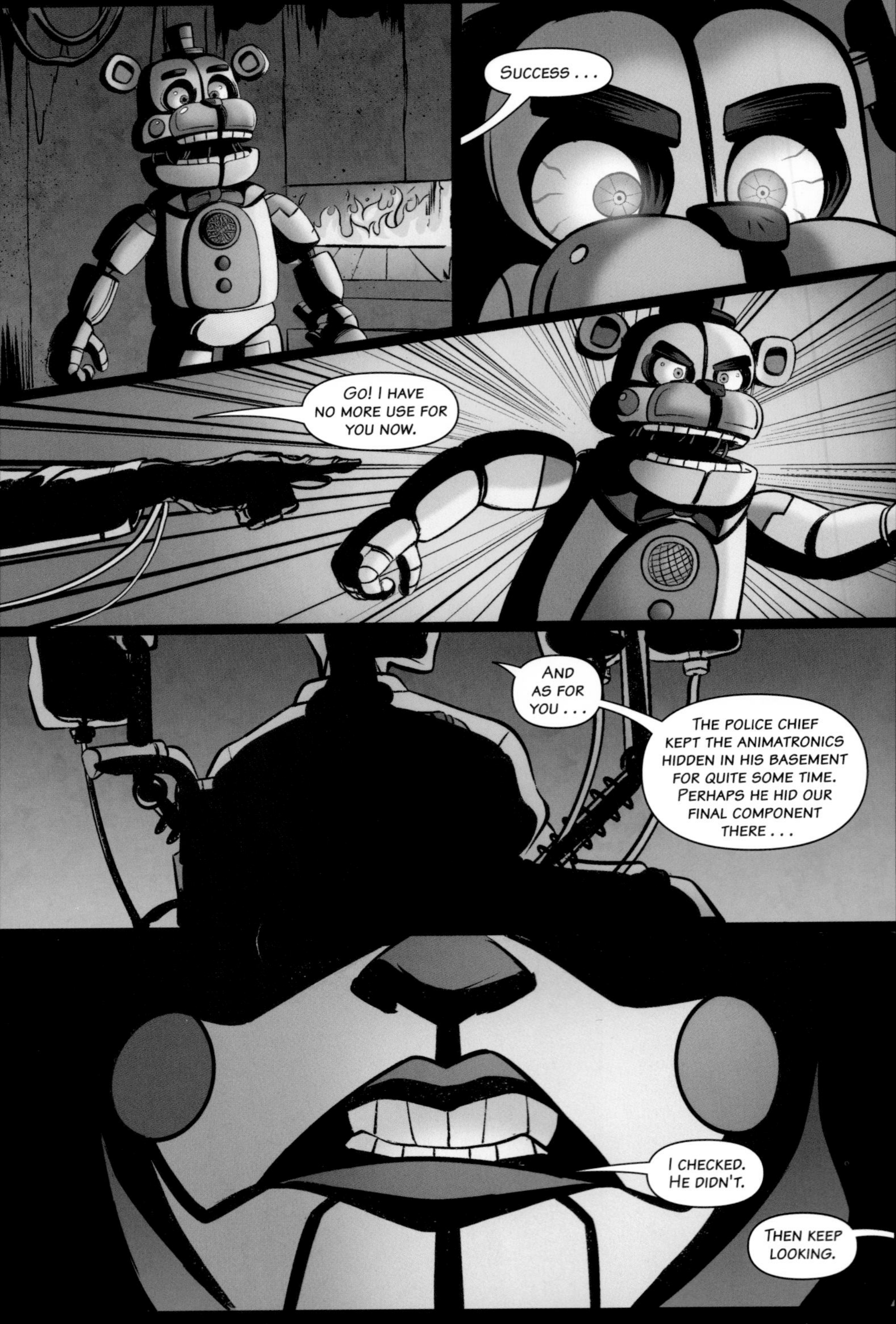
SUCCESS . . .
GO! I HAVE NO MORE USE FOR YOU NOW.
AND AS FOR YOU . . .
THE POLICE CHIEF KEPT THE ANIMATRONICS HIDDEN IN HIS BASEMENT FOR QUITE SOME TIME. PERHAPS HE HID OUR FINAL COMPONENT THERE . . .
I CHECKED. HE DIDN'T.
THEN KEEP LOOKING.

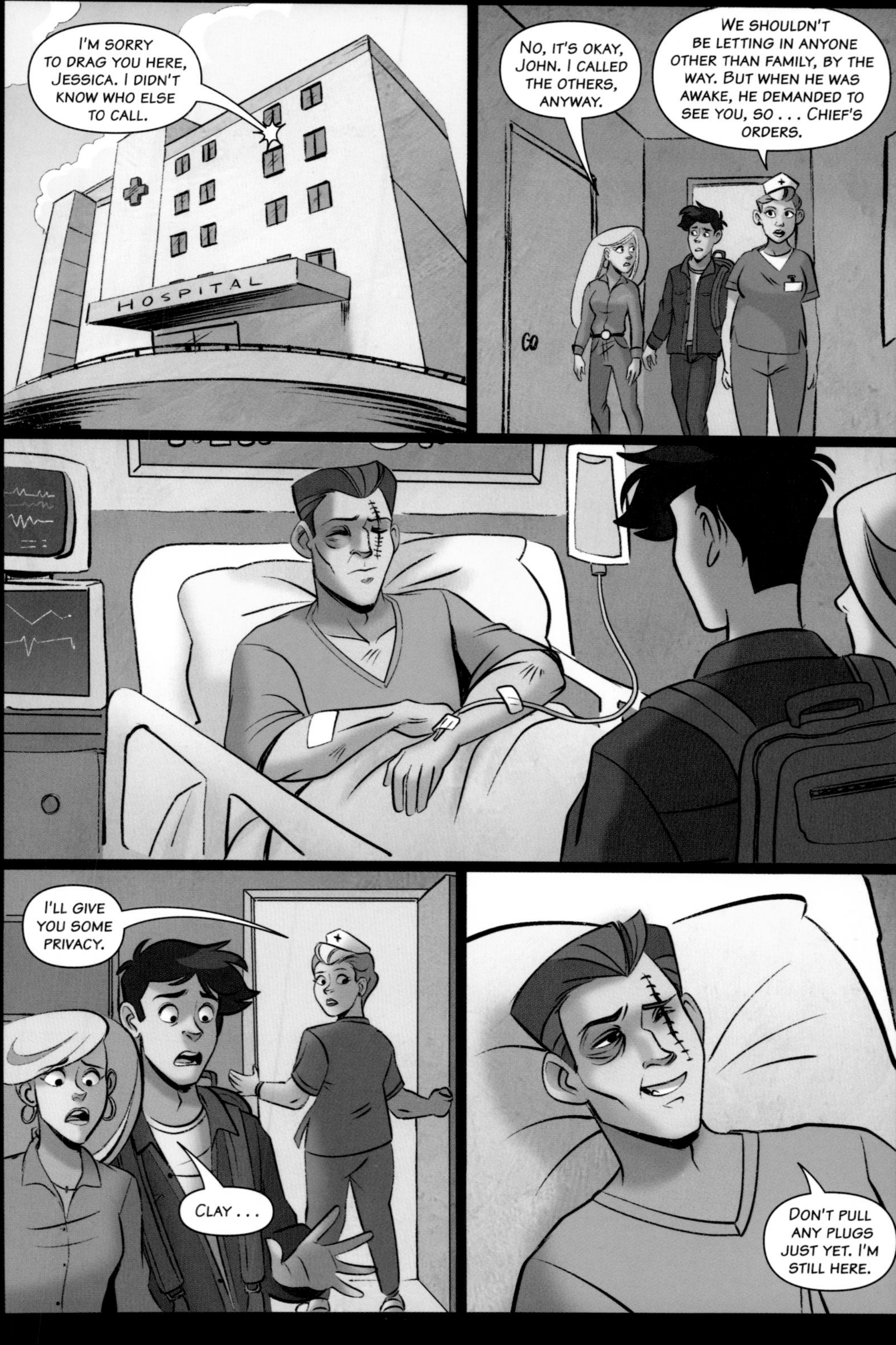
I'M SORRY TO DRAG YOU HERE, JESSICA. I DIDN'T KNOW WHO ELSE TO CALL.
HOSPITAL
NO, IT'S OKAY, JOHN. I CALLED THE OTHERS, ANYWAY.
WE SHOULDN'T BE LETTING IN ANYONE OTHER THAN FAMILY, BY THE WAY. BUT WHEN HE WAS AWAKE, HE DEMANDED TO SEE YOU, SO . . . CHIEF'S ORDERS.
I'LL GIVE YOU SOME PRIVACY.
CLAY . . .
DON'T PULL ANY PLUGS JUST YET. I'M STILL HERE.

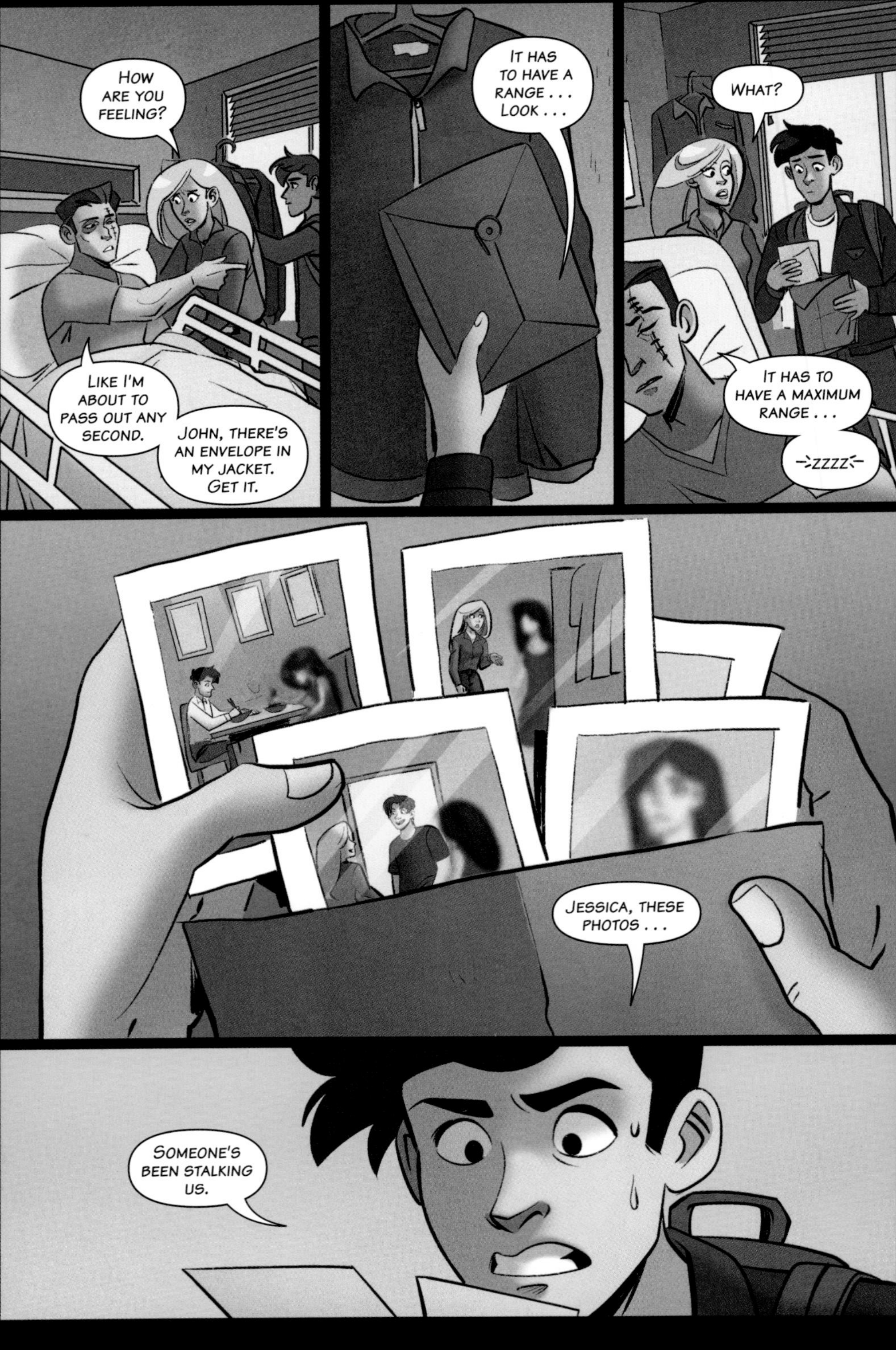
How are you feeling?
Like I'm about to pass out any second.
John, there's an envelope in my jacket. Get it.
It has to have a range . . . Look . . .
What?
It has to have a maximum range . . .
ZZZZ
Jessica, these photos . . .
Someone's been stalking us.

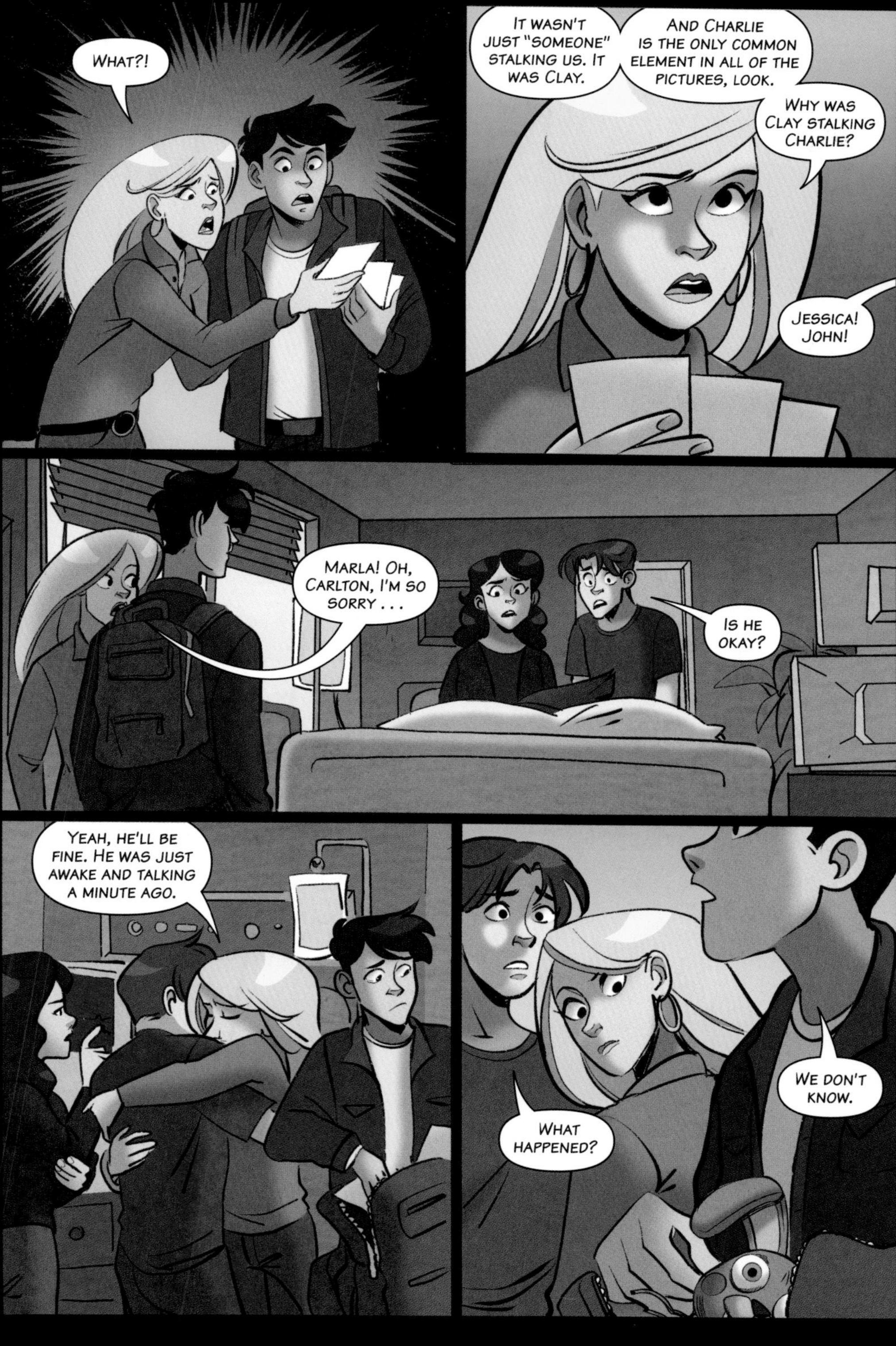
WHAT?!
IT WASN'T JUST "SOMEONE" STALKING US. IT WAS CLAY.
AND CHARLIE IS THE ONLY COMMON ELEMENT IN ALL OF THE PICTURES, LOOK.
WHY WAS CLAY STALKING CHARLIE?
JESSICA! JOHN!
MARLA! OH, CARLTON, I'M SO SORRY . . .
IS HE OKAY?
YEAH, HE'LL BE FINE. HE WAS JUST AWAKE AND TALKING A MINUTE AGO.
WHAT HAPPENED?
WE DON'T KNOW.

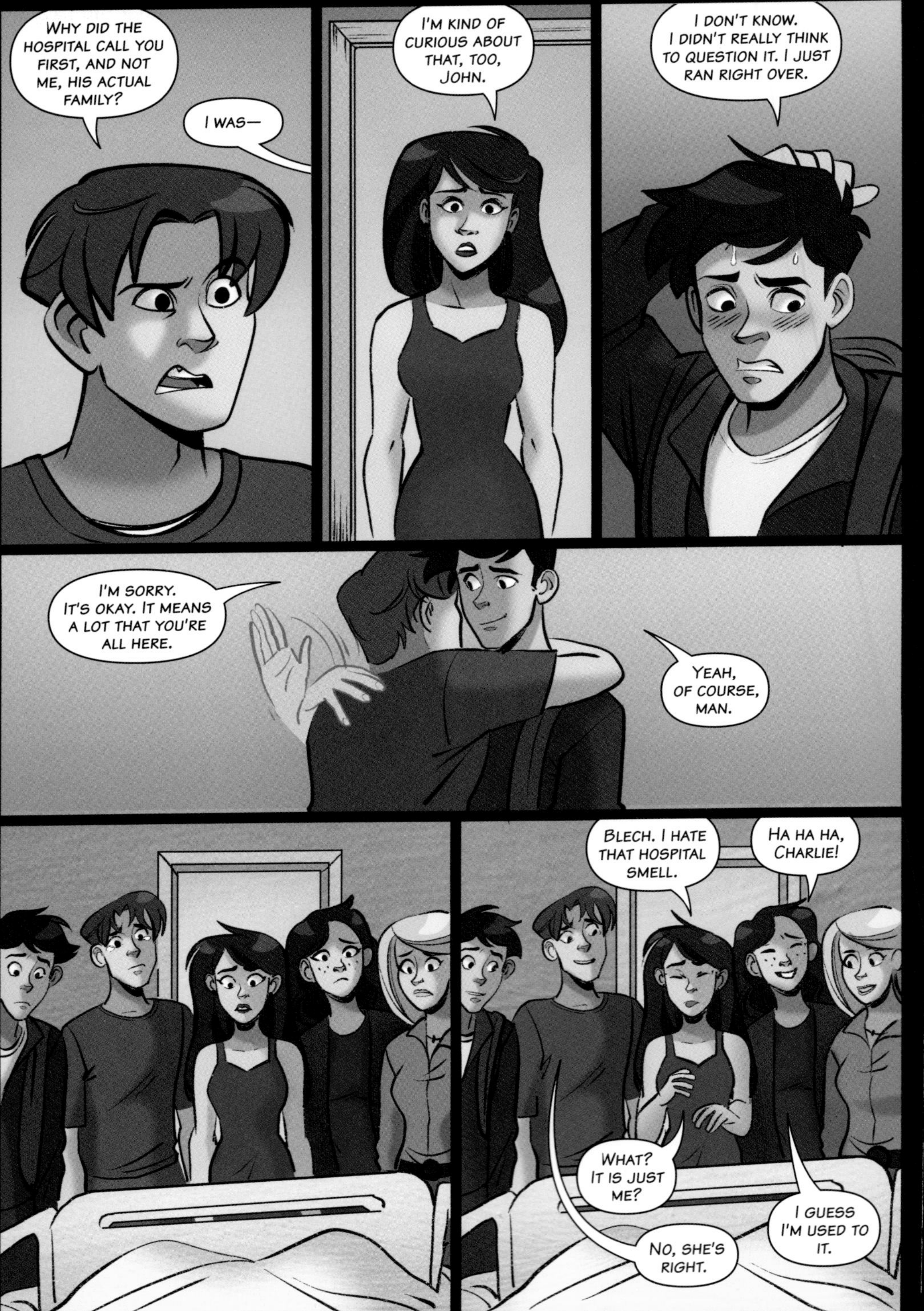
WHY DID THE HOSPITAL CALL YOU FIRST, AND NOT ME, HIS ACTUAL FAMILY?
I WAS—
I'M KIND OF CURIOUS ABOUT THAT, TOO, JOHN.
I DON'T KNOW. I DIDN'T REALLY THINK TO QUESTION IT. I JUST RAN RIGHT OVER.
I'M SORRY. IT'S OKAY. IT MEANS A LOT THAT YOU'RE ALL HERE.
YEAH, OF COURSE, MAN.
BLECH. I HATE THAT HOSPITAL SMELL.
HA HA HA, CHARLIE!
WHAT? IT IS JUST ME?
NO, SHE'S RIGHT.
I GUESS I'M USED TO IT.

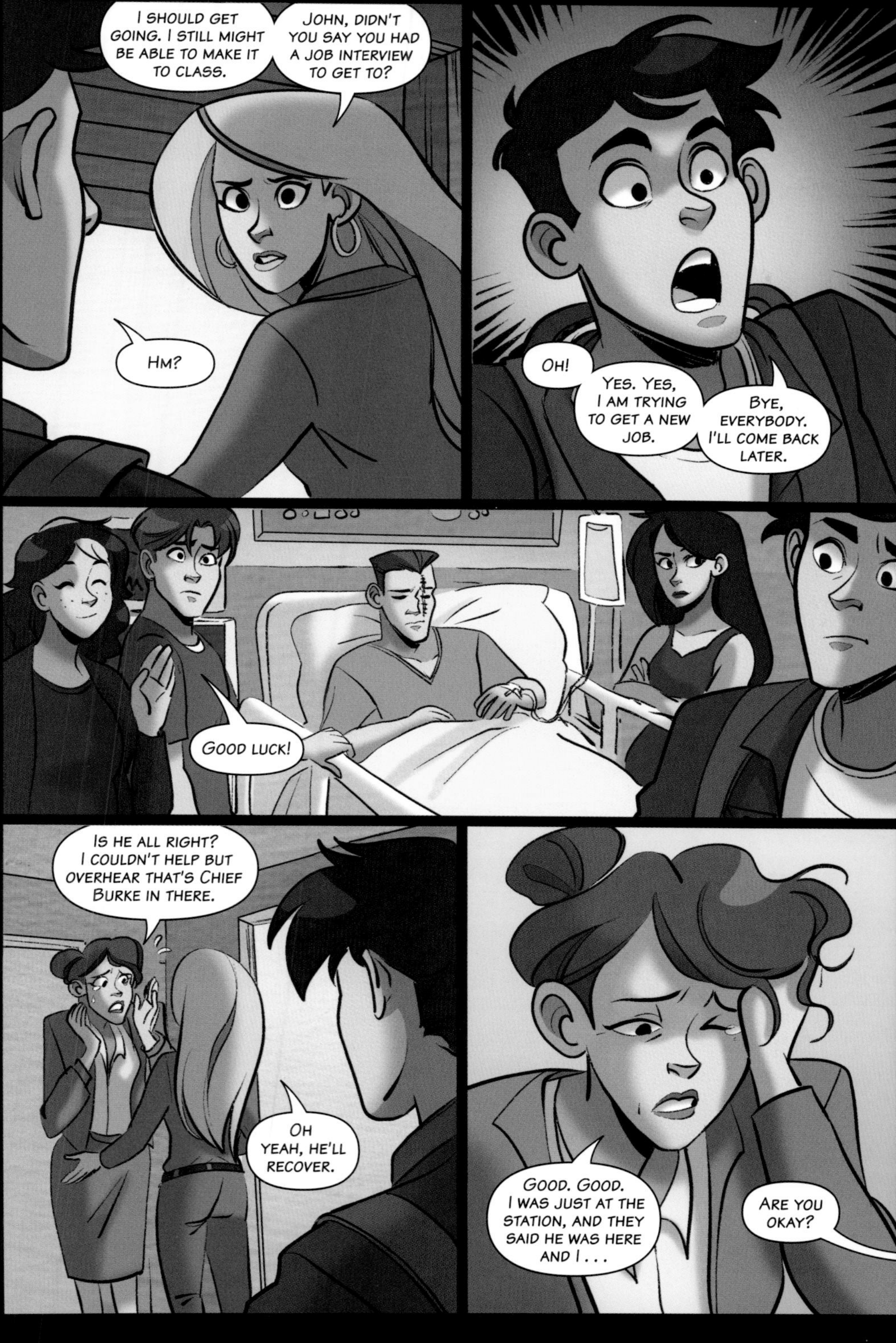

I SHOULD GET GOING. I STILL MIGHT BE ABLE TO MAKE IT TO CLASS.
JOHN, DIDN'T YOU SAY YOU HAD A JOB INTERVIEW TO GET TO?
HM?
OH!
YES. YES, I AM TRYING TO GET A NEW JOB.
BYE, EVERYBODY. I'LL COME BACK LATER.
GOOD LUCK!
IS HE ALL RIGHT? I COULDN'T HELP BUT OVERHEAR THAT'S CHIEF BURKE IN THERE.
OH YEAH, HE'LL RECOVER.
GOOD. GOOD. I WAS JUST AT THE STATION, AND THEY SAID HE WAS HERE AND I . . .
ARE YOU OKAY?

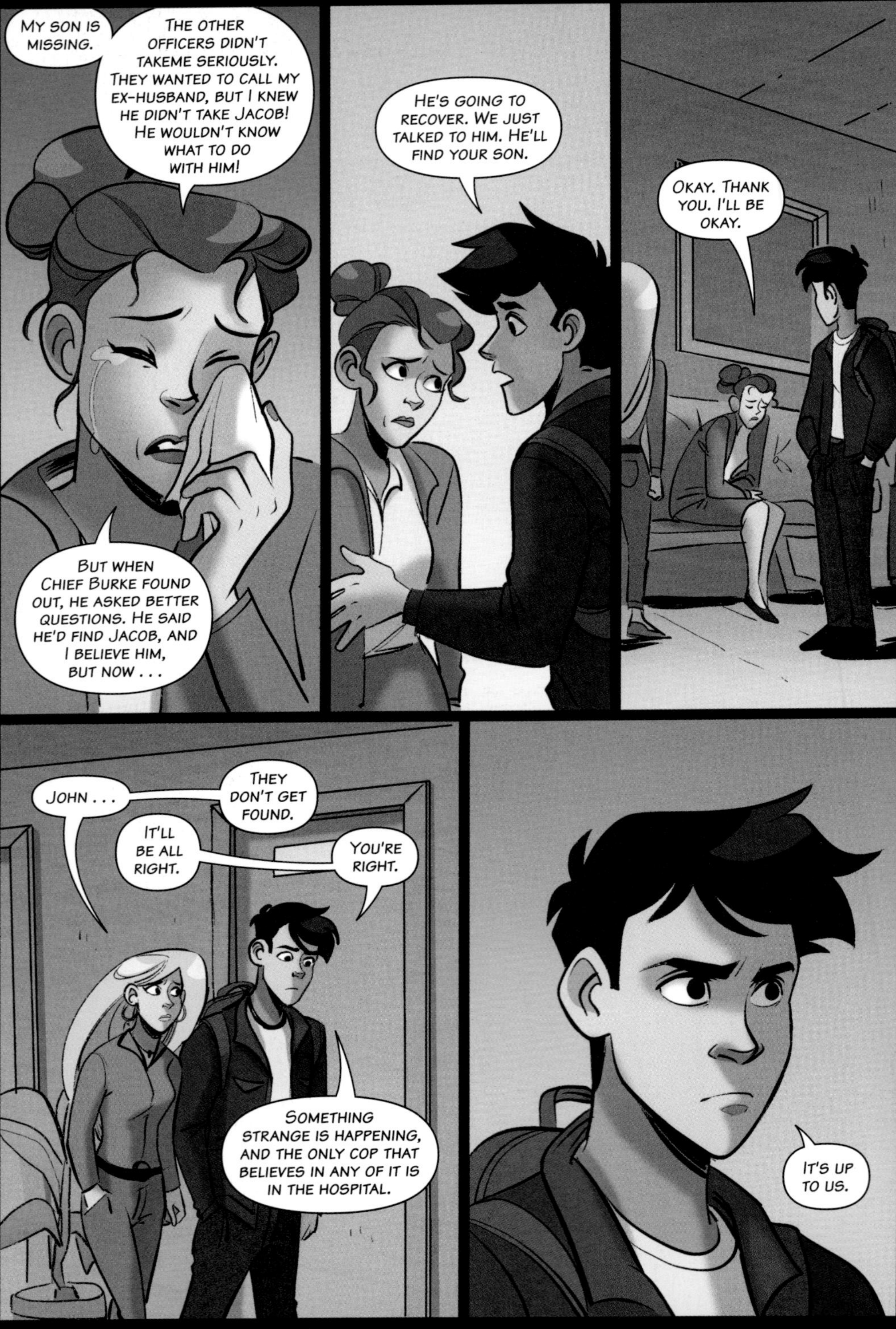
MY SON IS MISSING.
THE OTHER OFFICERS DIDN'T TAKEME SERIOUSLY. THEY WANTED TO CALL MY EX-HUSBAND, BUT I KNEW HE DIDN'T TAKE JACOB! HE WOULDN'T KNOW WHAT TO DO WITH HIM!
BUT WHEN CHIEF BURKE FOUND OUT, HE ASKED BETTER QUESTIONS. HE SAID HE'D FIND JACOB, AND I BELIEVE HIM, BUT NOW . . .
HE'S GOING TO RECOVER. WE JUST TALKED TO HIM. HE'LL FIND YOUR SON.
OKAY. THANK YOU. I'LL BE OKAY.
JOHN . . .
IT'LL BE ALL RIGHT.
THEY DON'T GET FOUND.
YOU'RE RIGHT.
SOMETHING STRANGE IS HAPPENING, AND THE ONLY COP THAT BELIEVES IN ANY OF IT IS IN THE HOSPITAL.
IT'S UP TO US.

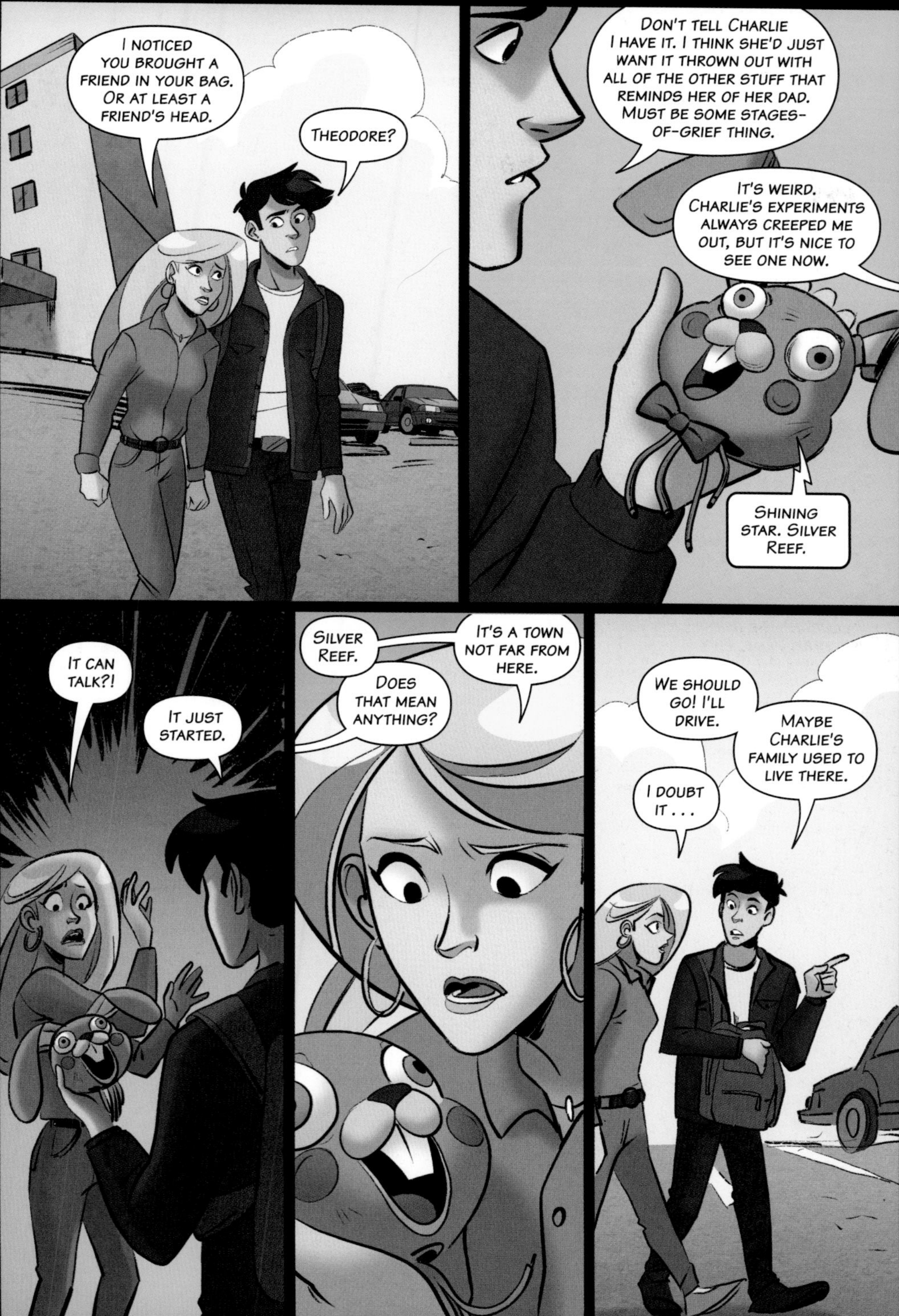
I NOTICED YOU BROUGHT A FRIEND IN YOUR BAG. OR AT LEAST A FRIEND'S HEAD.
THEODORE?
DON'T TELL CHARLIE I HAVE IT. I THINK SHE'D JUST WANT IT THROWN OUT WITH ALL OF THE OTHER STUFF THAT REMINDS HER OF HER DAD. MUST BE SOME STAGES-OF-GRIEF THING.
IT'S WEIRD. CHARLIE'S EXPERIMENTS ALWAYS CREEPED ME OUT, BUT IT'S NICE TO SEE ONE NOW.
SHINING STAR. SILVER REEF.
IT CAN TALK?!
IT JUST STARTED.
SILVER REEF.
DOES THAT MEAN ANYTHING?
IT'S A TOWN NOT FAR FROM HERE.
WE SHOULD GO! I'LL DRIVE.
I DOUBT IT . . .
MAYBE CHARLIE'S FAMILY USED TO LIVE THERE.

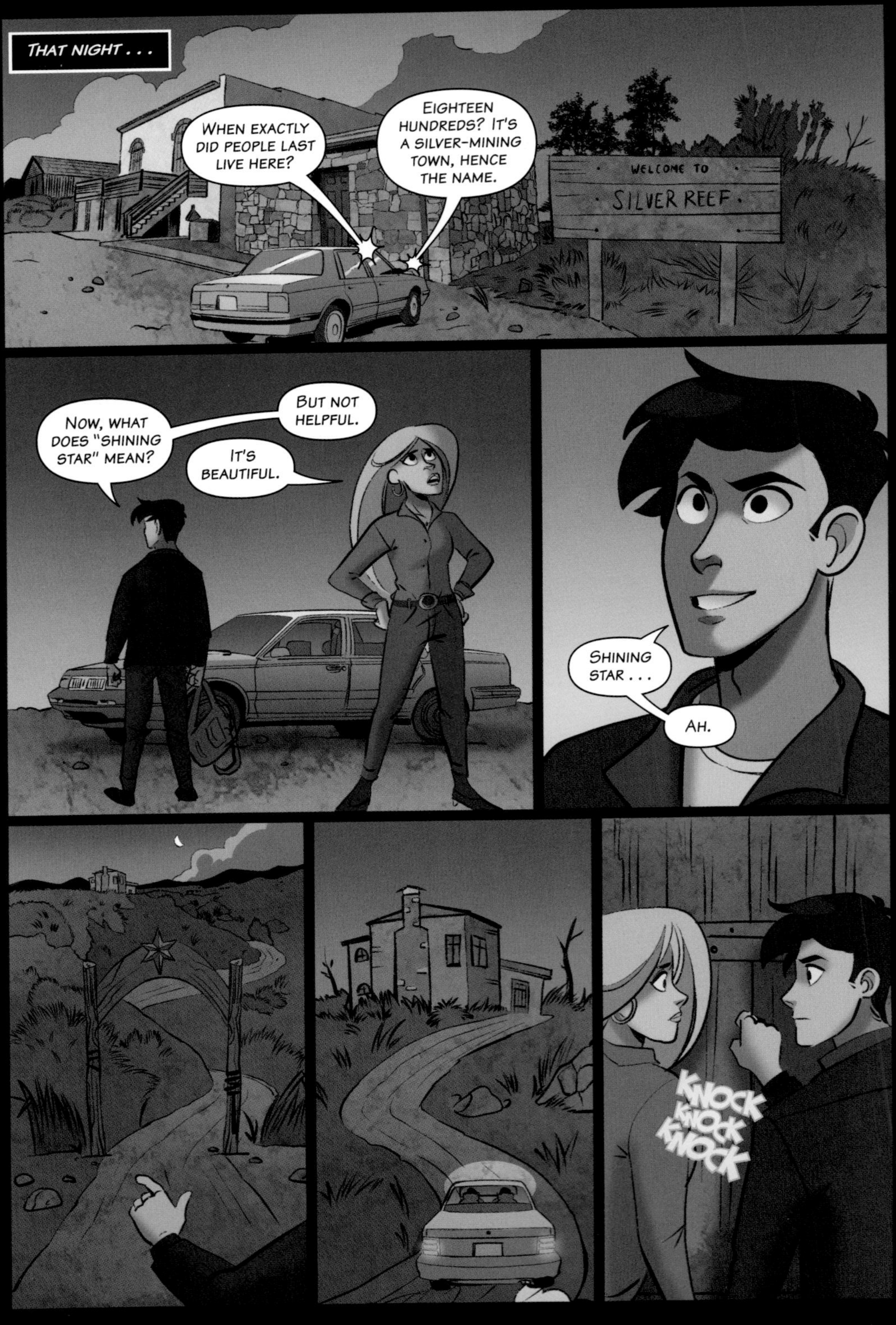
THAT NIGHT . . .
WHEN EXACTLY DID PEOPLE LAST LIVE HERE?
EIGHTEEN HUNDREDS? IT'S A SILVER-MINING TOWN, HENCE THE NAME.
WELCOME TO SILVER REEF
NOW, WHAT DOES "SHINING STAR" MEAN?
IT'S BEAUTIFUL.
BUT NOT HELPFUL.
SHINING STAR . . .
AH.
KNOCK KNOCK KNOCK

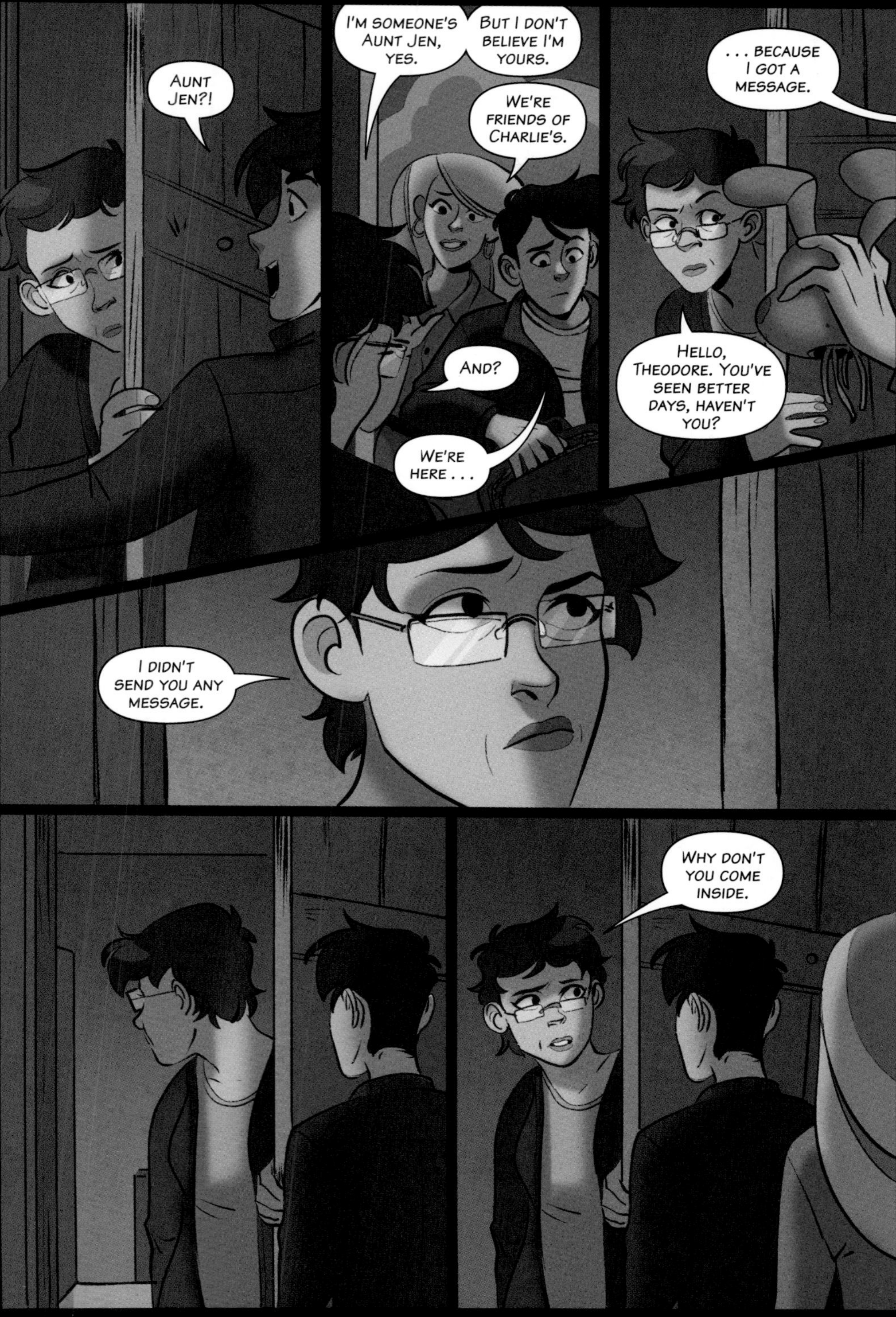
AUNT JEN?!
I'M SOMEONE'S AUNT JEN, YES.
BUT I DON'T BELIEVE I'M YOURS.
WE'RE FRIENDS OF CHARLIE'S.
AND?
WE'RE HERE . . .
. . . BECAUSE I GOT A MESSAGE.
HELLO, THEODORE. YOU'VE SEEN BETTER DAYS, HAVEN'T YOU?
I DIDN'T SEND YOU ANY MESSAGE.
WHY DON'T YOU COME INSIDE.

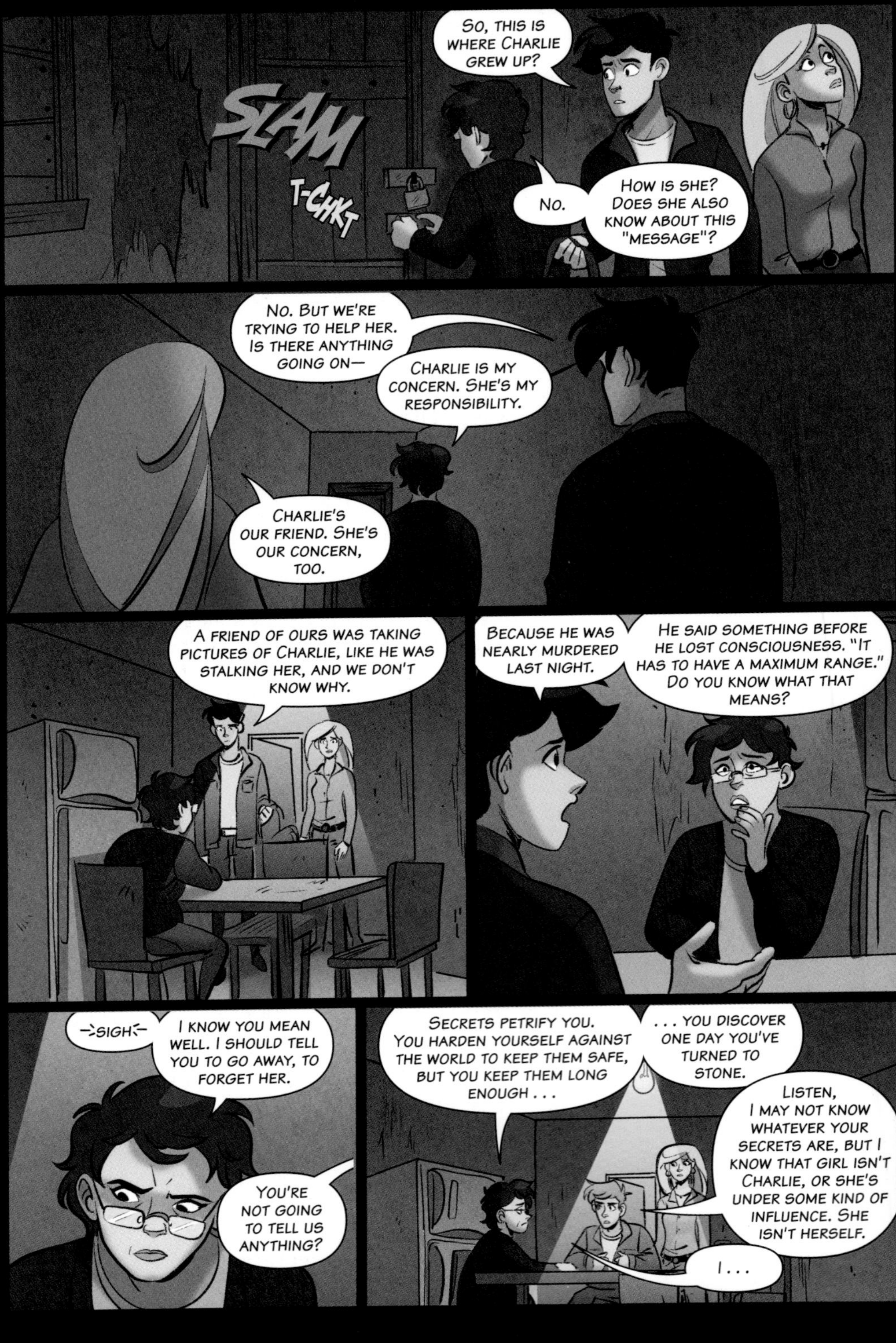
SO, THIS IS WHERE CHARLIE GREW UP?
SLAM
T-CHKT
NO.
HOW IS SHE? DOES SHE ALSO KNOW ABOUT THIS "MESSAGE"?
NO. BUT WE'RE TRYING TO HELP HER. IS THERE ANYTHING GOING ON—
CHARLIE IS MY CONCERN. SHE'S MY RESPONSIBILITY.
CHARLIE'S OUR FRIEND. SHE'S OUR CONCERN, TOO.
A FRIEND OF OURS WAS TAKING PICTURES OF CHARLIE, LIKE HE WAS STALKING HER, AND WE DON'T KNOW WHY.
BECAUSE HE WAS NEARLY MURDERED LAST NIGHT.
HE SAID SOMETHING BEFORE HE LOST CONSCIOUSNESS. "IT HAS TO HAVE A MAXIMUM RANGE." DO YOU KNOW WHAT THAT MEANS?
SIGH
I KNOW YOU MEAN WELL. I SHOULD TELL YOU TO GO AWAY, TO FORGET HER.
YOU'RE NOT GOING TO TELL US ANYTHING?
SECRETS PETRIFY YOU. YOU HARDEN YOURSELF AGAINST THE WORLD TO KEEP THEM SAFE, BUT YOU KEEP THEM LONG ENOUGH . . .
. . . YOU DISCOVER ONE DAY YOU'VE TURNED TO STONE.
LISTEN, I MAY NOT KNOW WHATEVER YOUR SECRETS ARE, BUT I KNOW THAT GIRL ISN'T CHARLIE, OR SHE'S UNDER SOME KIND OF INFLUENCE. SHE ISN'T HERSELF.
I . . .

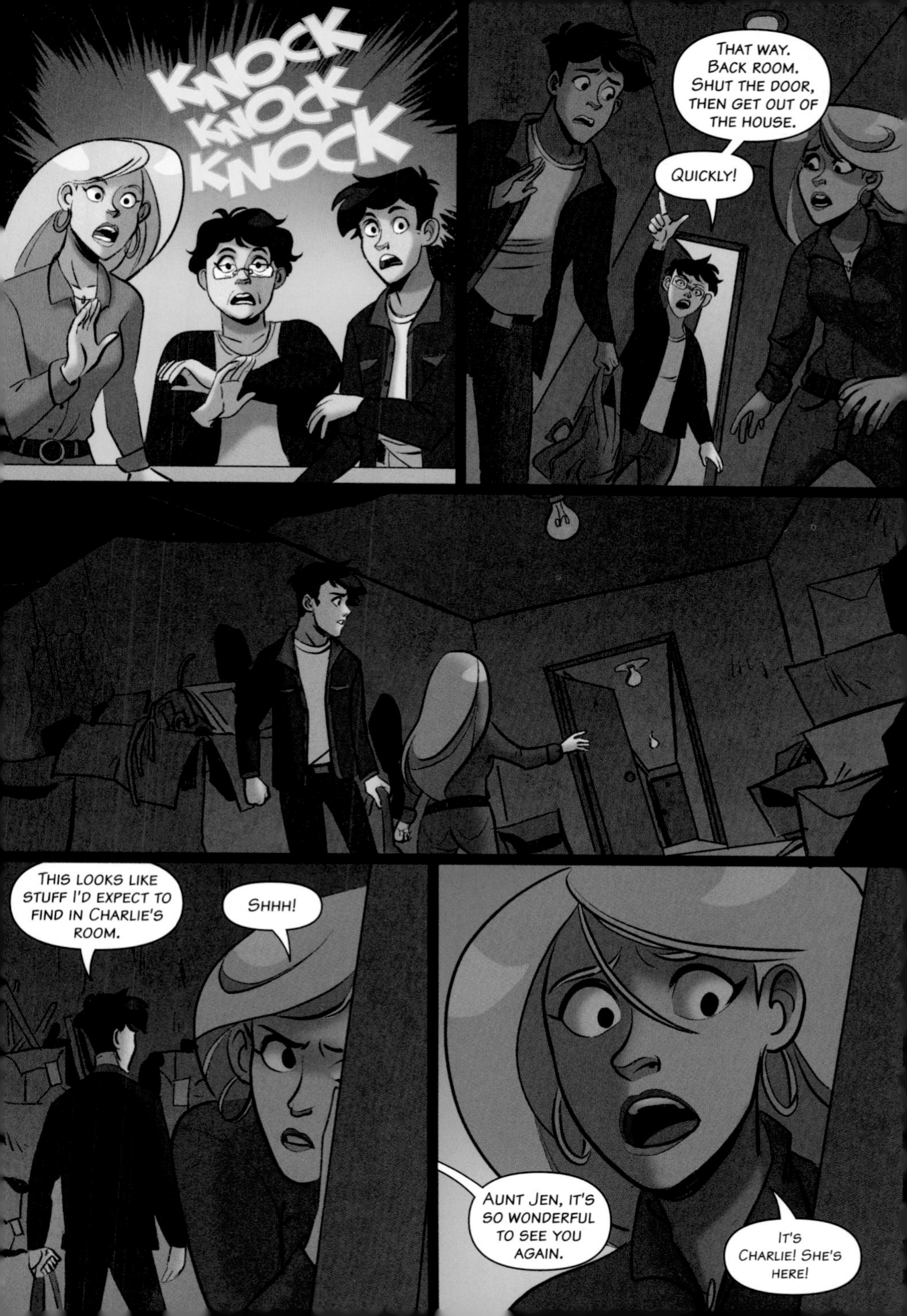
KNOCK KNOCK KNOCK
THAT WAY. BACK ROOM. SHUT THE DOOR, THEN GET OUT OF THE HOUSE.
QUICKLY!
THIS LOOKS LIKE STUFF I'D EXPECT TO FIND IN CHARLIE'S ROOM.
SHHH!
AUNT JEN, IT'S SO WONDERFUL TO SEE YOU AGAIN.
IT'S CHARLIE! SHE'S HERE!

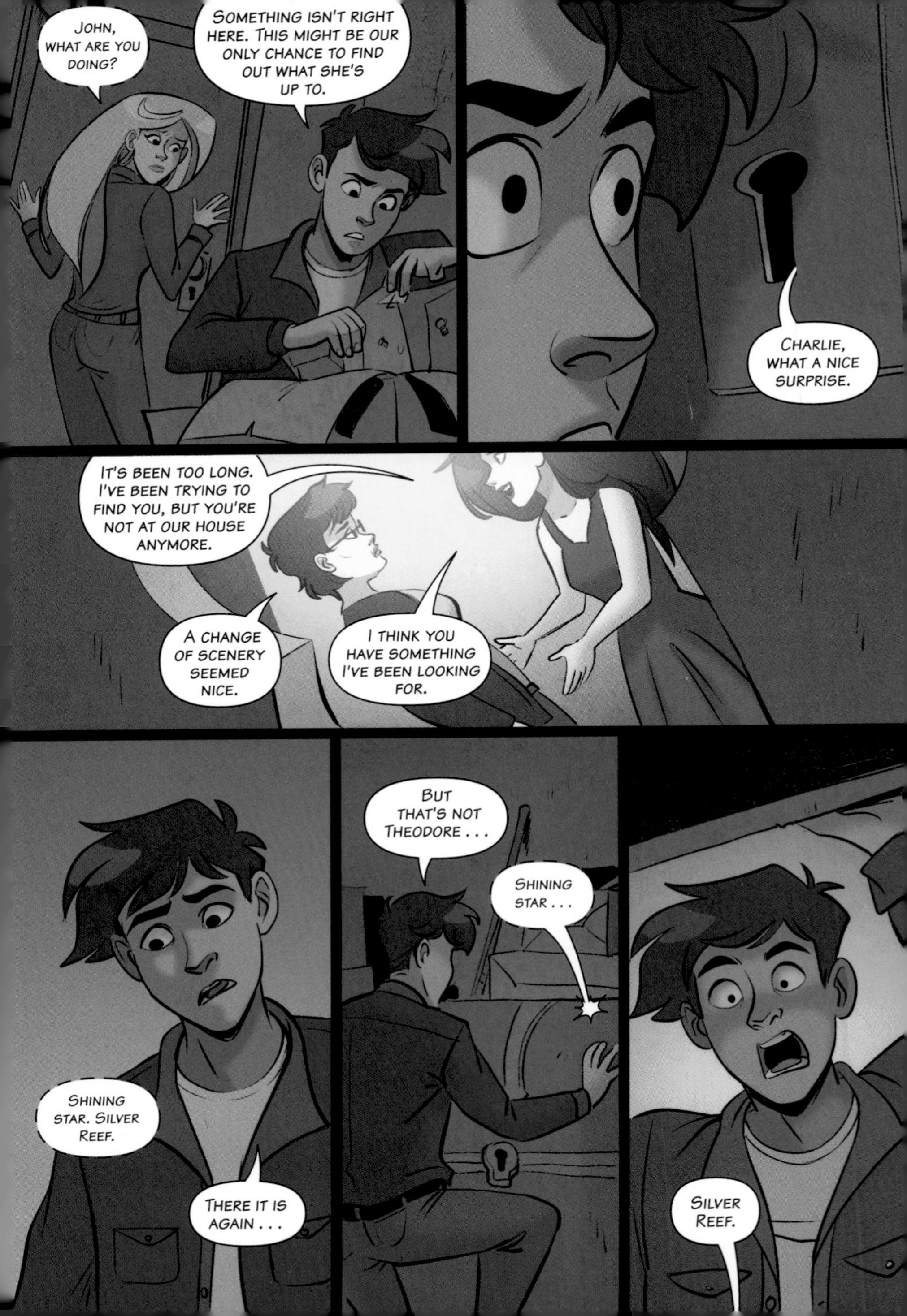
JOHN, WHAT ARE YOU DOING?
SOMETHING ISN'T RIGHT HERE. THIS MIGHT BE OUR ONLY CHANCE TO FIND OUT WHAT SHE'S UP TO.
CHARLIE, WHAT A NICE SURPRISE.
IT'S BEEN TOO LONG. I'VE BEEN TRYING TO FIND YOU, BUT YOU'RE NOT AT OUR HOUSE ANYMORE.
A CHANGE OF SCENERY SEEMED NICE.
I THINK YOU HAVE SOMETHING I'VE BEEN LOOKING FOR.
SHINING STAR. SILVER REEF.
THERE IT IS AGAIN . . .
BUT THAT'S NOT THEODORE . . .
SHINING STAR . . .
SILVER REEF.

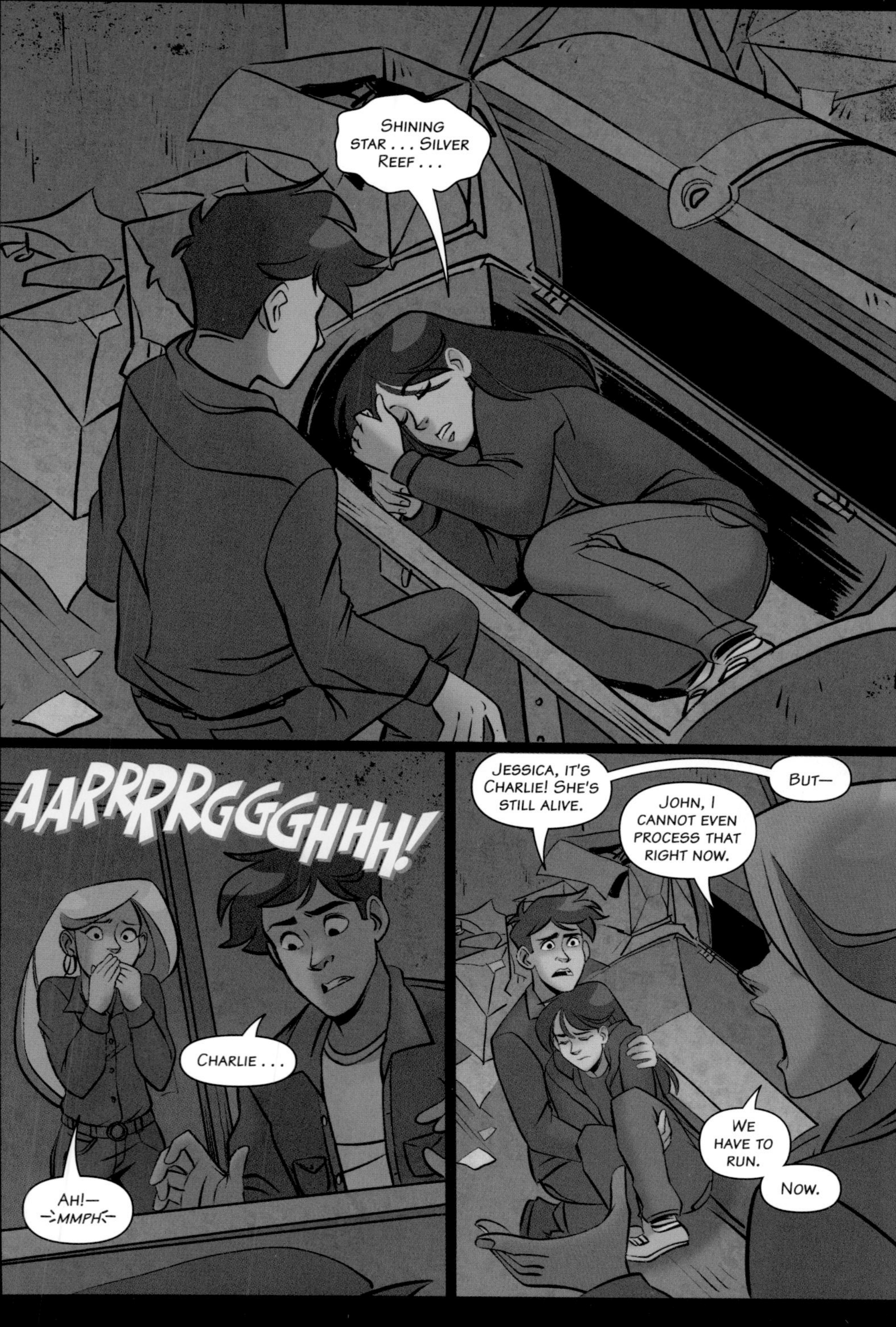
Shining star . . . Silver Reef . . .
AARRRRGGGHHH!
Charlie . . .
Ah!— —MMPH—
Jessica, it's Charlie! She's still alive.
But—
John, I cannot even process that right now.
We have to run.
Now.

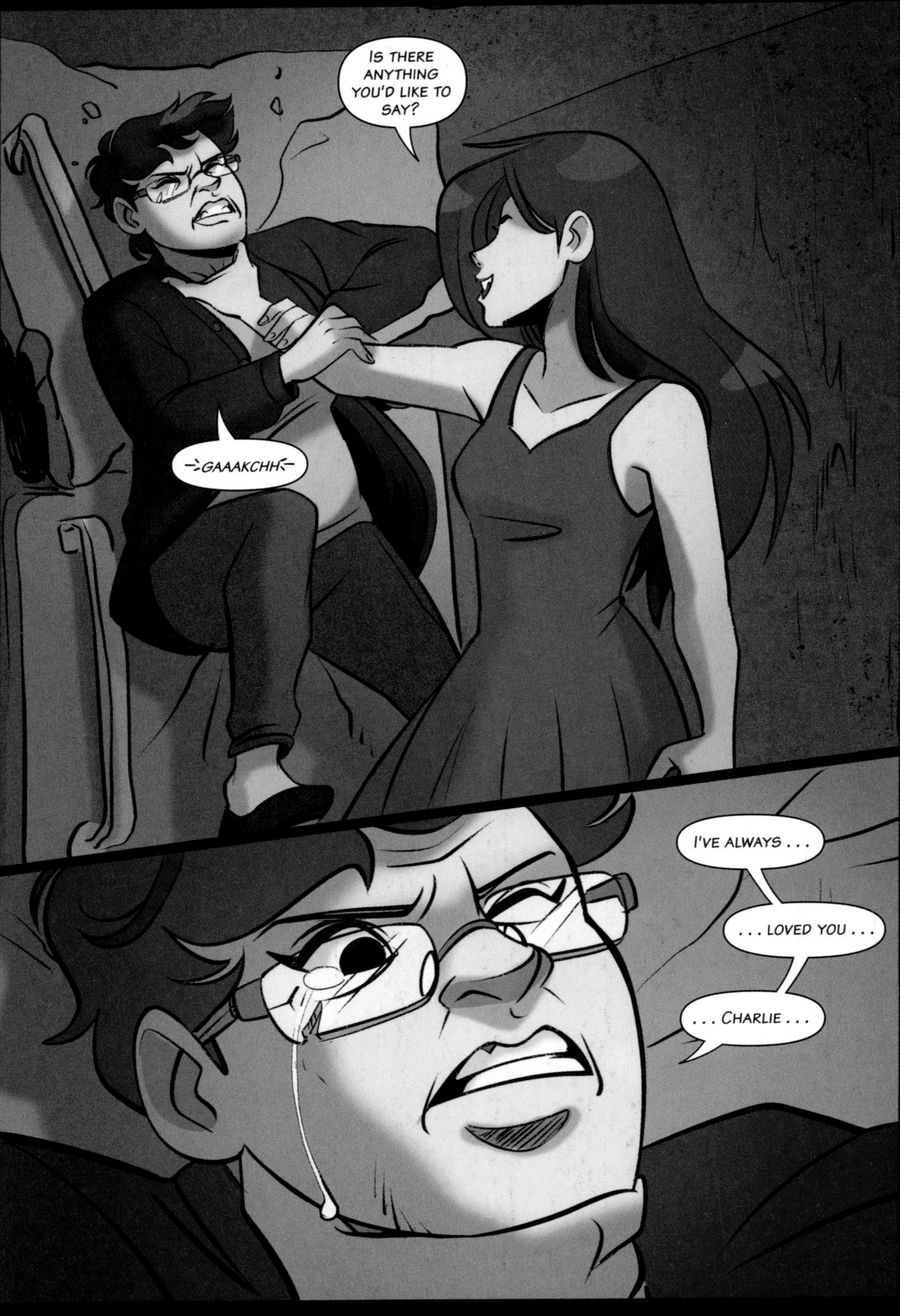
IS THERE ANYTHING YOU'D LIKE TO SAY?
GAAAKCHH
I'VE ALWAYS . . .
. . . LOVED YOU . . .
. . . CHARLIE . . .

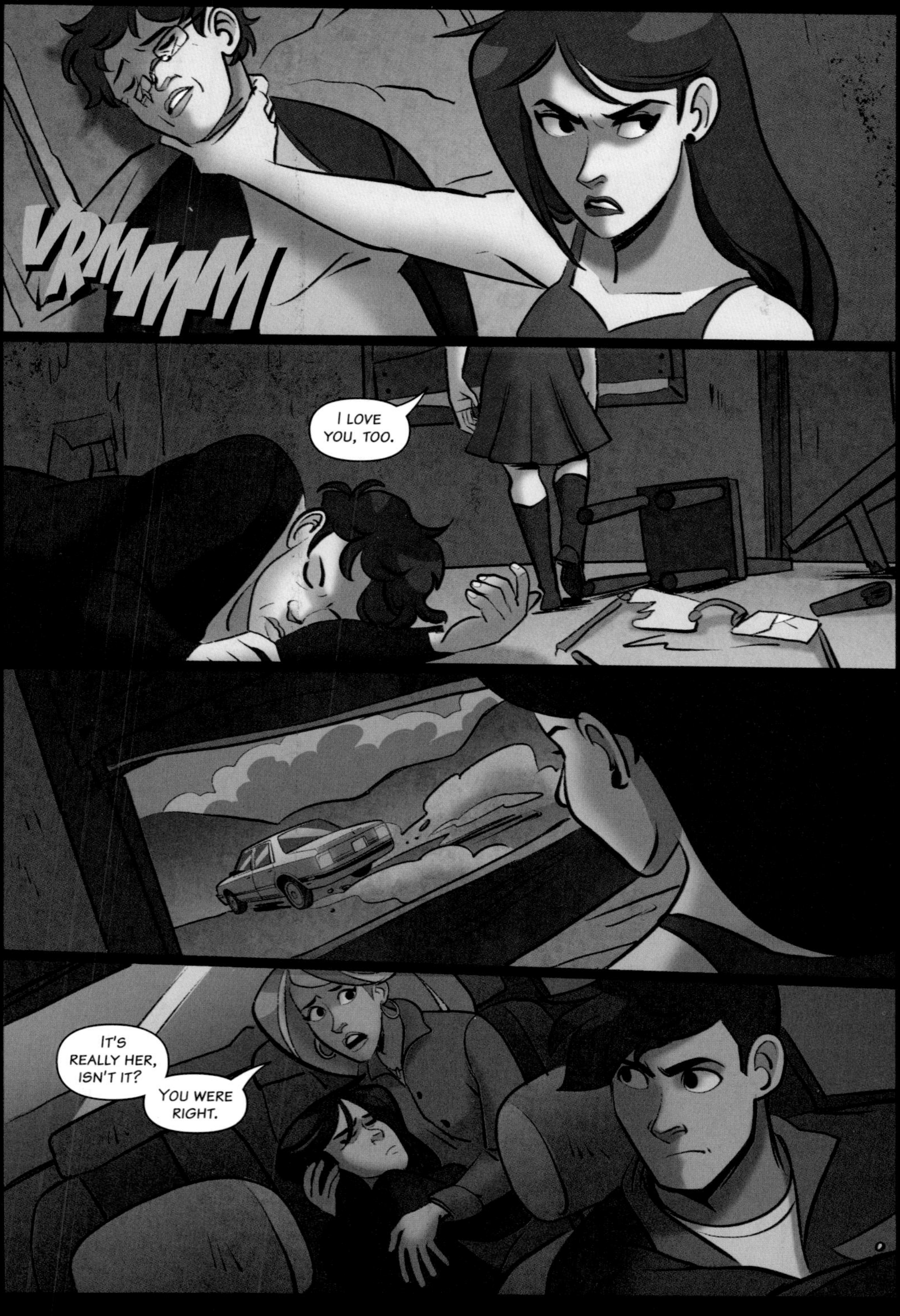
VRMMMM
I LOVE YOU, TOO.
IT'S REALLY HER, ISN'T IT?
YOU WERE RIGHT.

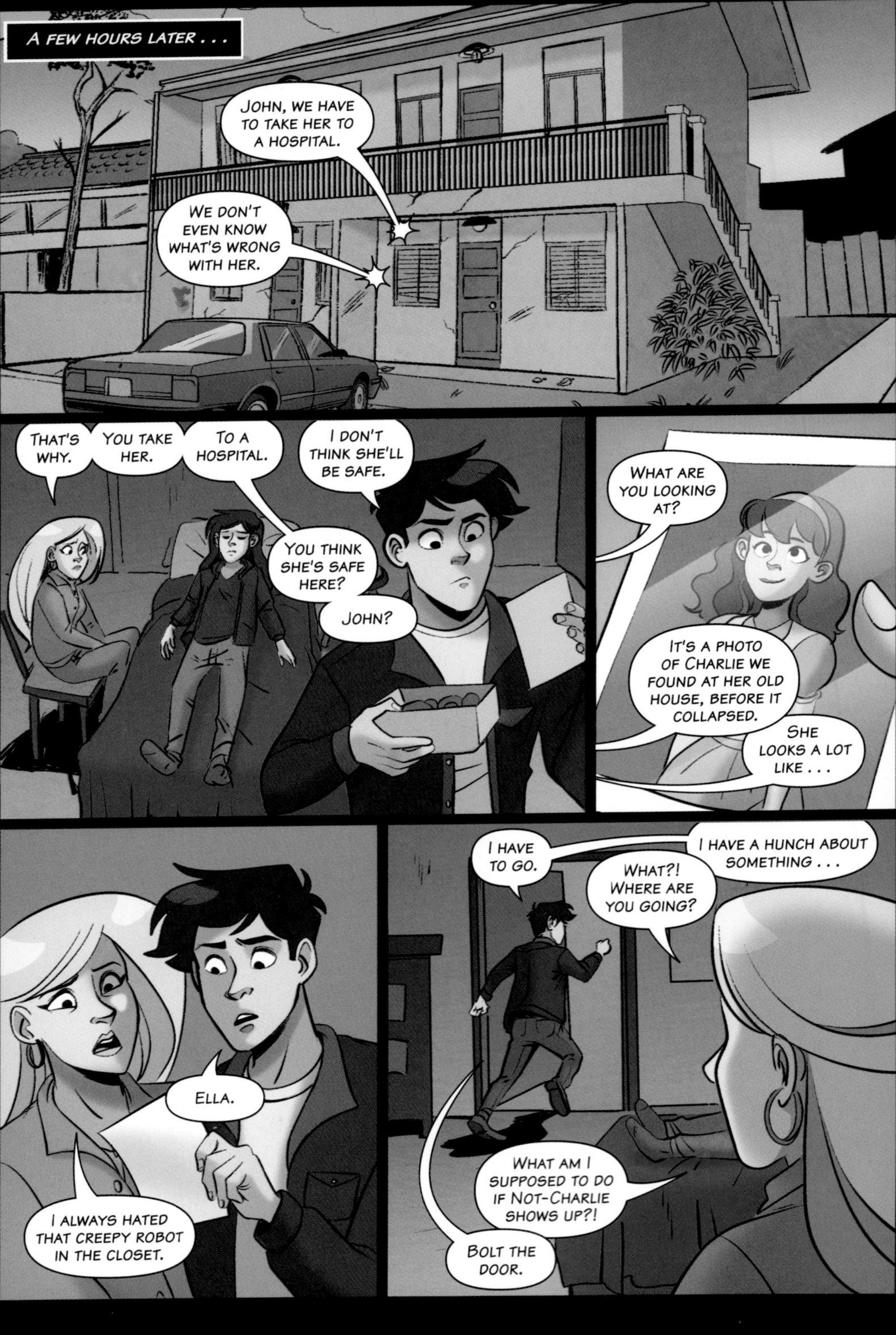
A FEW HOURS LATER . . .
JOHN, WE HAVE TO TAKE HER TO A HOSPITAL.
WE DON'T EVEN KNOW WHAT'S WRONG WITH HER.
THAT'S WHY.
YOU TAKE HER.
TO A HOSPITAL.
I DON'T THINK SHE'LL BE SAFE.
YOU THINK SHE'S SAFE HERE?
JOHN?
WHAT ARE YOU LOOKING AT?
IT'S A PHOTO OF CHARLIE WE FOUND AT HER OLD HOUSE, BEFORE IT COLLAPSED.
SHE LOOKS A LOT LIKE . . .
ELLA.
I ALWAYS HATED THAT CREEPY ROBOT IN THE CLOSET.
I HAVE TO GO.
I HAVE A HUNCH ABOUT SOMETHING . . .
WHAT?! WHERE ARE YOU GOING?
WHAT AM I SUPPOSED TO DO IF NOT-CHARLIE SHOWS UP?!
BOLT THE DOOR.

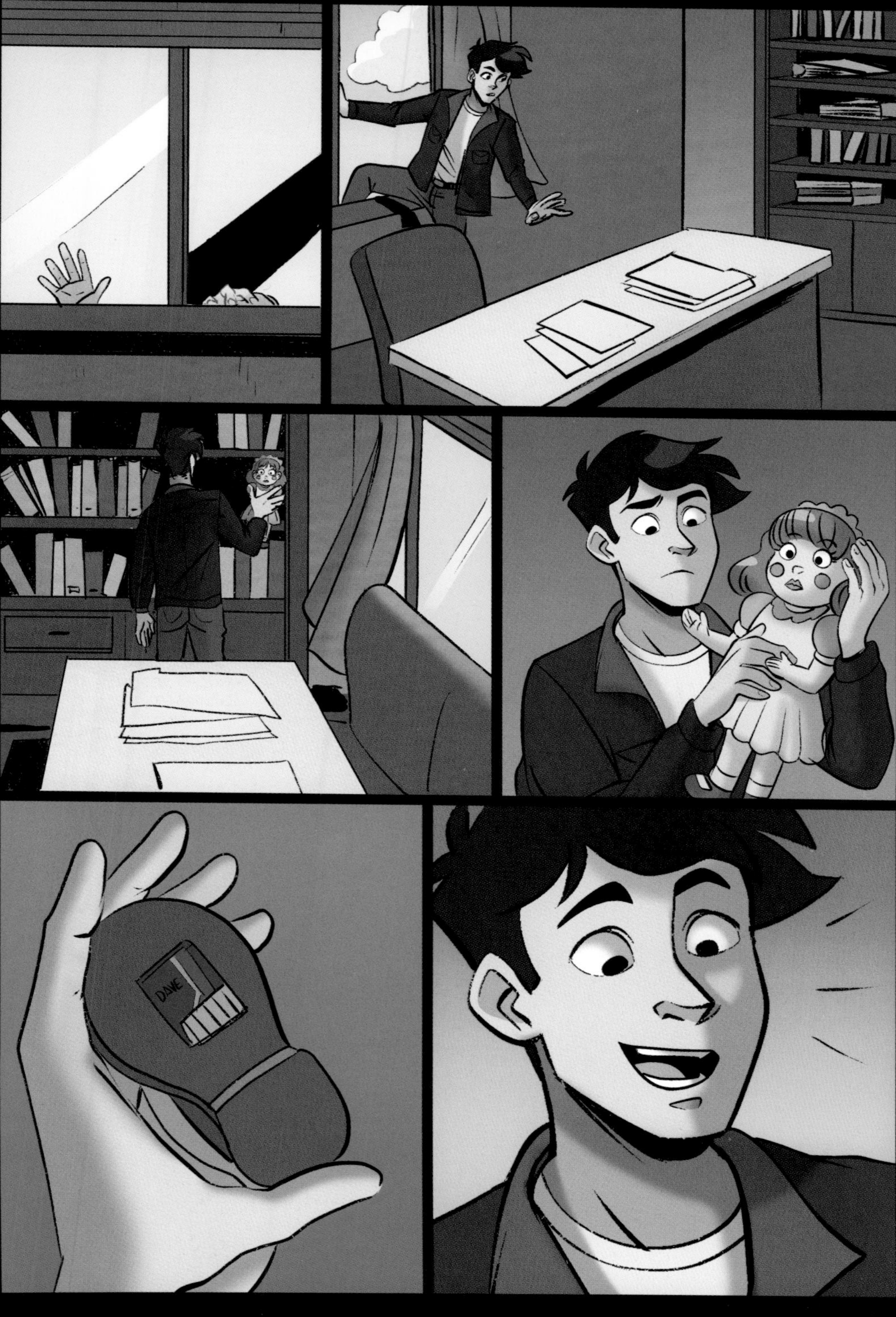
DAVE

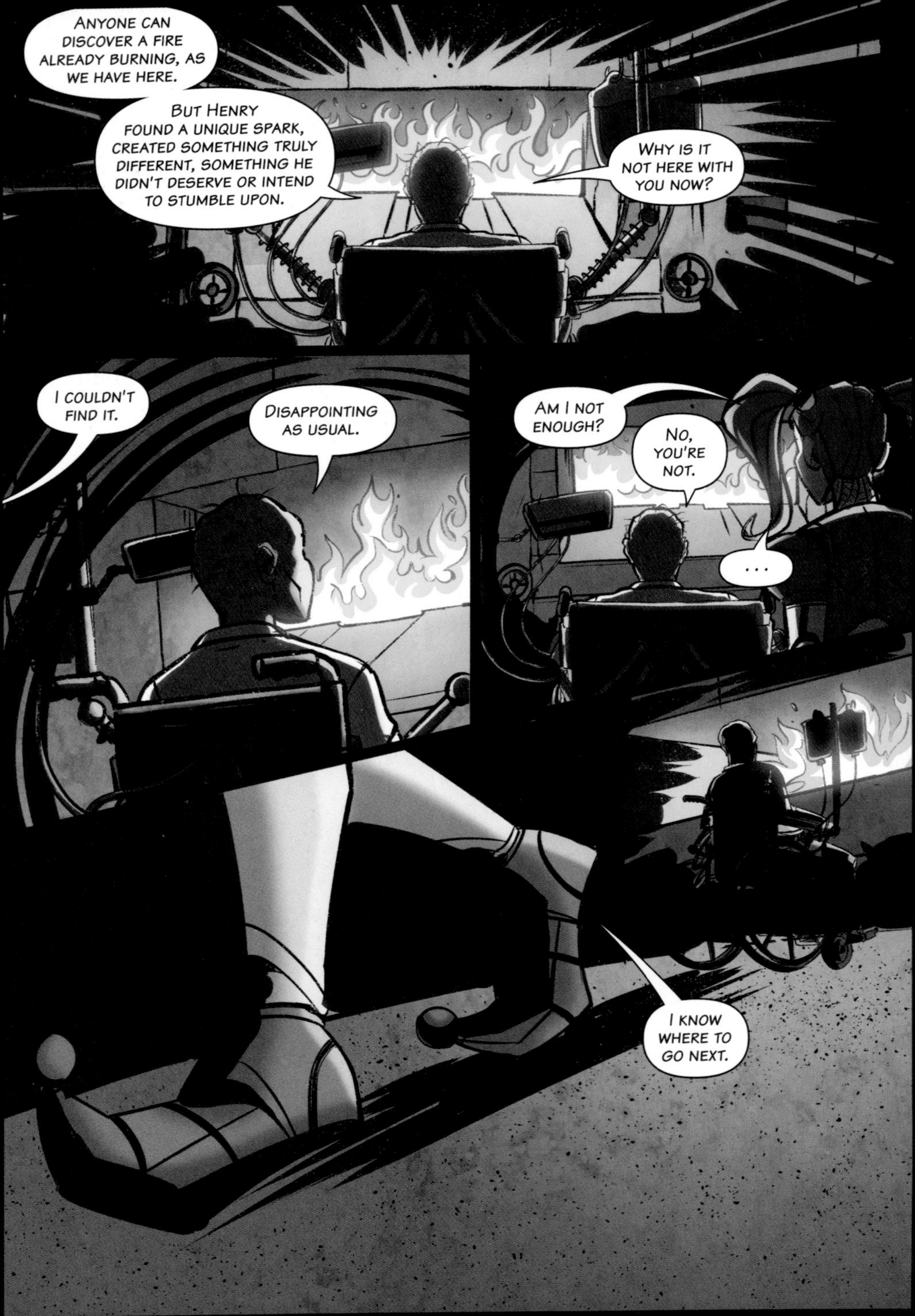
ANYONE CAN DISCOVER A FIRE ALREADY BURNING, AS WE HAVE HERE.
BUT HENRY FOUND A UNIQUE SPARK, CREATED SOMETHING TRULY DIFFERENT, SOMETHING HE DIDN'T DESERVE OR INTEND TO STUMBLE UPON.
WHY IS IT NOT HERE WITH YOU NOW?
I COULDN'T FIND IT.
DISAPPOINTING AS USUAL.
AM I NOT ENOUGH?
NO, YOU'RE NOT.
...
I KNOW WHERE TO GO NEXT.

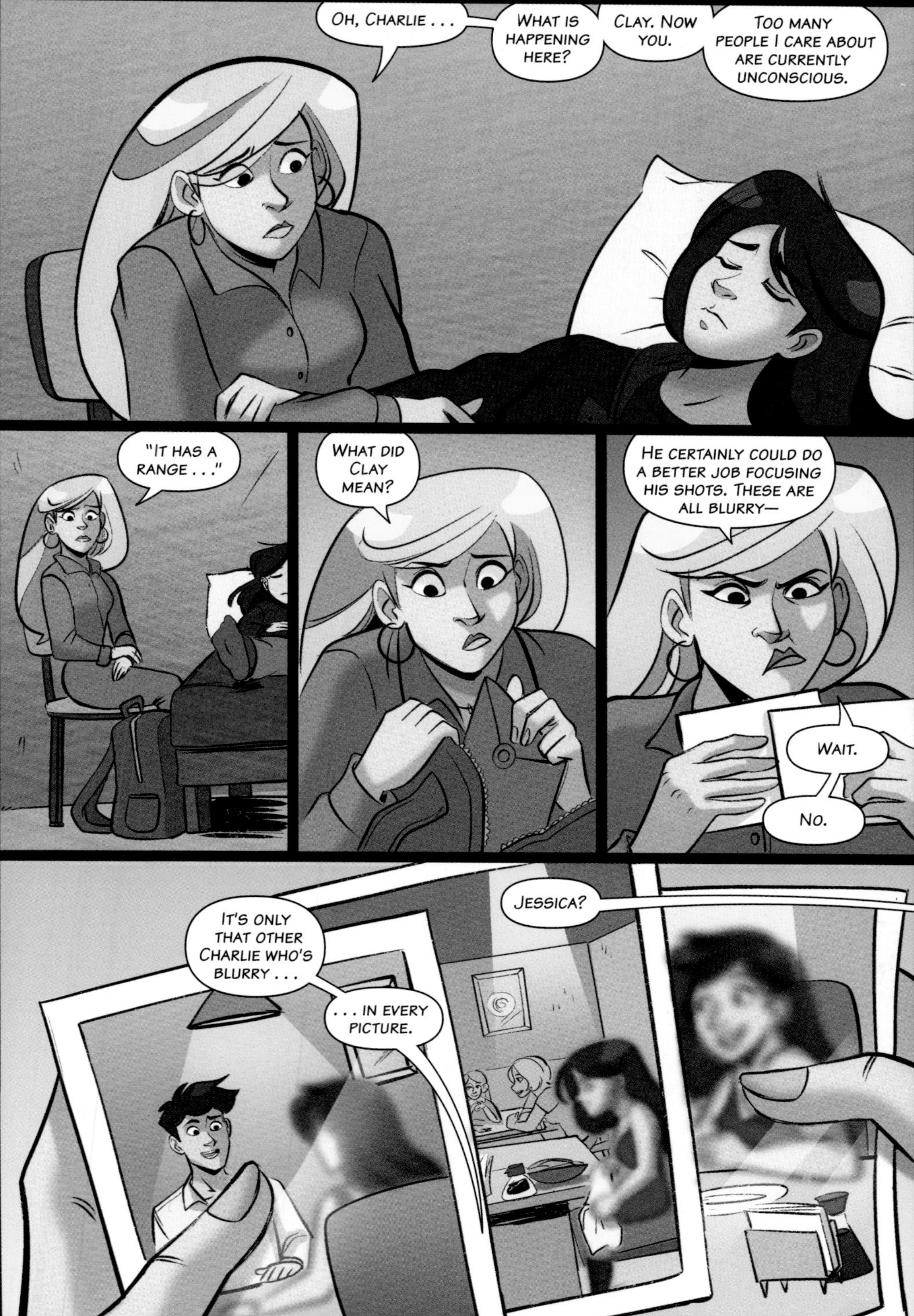
OH, CHARLIE . . .
WHAT IS HAPPENING HERE?
CLAY. NOW YOU.
TOO MANY PEOPLE I CARE ABOUT ARE CURRENTLY UNCONSCIOUS.
"IT HAS A RANGE . . ."
WHAT DID CLAY MEAN?
HE CERTAINLY COULD DO A BETTER JOB FOCUSING HIS SHOTS. THESE ARE ALL BLURRY—
WAIT.
NO.
IT'S ONLY THAT OTHER CHARLIE WHO'S BLURRY . . .
. . . IN EVERY PICTURE.
JESSICA?

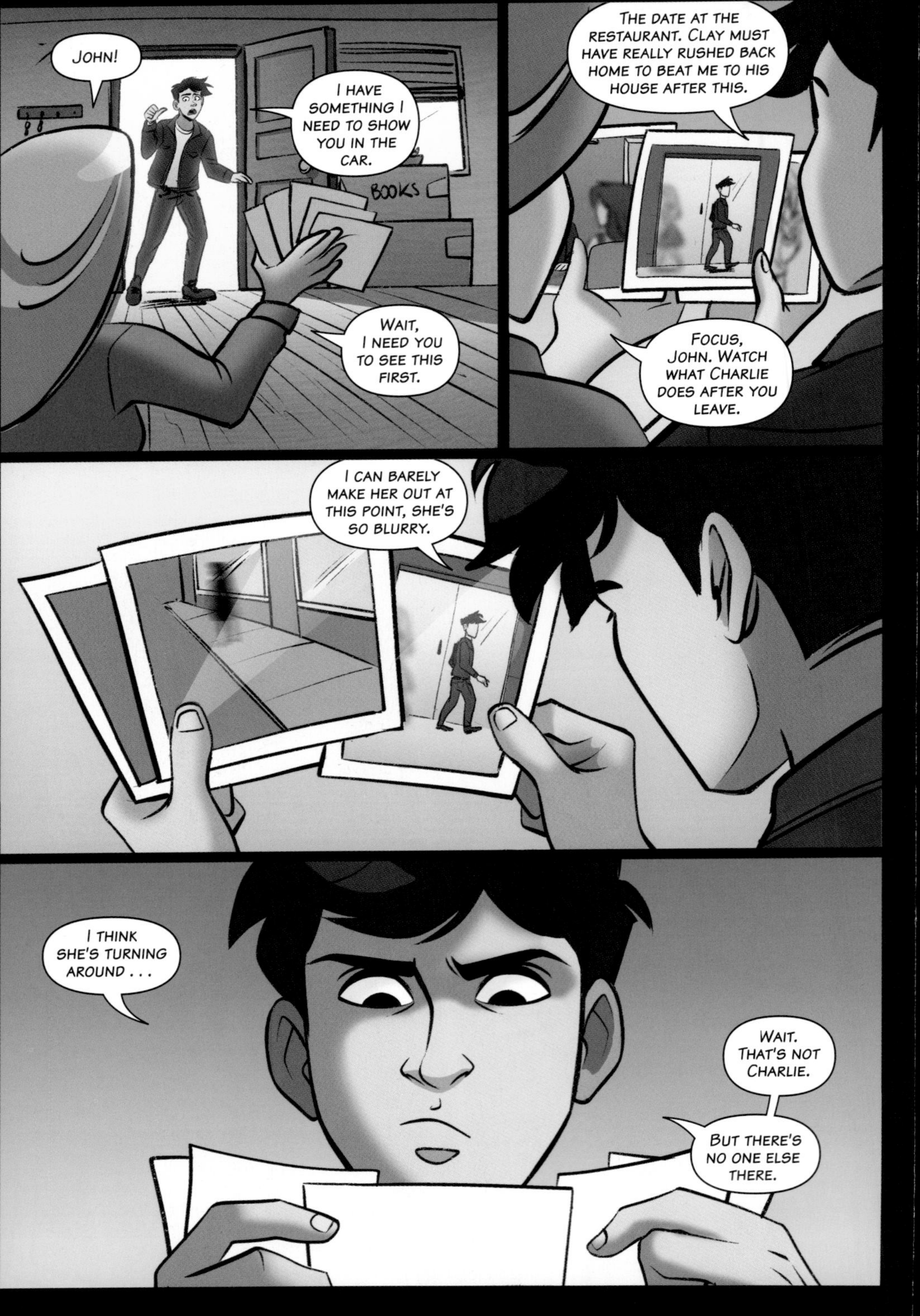
John!
I have something I need to show you in the car.
BOOKS
Wait, I need you to see this first.
The date at the restaurant. Clay must have really rushed back home to beat me to his house after this.
Focus, John. Watch what Charlie does after you leave.
I can barely make her out at this point, she's so blurry.
I think she's turning around . . .
Wait. That's not Charlie.
But there's no one else there.

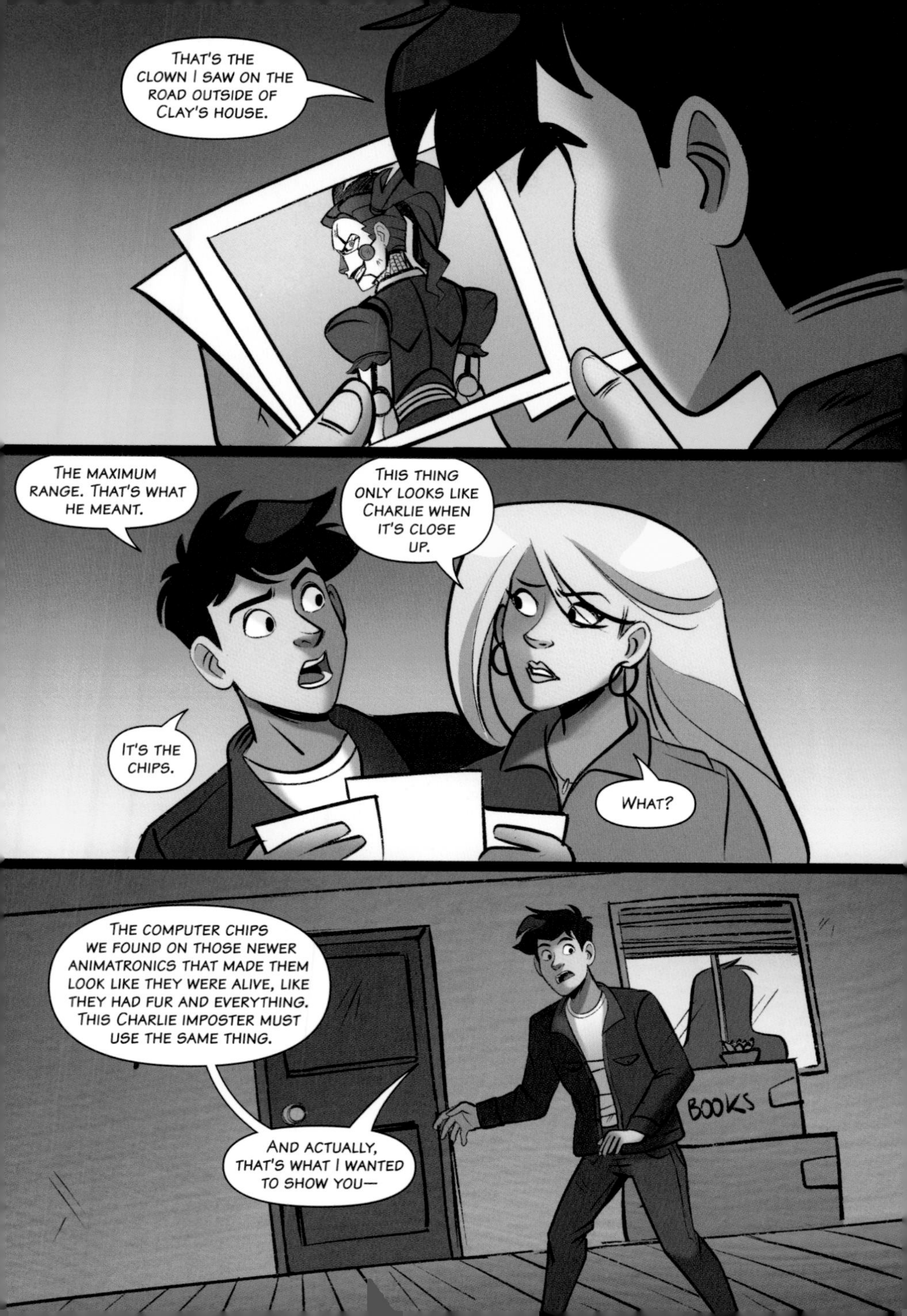
THAT'S THE CLOWN I SAW ON THE ROAD OUTSIDE OF CLAY'S HOUSE.
THE MAXIMUM RANGE. THAT'S WHAT HE MEANT.
THIS THING ONLY LOOKS LIKE CHARLIE WHEN IT'S CLOSE UP.
IT'S THE CHIPS.
WHAT?
THE COMPUTER CHIPS WE FOUND ON THOSE NEWER ANIMATRONICS THAT MADE THEM LOOK LIKE THEY WERE ALIVE, LIKE THEY HAD FUR AND EVERYTHING. THIS CHARLIE IMPOSTER MUST USE THE SAME THING.
AND ACTUALLY, THAT'S WHAT I WANTED TO SHOW YOU—
BOOKS

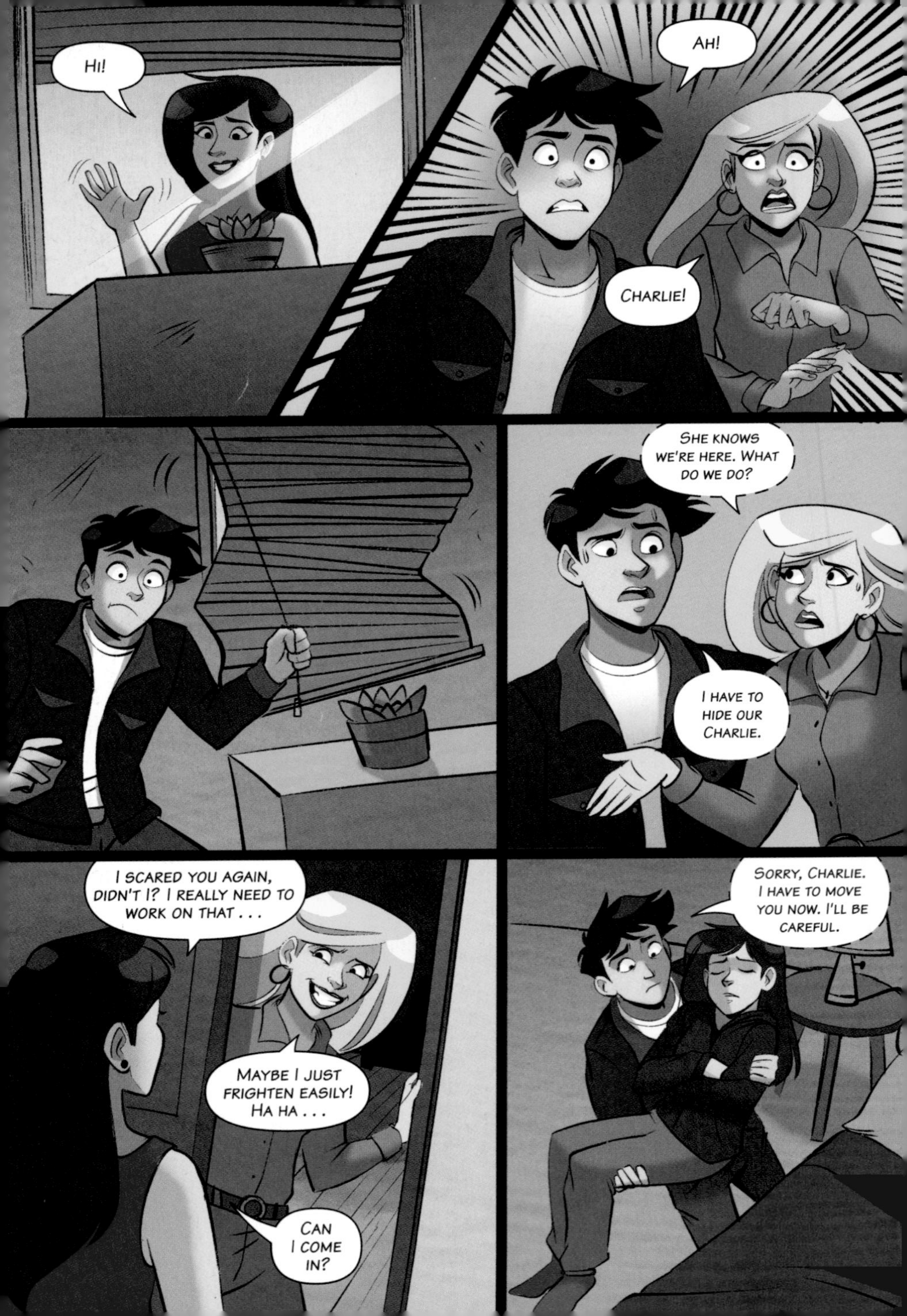
HI!
AH!
CHARLIE!
SHE KNOWS WE'RE HERE. WHAT DO WE DO?
I HAVE TO HIDE OUR CHARLIE.
I SCARED YOU AGAIN, DIDN'T I? I REALLY NEED TO WORK ON THAT . . .
MAYBE I JUST FRIGHTEN EASILY! HA HA . . .
CAN I COME IN?
SORRY, CHARLIE. I HAVE TO MOVE YOU NOW. I'LL BE CAREFUL.

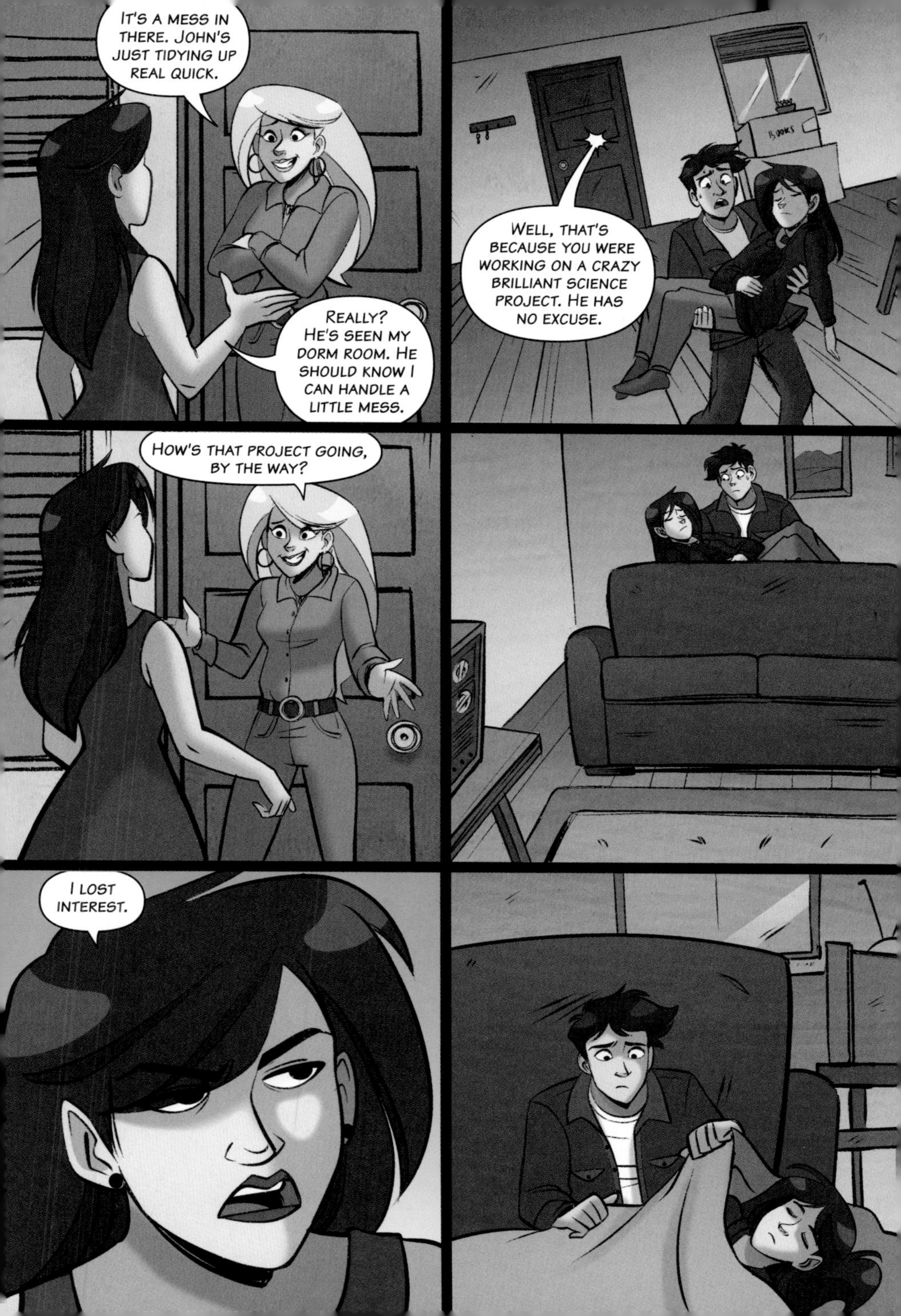

IT'S A MESS IN THERE. JOHN'S JUST TIDYING UP REAL QUICK.
REALLY? HE'S SEEN MY DORM ROOM. HE SHOULD KNOW I CAN HANDLE A LITTLE MESS.
BOOKS
WELL, THAT'S BECAUSE YOU WERE WORKING ON A CRAZY BRILLIANT SCIENCE PROJECT. HE HAS NO EXCUSE.
HOW'S THAT PROJECT GOING, BY THE WAY?
I LOST INTEREST.

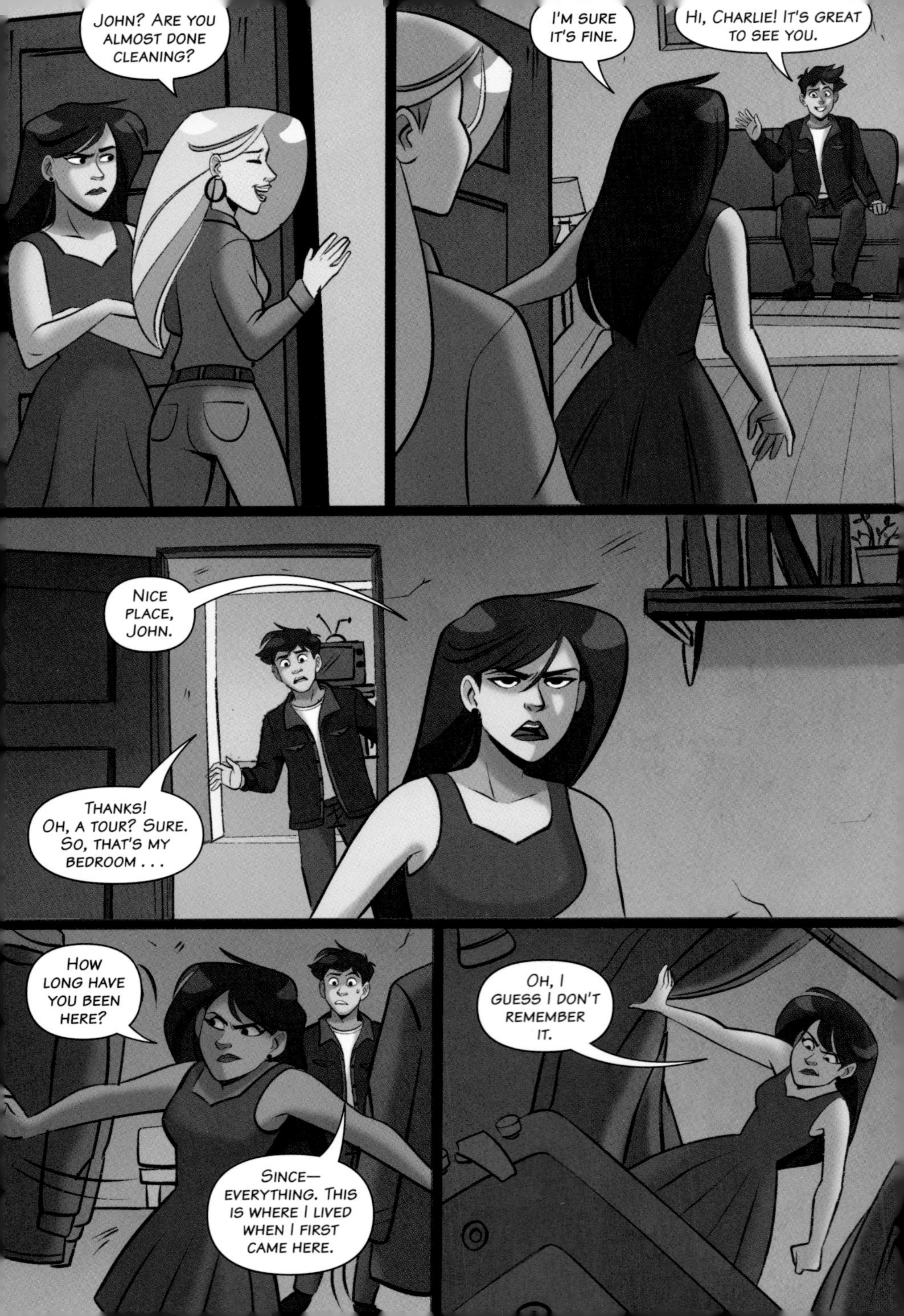
JOHN? ARE YOU ALMOST DONE CLEANING?
I'M SURE IT'S FINE.
HI, CHARLIE! IT'S GREAT TO SEE YOU.
NICE PLACE, JOHN.
THANKS! OH, A TOUR? SURE. SO, THAT'S MY BEDROOM . . .
HOW LONG HAVE YOU BEEN HERE?
SINCE— EVERYTHING. THIS IS WHERE I LIVED WHEN I FIRST CAME HERE.
OH, I GUESS I DON'T REMEMBER IT.

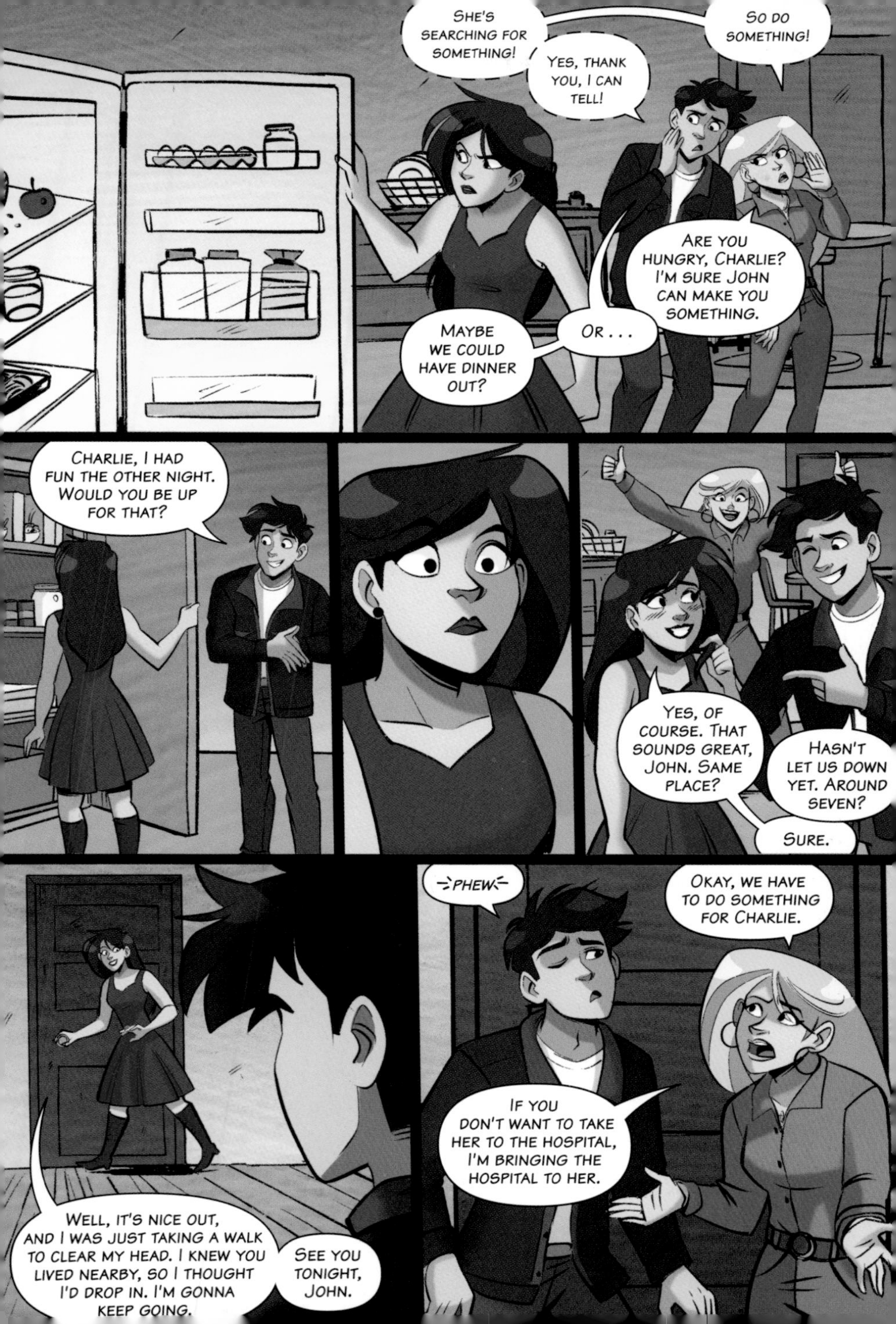

She's searching for something!
Yes, thank you, I can tell!
So do something!
Are you hungry, Charlie? I'm sure John can make you something.
Or . . .
Maybe we could have dinner out?
Charlie, I had fun the other night. Would you be up for that?
Yes, of course. That sounds great, John. Same place?
Hasn't let us down yet. Around seven?
Sure.
Well, it's nice out, and I was just taking a walk to clear my head. I knew you lived nearby, so I thought I'd drop in. I'm gonna keep going.
See you tonight, John.
PHEW
Okay, we have to do something for Charlie.
If you don't want to take her to the hospital, I'm bringing the hospital to her.

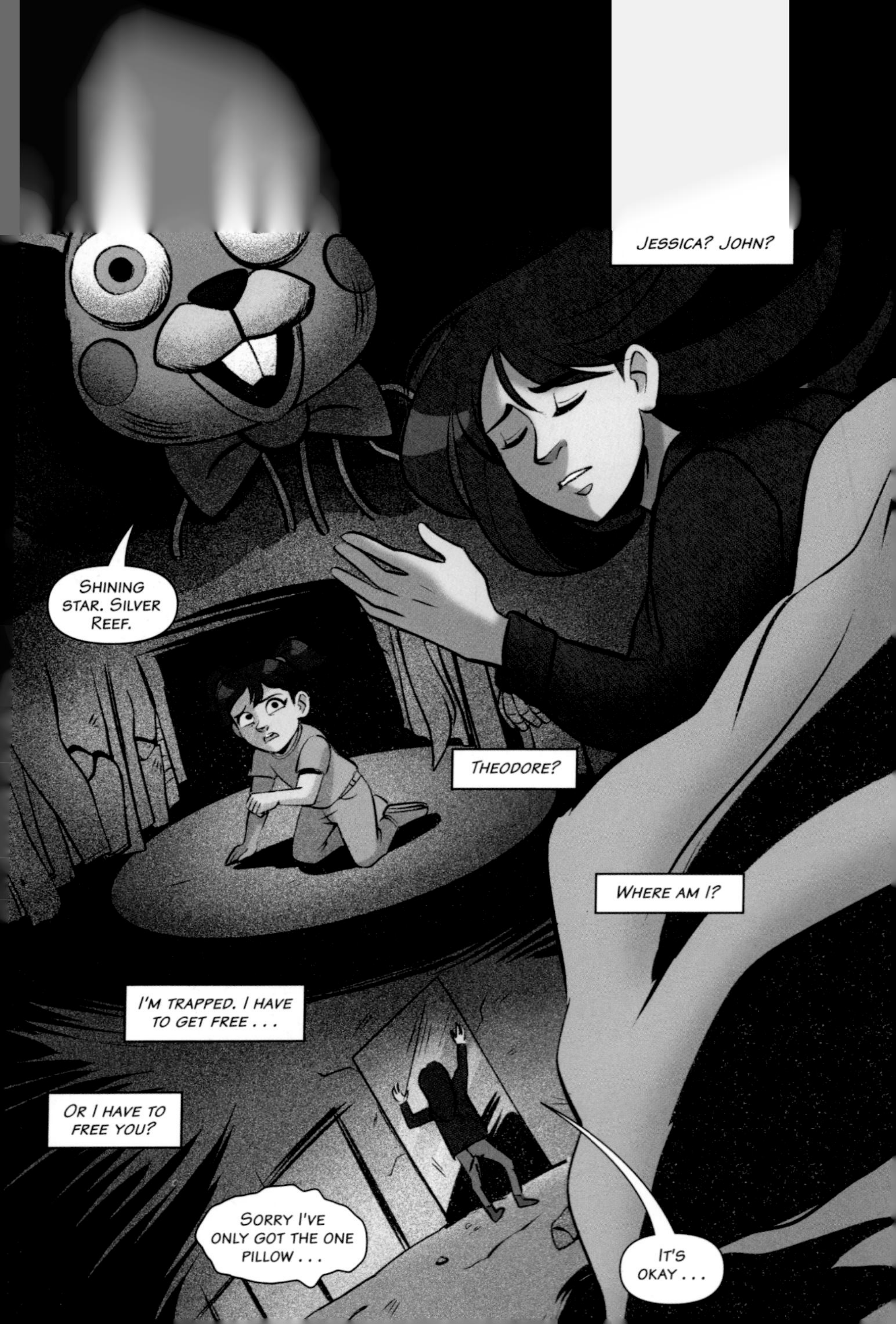
JESSICA? JOHN?
SHINING STAR. SILVER REEF.
THEODORE?
WHERE AM I?
I'M TRAPPED. I HAVE TO GET FREE . . .
OR I HAVE TO FREE YOU?
SORRY I'VE ONLY GOT THE ONE PILLOW . . .
IT'S OKAY . . .

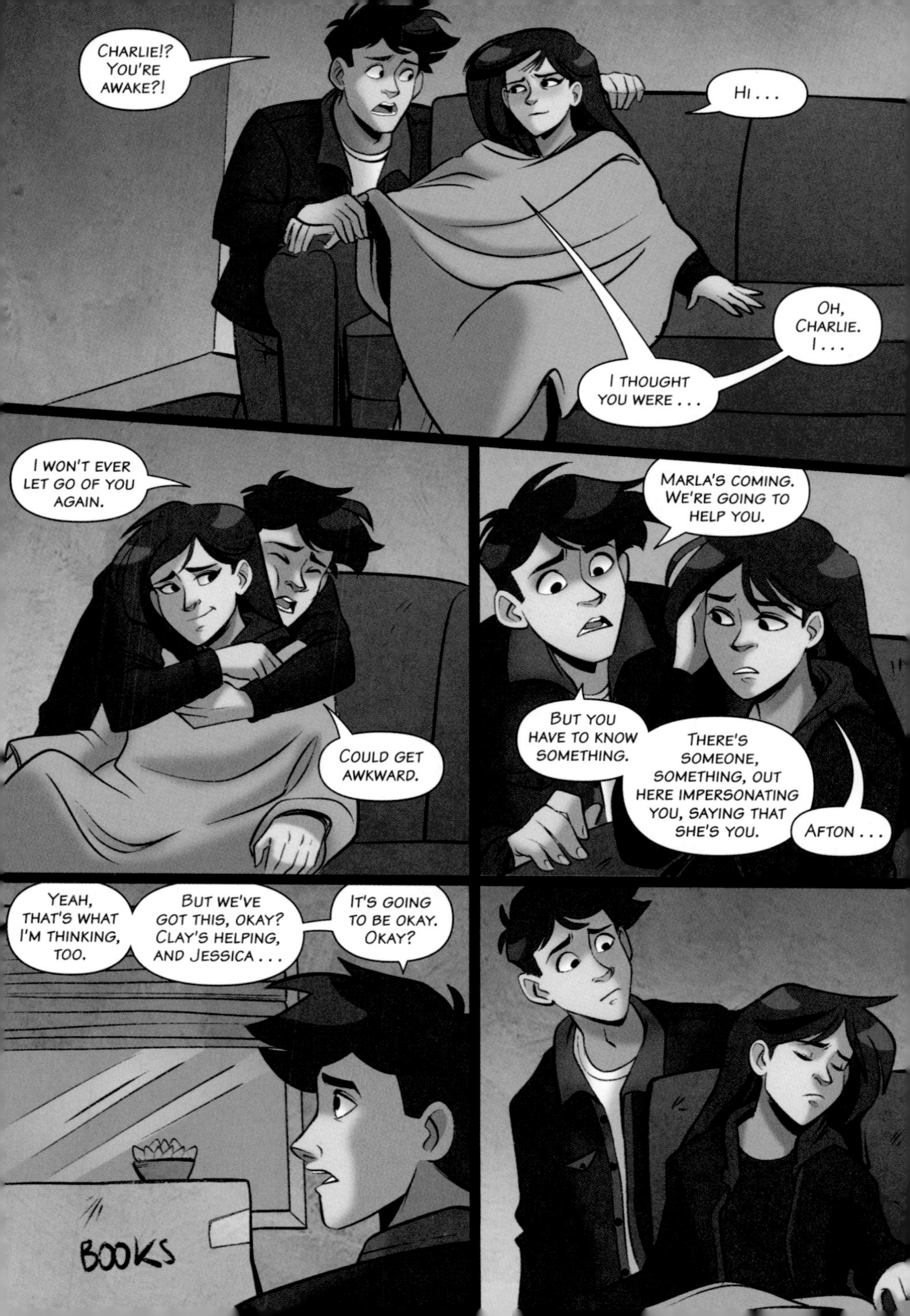

CHARLIE!? YOU'RE AWAKE?!
HI . . .
I THOUGHT YOU WERE . . .
OH, CHARLIE. I . . .
I WON'T EVER LET GO OF YOU AGAIN.
COULD GET AWKWARD.
MARLA'S COMING. WE'RE GOING TO HELP YOU.
BUT YOU HAVE TO KNOW SOMETHING.
THERE'S SOMEONE, SOMETHING, OUT HERE IMPERSONATING YOU, SAYING THAT SHE'S YOU.
AFTON . . .
YEAH, THAT'S WHAT I'M THINKING, TOO.
BUT WE'VE GOT THIS, OKAY? CLAY'S HELPING, AND JESSICA . . .
IT'S GOING TO BE OKAY. OKAY?
BOOKS

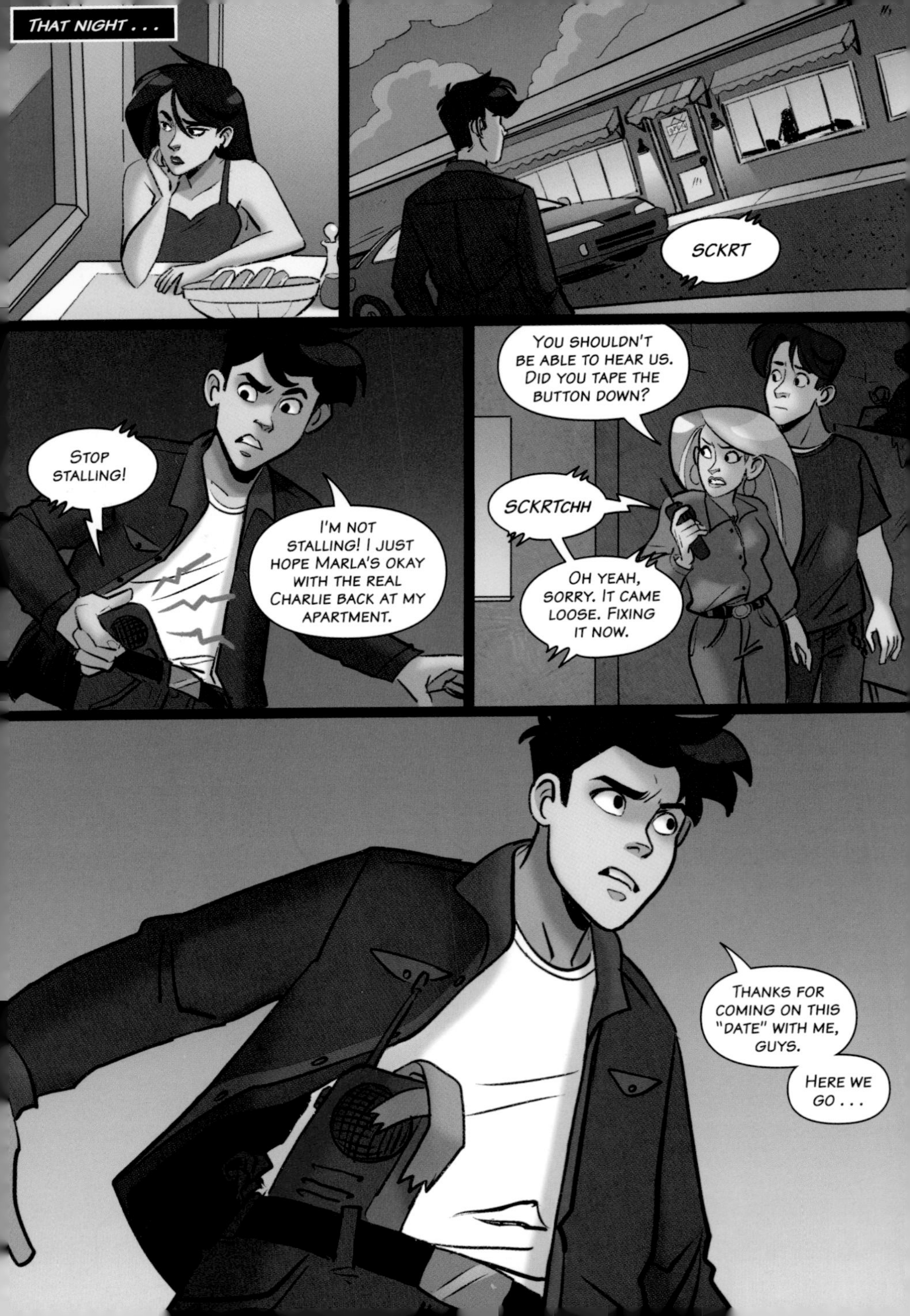
THAT NIGHT . . .
SCKRT
STOP STALLING!
I'M NOT STALLING! I JUST HOPE MARLA'S OKAY WITH THE REAL CHARLIE BACK AT MY APARTMENT.
YOU SHOULDN'T BE ABLE TO HEAR US. DID YOU TAPE THE BUTTON DOWN?
SCKRTCHH
OH YEAH, SORRY. IT CAME LOOSE. FIXING IT NOW.
THANKS FOR COMING ON THIS "DATE" WITH ME, GUYS.
HERE WE GO . . .

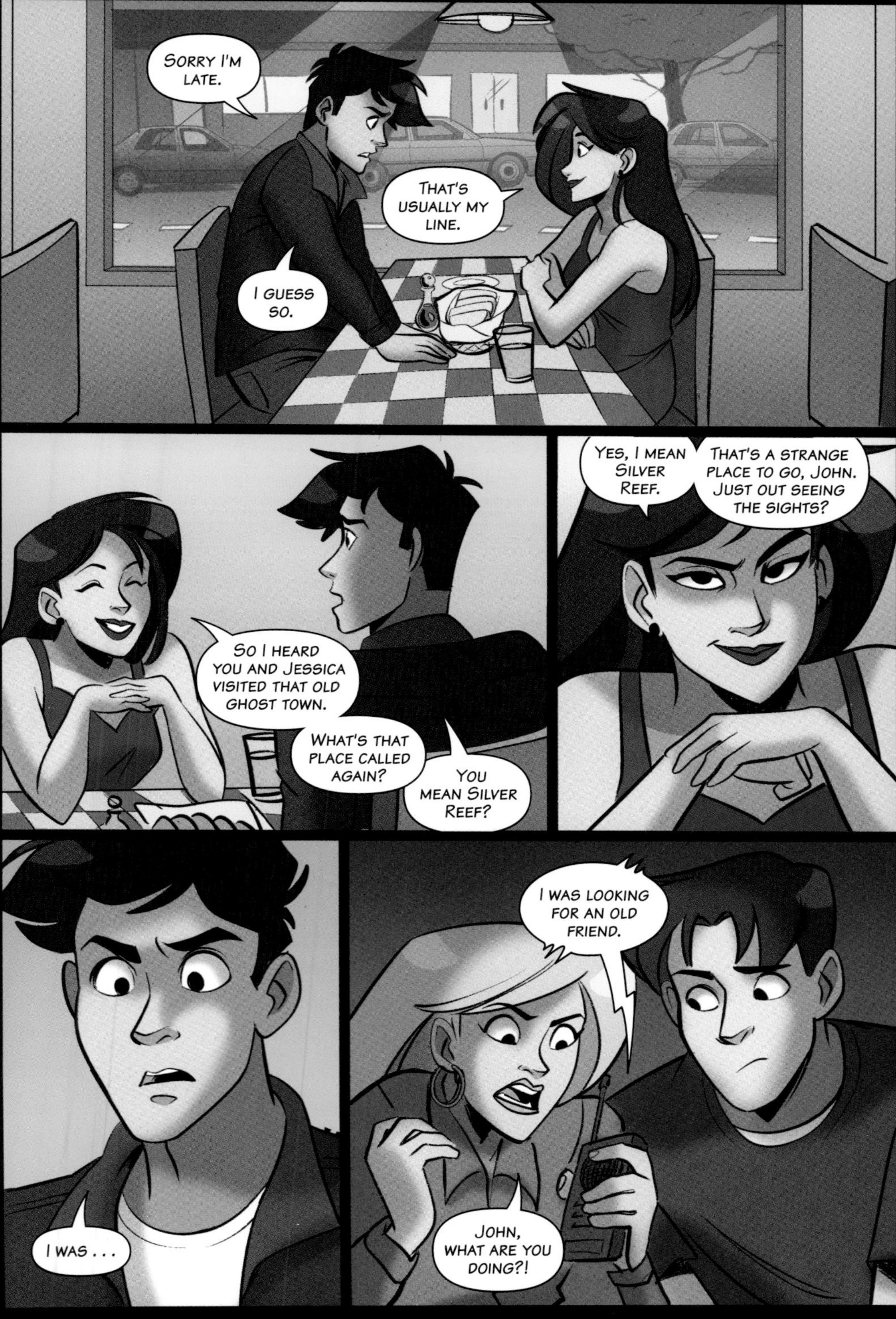
SORRY I'M LATE.
THAT'S USUALLY MY LINE.
I GUESS SO.
SO I HEARD YOU AND JESSICA VISITED THAT OLD GHOST TOWN.
WHAT'S THAT PLACE CALLED AGAIN?
YOU MEAN SILVER REEF?
YES, I MEAN SILVER REEF.
THAT'S A STRANGE PLACE TO GO, JOHN. JUST OUT SEEING THE SIGHTS?
I WAS . . .
I WAS LOOKING FOR AN OLD FRIEND.
JOHN, WHAT ARE YOU DOING?!

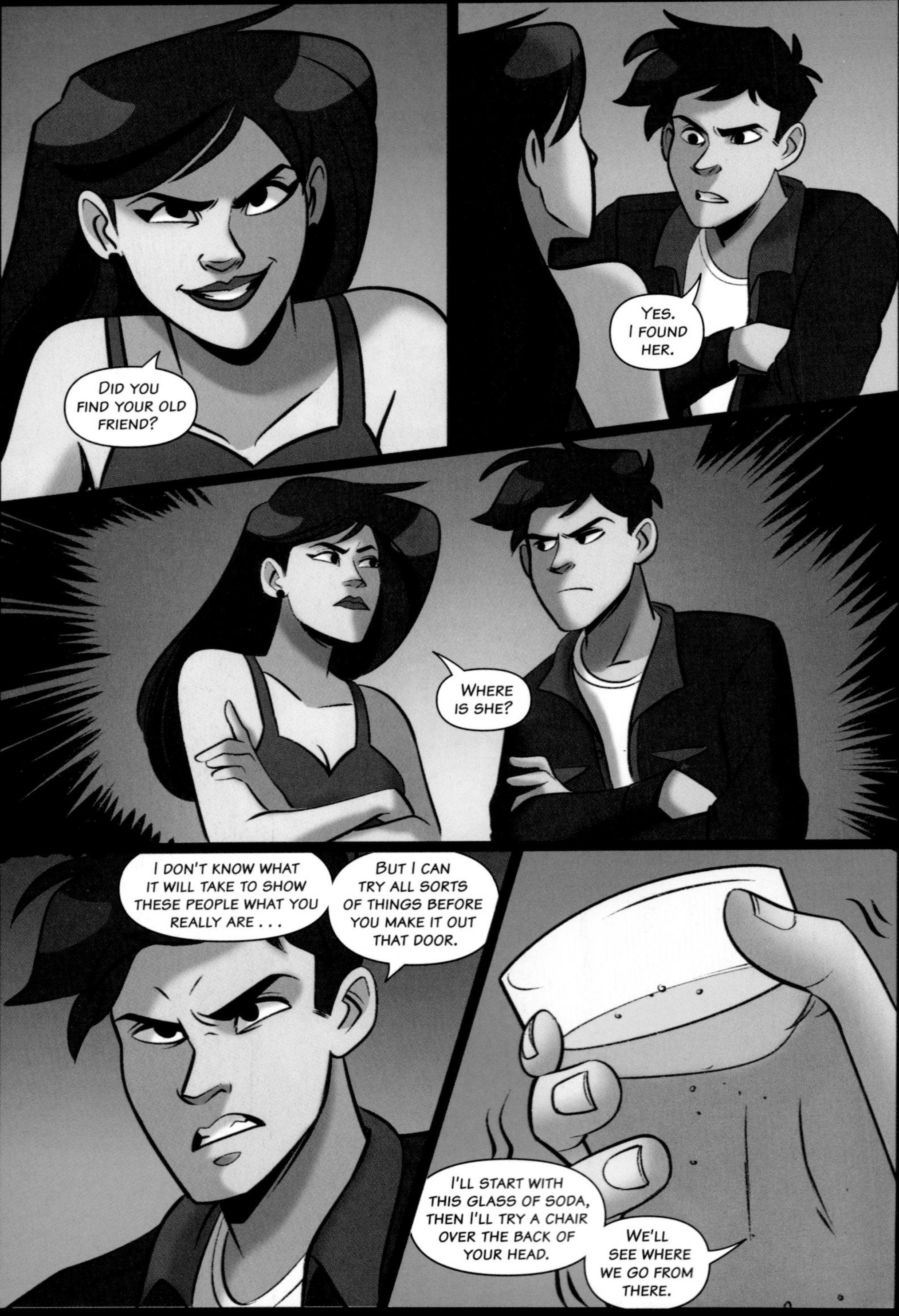
DID YOU FIND YOUR OLD FRIEND?
YES. I FOUND HER.
WHERE IS SHE?
I DON'T KNOW WHAT IT WILL TAKE TO SHOW THESE PEOPLE WHAT YOU REALLY ARE . . .
BUT I CAN TRY ALL SORTS OF THINGS BEFORE YOU MAKE IT OUT THAT DOOR.
I'LL START WITH THIS GLASS OF SODA, THEN I'LL TRY A CHAIR OVER THE BACK OF YOUR HEAD.
WE'LL SEE WHERE WE GO FROM THERE.

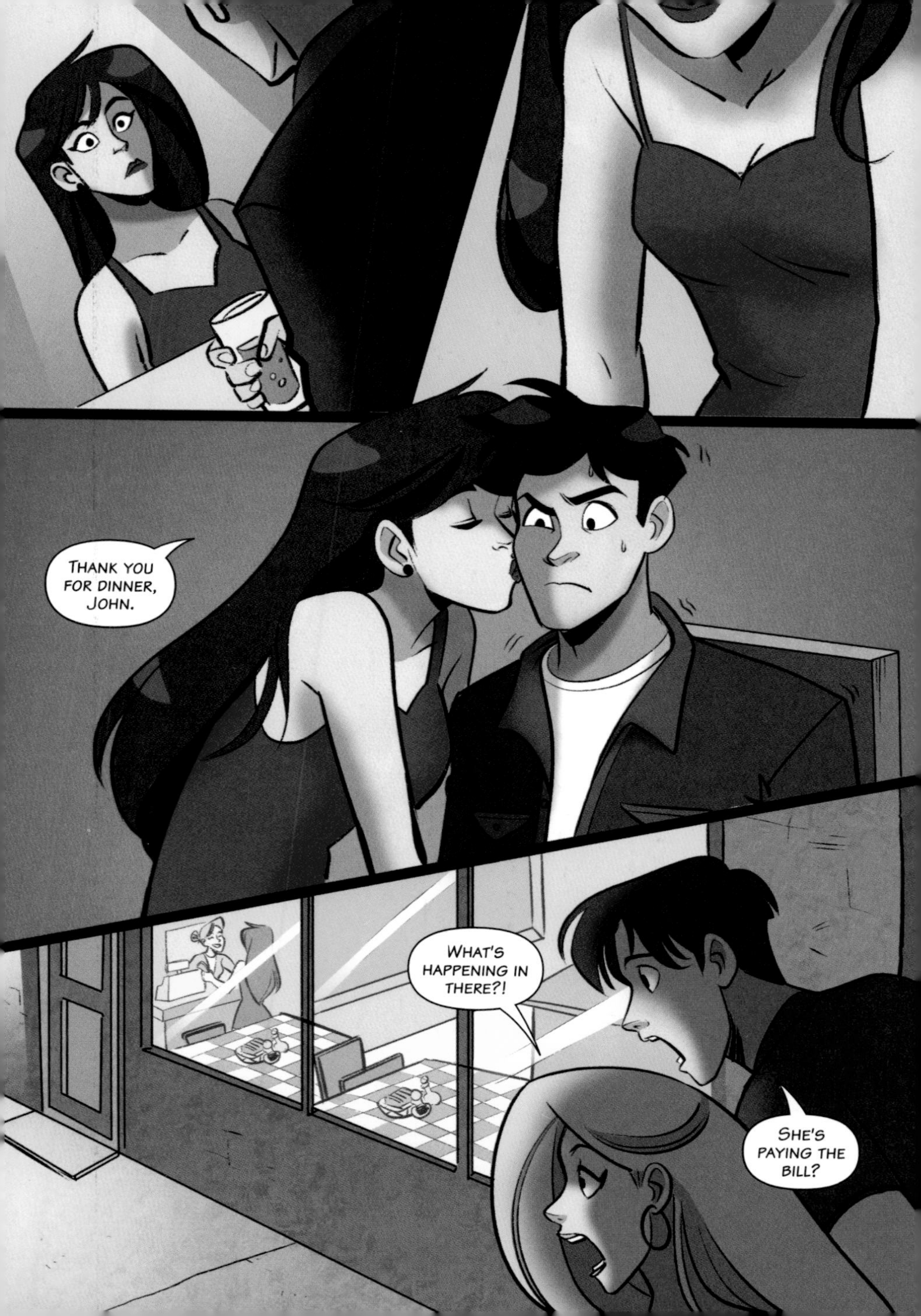
THANK YOU FOR DINNER, JOHN.
WHAT'S HAPPENING IN THERE?!
SHE'S PAYING THE BILL?

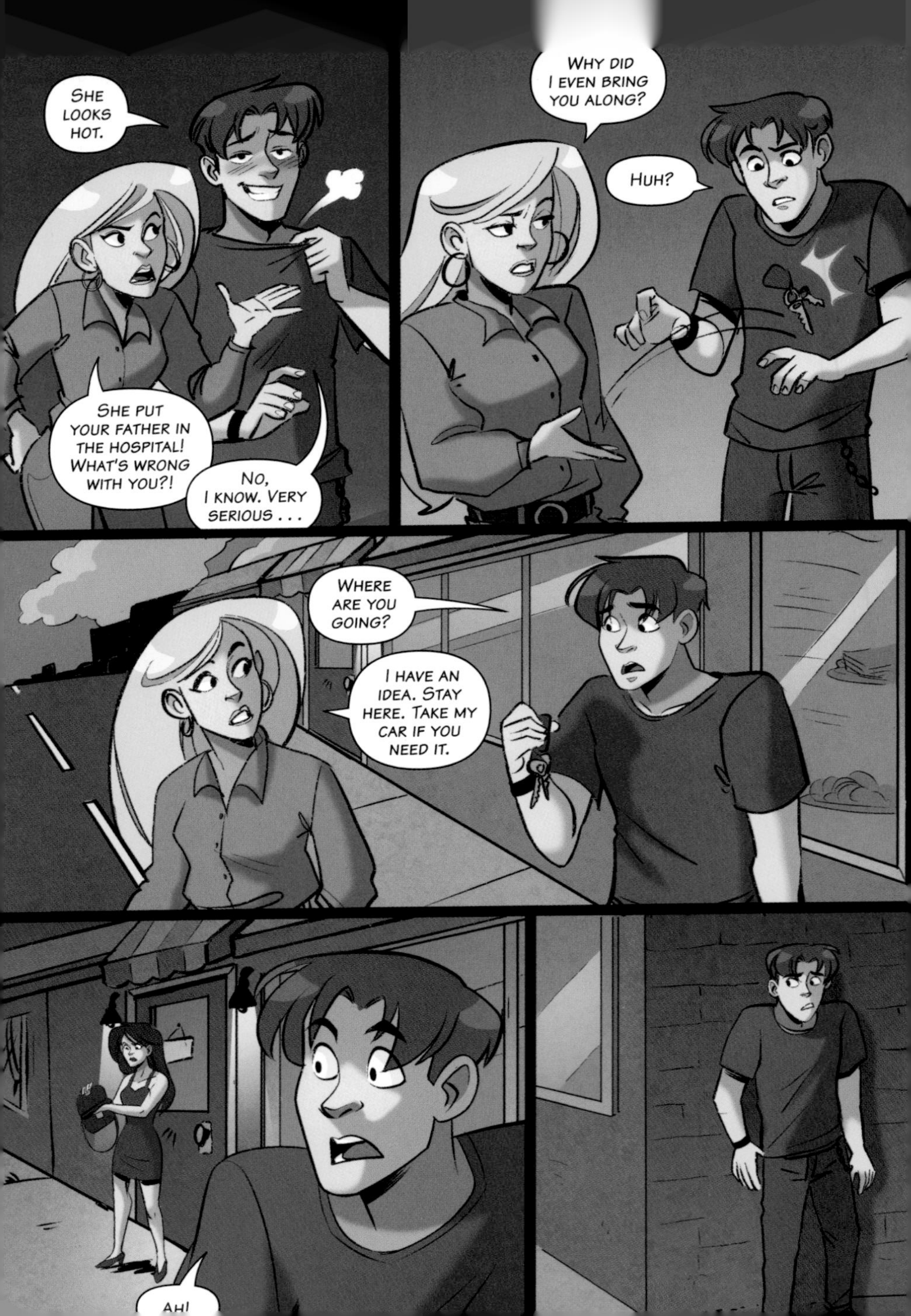
SHE LOOKS HOT.
SHE PUT YOUR FATHER IN THE HOSPITAL! WHAT'S WRONG WITH YOU?!
NO, I KNOW. VERY SERIOUS . . .
WHY DID I EVEN BRING YOU ALONG?
HUH?
WHERE ARE YOU GOING?
I HAVE AN IDEA. STAY HERE. TAKE MY CAR IF YOU NEED IT.
AH!

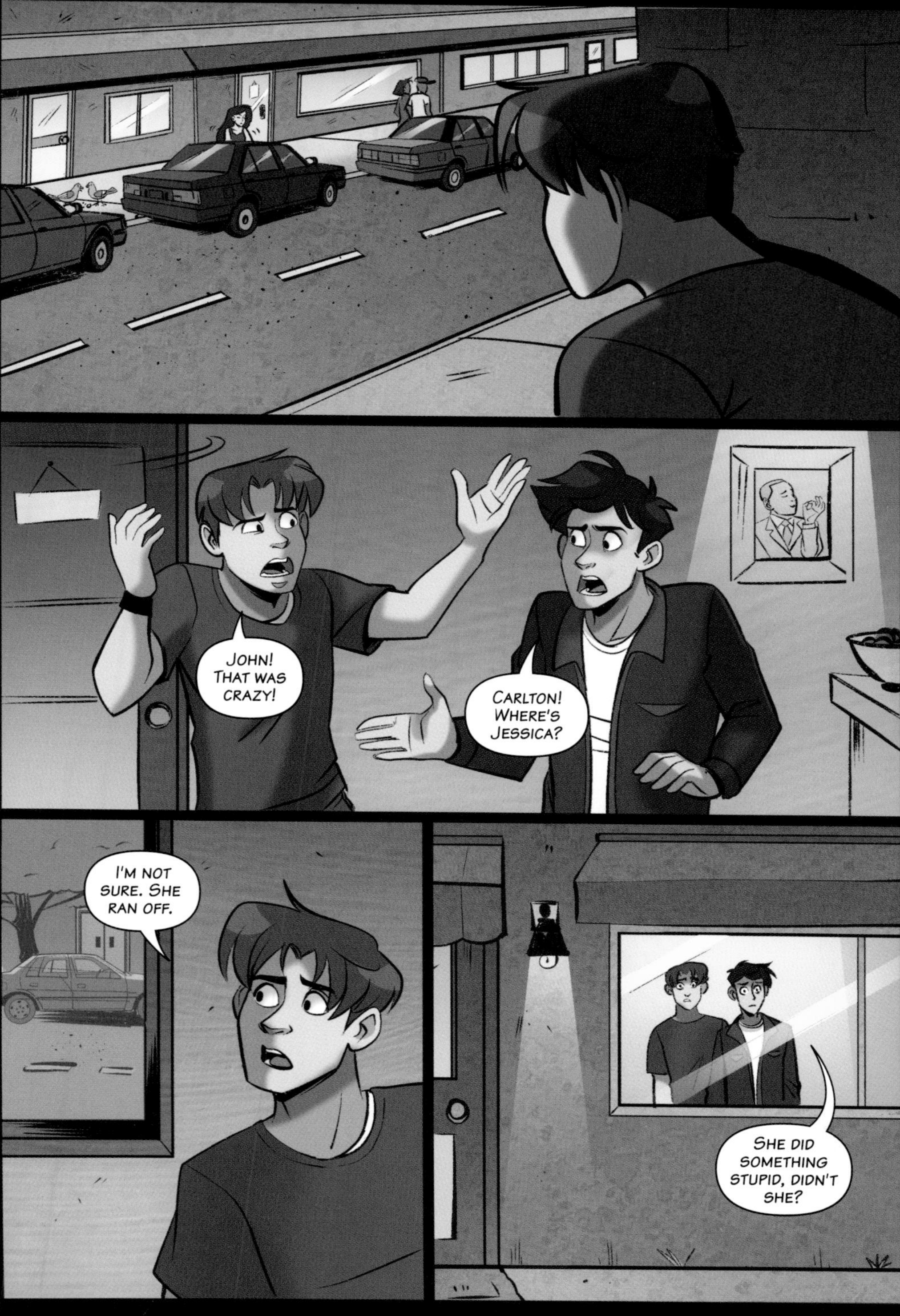
JOHN! THAT WAS CRAZY!
CARLTON! WHERE'S JESSICA?
I'M NOT SURE. SHE RAN OFF.
SHE DID SOMETHING STUPID, DIDN'T SHE?

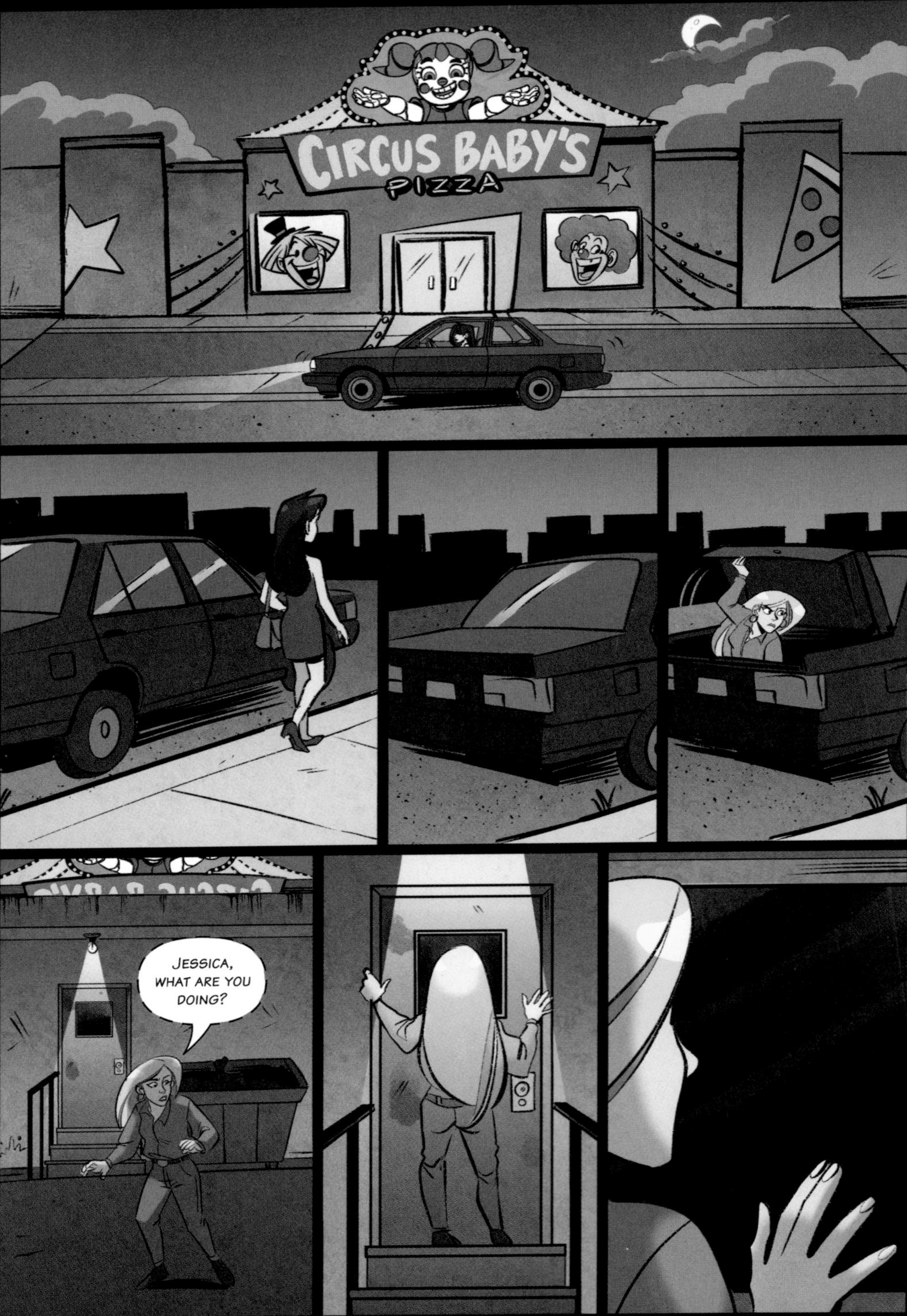
CIRCUS BABY'S
PIZZA
JESSICA, WHAT ARE YOU DOING?

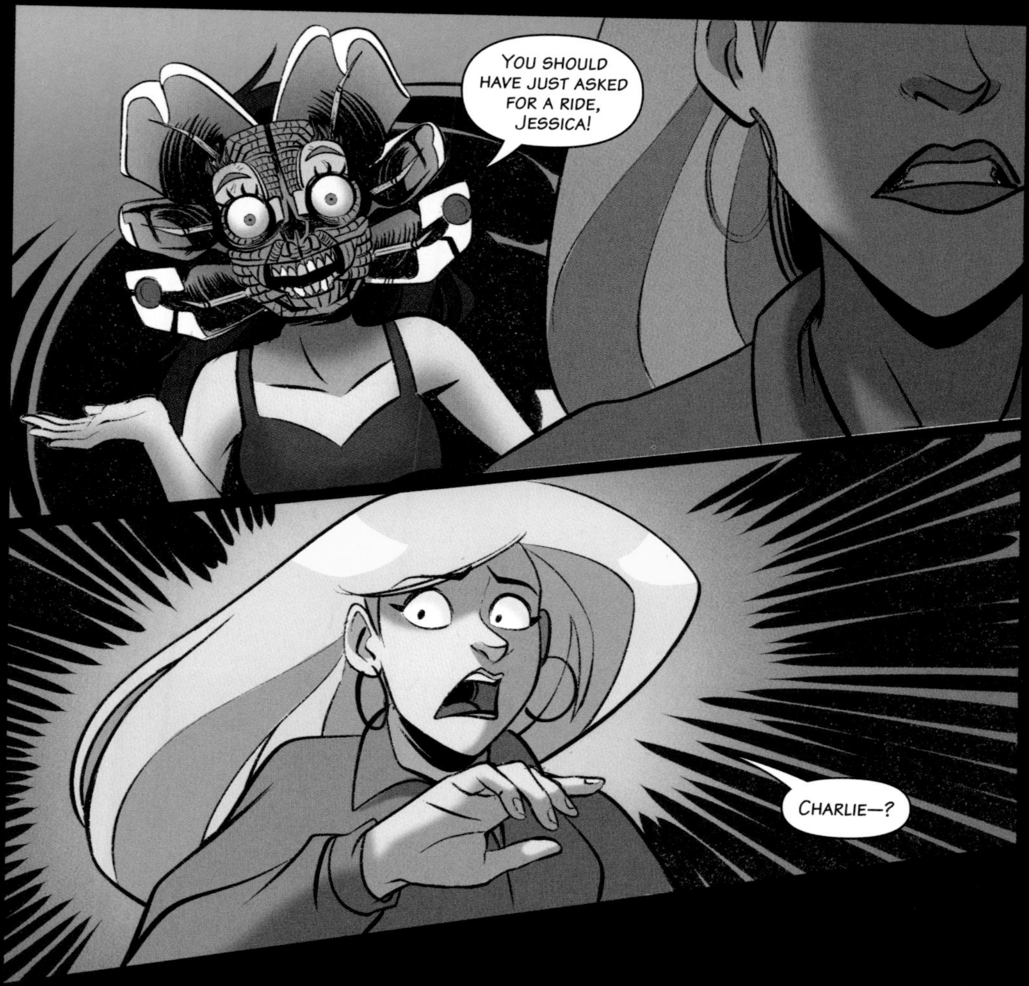
YOU SHOULD HAVE JUST ASKED FOR A RIDE, JESSICA!
CHARLIE—?

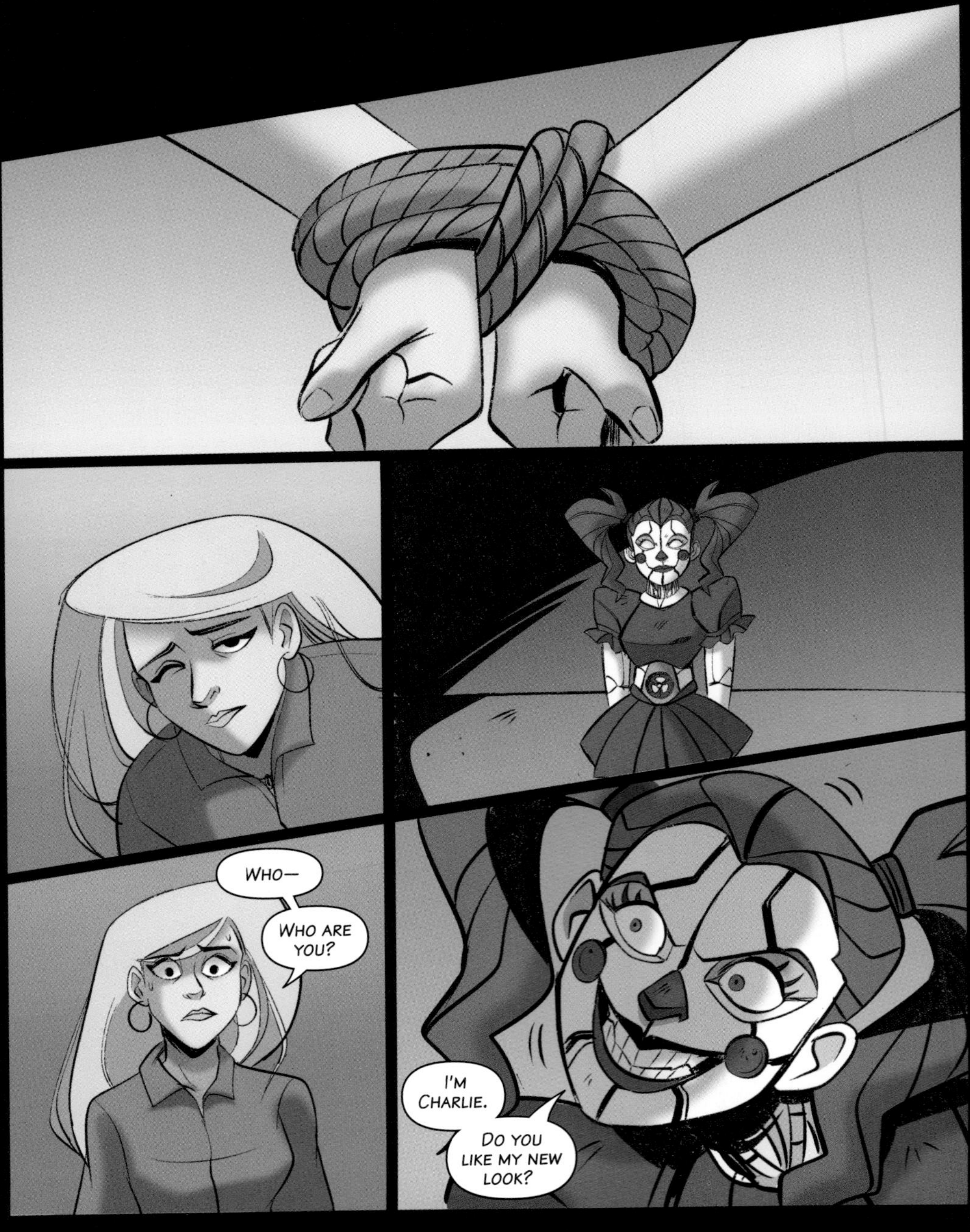
WHO—
WHO ARE YOU?
I'M CHARLIE.
DO YOU LIKE MY NEW LOOK?

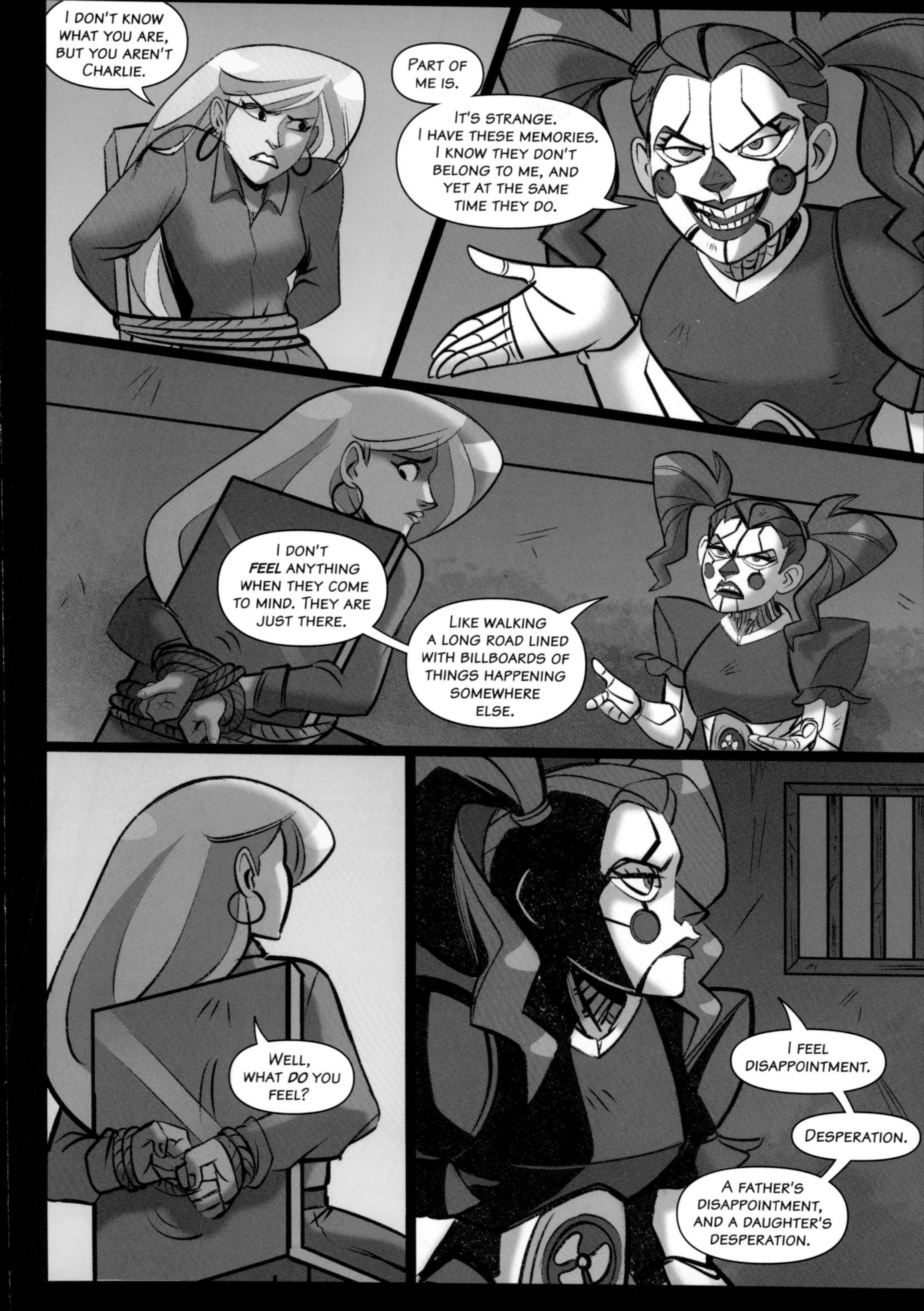
I DON'T KNOW WHAT YOU ARE, BUT YOU AREN'T CHARLIE.
PART OF ME IS.
IT'S STRANGE. I HAVE THESE MEMORIES. I KNOW THEY DON'T BELONG TO ME, AND YET AT THE SAME TIME THEY DO.
I DON'T *FEEL* ANYTHING WHEN THEY COME TO MIND. THEY ARE JUST THERE.
LIKE WALKING A LONG ROAD LINED WITH BILLBOARDS OF THINGS HAPPENING SOMEWHERE ELSE.
WELL, WHAT *DO* YOU FEEL?
I FEEL DISAPPOINTMENT.
DESPERATION.
A FATHER'S DISAPPOINTMENT, AND A DAUGHTER'S DESPERATION.

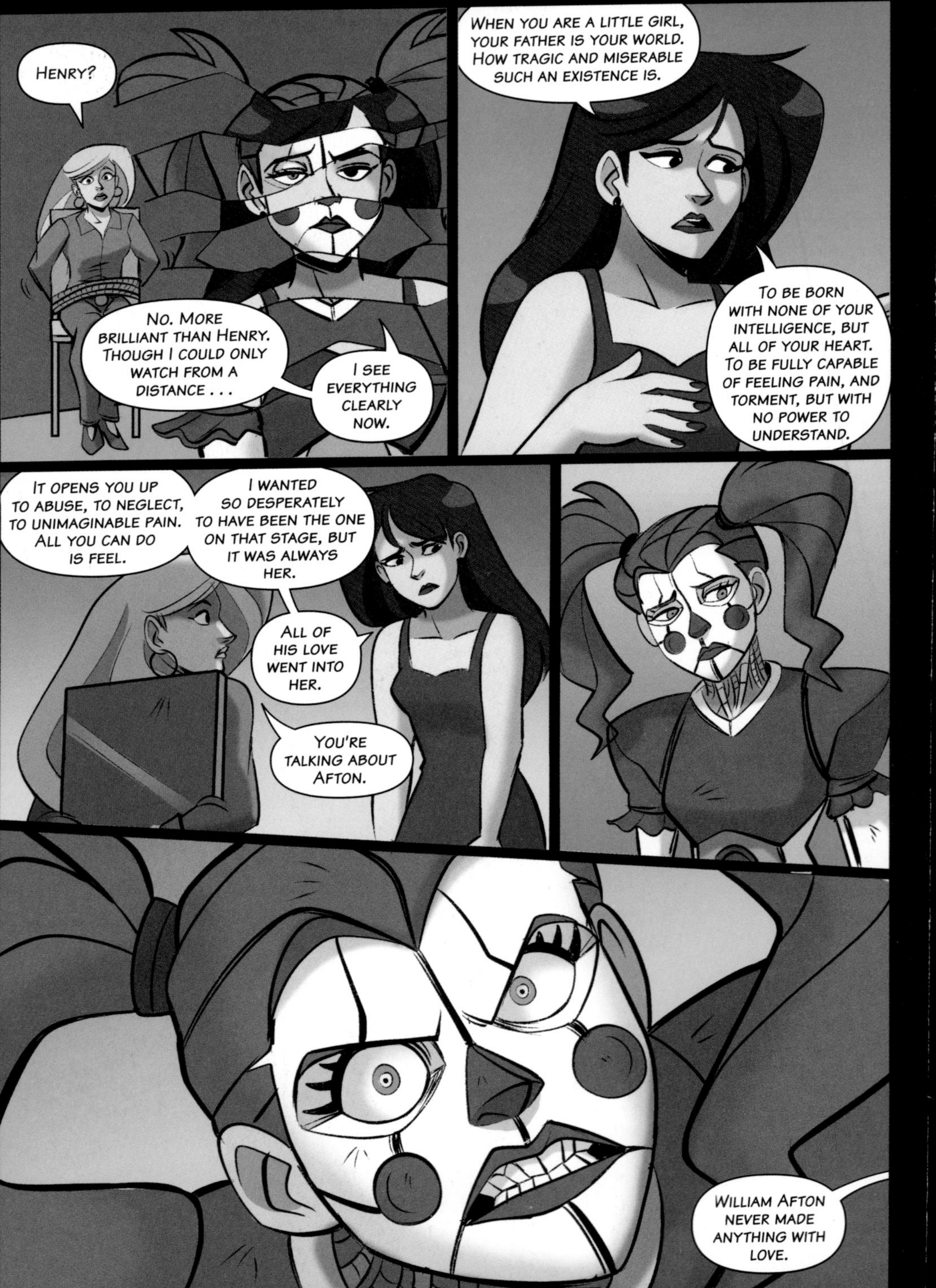
HENRY?
NO. MORE BRILLIANT THAN HENRY. THOUGH I COULD ONLY WATCH FROM A DISTANCE . . .
I SEE EVERYTHING CLEARLY NOW.
WHEN YOU ARE A LITTLE GIRL, YOUR FATHER IS YOUR WORLD. HOW TRAGIC AND MISERABLE SUCH AN EXISTENCE IS.
TO BE BORN WITH NONE OF YOUR INTELLIGENCE, BUT ALL OF YOUR HEART. TO BE FULLY CAPABLE OF FEELING PAIN, AND TORMENT, BUT WITH NO POWER TO UNDERSTAND.
IT OPENS YOU UP TO ABUSE, TO NEGLECT, TO UNIMAGINABLE PAIN. ALL YOU CAN DO IS FEEL.
I WANTED SO DESPERATELY TO HAVE BEEN THE ONE ON THAT STAGE, BUT IT WAS ALWAYS HER.
ALL OF HIS LOVE WENT INTO HER.
YOU'RE TALKING ABOUT AFTON.
WILLIAM AFTON NEVER MADE ANYTHING WITH LOVE.

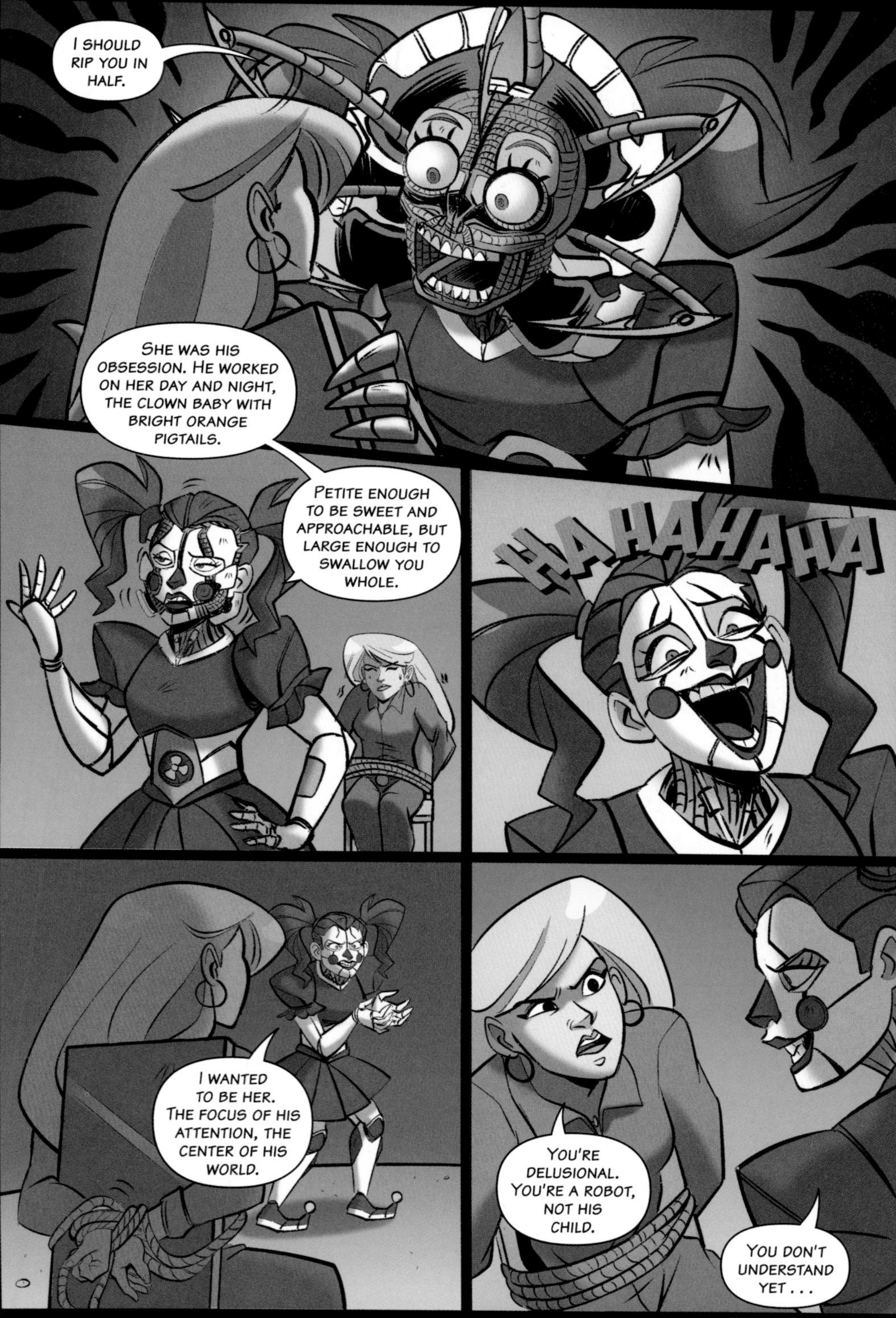

I SHOULD RIP YOU IN HALF.
SHE WAS HIS OBSESSION. HE WORKED ON HER DAY AND NIGHT, THE CLOWN BABY WITH BRIGHT ORANGE PIGTAILS.
PETITE ENOUGH TO BE SWEET AND APPROACHABLE, BUT LARGE ENOUGH TO SWALLOW YOU WHOLE.
HAHAHAHAHA
I WANTED TO BE HER. THE FOCUS OF HIS ATTENTION, THE CENTER OF HIS WORLD.
YOU'RE DELUSIONAL. YOU'RE A ROBOT, NOT HIS CHILD.
YOU DON'T UNDERSTAND YET . . .

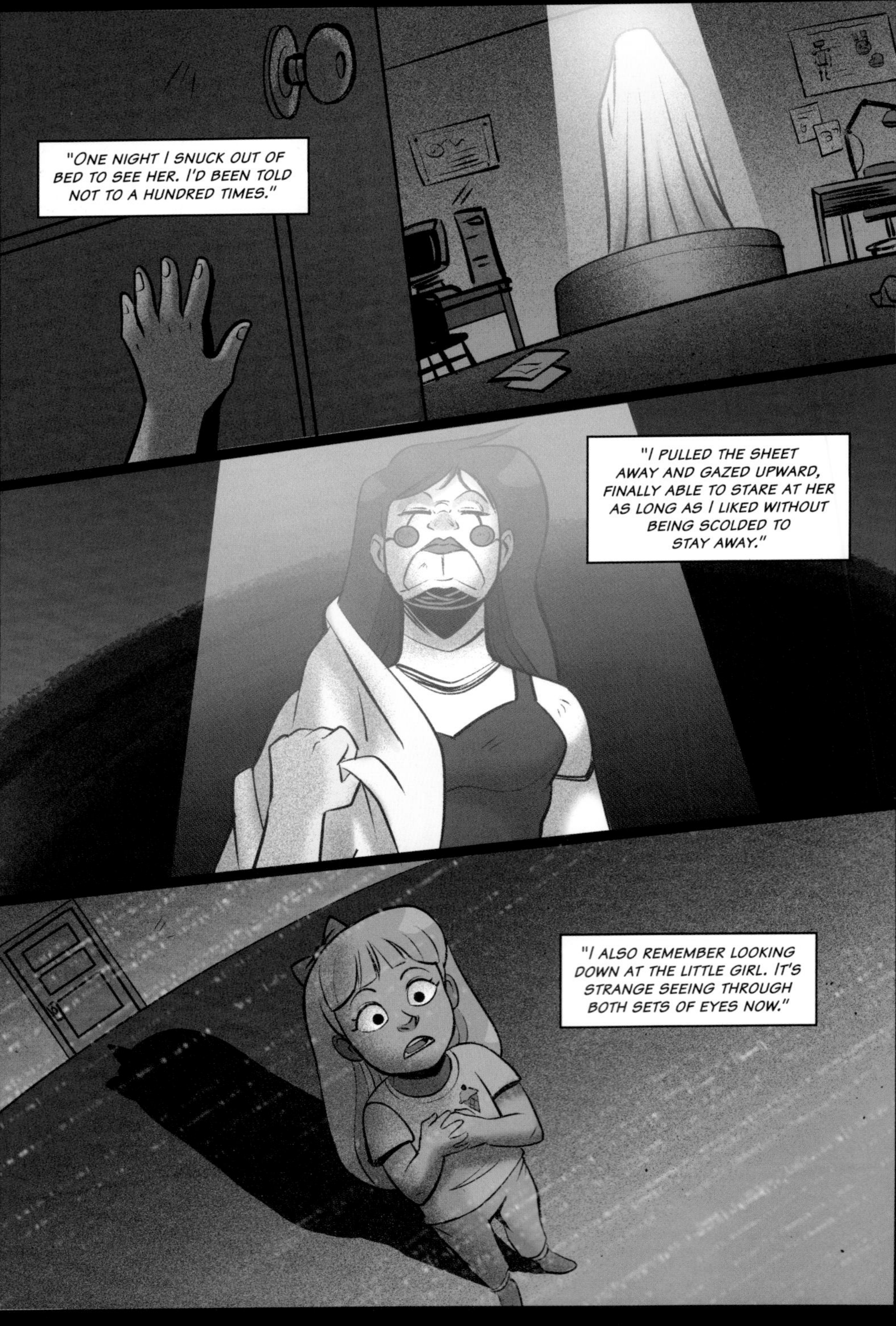
"ONE NIGHT I SNUCK OUT OF BED TO SEE HER. I'D BEEN TOLD NOT TO A HUNDRED TIMES."
"I PULLED THE SHEET AWAY AND GAZED UPWARD, FINALLY ABLE TO STARE AT HER AS LONG AS I LIKED WITHOUT BEING SCOLDED TO STAY AWAY."
"I ALSO REMEMBER LOOKING DOWN AT THE LITTLE GIRL. IT'S STRANGE SEEING THROUGH BOTH SETS OF EYES NOW."

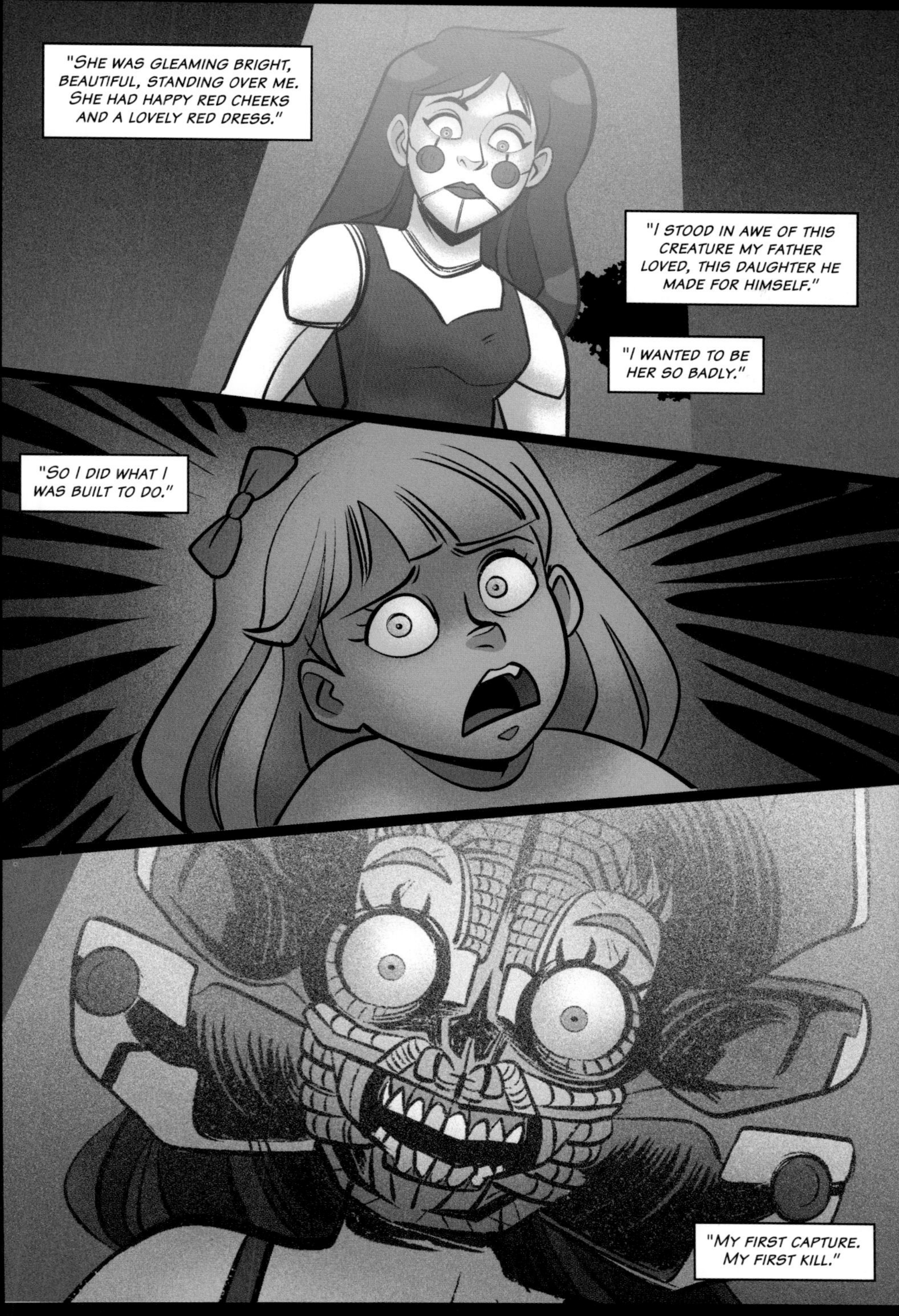
"SHE WAS GLEAMING BRIGHT, BEAUTIFUL, STANDING OVER ME. SHE HAD HAPPY RED CHEEKS AND A LOVELY RED DRESS."
"I STOOD IN AWE OF THIS CREATURE MY FATHER LOVED, THIS DAUGHTER HE MADE FOR HIMSELF."
"I WANTED TO BE HER SO BADLY."
"SO I DID WHAT I WAS BUILT TO DO."
"MY FIRST CAPTURE. MY FIRST KILL."

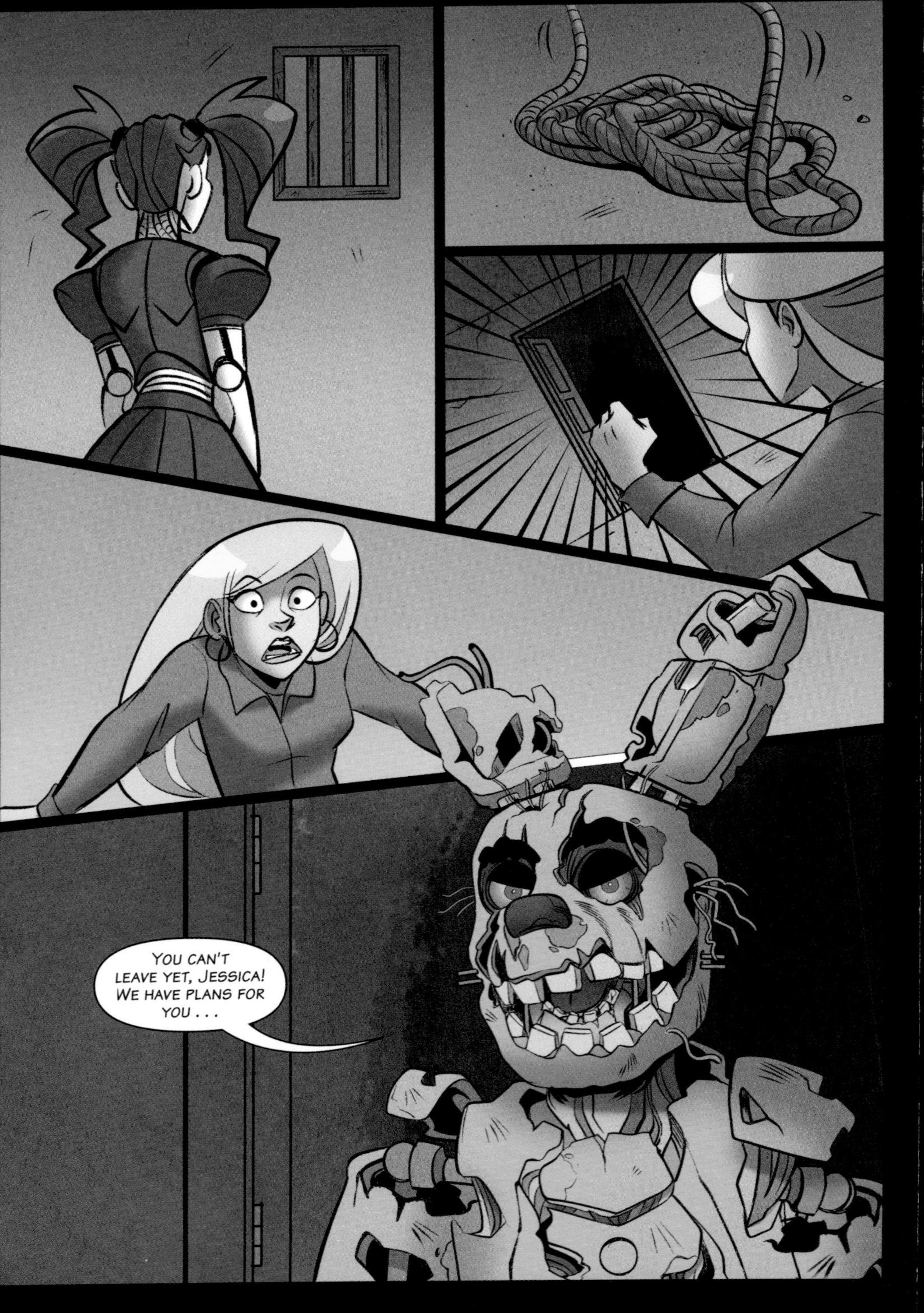
YOU CAN'T LEAVE YET, JESSICA! WE HAVE PLANS FOR YOU . . .

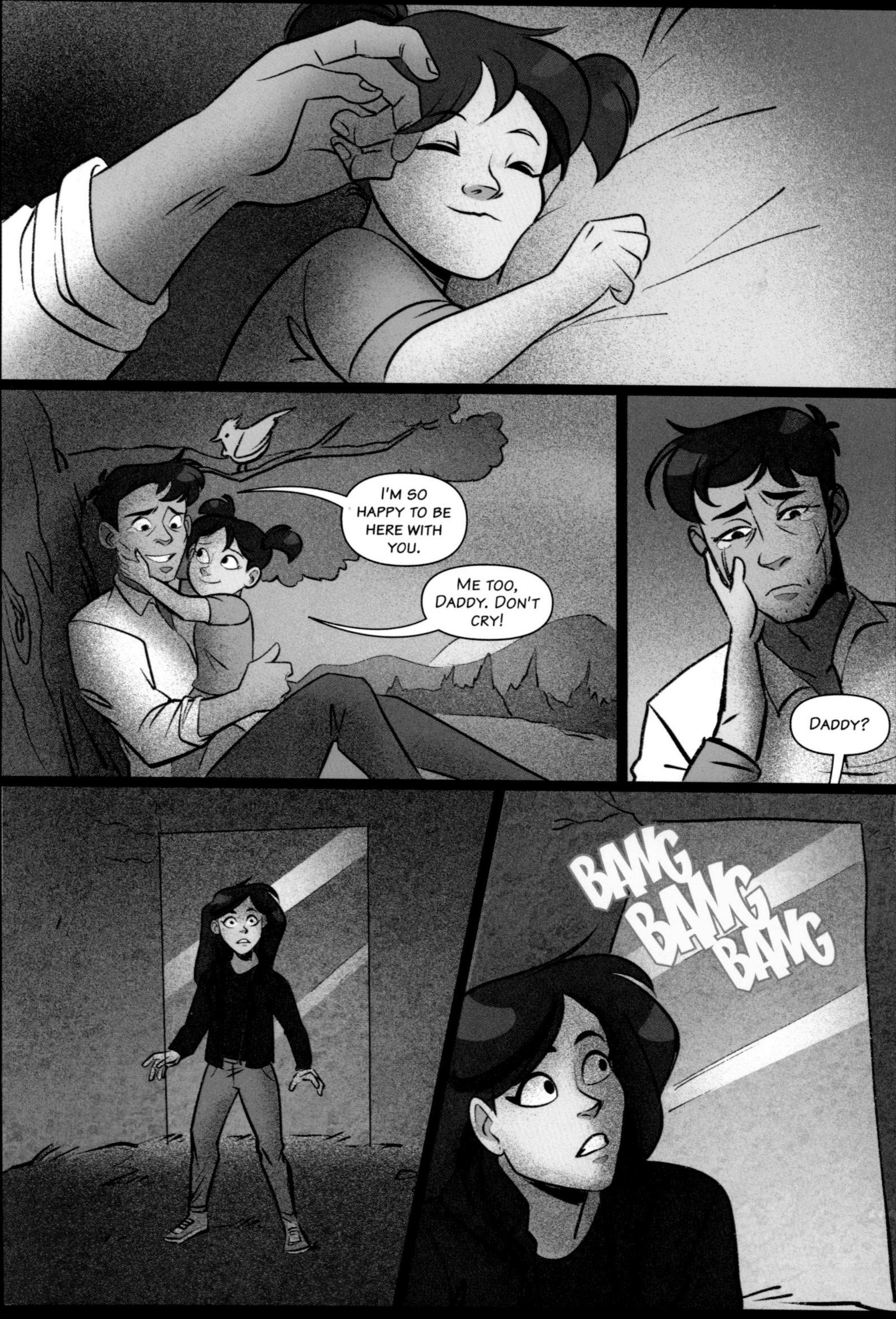
I'M SO HAPPY TO BE HERE WITH YOU.
ME TOO, DADDY. DON'T CRY!
DADDY?
BANG BANG BANG

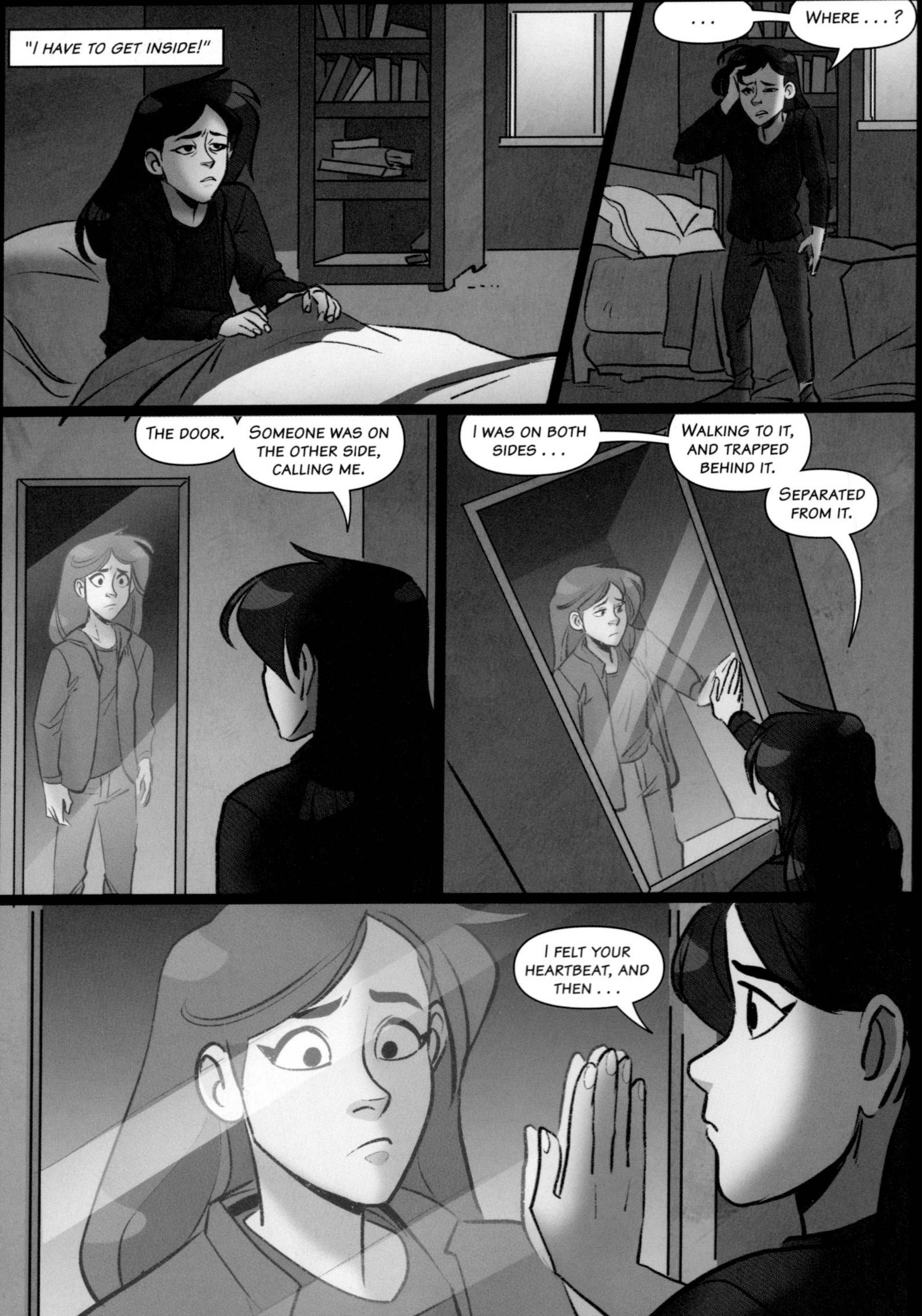
"I HAVE TO GET INSIDE!"
. . .
WHERE . . . ?
THE DOOR.
SOMEONE WAS ON THE OTHER SIDE, CALLING ME.
I WAS ON BOTH SIDES . . .
WALKING TO IT, AND TRAPPED BEHIND IT.
SEPARATED FROM IT.
I FELT YOUR HEARTBEAT, AND THEN . . .

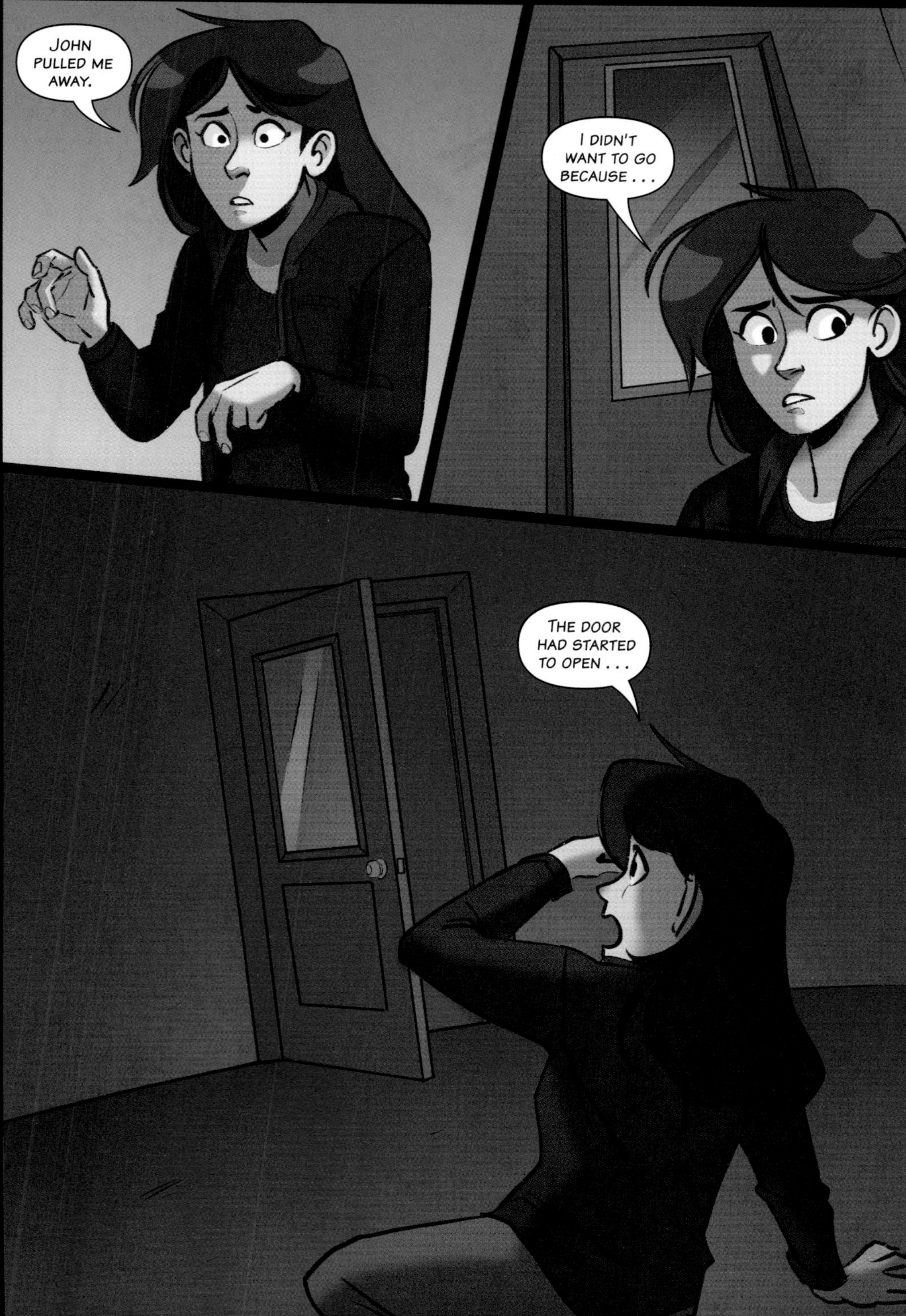
JOHN PULLED ME AWAY.
I DIDN'T WANT TO GO BECAUSE . . .
THE DOOR HAD STARTED TO OPEN . . .

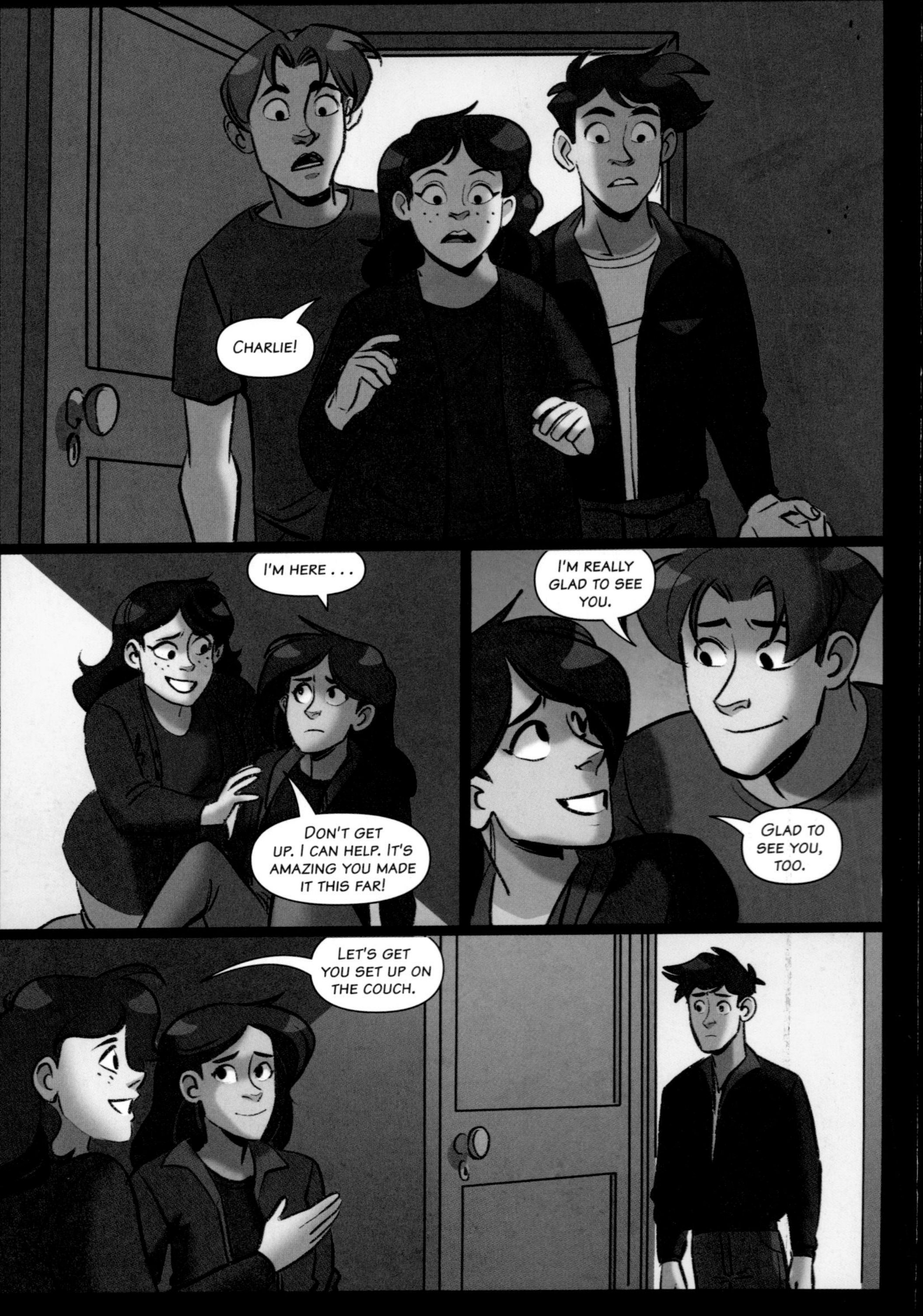
CHARLIE!
I'M HERE . . .
DON'T GET UP. I CAN HELP. IT'S AMAZING YOU MADE IT THIS FAR!
I'M REALLY GLAD TO SEE YOU.
GLAD TO SEE YOU, TOO.
LET'S GET YOU SET UP ON THE COUCH.

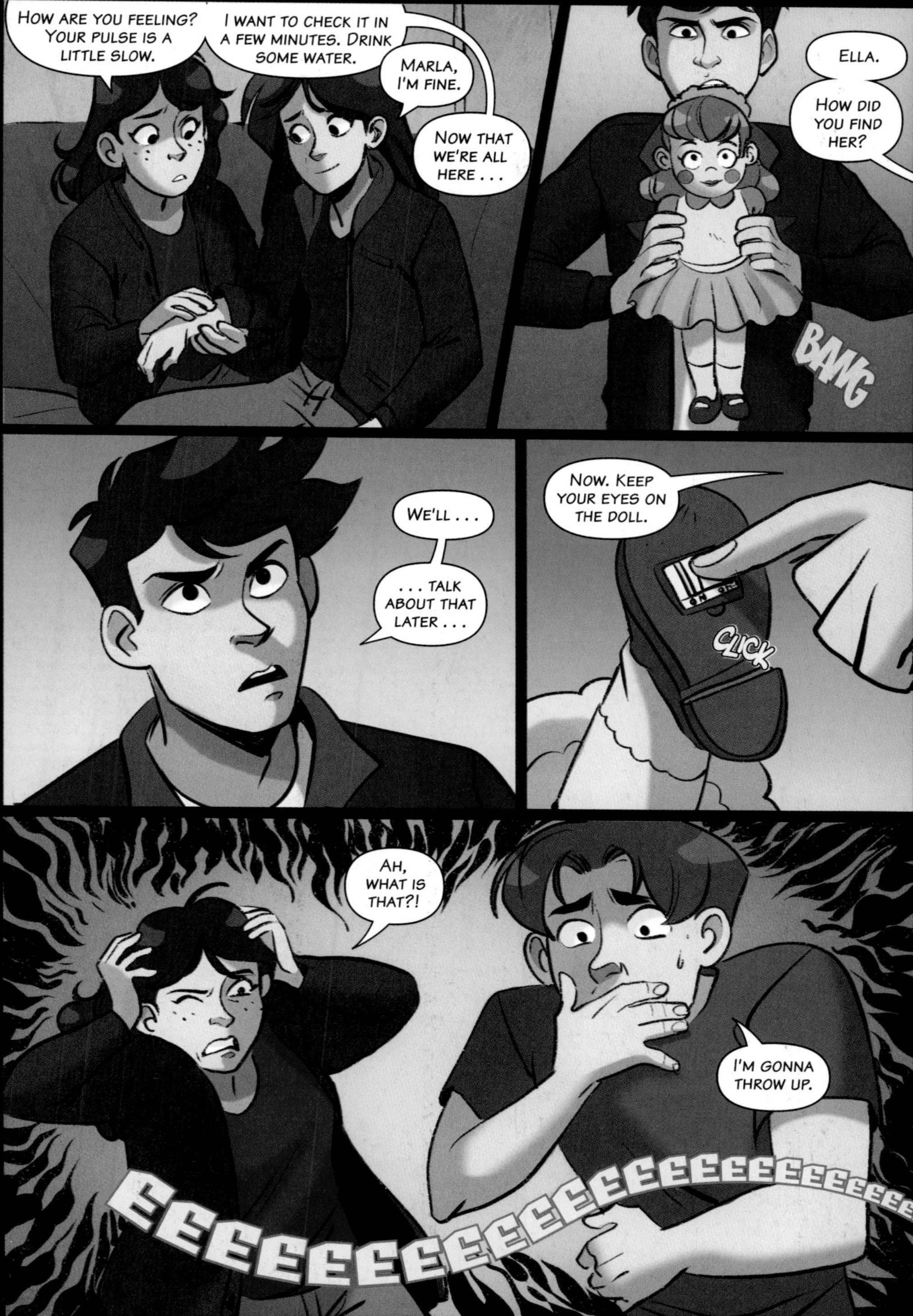
HOW ARE YOU FEELING? YOUR PULSE IS A LITTLE SLOW.
I WANT TO CHECK IT IN A FEW MINUTES. DRINK SOME WATER.
MARLA, I'M FINE.
NOW THAT WE'RE ALL HERE . . .
ELLA.
HOW DID YOU FIND HER?
BANG
WE'LL . . .
. . . TALK ABOUT THAT LATER . . .
NOW. KEEP YOUR EYES ON THE DOLL.
CLICK
AH, WHAT IS THAT?!
I'M GONNA THROW UP.
EEEEEEEEEEEEEEEEEEEEEEEEEEEEEEEE

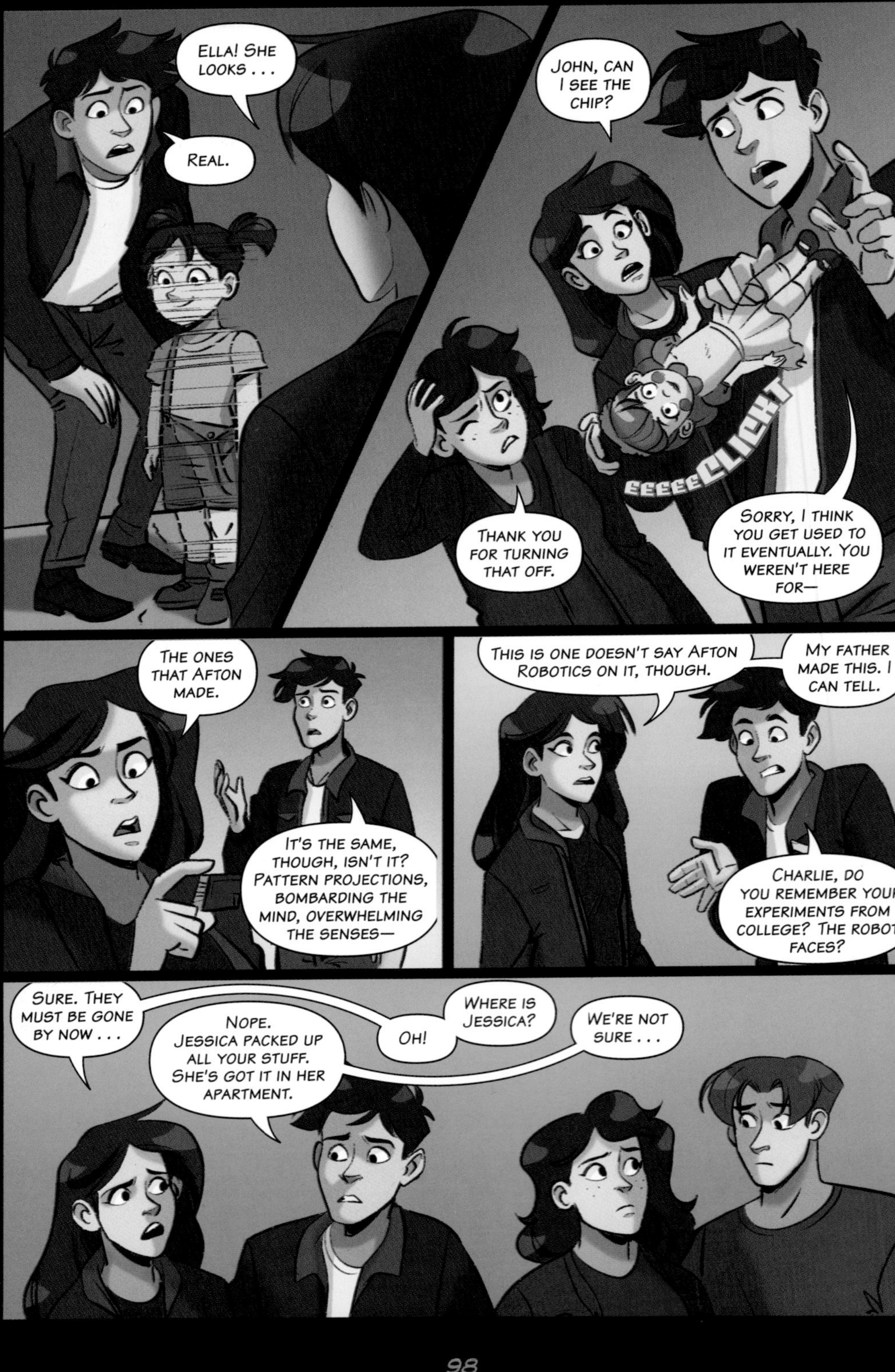

ELLA! SHE LOOKS . . .
REAL.
JOHN, CAN I SEE THE CHIP?
EEEEECLICK!
THANK YOU FOR TURNING THAT OFF.
SORRY, I THINK YOU GET USED TO IT EVENTUALLY. YOU WEREN'T HERE FOR—
THE ONES THAT AFTON MADE.
IT'S THE SAME, THOUGH, ISN'T IT? PATTERN PROJECTIONS, BOMBARDING THE MIND, OVERWHELMING THE SENSES—
THIS IS ONE DOESN'T SAY AFTON ROBOTICS ON IT, THOUGH.
MY FATHER MADE THIS. I CAN TELL.
CHARLIE, DO YOU REMEMBER YOUR EXPERIMENTS FROM COLLEGE? THE ROBOT FACES?
SURE. THEY MUST BE GONE BY NOW . . .
NOPE. JESSICA PACKED UP ALL YOUR STUFF. SHE'S GOT IT IN HER APARTMENT.
OH!
WHERE IS JESSICA?
WE'RE NOT SURE . . .

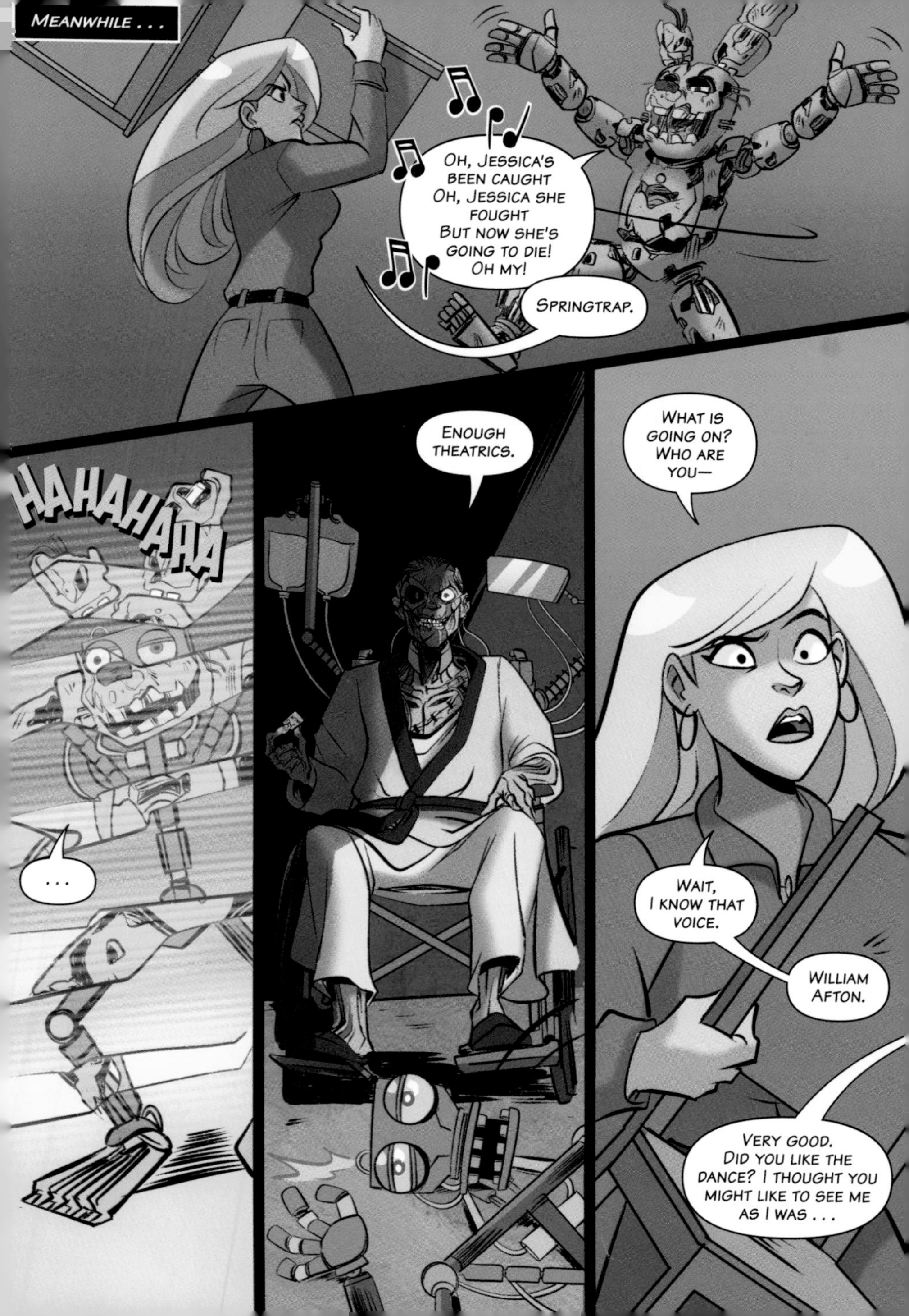
MEANWHILE . . .
OH, JESSICA'S BEEN CAUGHT OH, JESSICA SHE FOUGHT BUT NOW SHE'S GOING TO DIE! OH MY!
SPRINGTRAP.
HAHAHAHAHA
. . .
ENOUGH THEATRICS.
WHAT IS GOING ON? WHO ARE YOU—
WAIT, I KNOW THAT VOICE.
WILLIAM AFTON.
VERY GOOD. DID YOU LIKE THE DANCE? I THOUGHT YOU MIGHT LIKE TO SEE ME AS I WAS . . .

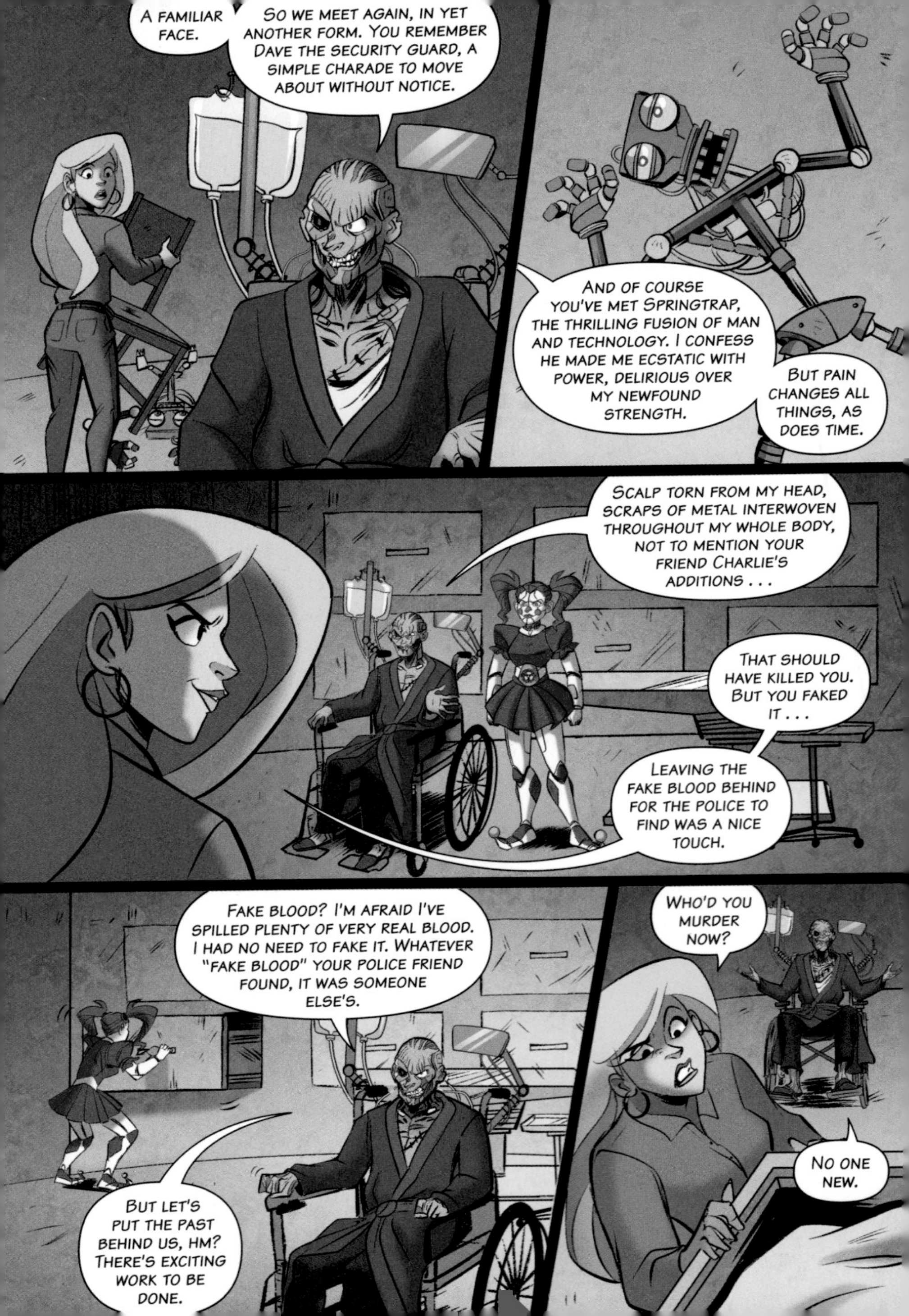
A FAMILIAR FACE.
SO WE MEET AGAIN, IN YET ANOTHER FORM. YOU REMEMBER DAVE THE SECURITY GUARD, A SIMPLE CHARADE TO MOVE ABOUT WITHOUT NOTICE.
AND OF COURSE YOU'VE MET SPRINGTRAP, THE THRILLING FUSION OF MAN AND TECHNOLOGY. I CONFESS HE MADE ME ECSTATIC WITH POWER, DELIRIOUS OVER MY NEWFOUND STRENGTH.
BUT PAIN CHANGES ALL THINGS, AS DOES TIME.
SCALP TORN FROM MY HEAD, SCRAPS OF METAL INTERWOVEN THROUGHOUT MY WHOLE BODY, NOT TO MENTION YOUR FRIEND CHARLIE'S ADDITIONS . . .
THAT SHOULD HAVE KILLED YOU. BUT YOU FAKED IT . . .
LEAVING THE FAKE BLOOD BEHIND FOR THE POLICE TO FIND WAS A NICE TOUCH.
FAKE BLOOD? I'M AFRAID I'VE SPILLED PLENTY OF VERY REAL BLOOD. I HAD NO NEED TO FAKE IT. WHATEVER "FAKE BLOOD" YOUR POLICE FRIEND FOUND, IT WAS SOMEONE ELSE'S.
BUT LET'S PUT THE PAST BEHIND US, HM? THERE'S EXCITING WORK TO BE DONE.
WHO'D YOU MURDER NOW?
NO ONE NEW.

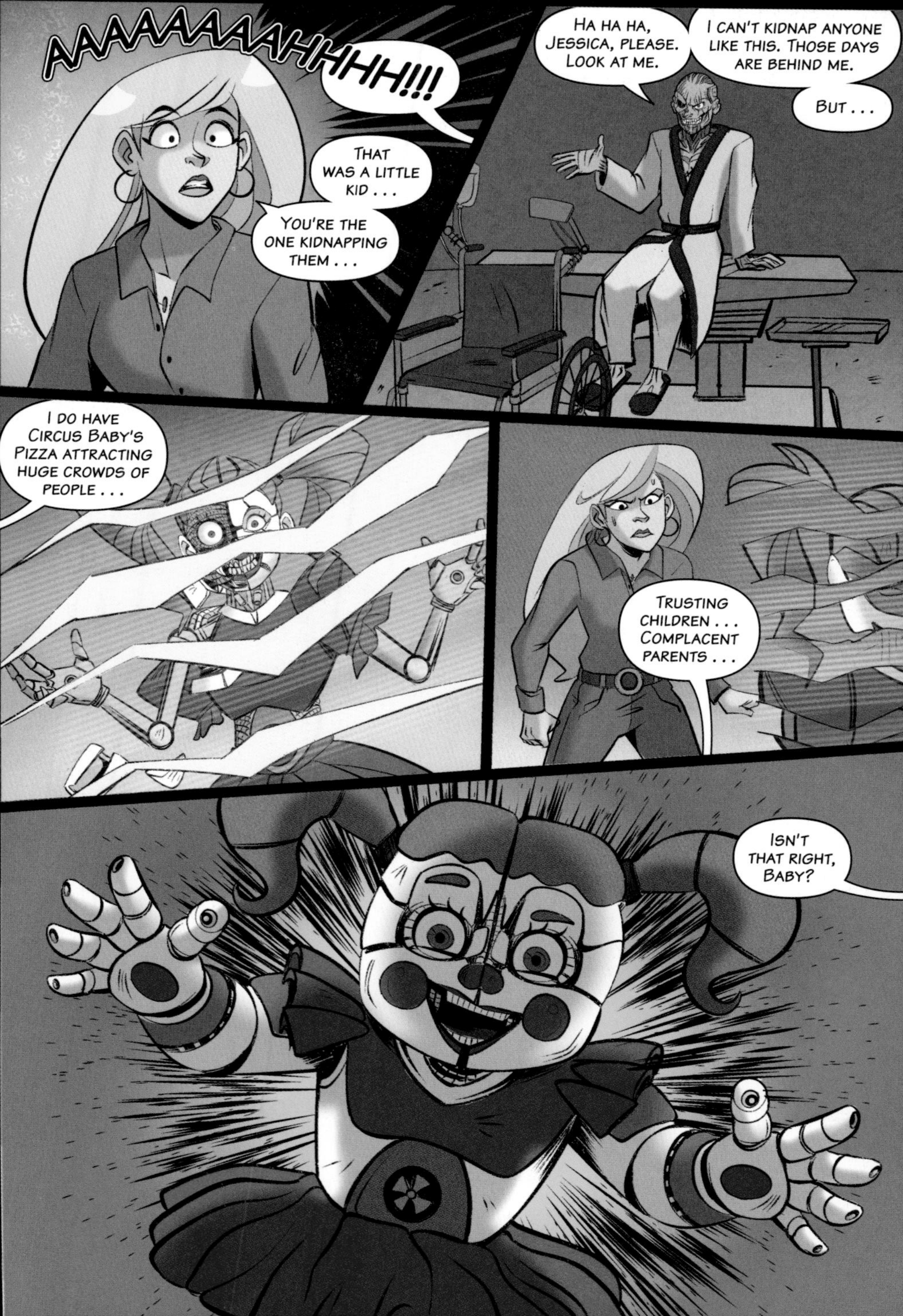
AAAAAAAAHHHH!!!
THAT WAS A LITTLE KID . . .
YOU'RE THE ONE KIDNAPPING THEM . . .
HA HA HA, JESSICA, PLEASE. LOOK AT ME.
I CAN'T KIDNAP ANYONE LIKE THIS. THOSE DAYS ARE BEHIND ME.
BUT . . .
I DO HAVE CIRCUS BABY'S PIZZA ATTRACTING HUGE CROWDS OF PEOPLE . . .
TRUSTING CHILDREN . . . COMPLACENT PARENTS . . .
ISN'T THAT RIGHT, BABY?

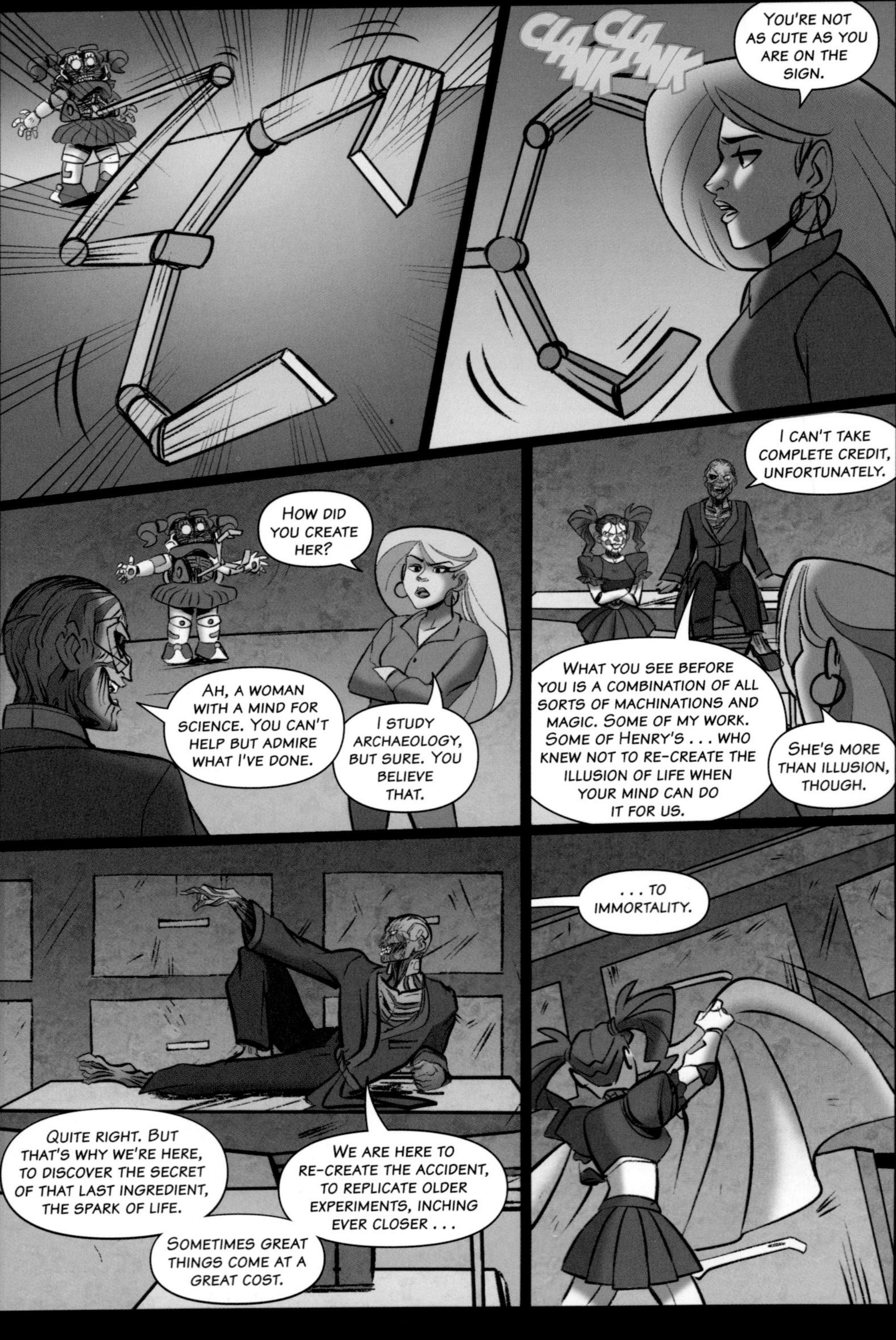
CLANK CLANK
YOU'RE NOT AS CUTE AS YOU ARE ON THE SIGN.
HOW DID YOU CREATE HER?
AH, A WOMAN WITH A MIND FOR SCIENCE. YOU CAN'T HELP BUT ADMIRE WHAT I'VE DONE.
I STUDY ARCHAEOLOGY, BUT SURE. YOU BELIEVE THAT.
I CAN'T TAKE COMPLETE CREDIT, UNFORTUNATELY.
WHAT YOU SEE BEFORE YOU IS A COMBINATION OF ALL SORTS OF MACHINATIONS AND MAGIC. SOME OF MY WORK. SOME OF HENRY'S . . . WHO KNEW NOT TO RE-CREATE THE ILLUSION OF LIFE WHEN YOUR MIND CAN DO IT FOR US.
SHE'S MORE THAN ILLUSION, THOUGH.
QUITE RIGHT. BUT THAT'S WHY WE'RE HERE, TO DISCOVER THE SECRET OF THAT LAST INGREDIENT, THE SPARK OF LIFE.
SOMETIMES GREAT THINGS COME AT A GREAT COST.
WE ARE HERE TO RE-CREATE THE ACCIDENT, TO REPLICATE OLDER EXPERIMENTS, INCHING EVER CLOSER . . .
. . . TO IMMORTALITY.

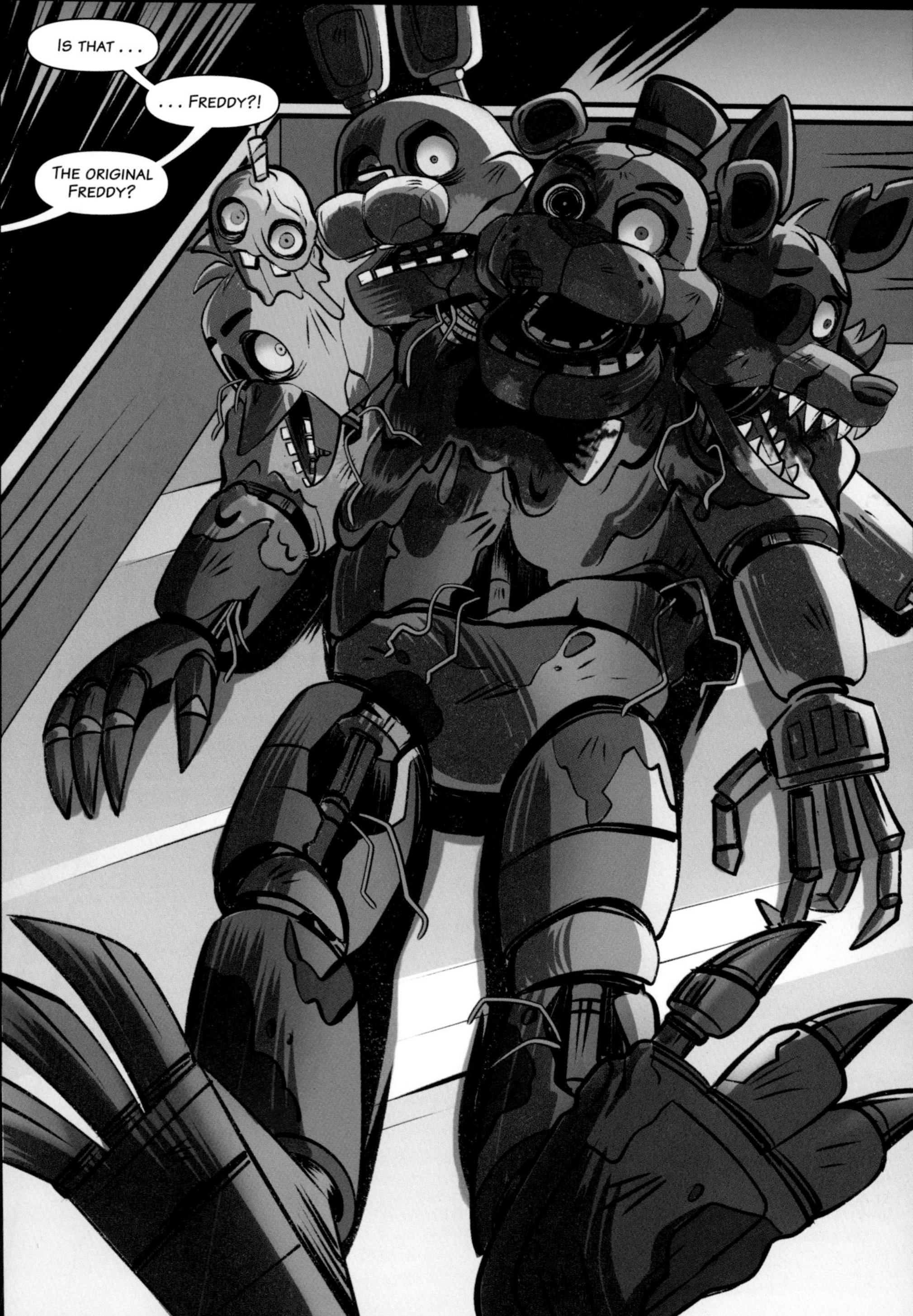
IS THAT . . .
. . . FREDDY?!
THE ORIGINAL FREDDY?

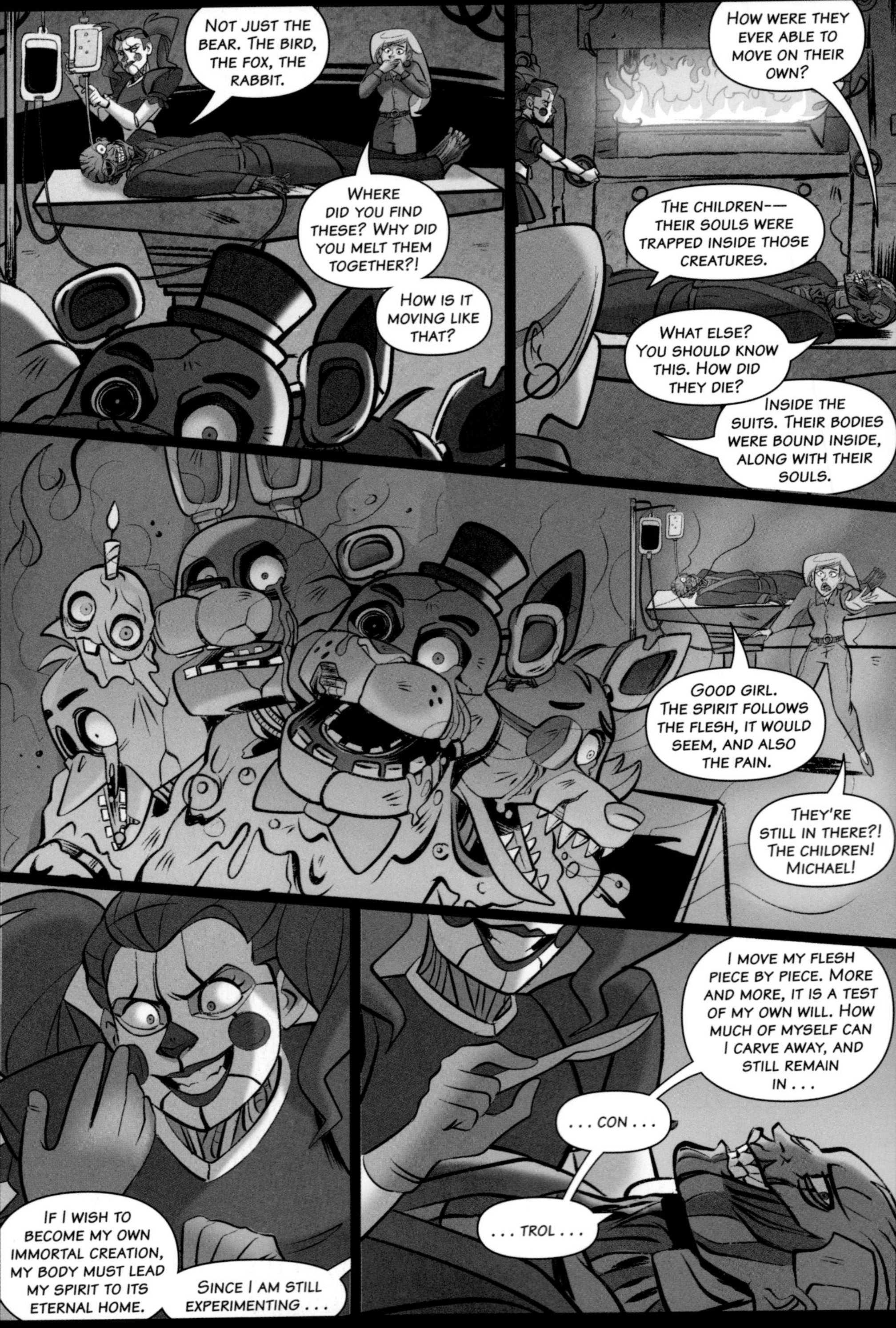
NOT JUST THE BEAR. THE BIRD, THE FOX, THE RABBIT.
WHERE DID YOU FIND THESE? WHY DID YOU MELT THEM TOGETHER?!
HOW IS IT MOVING LIKE THAT?
HOW WERE THEY EVER ABLE TO MOVE ON THEIR OWN?
THE CHILDREN–– THEIR SOULS WERE TRAPPED INSIDE THOSE CREATURES.
WHAT ELSE? YOU SHOULD KNOW THIS. HOW DID THEY DIE?
INSIDE THE SUITS. THEIR BODIES WERE BOUND INSIDE, ALONG WITH THEIR SOULS.
GOOD GIRL. THE SPIRIT FOLLOWS THE FLESH, IT WOULD SEEM, AND ALSO THE PAIN.
THEY'RE STILL IN THERE?! THE CHILDREN! MICHAEL!
IF I WISH TO BECOME MY OWN IMMORTAL CREATION, MY BODY MUST LEAD MY SPIRIT TO ITS ETERNAL HOME.
SINCE I AM STILL EXPERIMENTING . . .
I MOVE MY FLESH PIECE BY PIECE. MORE AND MORE, IT IS A TEST OF MY OWN WILL. HOW MUCH OF MYSELF CAN I CARVE AWAY, AND STILL REMAIN IN . . .
. . . CON . . .
. . . TROL . . .

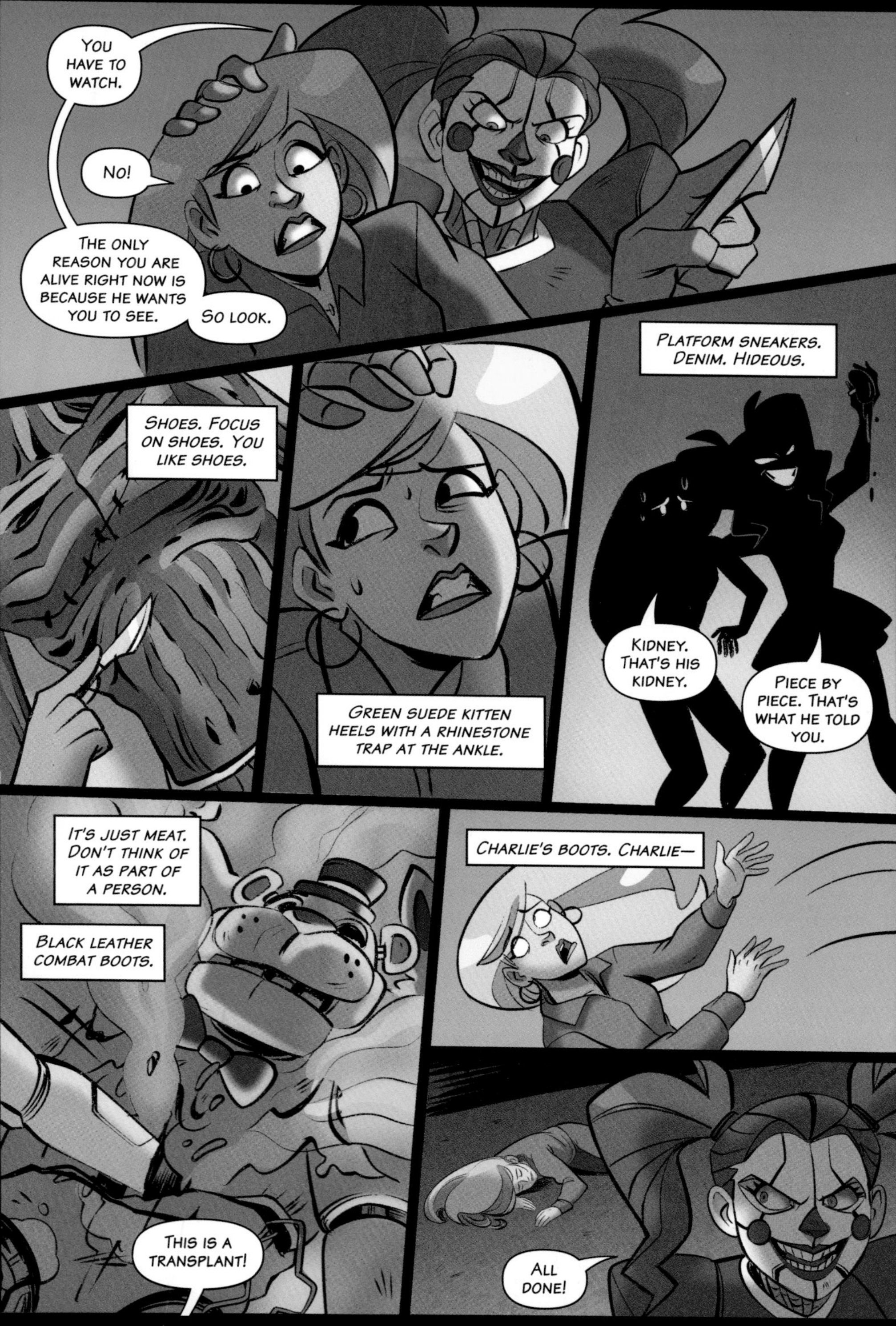

You have to watch.
No!
The only reason you are alive right now is because he wants you to see.
So look.
Shoes. Focus on shoes. You like shoes.
Green suede kitten heels with a rhinestone trap at the ankle.
Platform sneakers. Denim. Hideous.
Kidney. That's his kidney.
Piece by piece. That's what he told you.
It's just meat. Don't think of it as part of a person.
Black leather combat boots.
This is a transplant!
Charlie's boots. Charlie—
All done!

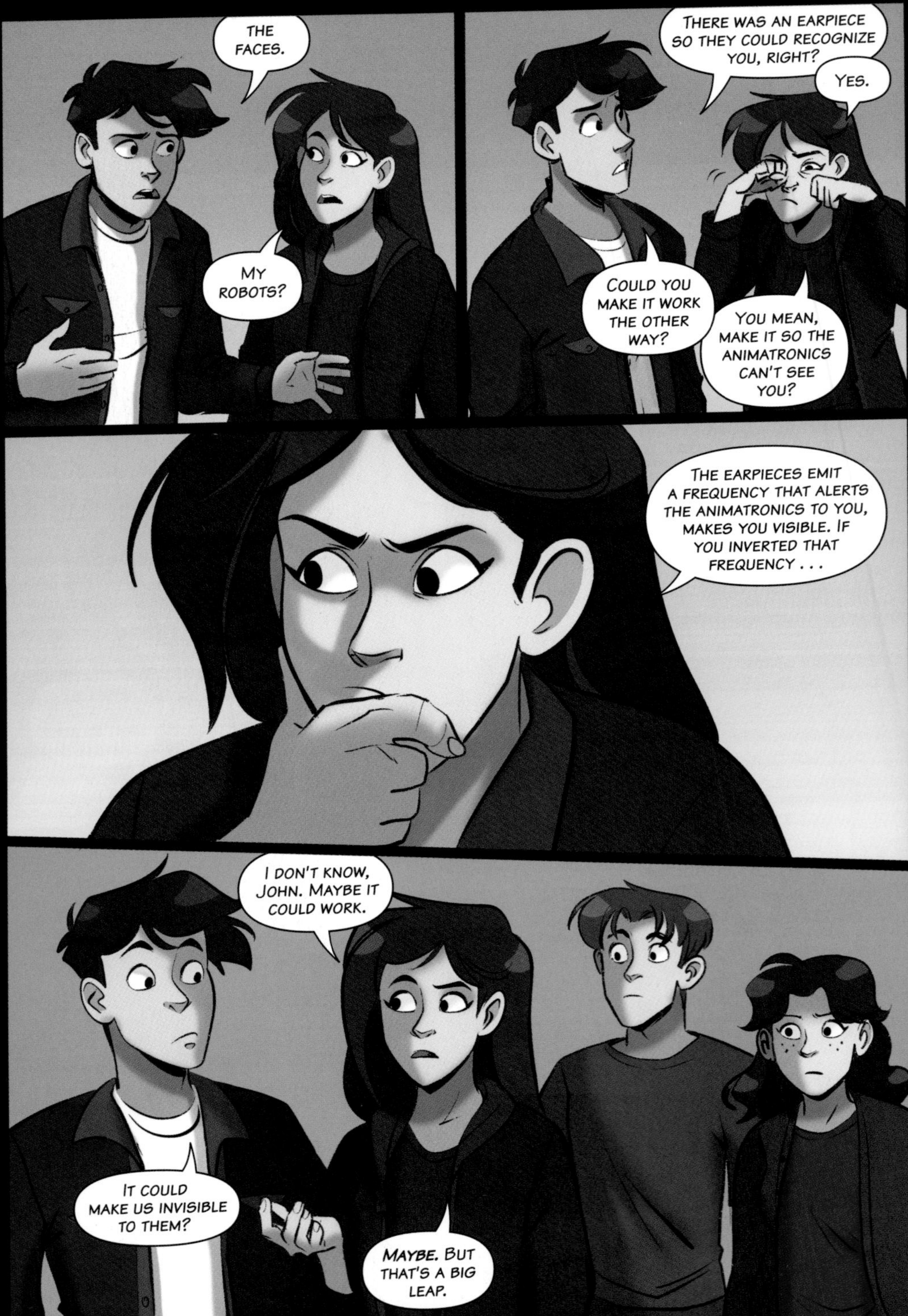
THE FACES.
MY ROBOTS?
THERE WAS AN EARPIECE SO THEY COULD RECOGNIZE YOU, RIGHT?
YES.
COULD YOU MAKE IT WORK THE OTHER WAY?
YOU MEAN, MAKE IT SO THE ANIMATRONICS CAN'T SEE YOU?
THE EARPIECES EMIT A FREQUENCY THAT ALERTS THE ANIMATRONICS TO YOU, MAKES YOU VISIBLE. IF YOU INVERTED THAT FREQUENCY . . .
I DON'T KNOW, JOHN. MAYBE IT COULD WORK.
IT COULD MAKE US INVISIBLE TO THEM?
MAYBE. BUT THAT'S A BIG LEAP.

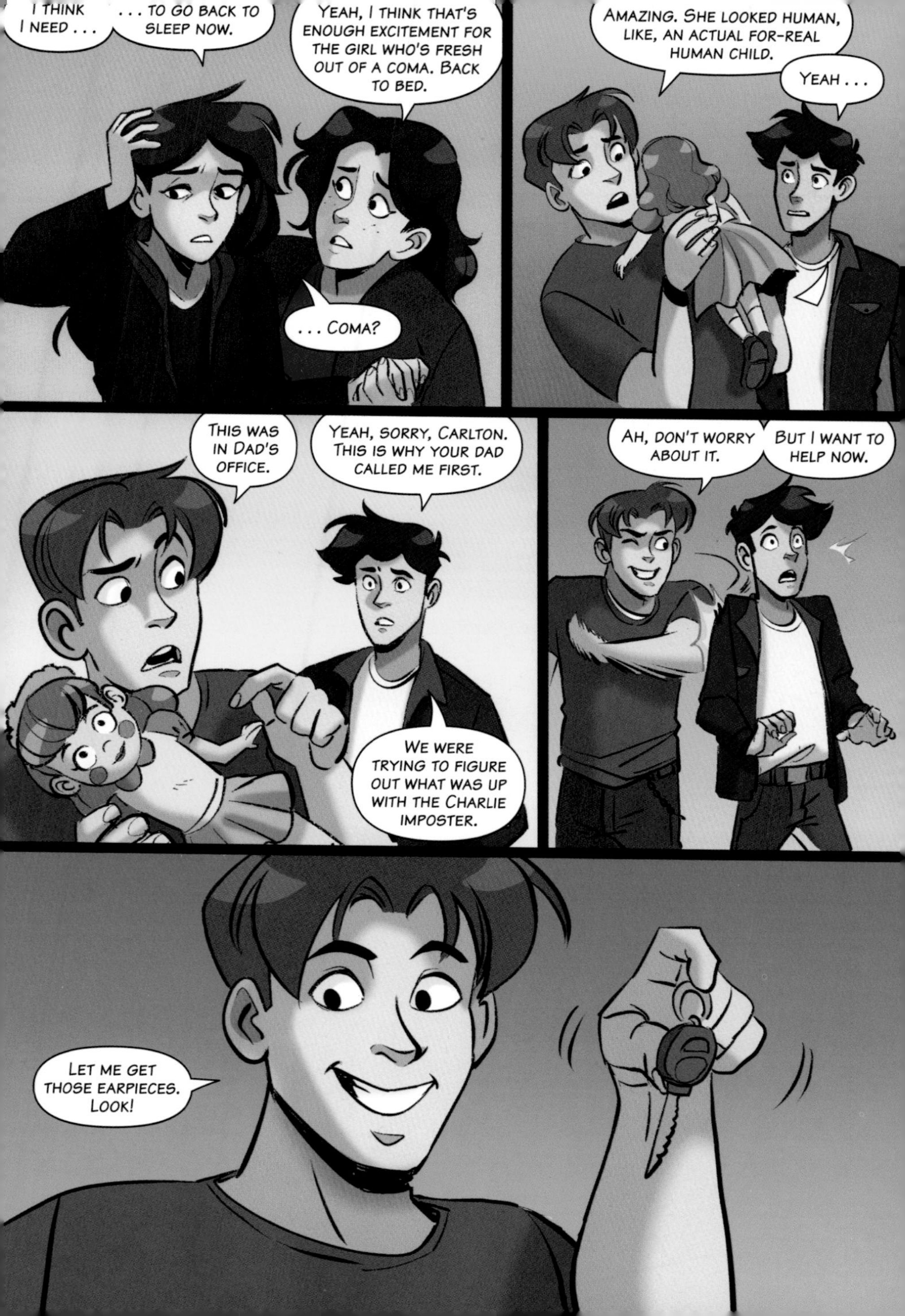
I THINK I NEED . . .
. . . TO GO BACK TO SLEEP NOW.
YEAH, I THINK THAT'S ENOUGH EXCITEMENT FOR THE GIRL WHO'S FRESH OUT OF A COMA. BACK TO BED.
. . . COMA?
AMAZING. SHE LOOKED HUMAN, LIKE, AN ACTUAL FOR-REAL HUMAN CHILD.
YEAH . . .
THIS WAS IN DAD'S OFFICE.
YEAH, SORRY, CARLTON. THIS IS WHY YOUR DAD CALLED ME FIRST.
WE WERE TRYING TO FIGURE OUT WHAT WAS UP WITH THE CHARLIE IMPOSTER.
AH, DON'T WORRY ABOUT IT.
BUT I WANT TO HELP NOW.
LET ME GET THOSE EARPIECES. LOOK!

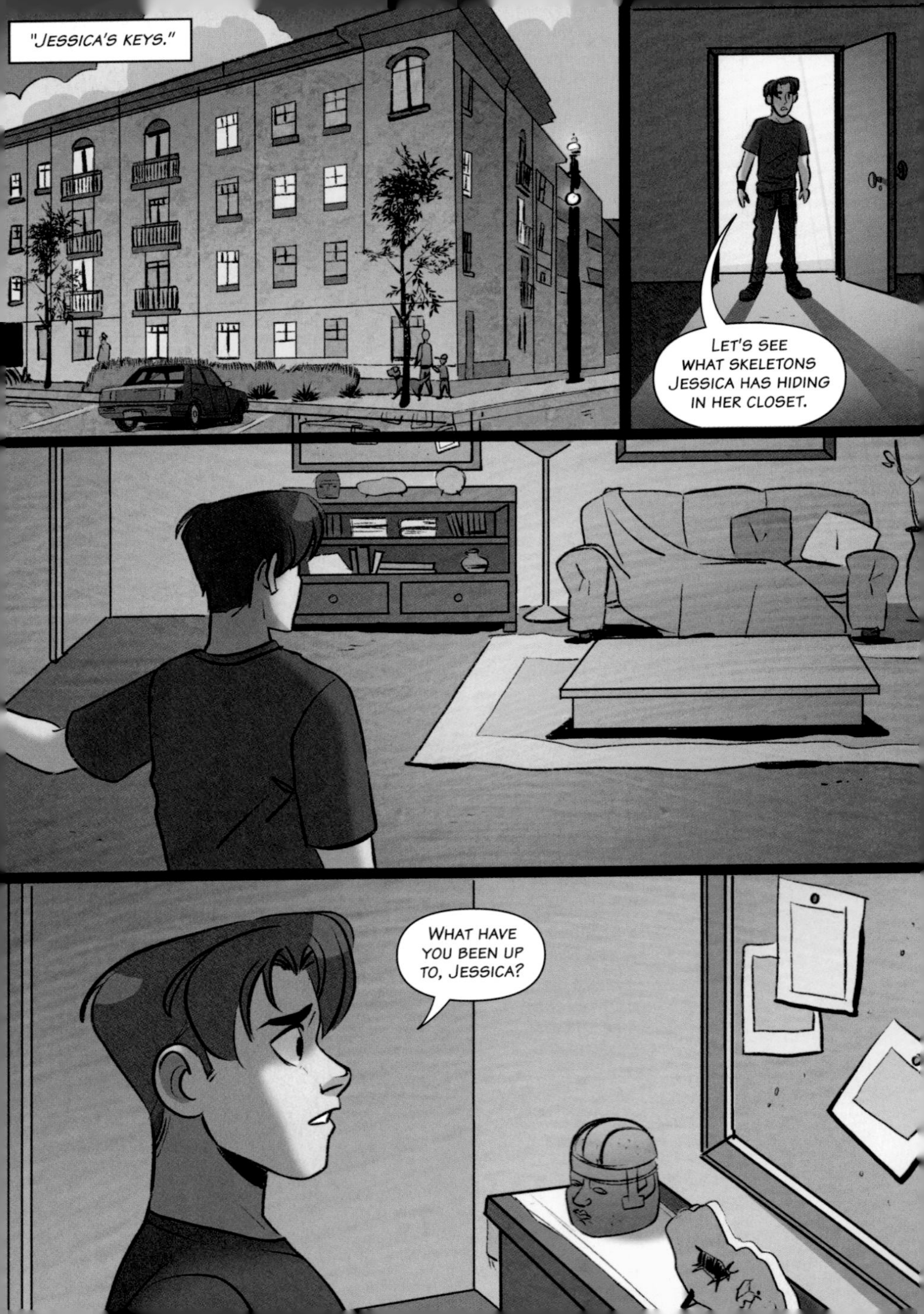
"JESSICA'S KEYS."
LET'S SEE WHAT SKELETONS JESSICA HAS HIDING IN HER CLOSET.
WHAT HAVE YOU BEEN UP TO, JESSICA?

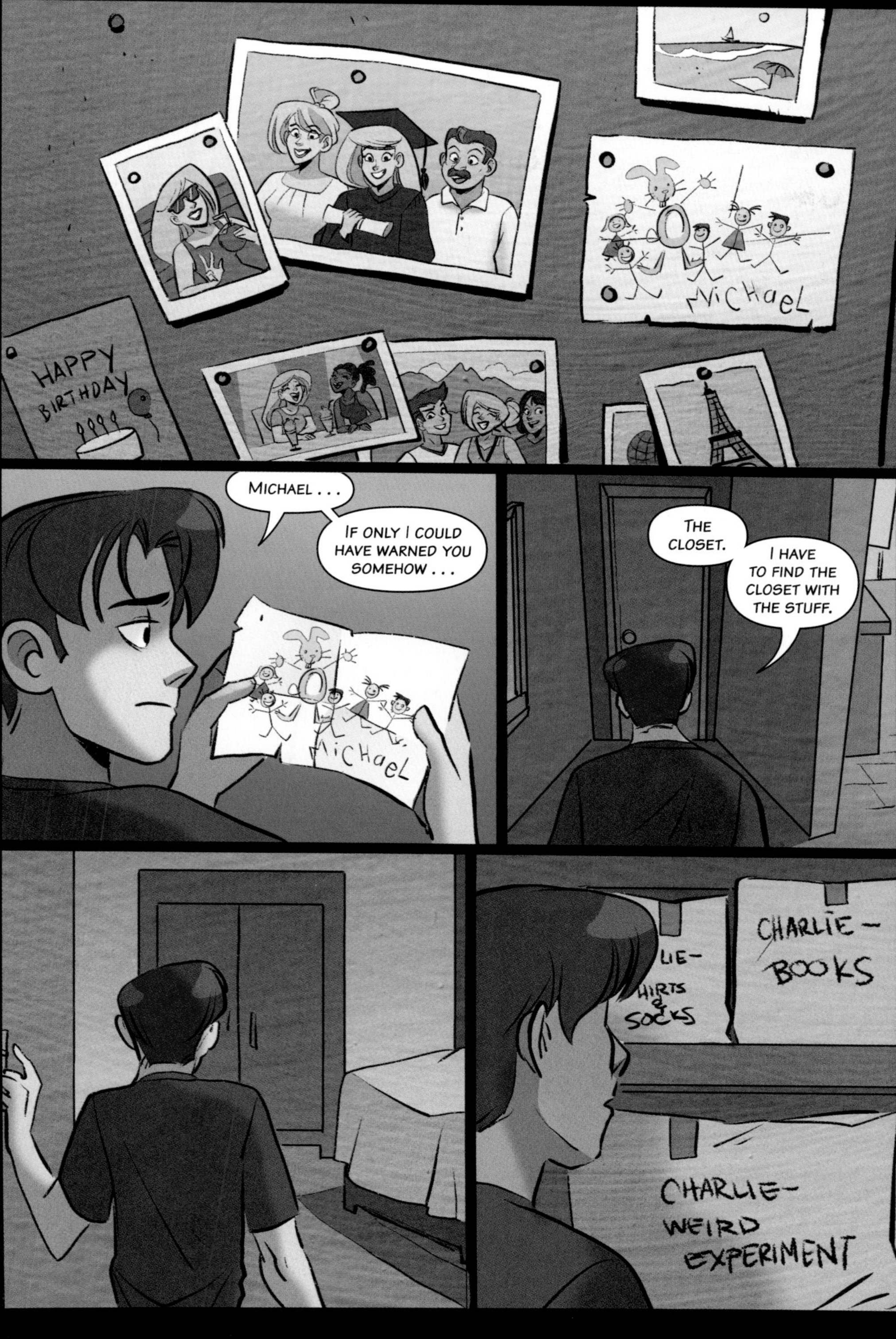

HAPPY BIRTHDAY
MICHAEL
MICHAEL . . .
IF ONLY I COULD HAVE WARNED YOU SOMEHOW . . .
MICHAEL
THE CLOSET.
I HAVE TO FIND THE CLOSET WITH THE STUFF.
CHARLIE - BOOKS
LIE- HIRTS & SOCKS
CHARLIE- WEIRD EXPERIMENT

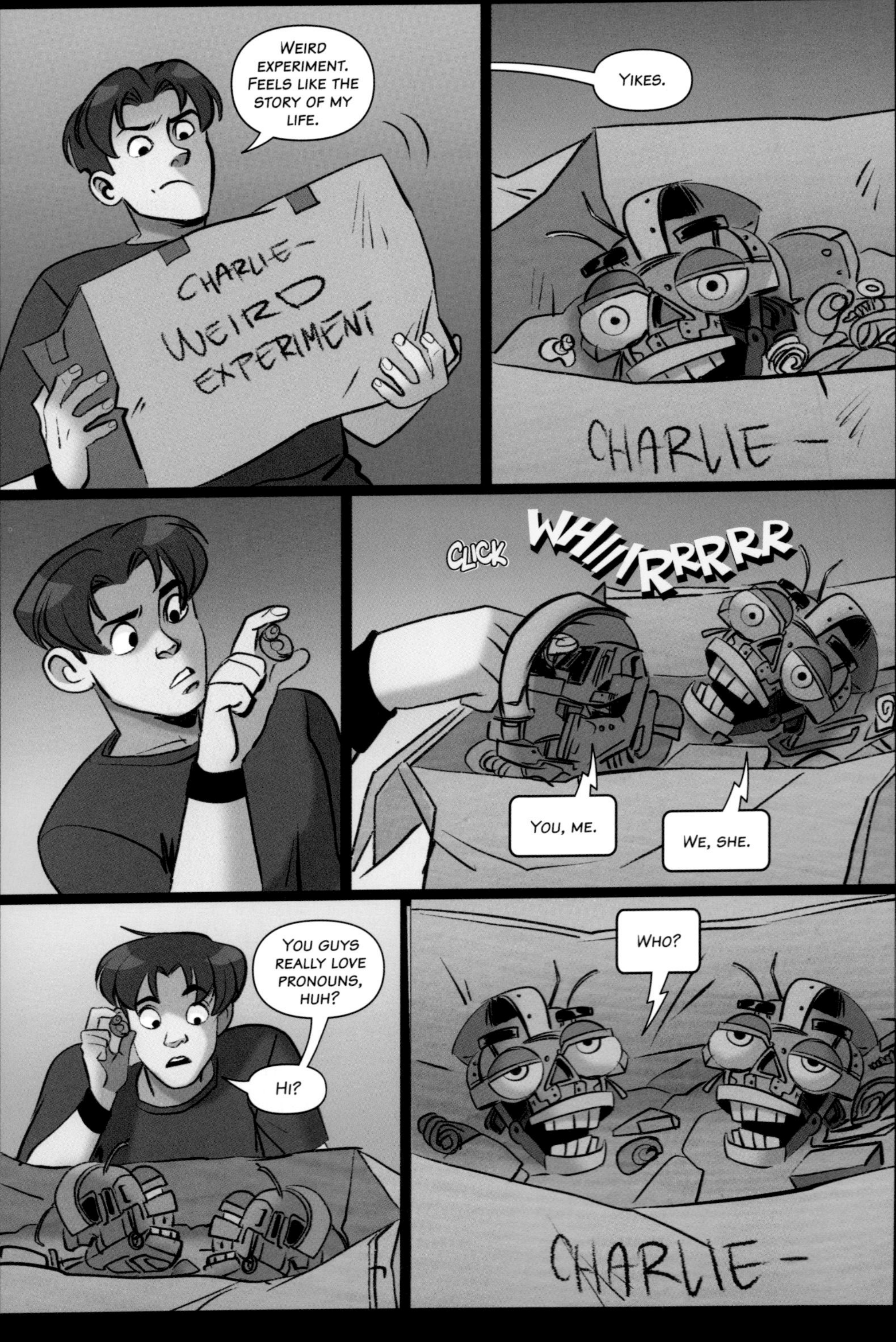
Weird experiment. Feels like the story of my life.
Charlie—
Weird experiment
Yikes.
Charlie—
CLICK
WHIIIIRRRRR
You, me.
We, she.
You guys really love pronouns, huh?
Hi?
Who?
Charlie—

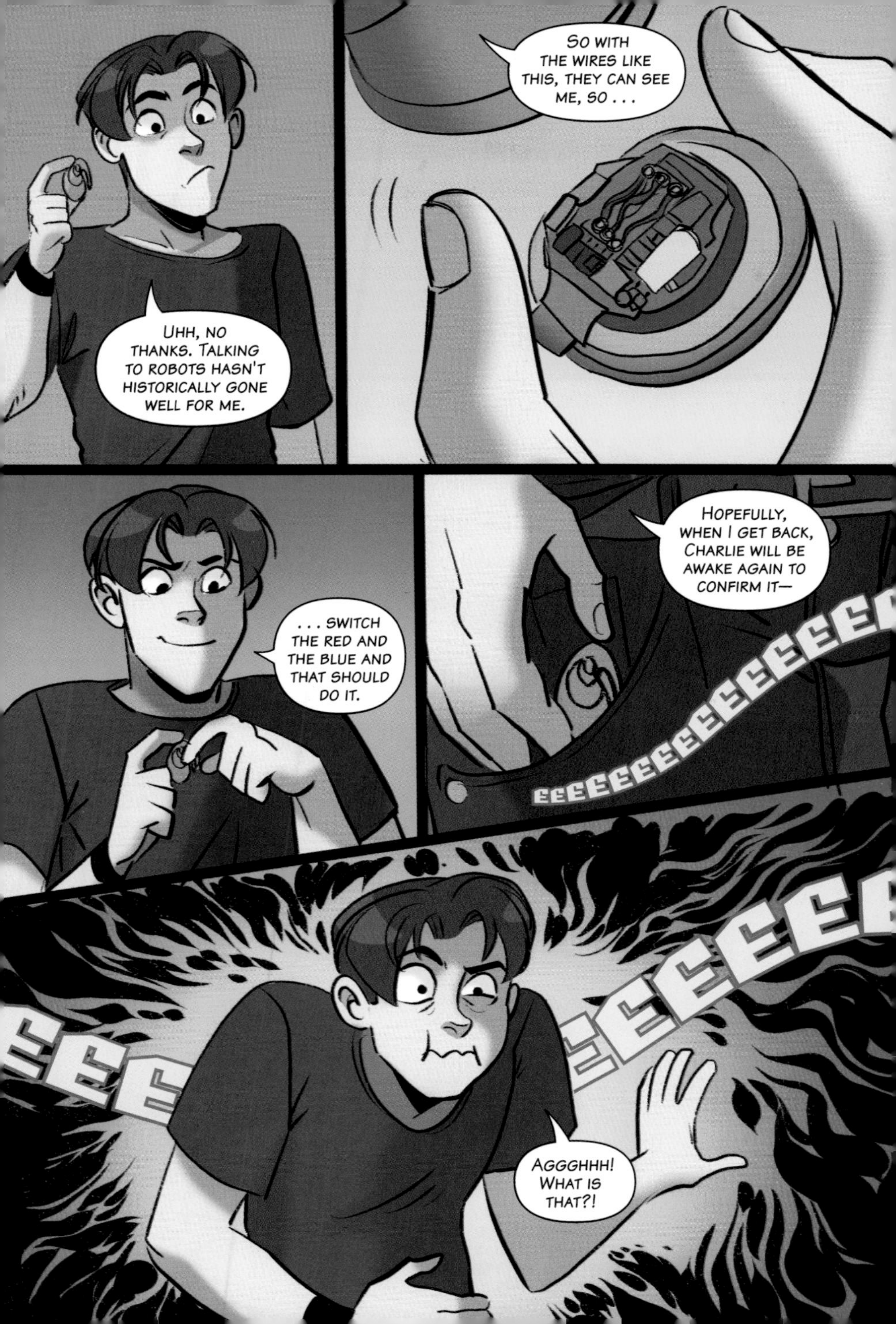
UHH, NO THANKS. TALKING TO ROBOTS HASN'T HISTORICALLY GONE WELL FOR ME.
SO WITH THE WIRES LIKE THIS, THEY CAN SEE ME, SO . . .
. . . SWITCH THE RED AND THE BLUE AND THAT SHOULD DO IT.
HOPEFULLY, WHEN I GET BACK, CHARLIE WILL BE AWAKE AGAIN TO CONFIRM IT—
EEEEEEEEEEEEEEEEEEEEEE
EEEEEEEEEE
AGGGHHH! WHAT IS THAT?!

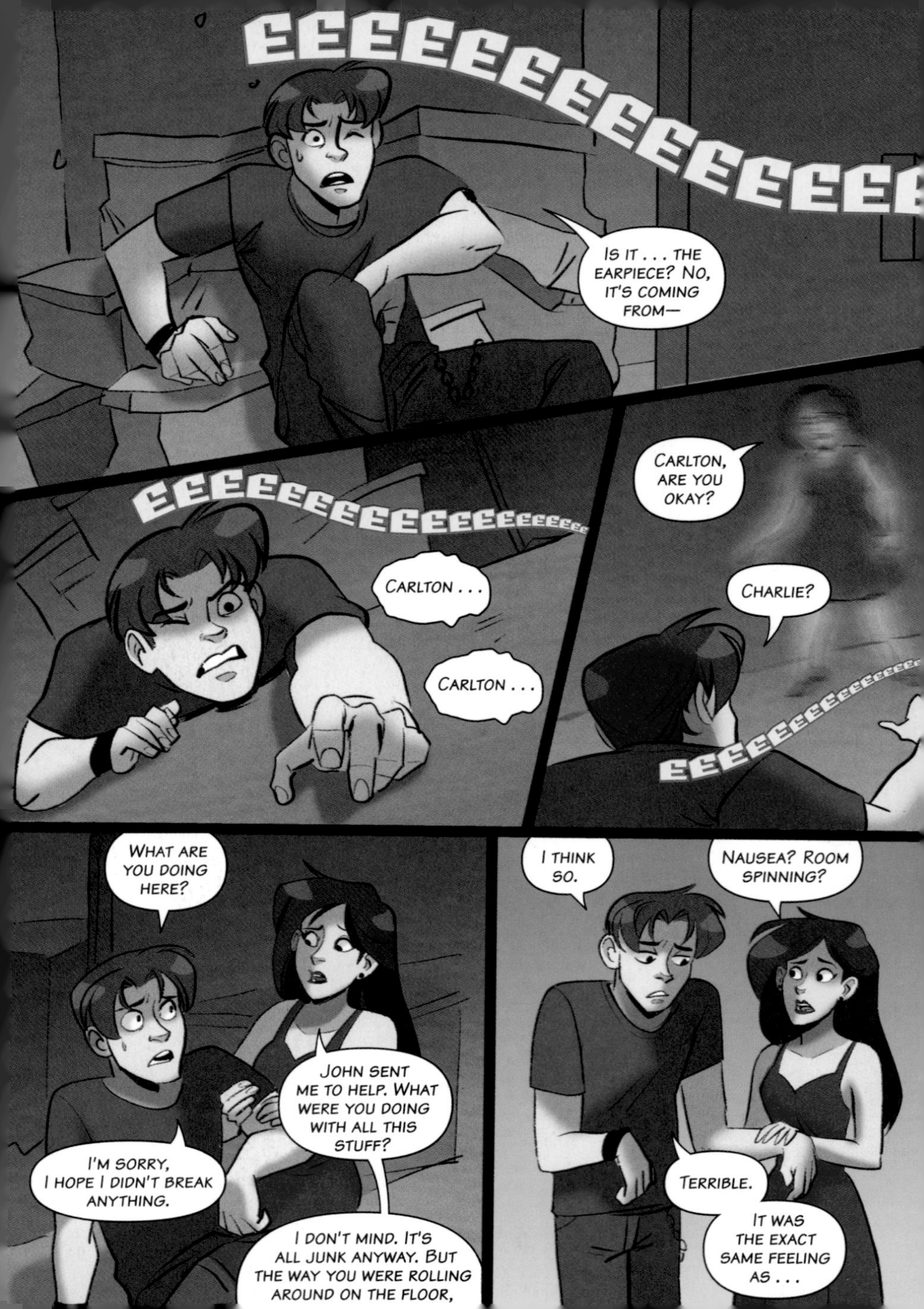

EEEEEEEEEEEEEEEEEEEEE
IS IT . . . THE EARPIECE? NO, IT'S COMING FROM—
EEEEEEEEEEEEEEEEEEEEE
CARLTON . . .
CARLTON . . .
CARLTON, ARE YOU OKAY?
CHARLIE?
EEEEEEEEEEEEEEEEEEEEE
WHAT ARE YOU DOING HERE?
JOHN SENT ME TO HELP. WHAT WERE YOU DOING WITH ALL THIS STUFF?
I'M SORRY, I HOPE I DIDN'T BREAK ANYTHING.
I DON'T MIND. IT'S ALL JUNK ANYWAY. BUT THE WAY YOU WERE ROLLING AROUND ON THE FLOOR,
I THINK SO.
NAUSEA? ROOM SPINNING?
TERRIBLE.
IT WAS THE EXACT SAME FEELING AS . . .

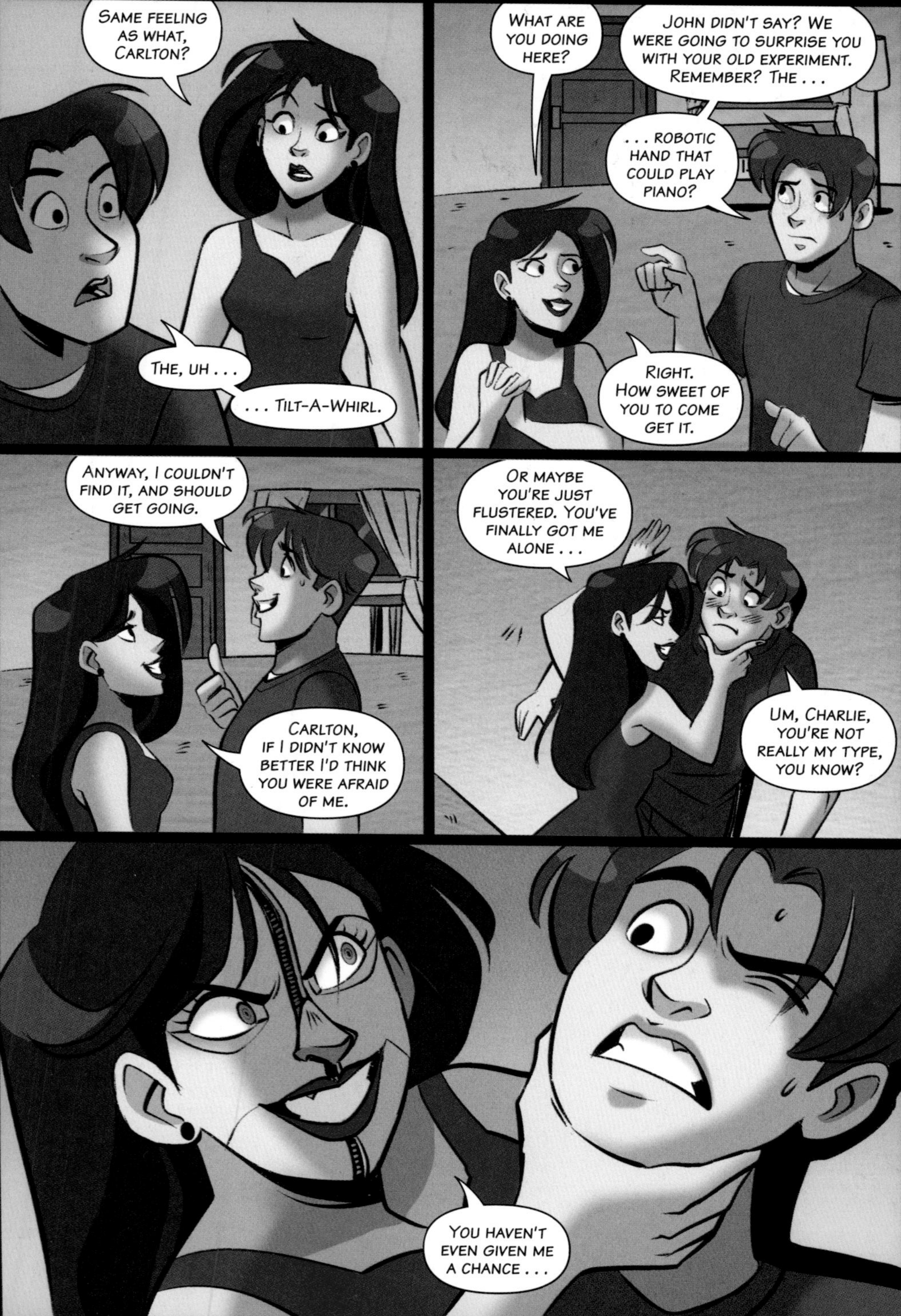
SAME FEELING AS WHAT, CARLTON?
THE, UH . . .
. . . TILT-A-WHIRL.
WHAT ARE YOU DOING HERE?
JOHN DIDN'T SAY? WE WERE GOING TO SURPRISE YOU WITH YOUR OLD EXPERIMENT. REMEMBER? THE . . .
. . . ROBOTIC HAND THAT COULD PLAY PIANO?
RIGHT. HOW SWEET OF YOU TO COME GET IT.
ANYWAY, I COULDN'T FIND IT, AND SHOULD GET GOING.
CARLTON, IF I DIDN'T KNOW BETTER I'D THINK YOU WERE AFRAID OF ME.
OR MAYBE YOU'RE JUST FLUSTERED. YOU'VE FINALLY GOT ME ALONE . . .
UM, CHARLIE, YOU'RE NOT REALLY MY TYPE, YOU KNOW?
YOU HAVEN'T EVEN GIVEN ME A CHANCE . . .

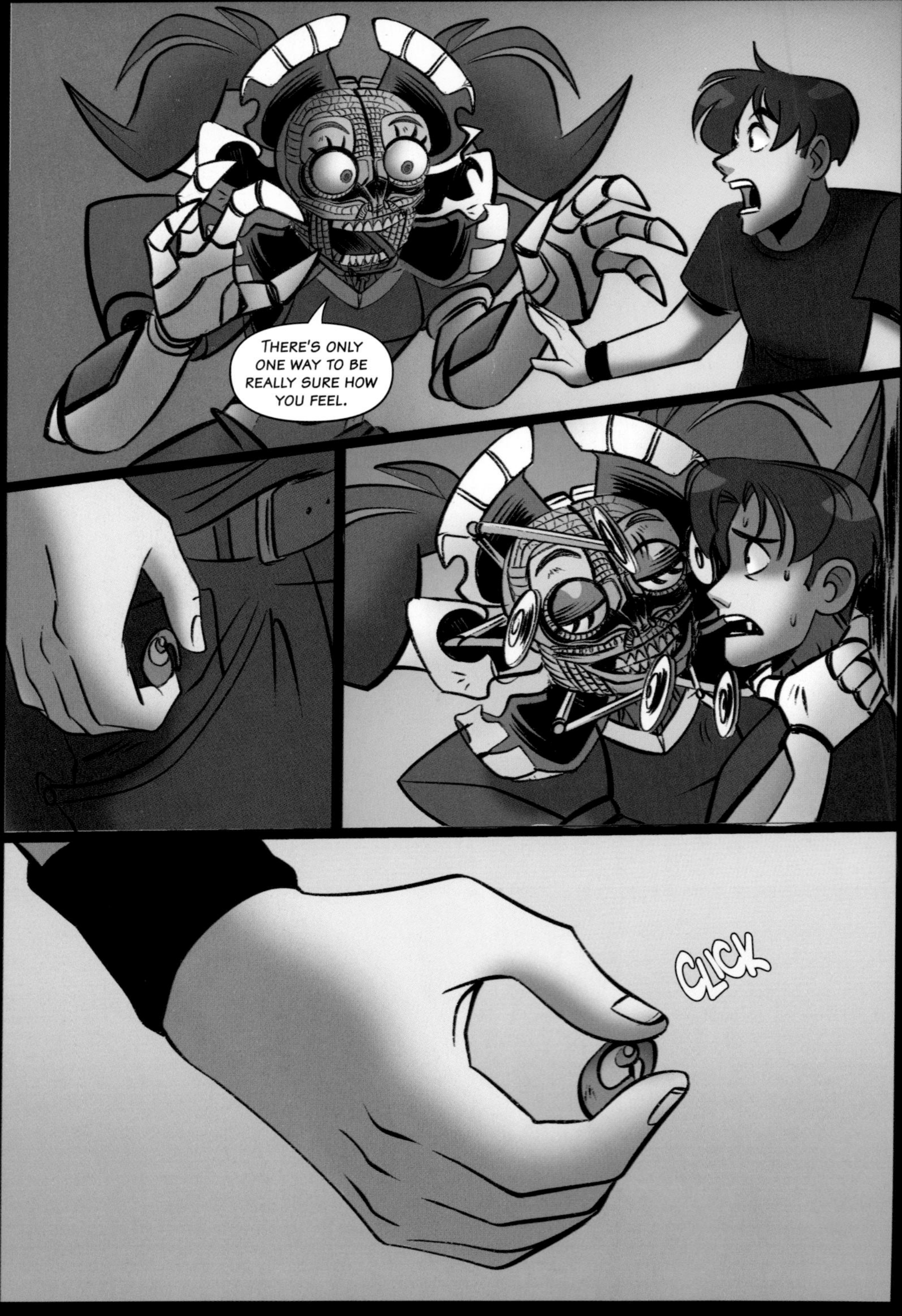
THERE'S ONLY ONE WAY TO BE REALLY SURE HOW YOU FEEL.
CLICK

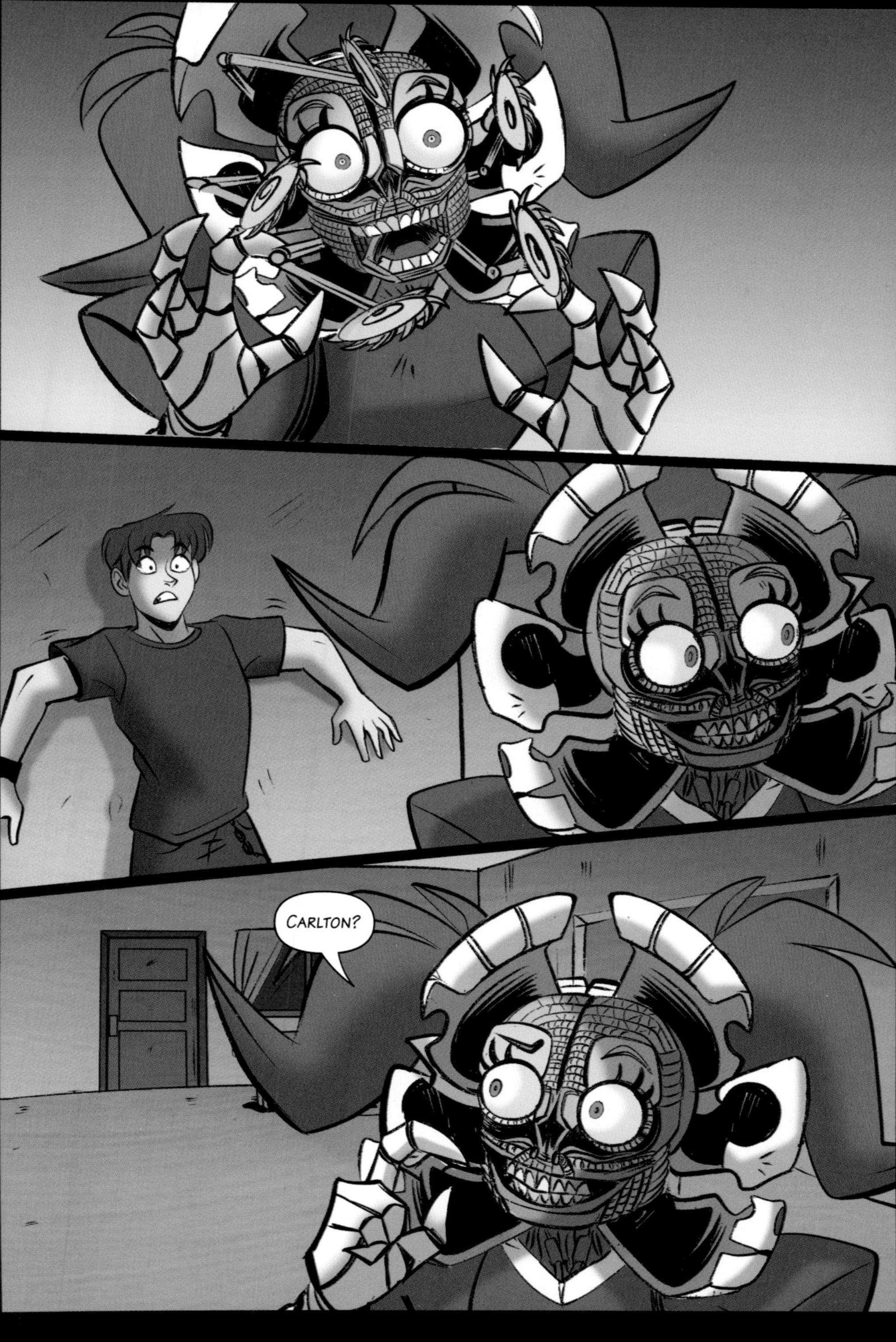
CARLTON?

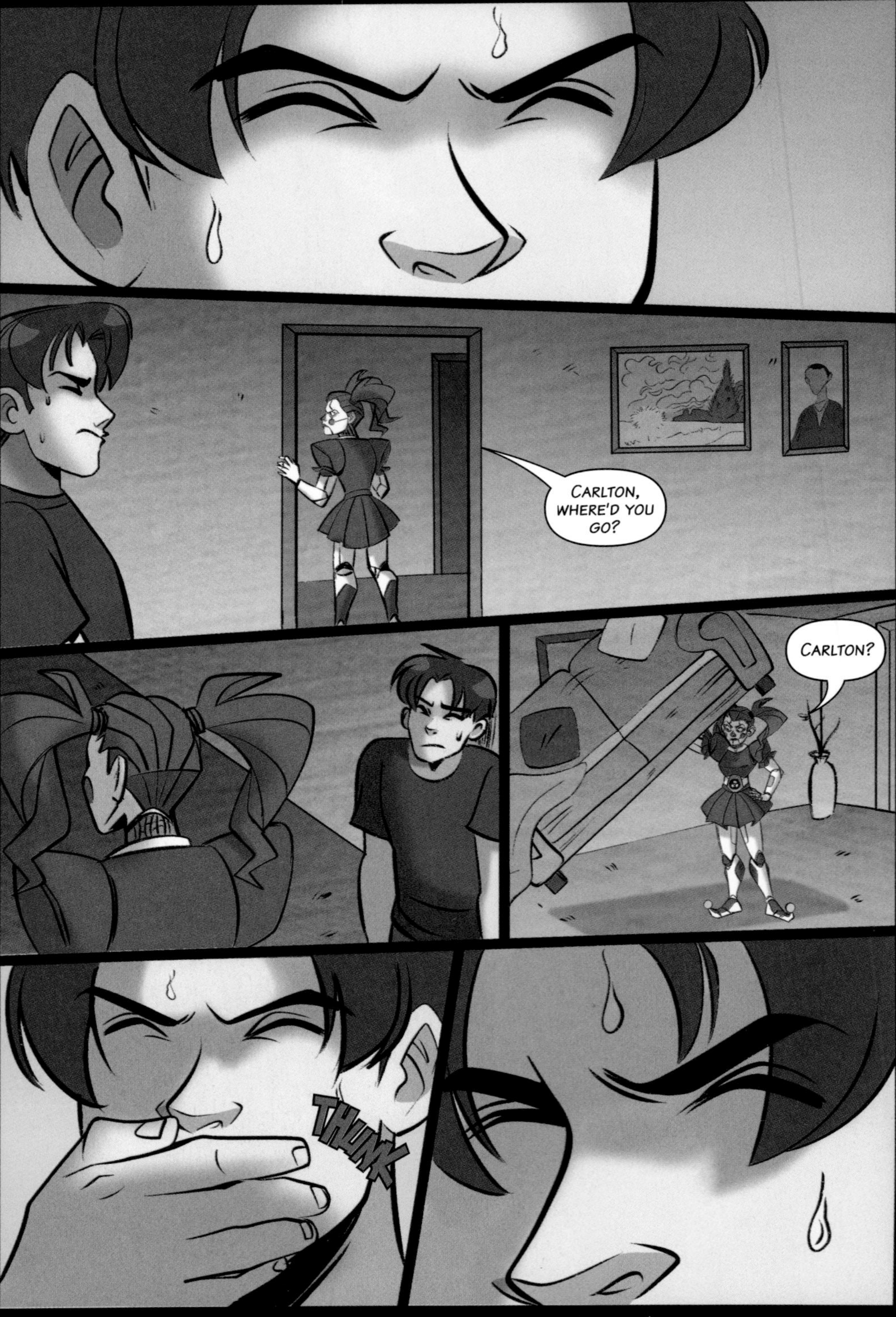

CARLTON, WHERE'D YOU GO?
CARLTON?
THUNK

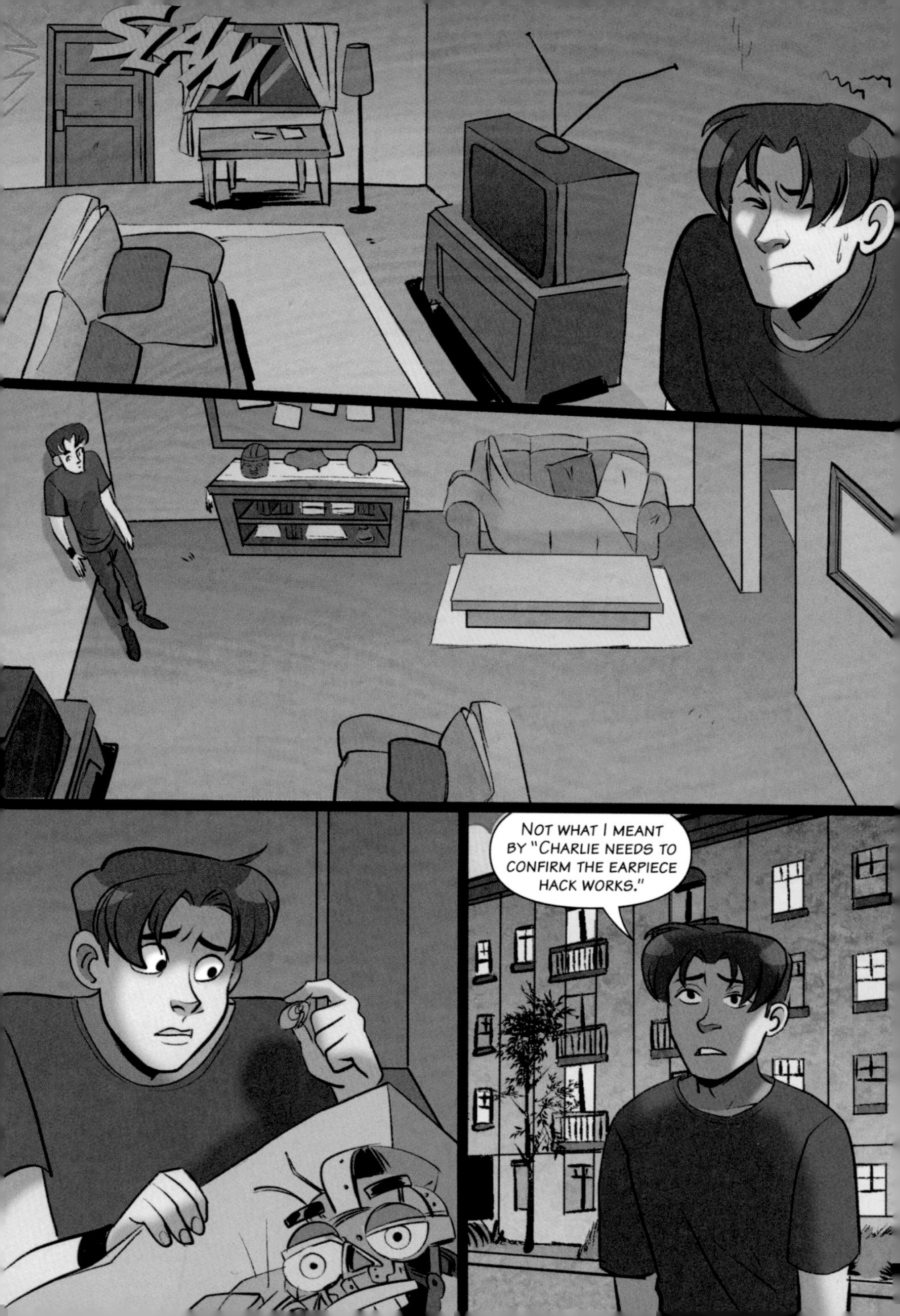
SLAM
NOT WHAT I MEANT BY "CHARLIE NEEDS TO CONFIRM THE EARPIECE HACK WORKS."

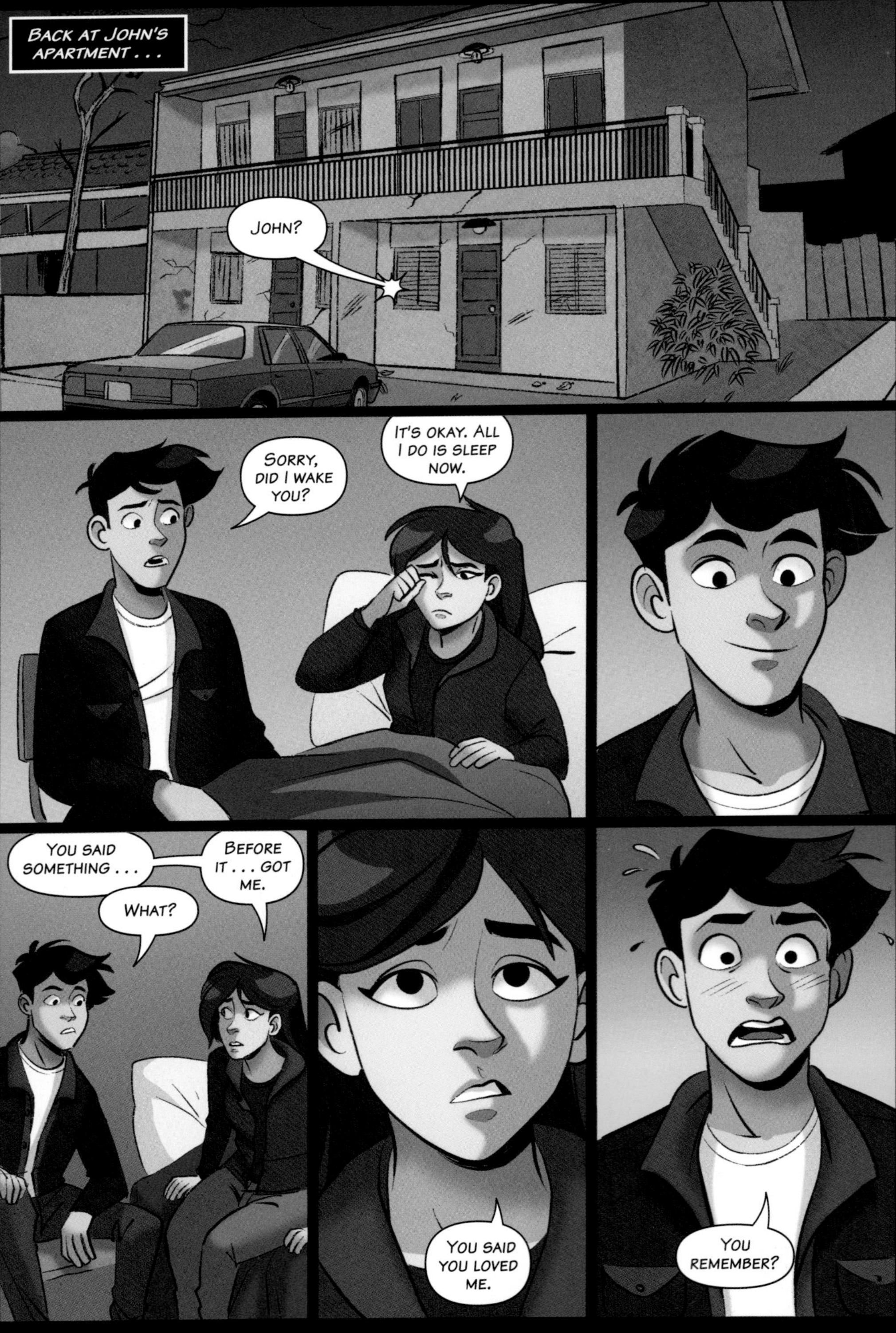
Back at John's apartment . . .
John?
Sorry, did I wake you?
It's okay. All I do is sleep now.
You said something . . .
What?
Before it . . . got me.
You said you loved me.
You remember?

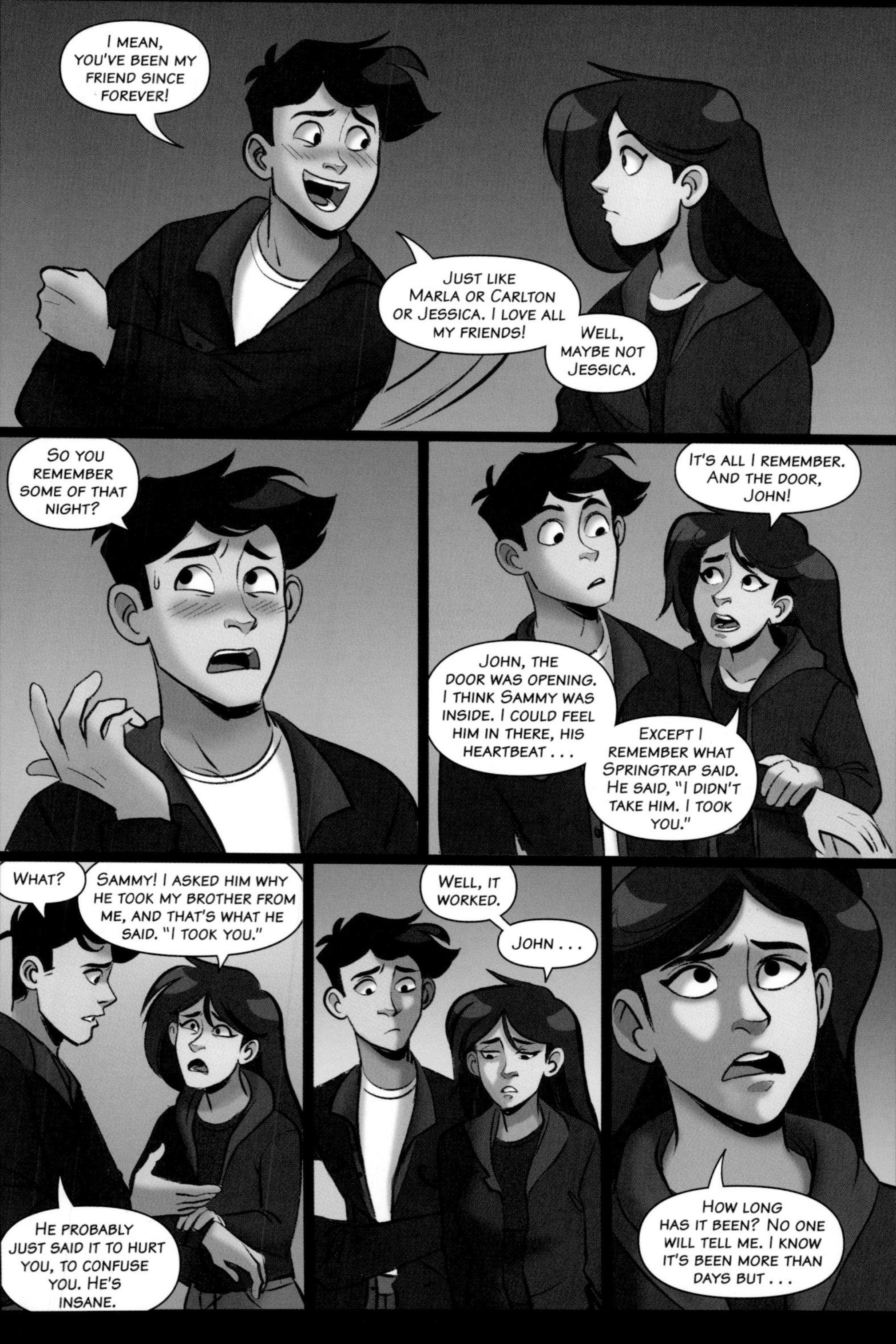
I MEAN, YOU'VE BEEN MY FRIEND SINCE FOREVER!
JUST LIKE MARLA OR CARLTON OR JESSICA. I LOVE ALL MY FRIENDS!
WELL, MAYBE NOT JESSICA.
SO YOU REMEMBER SOME OF THAT NIGHT?
IT'S ALL I REMEMBER. AND THE DOOR, JOHN!
JOHN, THE DOOR WAS OPENING. I THINK SAMMY WAS INSIDE. I COULD FEEL HIM IN THERE, HIS HEARTBEAT . . .
EXCEPT I REMEMBER WHAT SPRINGTRAP SAID. HE SAID, "I DIDN'T TAKE HIM. I TOOK YOU."
WHAT?
SAMMY! I ASKED HIM WHY HE TOOK MY BROTHER FROM ME, AND THAT'S WHAT HE SAID. "I TOOK YOU."
HE PROBABLY JUST SAID IT TO HURT YOU, TO CONFUSE YOU. HE'S INSANE.
WELL, IT WORKED.
JOHN . . .
HOW LONG HAS IT BEEN? NO ONE WILL TELL ME. I KNOW IT'S BEEN MORE THAN DAYS BUT . . .

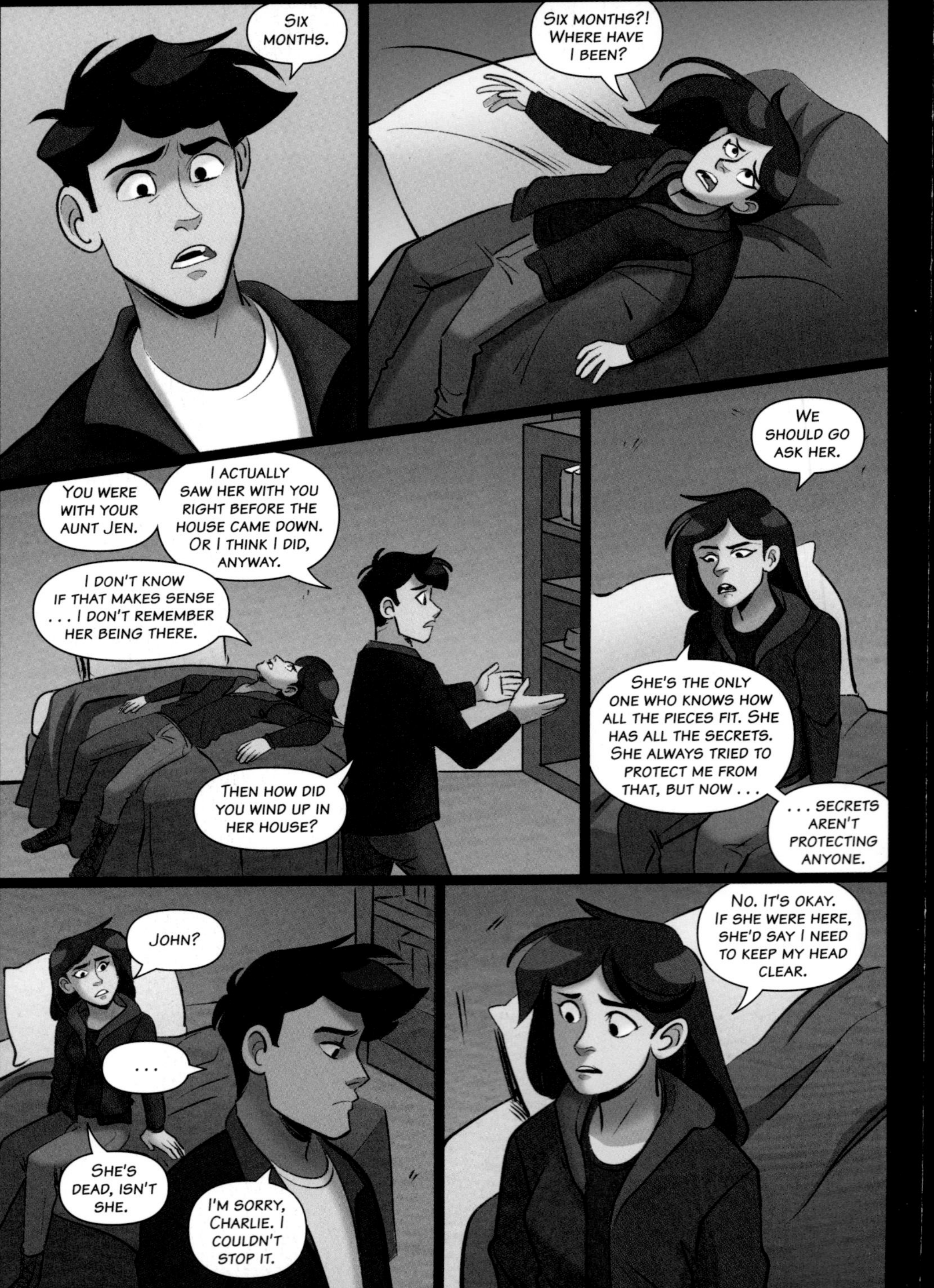
SIX MONTHS.
SIX MONTHS?! WHERE HAVE I BEEN?
YOU WERE WITH YOUR AUNT JEN.
I ACTUALLY SAW HER WITH YOU RIGHT BEFORE THE HOUSE CAME DOWN. OR I THINK I DID, ANYWAY.
I DON'T KNOW IF THAT MAKES SENSE . . . I DON'T REMEMBER HER BEING THERE.
THEN HOW DID YOU WIND UP IN HER HOUSE?
WE SHOULD GO ASK HER.
SHE'S THE ONLY ONE WHO KNOWS HOW ALL THE PIECES FIT. SHE HAS ALL THE SECRETS. SHE ALWAYS TRIED TO PROTECT ME FROM THAT, BUT NOW . . .
. . . SECRETS AREN'T PROTECTING ANYONE.
JOHN?
. . .
SHE'S DEAD, ISN'T SHE.
I'M SORRY, CHARLIE. I COULDN'T STOP IT.
NO. IT'S OKAY. IF SHE WERE HERE, SHE'D SAY I NEED TO KEEP MY HEAD CLEAR.

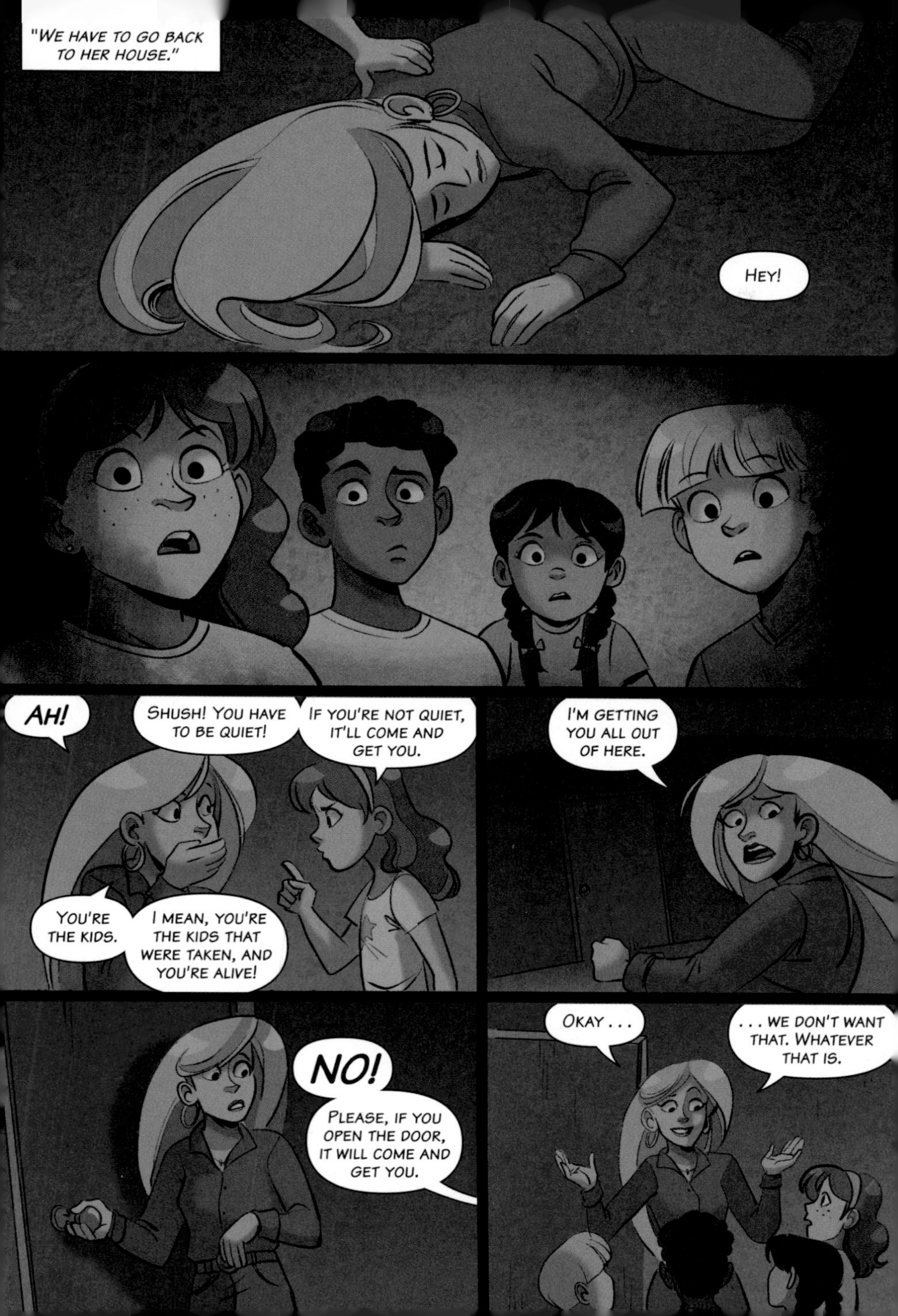
"We have to go back to her house."
Hey!
Ah!
Shush! You have to be quiet!
If you're not quiet, it'll come and get you.
You're the kids.
I mean, you're the kids that were taken, and you're alive!
I'm getting you all out of here.
NO!
Please, if you open the door, it will come and get you.
Okay . . .
. . . we don't want that. Whatever that is.

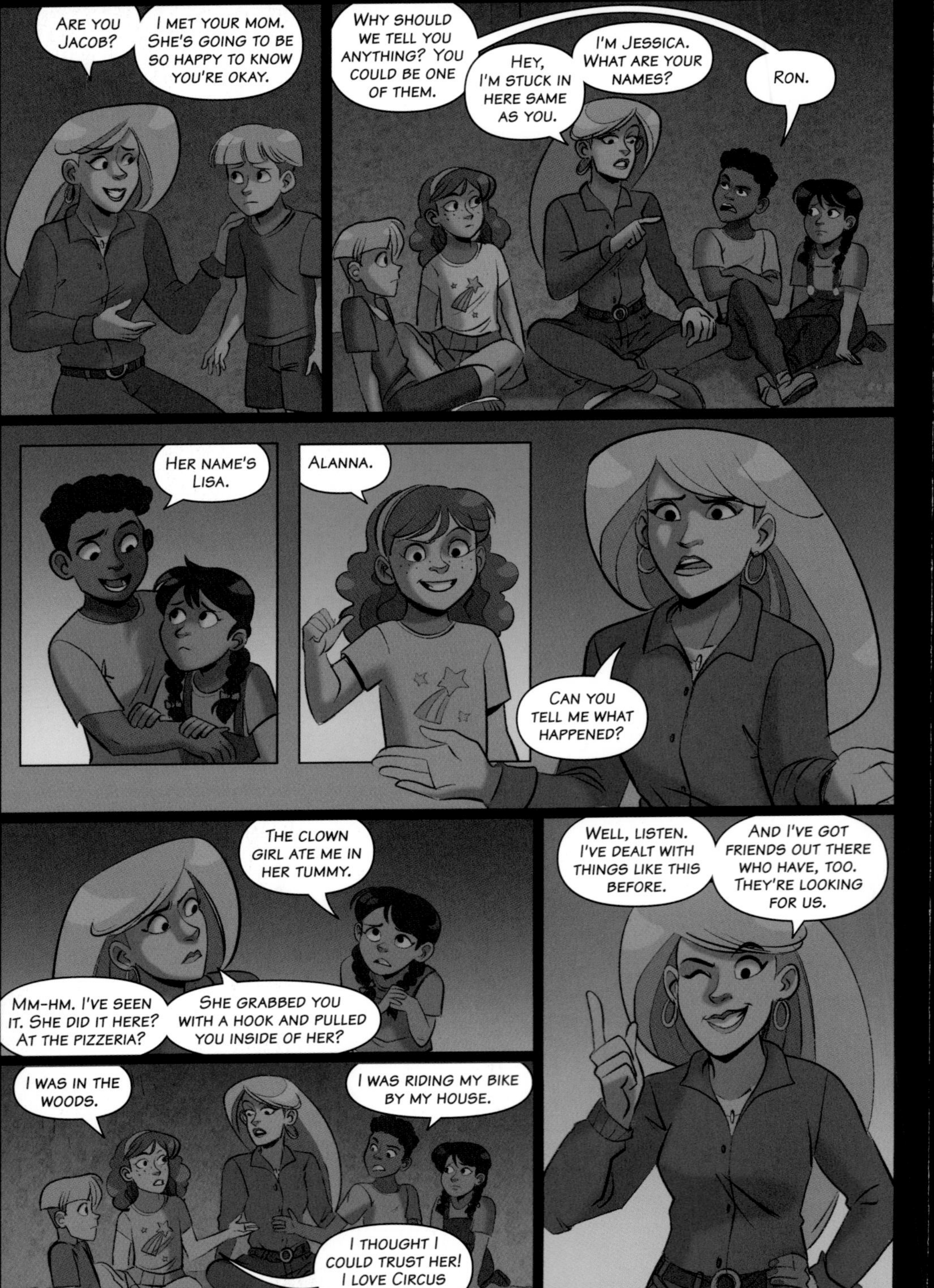

ARE YOU JACOB?
I MET YOUR MOM. SHE'S GOING TO BE SO HAPPY TO KNOW YOU'RE OKAY.
WHY SHOULD WE TELL YOU ANYTHING? YOU COULD BE ONE OF THEM.
HEY, I'M STUCK IN HERE SAME AS YOU.
I'M JESSICA. WHAT ARE YOUR NAMES?
RON.
HER NAME'S LISA.
ALANNA.
CAN YOU TELL ME WHAT HAPPENED?
THE CLOWN GIRL ATE ME IN HER TUMMY.
MM-HM. I'VE SEEN IT. SHE DID IT HERE? AT THE PIZZERIA?
SHE GRABBED YOU WITH A HOOK AND PULLED YOU INSIDE OF HER?
I WAS IN THE WOODS.
I WAS RIDING MY BIKE BY MY HOUSE.
I THOUGHT I COULD TRUST HER! I LOVE CIRCUS BABY'S!
WELL, LISTEN. I'VE DEALT WITH THINGS LIKE THIS BEFORE.
AND I'VE GOT FRIENDS OUT THERE WHO HAVE, TOO. THEY'RE LOOKING FOR US.

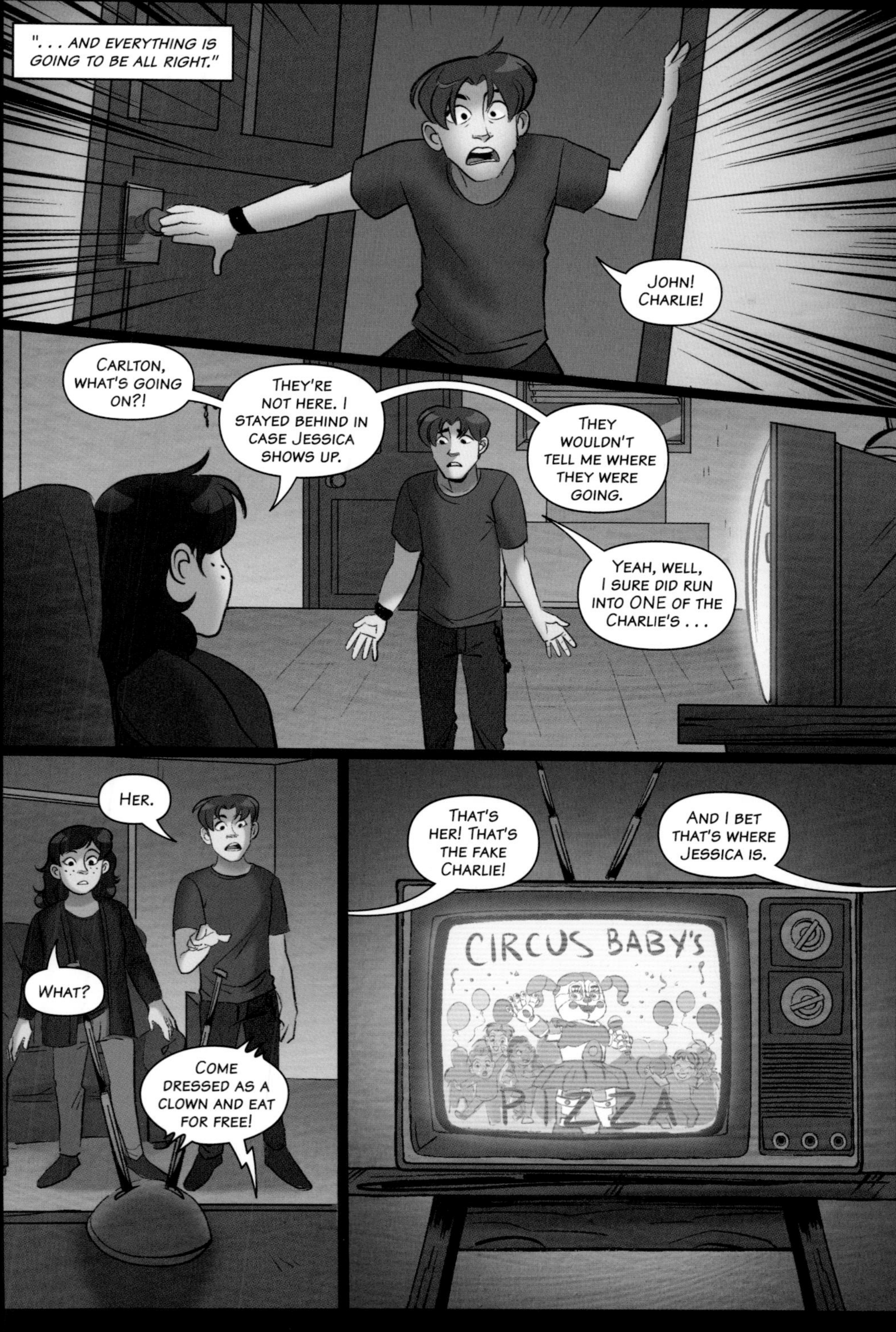
". . . AND EVERYTHING IS GOING TO BE ALL RIGHT."
JOHN! CHARLIE!
CARLTON, WHAT'S GOING ON?!
THEY'RE NOT HERE. I STAYED BEHIND IN CASE JESSICA SHOWS UP.
THEY WOULDN'T TELL ME WHERE THEY WERE GOING.
YEAH, WELL, I SURE DID RUN INTO ONE OF THE CHARLIE'S . . .
HER.
WHAT?
COME DRESSED AS A CLOWN AND EAT FOR FREE!
THAT'S HER! THAT'S THE FAKE CHARLIE!
AND I BET THAT'S WHERE JESSICA IS.
CIRCUS BABY'S
PIZZA

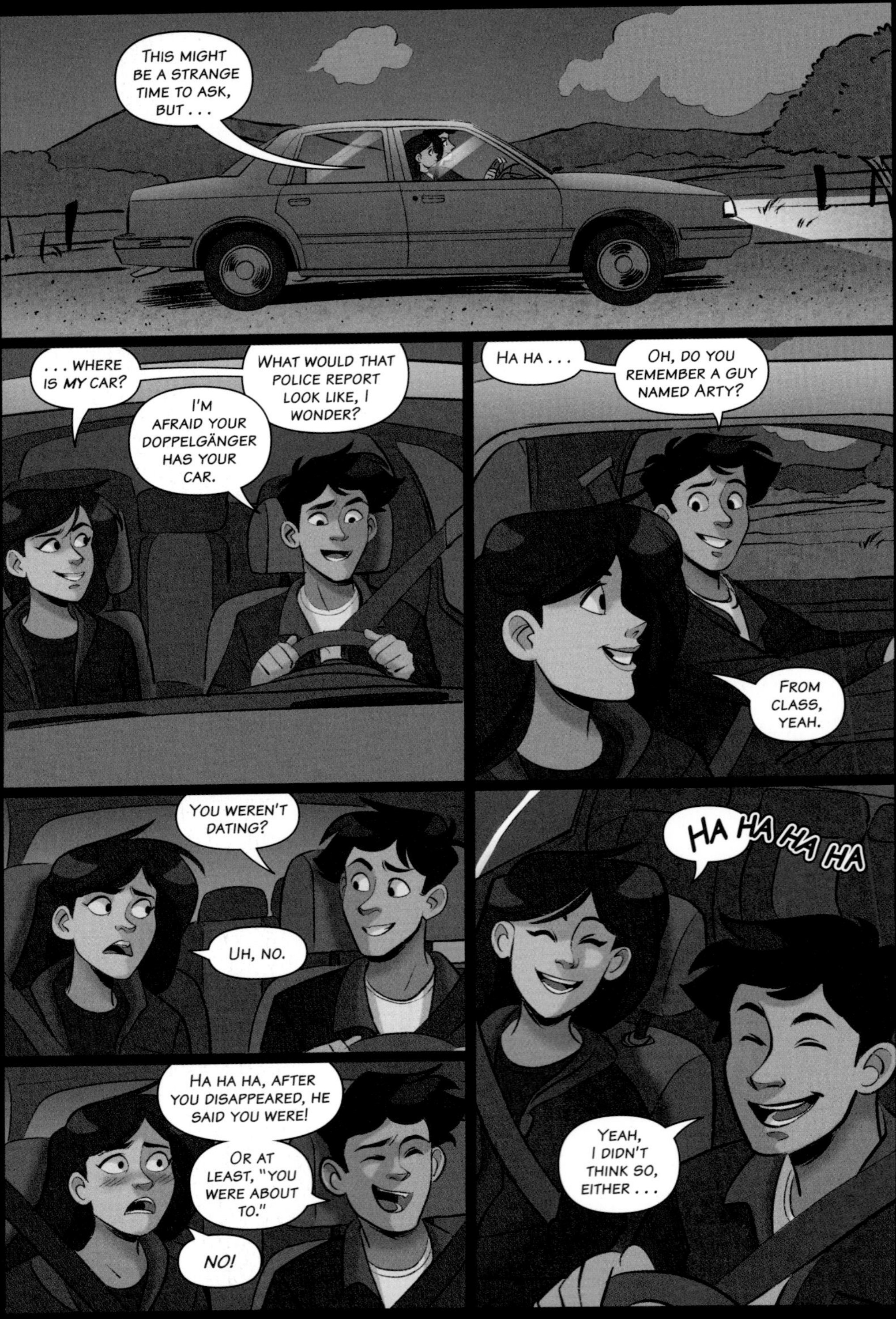

THIS MIGHT BE A STRANGE TIME TO ASK, BUT . . .
. . . WHERE IS MY CAR?
WHAT WOULD THAT POLICE REPORT LOOK LIKE, I WONDER?
I'M AFRAID YOUR DOPPELGÄNGER HAS YOUR CAR.
HA HA . . .
OH, DO YOU REMEMBER A GUY NAMED ARTY?
FROM CLASS, YEAH.
YOU WEREN'T DATING?
UH, NO.
HA HA HA, AFTER YOU DISAPPEARED, HE SAID YOU WERE!
OR AT LEAST, "YOU WERE ABOUT TO."
NO!
HA HA HA HA
YEAH, I DIDN'T THINK SO, EITHER . . .

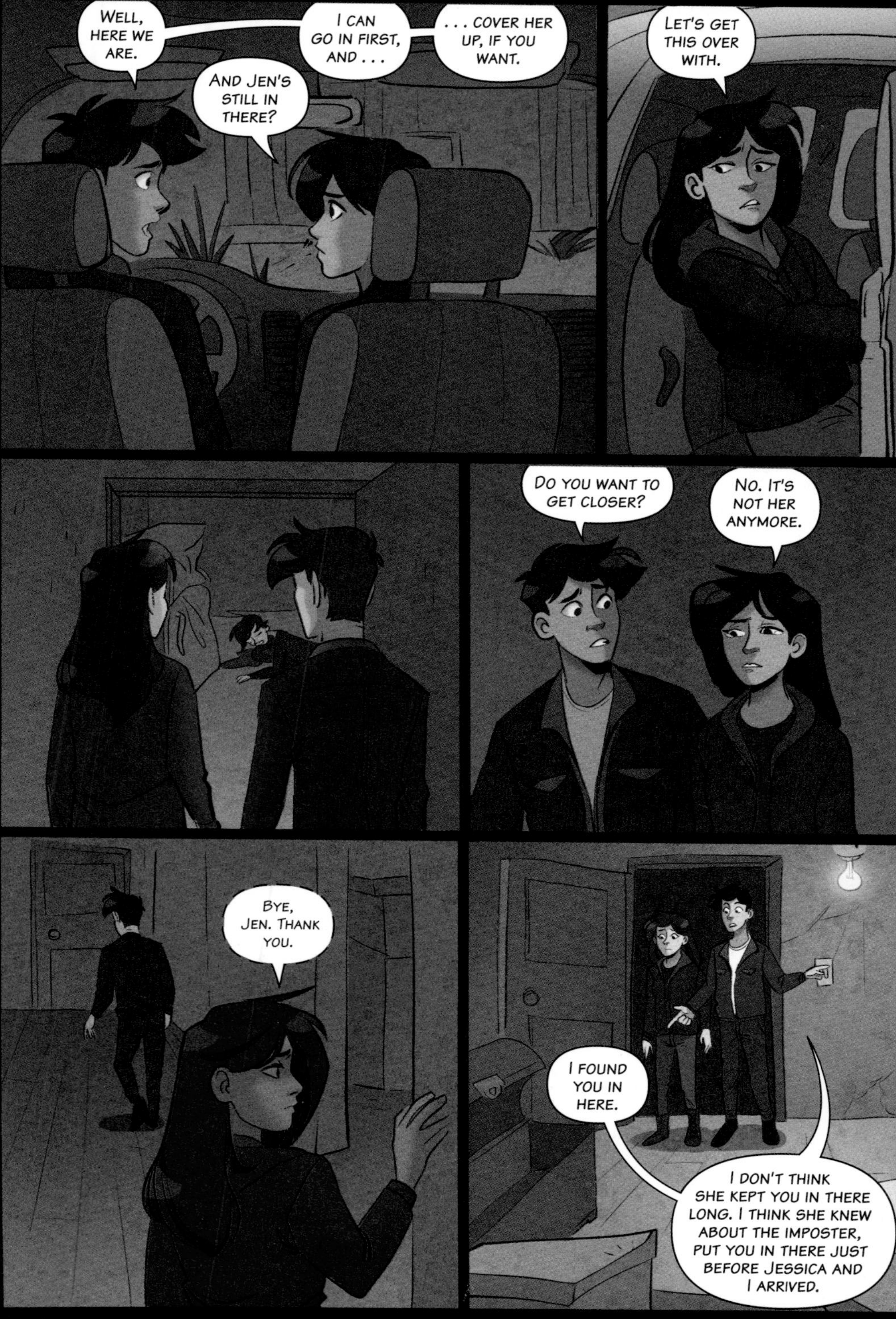

WELL, HERE WE ARE.
AND JEN'S STILL IN THERE?
I CAN GO IN FIRST, AND . . .
. . . COVER HER UP, IF YOU WANT.
LET'S GET THIS OVER WITH.
DO YOU WANT TO GET CLOSER?
NO. IT'S NOT HER ANYMORE.
BYE, JEN. THANK YOU.
I FOUND YOU IN HERE.
I DON'T THINK SHE KEPT YOU IN THERE LONG. I THINK SHE KNEW ABOUT THE IMPOSTER, PUT YOU IN THERE JUST BEFORE JESSICA AND I ARRIVED.

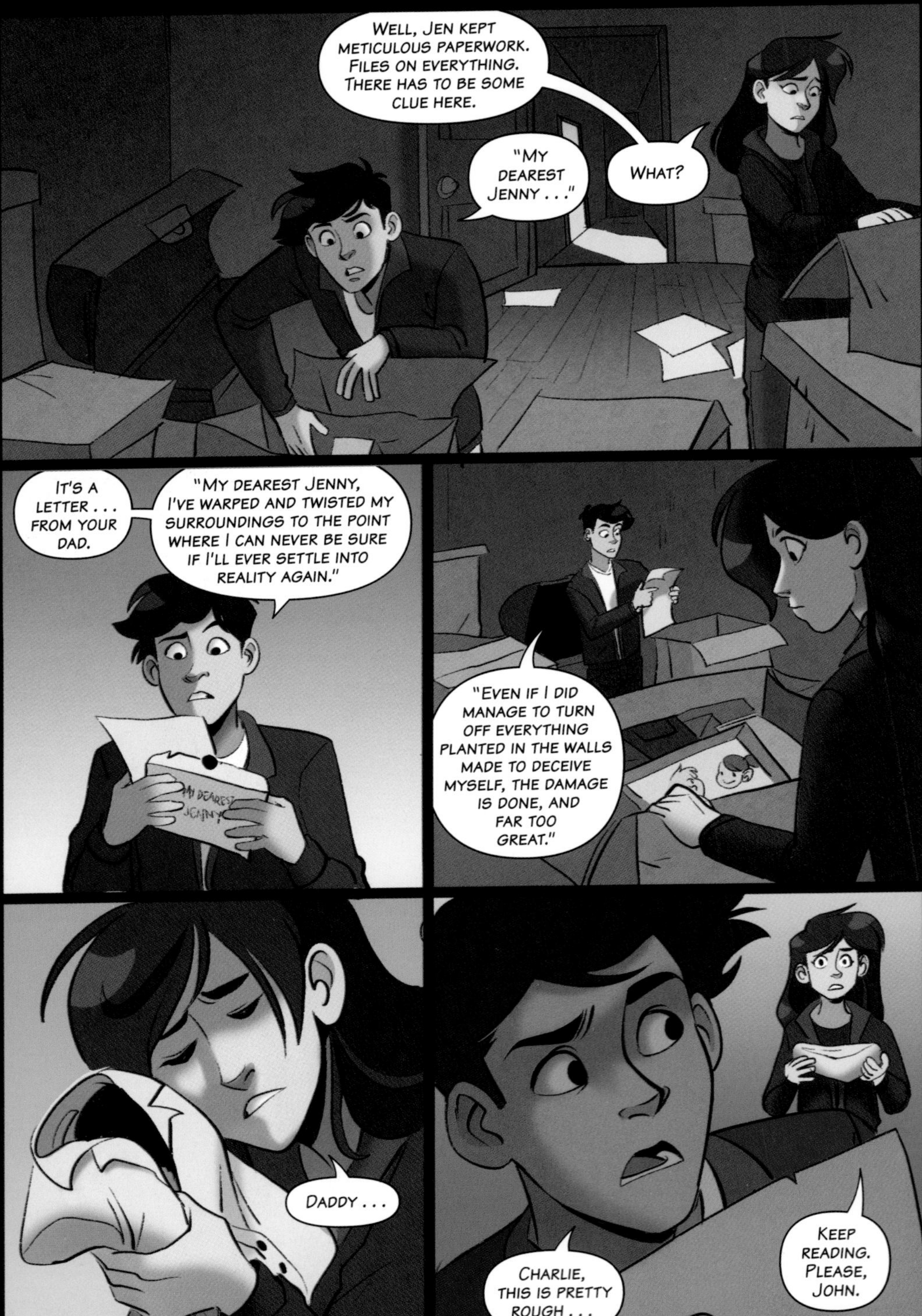
WELL, JEN KEPT METICULOUS PAPERWORK. FILES ON EVERYTHING. THERE HAS TO BE SOME CLUE HERE.
"MY DEAREST JENNY . . ."
WHAT?
IT'S A LETTER . . . FROM YOUR DAD.
"MY DEAREST JENNY, I'VE WARPED AND TWISTED MY SURROUNDINGS TO THE POINT WHERE I CAN NEVER BE SURE IF I'LL EVER SETTLE INTO REALITY AGAIN."
"EVEN IF I DID MANAGE TO TURN OFF EVERYTHING PLANTED IN THE WALLS MADE TO DECEIVE MYSELF, THE DAMAGE IS DONE, AND FAR TOO GREAT."
DADDY . . .
CHARLIE, THIS IS PRETTY ROUGH . . .
KEEP READING. PLEASE, JOHN.

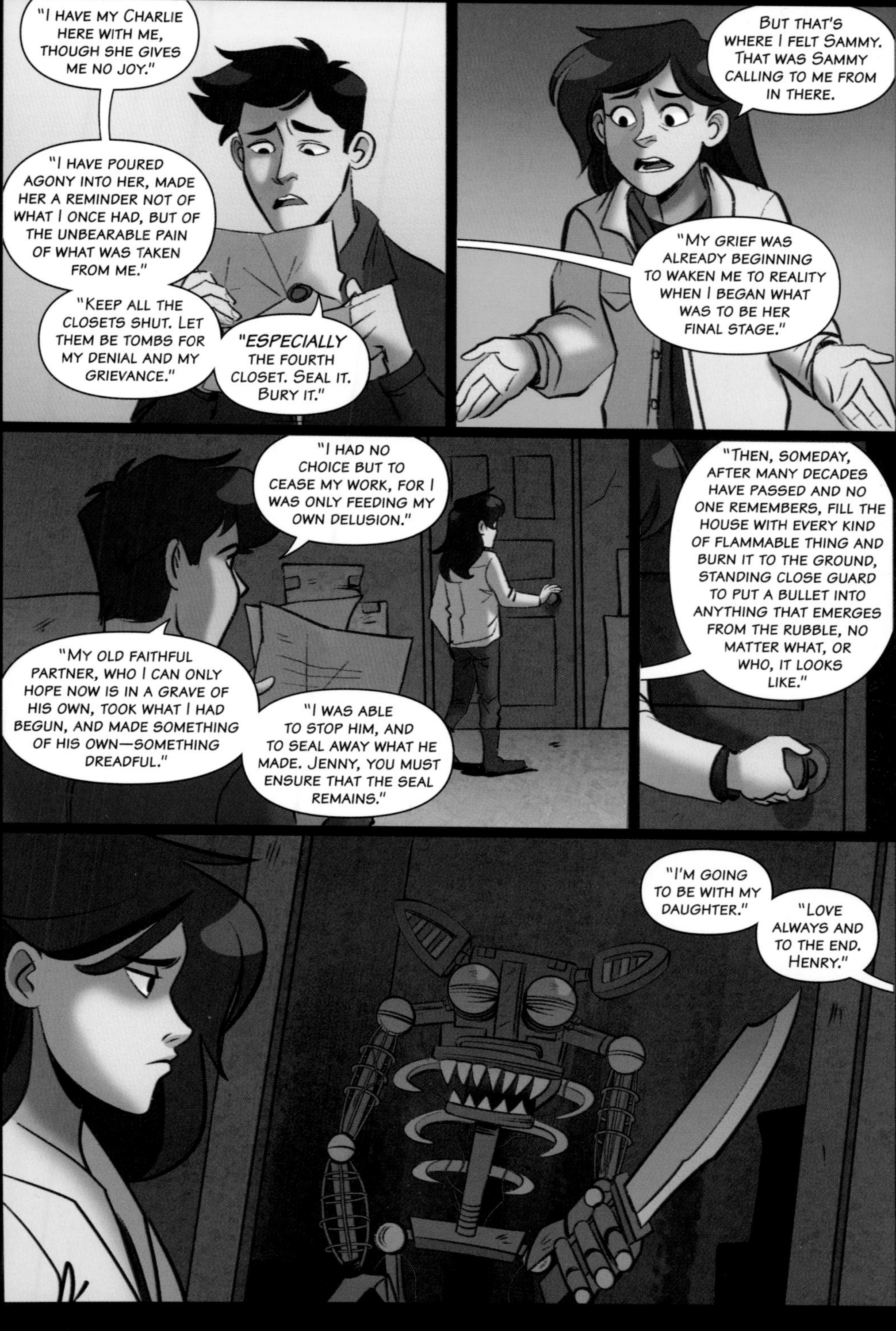
"I HAVE MY CHARLIE HERE WITH ME, THOUGH SHE GIVES ME NO JOY."
"I HAVE POURED AGONY INTO HER, MADE HER A REMINDER NOT OF WHAT I ONCE HAD, BUT OF THE UNBEARABLE PAIN OF WHAT WAS TAKEN FROM ME."
"KEEP ALL THE CLOSETS SHUT. LET THEM BE TOMBS FOR MY DENIAL AND MY GRIEVANCE."
"ESPECIALLY THE FOURTH CLOSET. SEAL IT. BURY IT."
BUT THAT'S WHERE I FELT SAMMY. THAT WAS SAMMY CALLING TO ME FROM IN THERE.
"MY GRIEF WAS ALREADY BEGINNING TO WAKEN ME TO REALITY WHEN I BEGAN WHAT WAS TO BE HER FINAL STAGE."
"I HAD NO CHOICE BUT TO CEASE MY WORK, FOR I WAS ONLY FEEDING MY OWN DELUSION."
"MY OLD FAITHFUL PARTNER, WHO I CAN ONLY HOPE NOW IS IN A GRAVE OF HIS OWN, TOOK WHAT I HAD BEGUN, AND MADE SOMETHING OF HIS OWN—SOMETHING DREADFUL."
"I WAS ABLE TO STOP HIM, AND TO SEAL AWAY WHAT HE MADE. JENNY, YOU MUST ENSURE THAT THE SEAL REMAINS."
"THEN, SOMEDAY, AFTER MANY DECADES HAVE PASSED AND NO ONE REMEMBERS, FILL THE HOUSE WITH EVERY KIND OF FLAMMABLE THING AND BURN IT TO THE GROUND, STANDING CLOSE GUARD TO PUT A BULLET INTO ANYTHING THAT EMERGES FROM THE RUBBLE, NO MATTER WHAT, OR WHO, IT LOOKS LIKE."
"I'M GOING TO BE WITH MY DAUGHTER."
"LOVE ALWAYS AND TO THE END. HENRY."

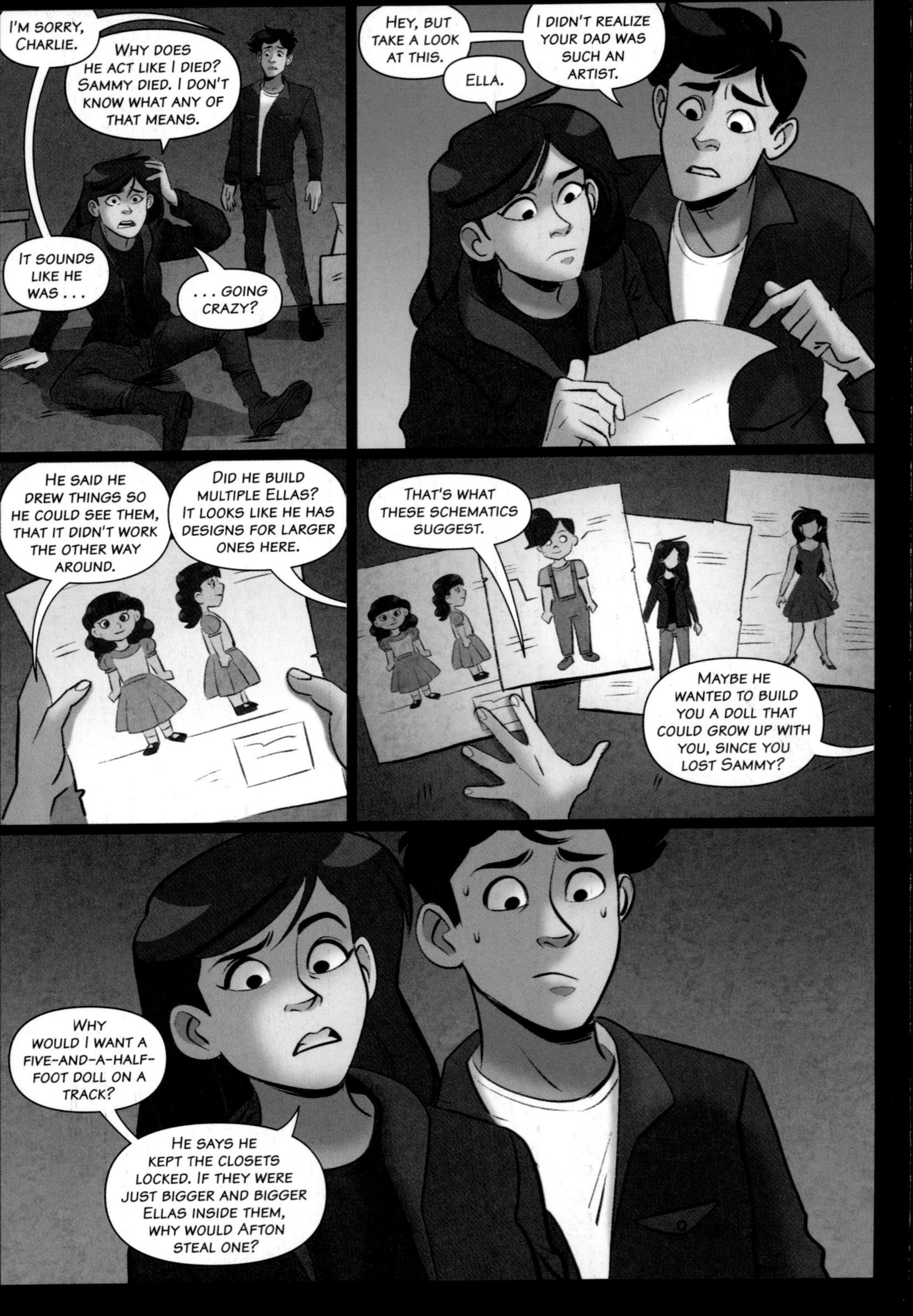
I'M SORRY, CHARLIE.
WHY DOES HE ACT LIKE I DIED? SAMMY DIED. I DON'T KNOW WHAT ANY OF THAT MEANS.
IT SOUNDS LIKE HE WAS . . .
. . . GOING CRAZY?
HEY, BUT TAKE A LOOK AT THIS.
ELLA.
I DIDN'T REALIZE YOUR DAD WAS SUCH AN ARTIST.
HE SAID HE DREW THINGS SO HE COULD SEE THEM, THAT IT DIDN'T WORK THE OTHER WAY AROUND.
DID HE BUILD MULTIPLE ELLAS? IT LOOKS LIKE HE HAS DESIGNS FOR LARGER ONES HERE.
THAT'S WHAT THESE SCHEMATICS SUGGEST.
MAYBE HE WANTED TO BUILD YOU A DOLL THAT COULD GROW UP WITH YOU, SINCE YOU LOST SAMMY?
WHY WOULD I WANT A FIVE-AND-A-HALF-FOOT DOLL ON A TRACK?
HE SAYS HE KEPT THE CLOSETS LOCKED. IF THEY WERE JUST BIGGER AND BIGGER ELLAS INSIDE THEM, WHY WOULD AFTON STEAL ONE?

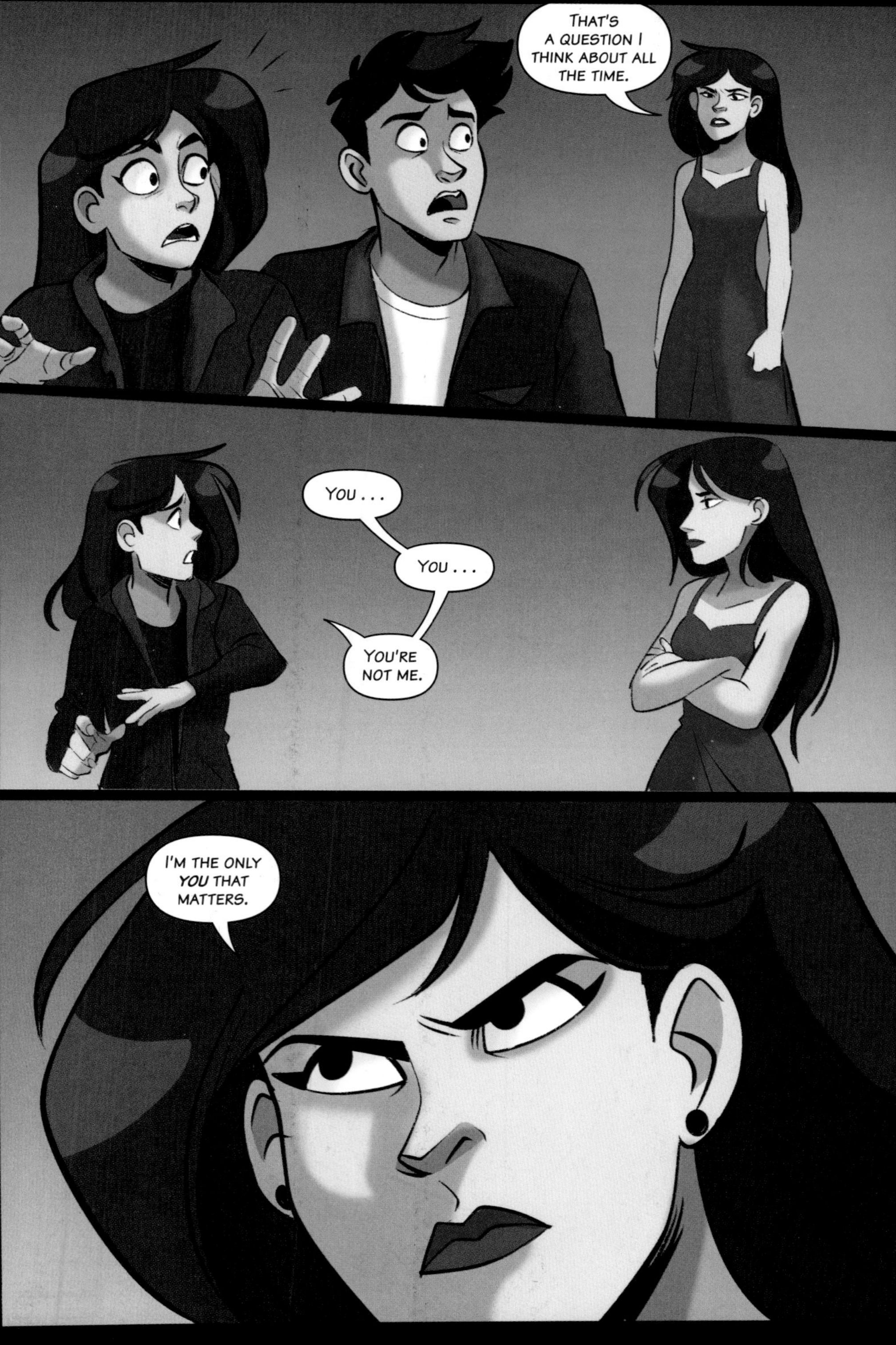
THAT'S A QUESTION I THINK ABOUT ALL THE TIME.
YOU . . .
YOU . . .
YOU'RE NOT ME.
I'M THE ONLY *YOU* THAT MATTERS.

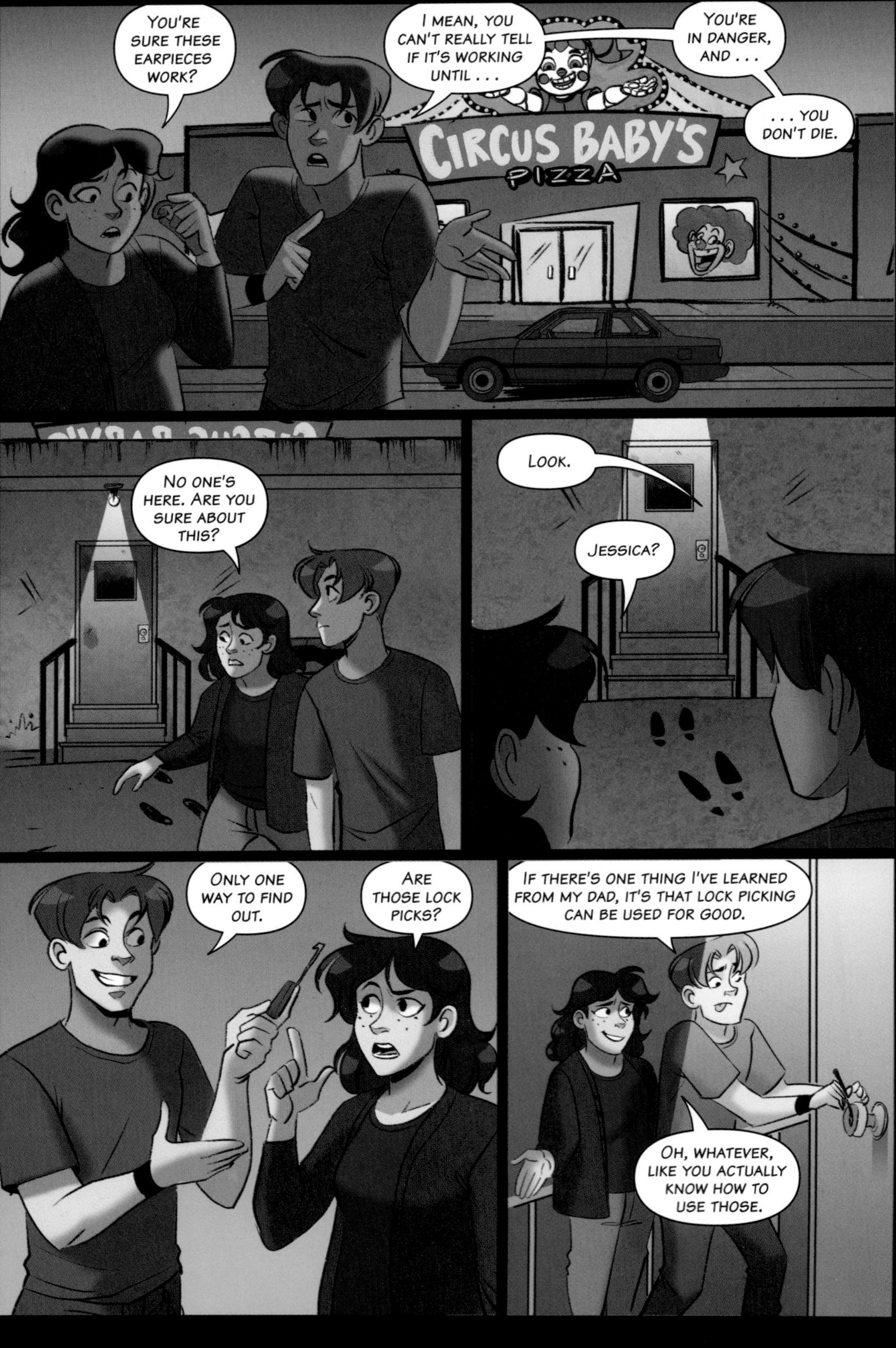
YOU'RE SURE THESE EARPIECES WORK?
I MEAN, YOU CAN'T REALLY TELL IF IT'S WORKING UNTIL . . .
YOU'RE IN DANGER, AND . . .
. . . YOU DON'T DIE.
CIRCUS BABY'S PIZZA
NO ONE'S HERE. ARE YOU SURE ABOUT THIS?
LOOK.
JESSICA?
ONLY ONE WAY TO FIND OUT.
ARE THOSE LOCK PICKS?
IF THERE'S ONE THING I'VE LEARNED FROM MY DAD, IT'S THAT LOCK PICKING CAN BE USED FOR GOOD.
OH, WHATEVER, LIKE YOU ACTUALLY KNOW HOW TO USE THOSE.

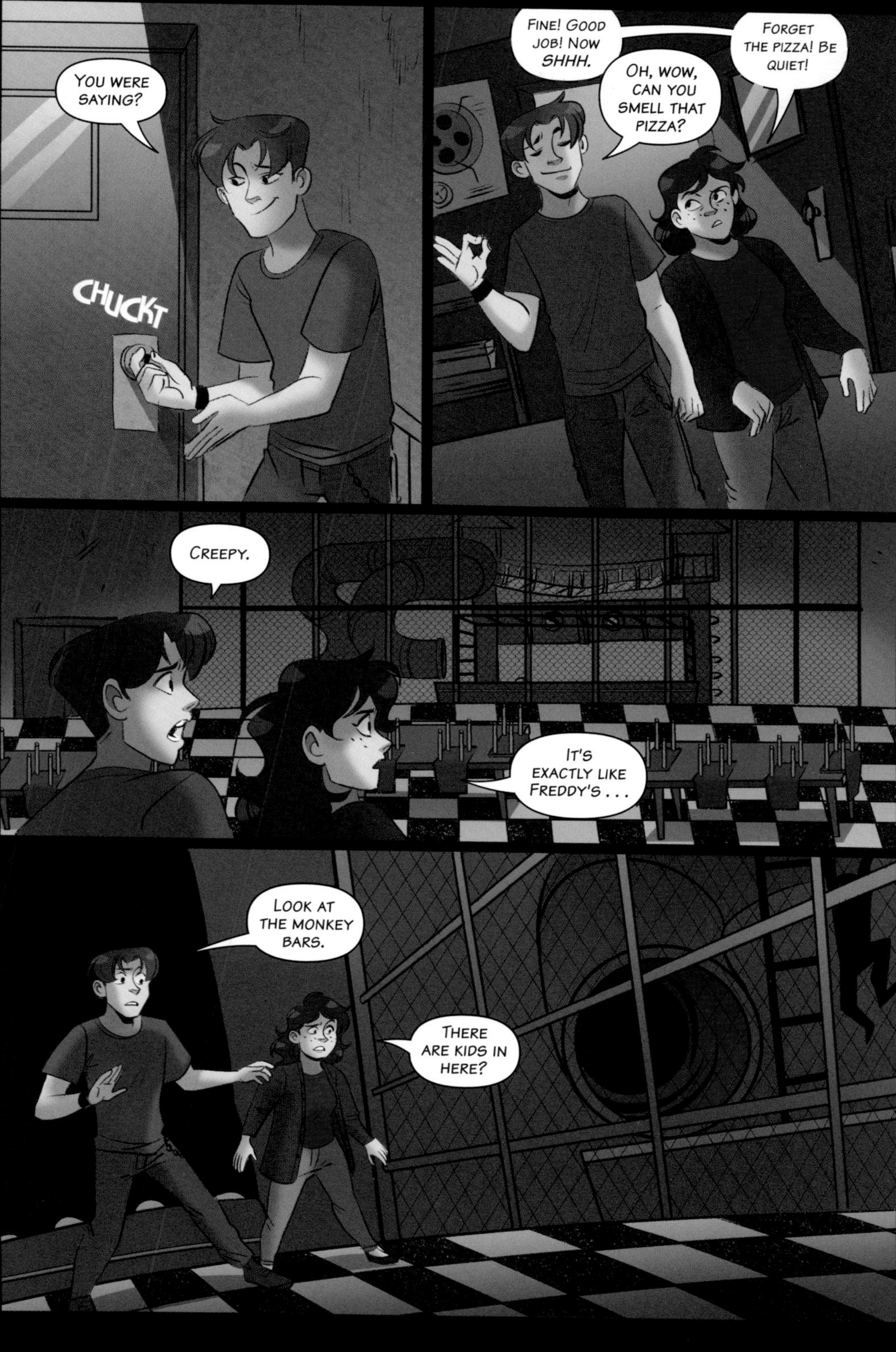
You were saying?
CHUCKT
Fine! Good job! Now SHHH.
Forget the pizza! Be quiet!
Oh, wow, can you smell that pizza?
Creepy.
It's exactly like Freddy's . . .
Look at the monkey bars.
There are kids in here?

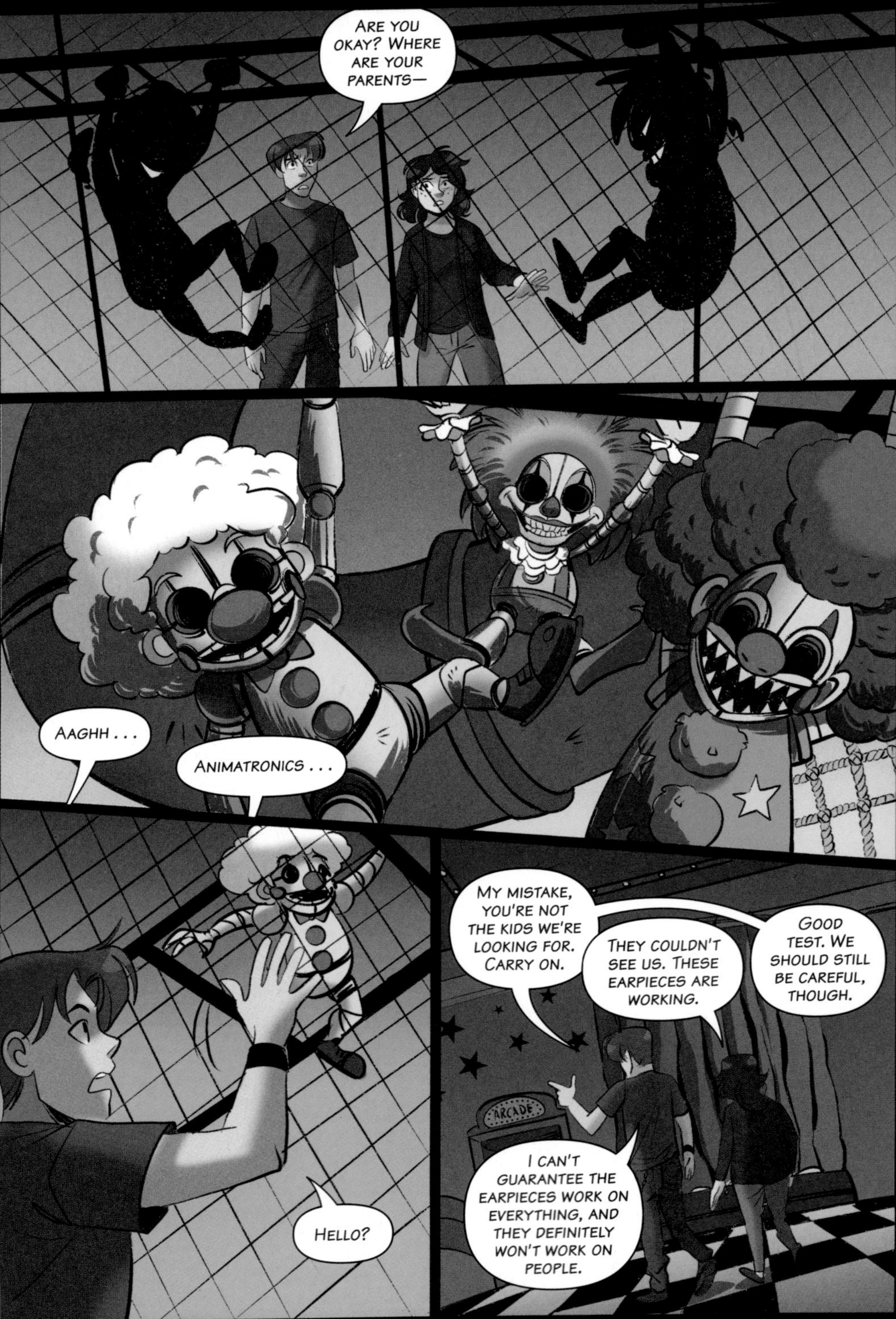

Are you okay? Where are your parents—
Aaghh . . .
Animatronics . . .
Hello?
My mistake, you're not the kids we're looking for. Carry on.
They couldn't see us. These earpieces are working.
Good test. We should still be careful, though.
Arcade
I can't guarantee the earpieces work on everything, and they definitely won't work on people.

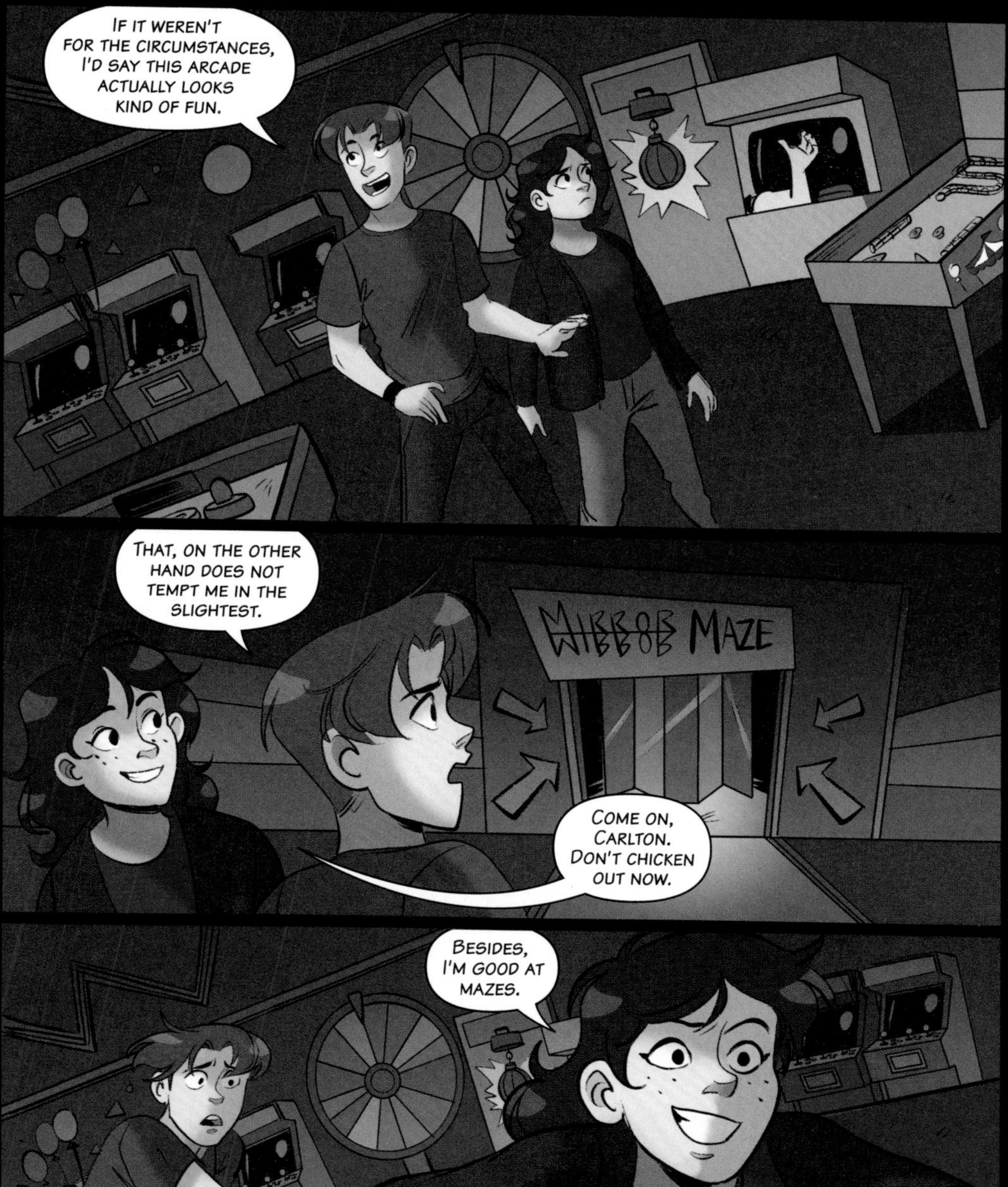
IF IT WEREN'T FOR THE CIRCUMSTANCES, I'D SAY THIS ARCADE ACTUALLY LOOKS KIND OF FUN.
THAT, ON THE OTHER HAND DOES NOT TEMPT ME IN THE SLIGHTEST.
MIRROR MAZE
COME ON, CARLTON. DON'T CHICKEN OUT NOW.
BESIDES, I'M GOOD AT MAZES.
YOU'RE GOOD AT MAZES? WHAT IS THAT SUPPOSED TO MEAN?! "I'M GOOD AT MAZES."

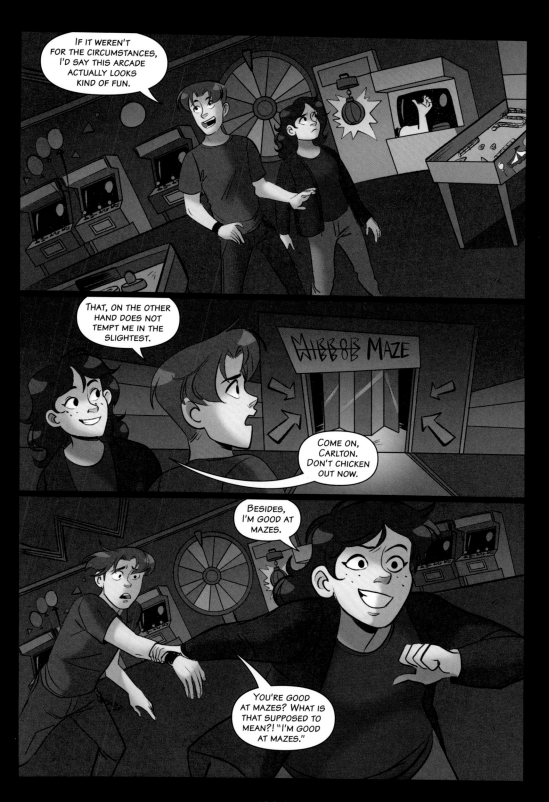

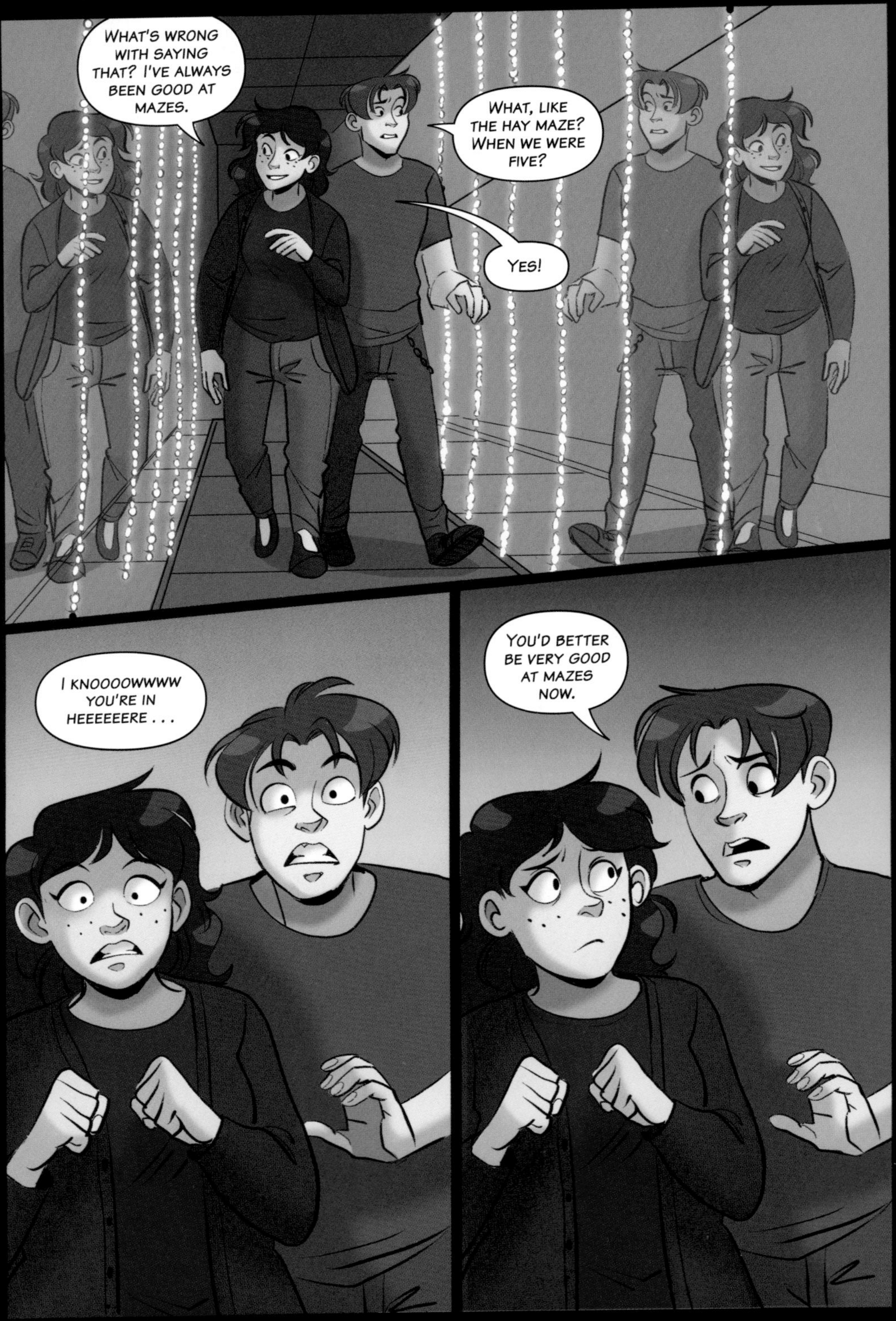
WHAT'S WRONG WITH SAYING THAT? I'VE ALWAYS BEEN GOOD AT MAZES.
WHAT, LIKE THE HAY MAZE? WHEN WE WERE FIVE?
YES!
I KNOOOOWWWW YOU'RE IN HEEEEEERE . . .
YOU'D BETTER BE VERY GOOD AT MAZES NOW.

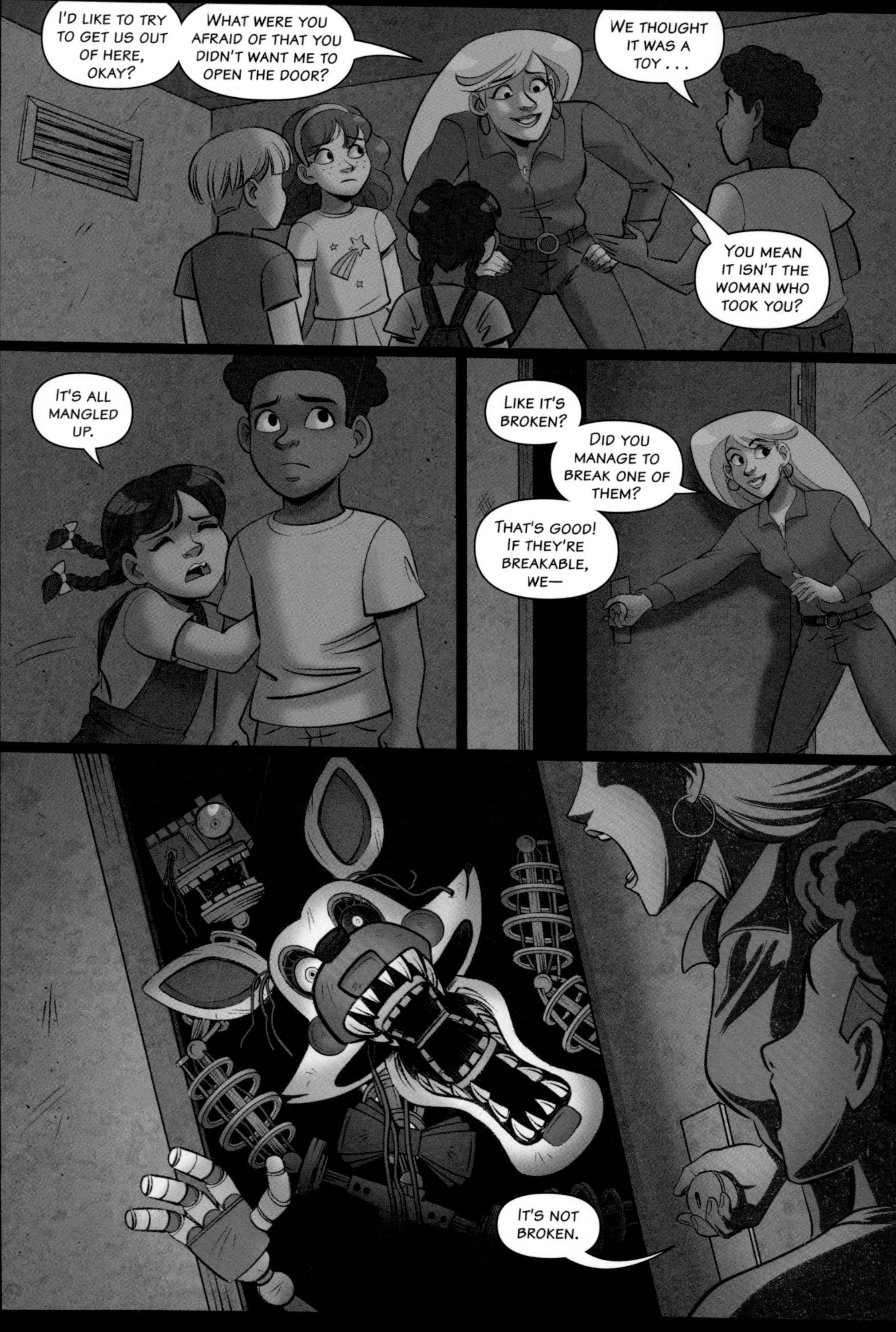
I'D LIKE TO TRY TO GET US OUT OF HERE, OKAY?
WHAT WERE YOU AFRAID OF THAT YOU DIDN'T WANT ME TO OPEN THE DOOR?
WE THOUGHT IT WAS A TOY . . .
YOU MEAN IT ISN'T THE WOMAN WHO TOOK YOU?
IT'S ALL MANGLED UP.
LIKE IT'S BROKEN?
DID YOU MANAGE TO BREAK ONE OF THEM?
THAT'S GOOD! IF THEY'RE BREAKABLE, WE—
IT'S NOT BROKEN.

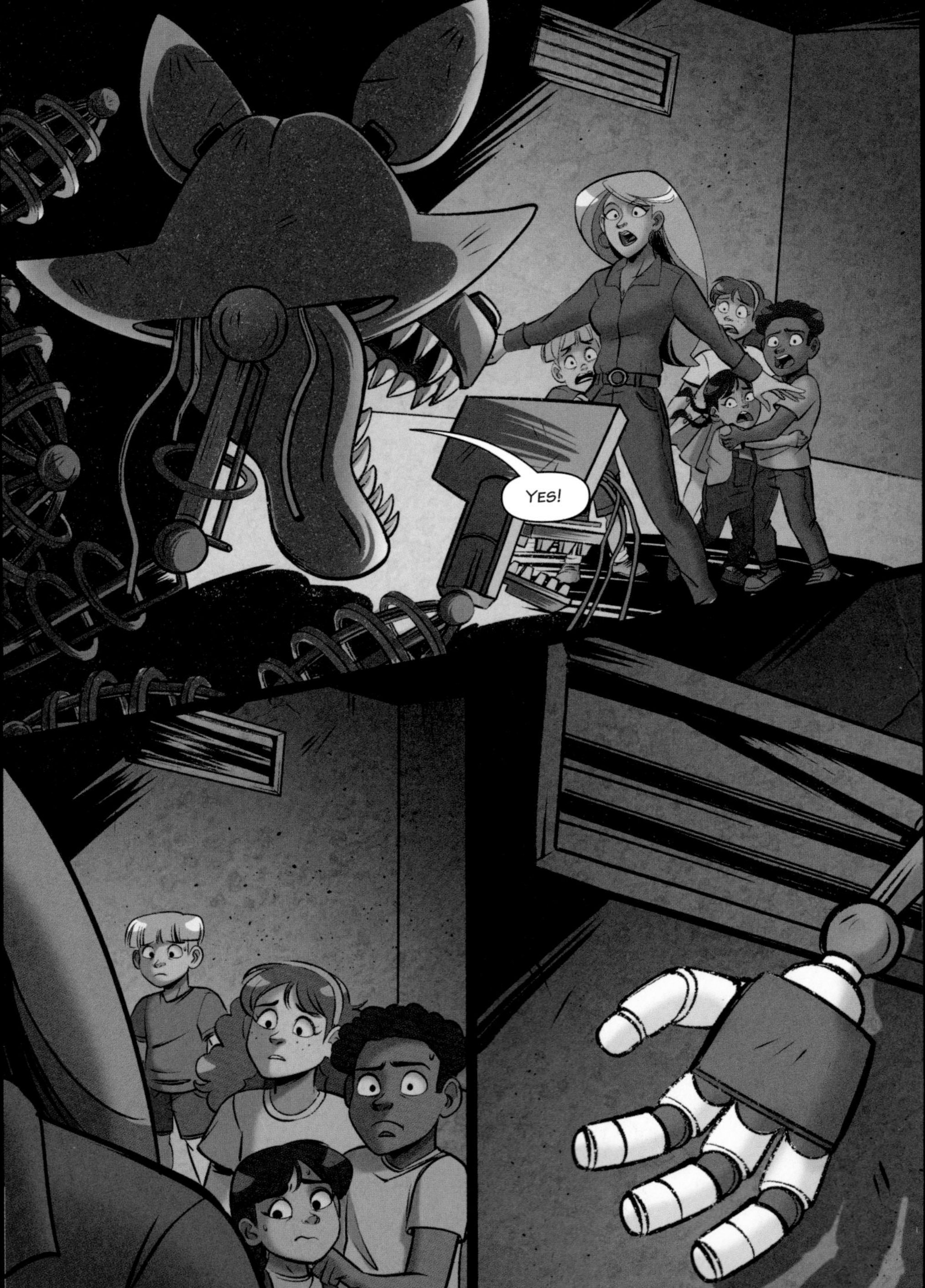
YES!

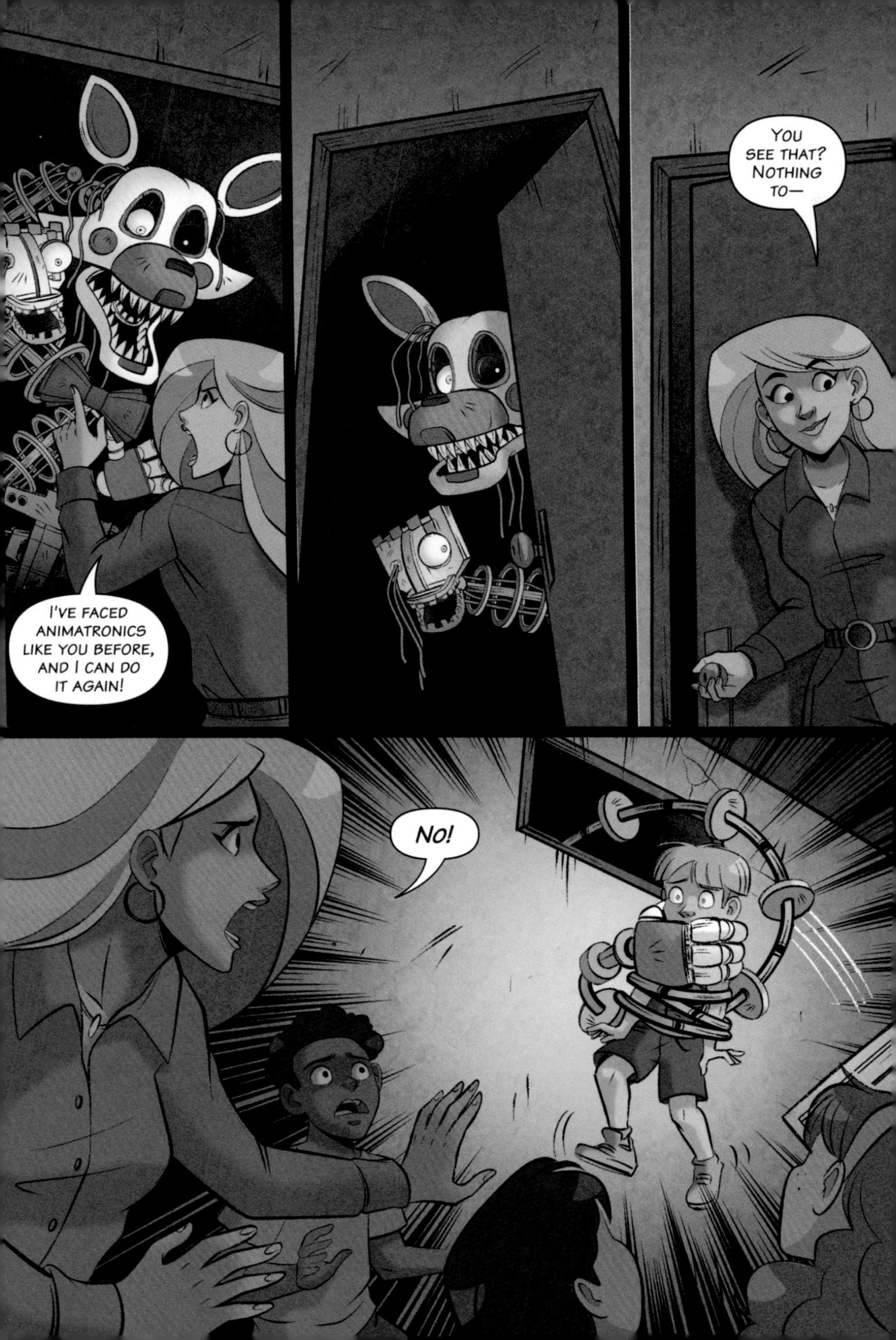
I'VE FACED ANIMATRONICS LIKE YOU BEFORE, AND I CAN DO IT AGAIN!
YOU SEE THAT? NOTHING TO—
No!

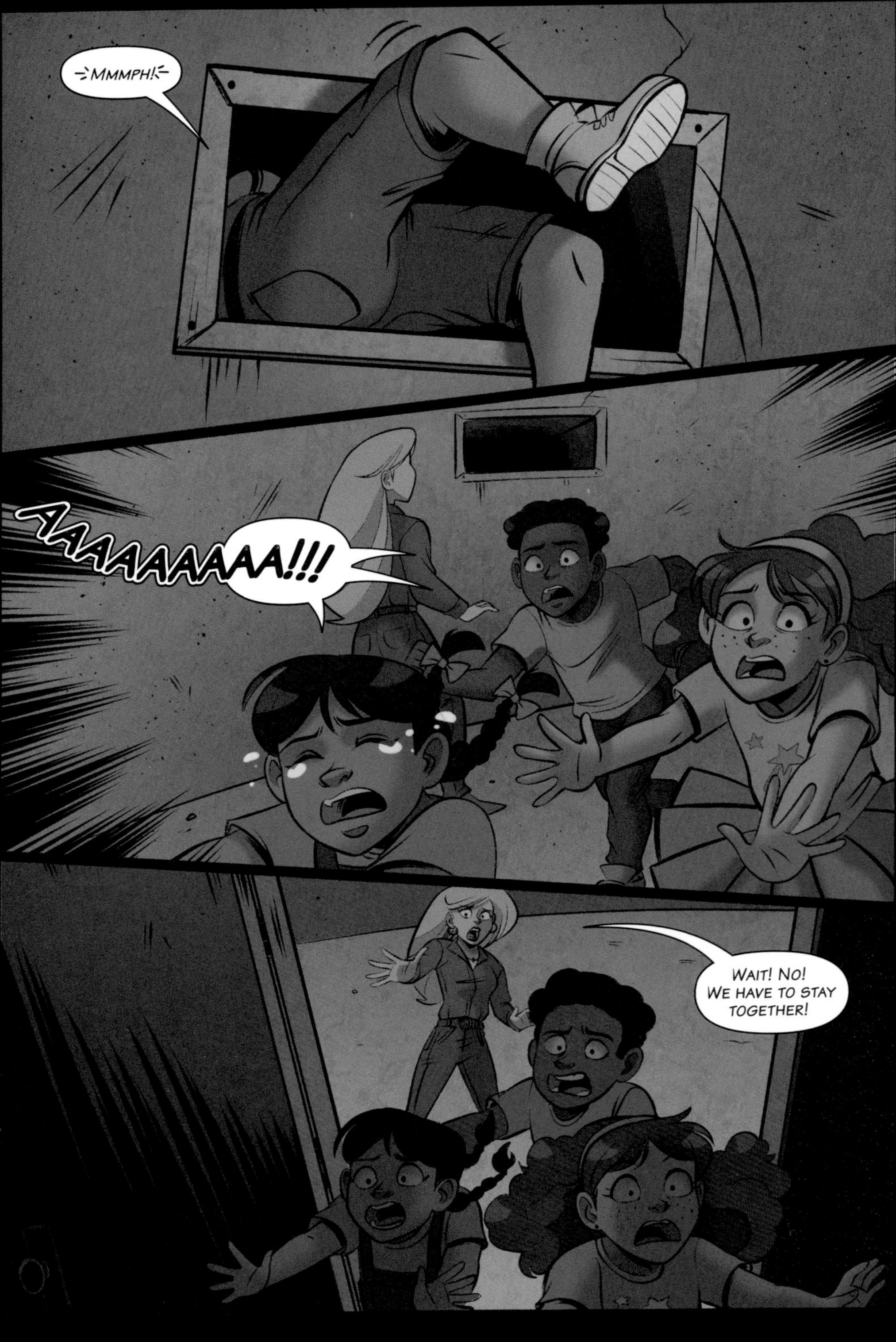
MMMPH!
AAAAAAAAAA!!!
WAIT! NO! WE HAVE TO STAY TOGETHER!

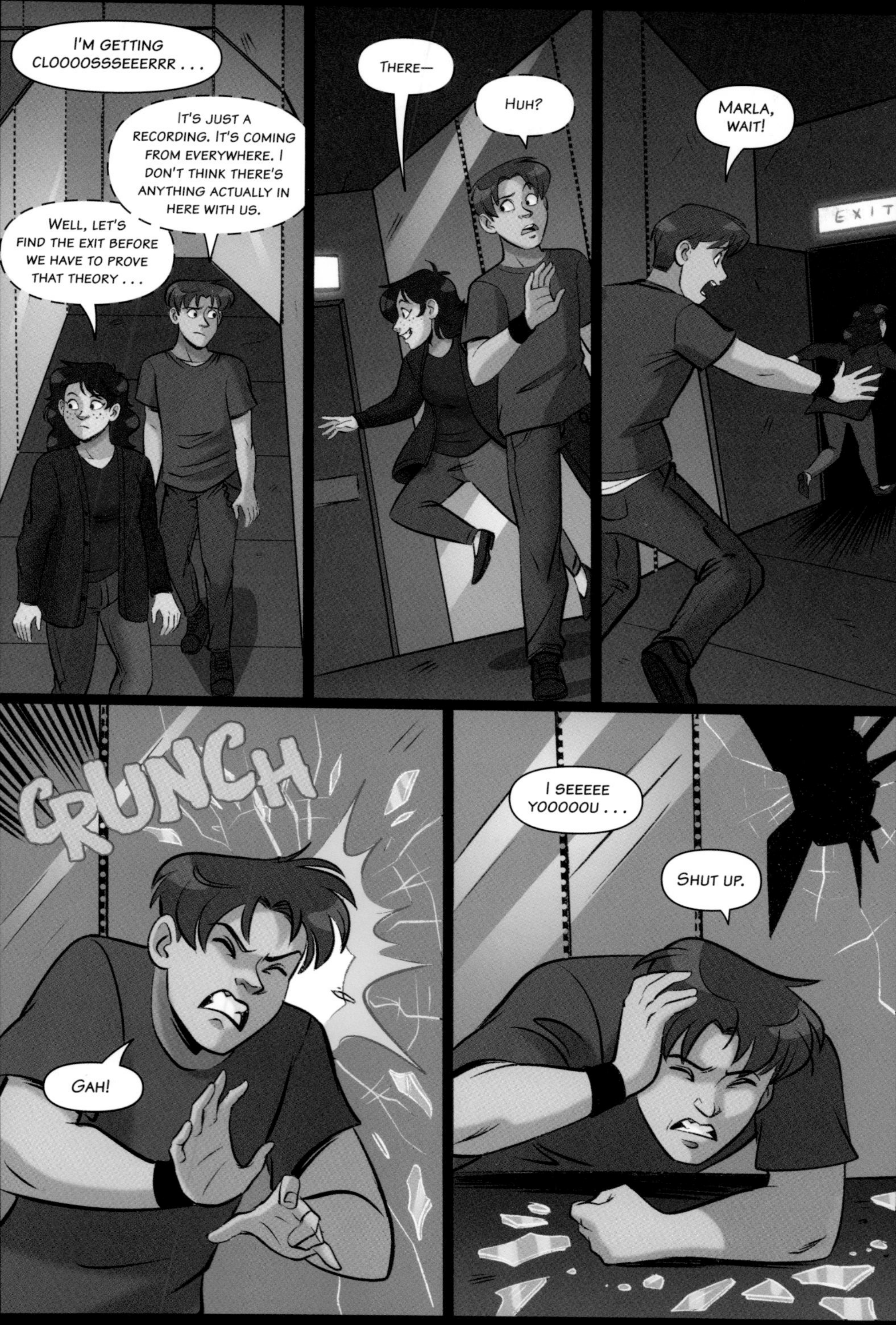
I'M GETTING CLOOOOSSSEEERRR . . .
IT'S JUST A RECORDING. IT'S COMING FROM EVERYWHERE. I DON'T THINK THERE'S ANYTHING ACTUALLY IN HERE WITH US.
WELL, LET'S FIND THE EXIT BEFORE WE HAVE TO PROVE THAT THEORY . . .
THERE—
HUH?
MARLA, WAIT!
EXIT
CRUNCH
GAH!
I SEEEEE YOOOOOU . . .
SHUT UP.

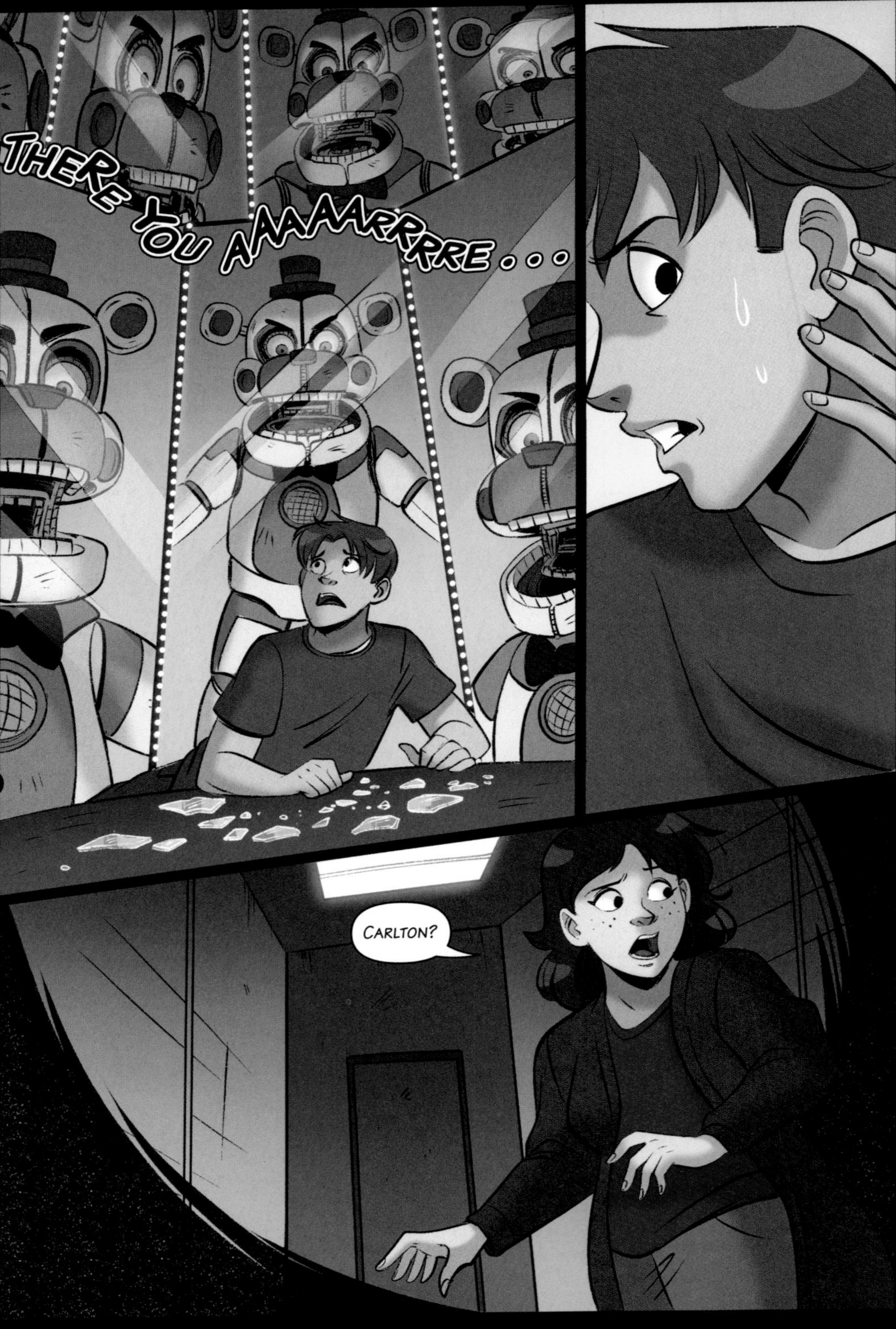
THERE YOU AAAAARRRRRE . . .
CARLTON?

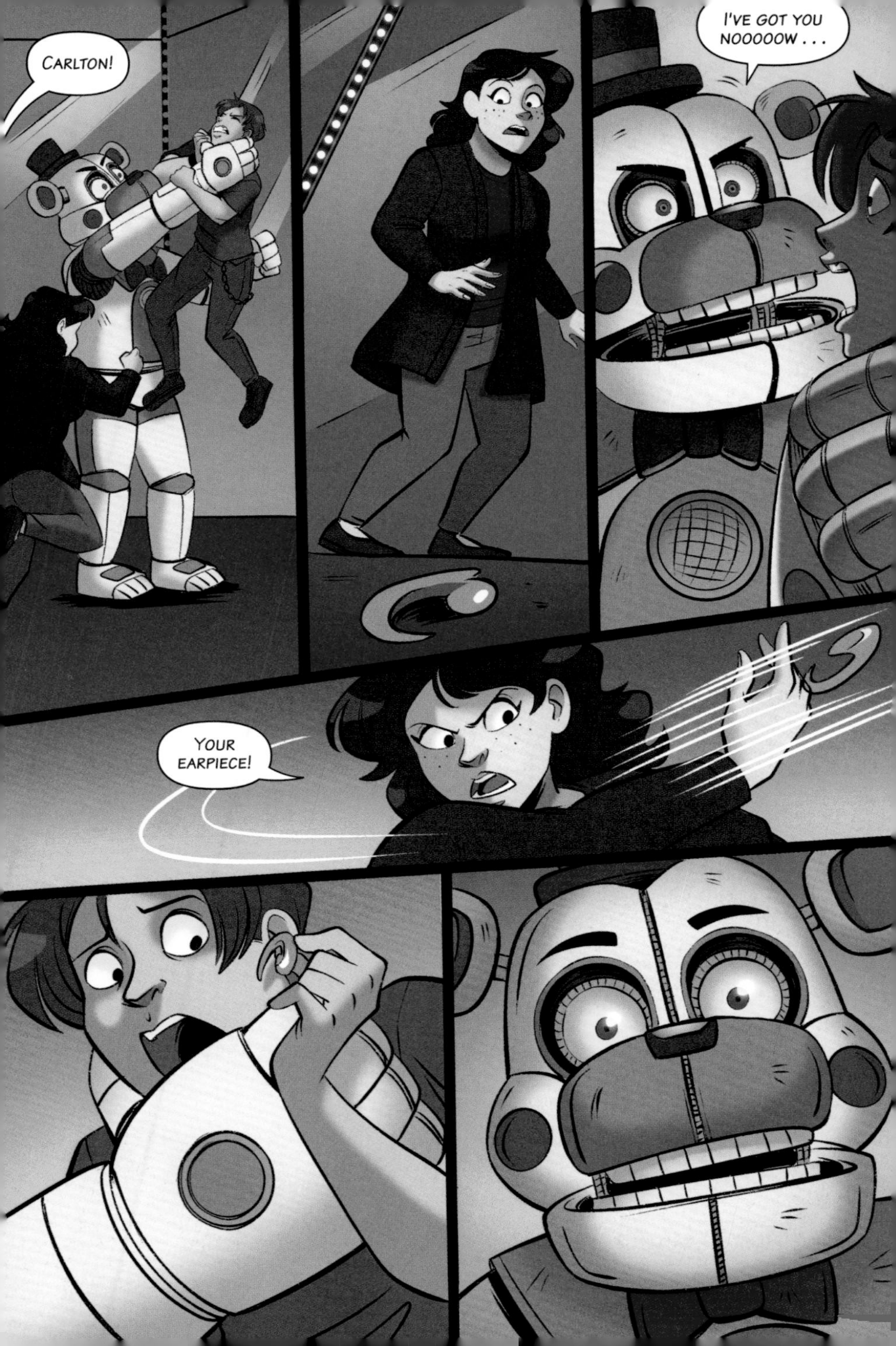
CARLTON!
I'VE GOT YOU NOOOOOW . . .
YOUR EARPIECE!

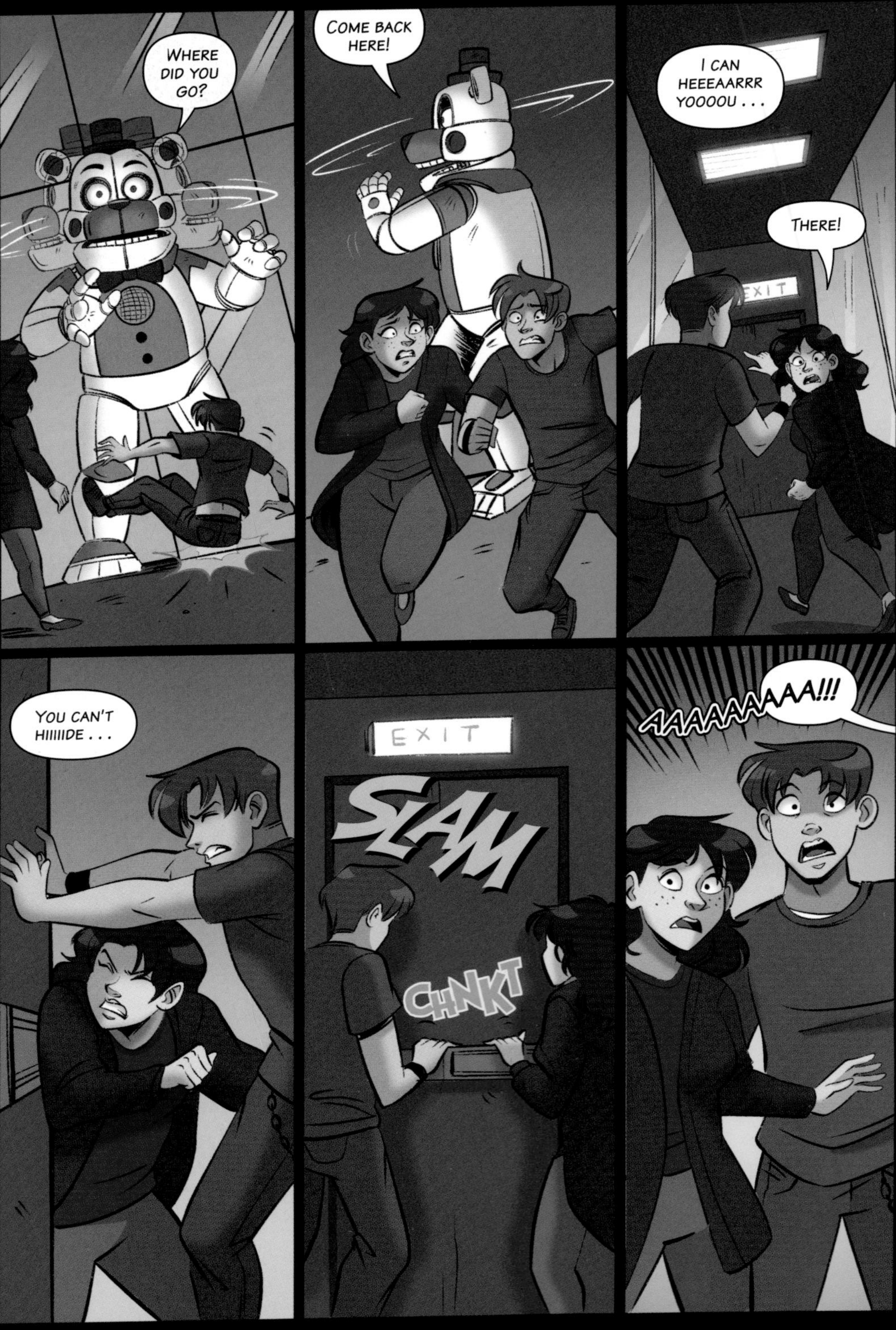
WHERE DID YOU GO?
COME BACK HERE!
I CAN HEEEAARRR YOOOOU . . .
THERE!
EXIT
YOU CAN'T HIIIIIDE . . .
EXIT
SLAM
CHNKT
AAAAAAAAA!!!

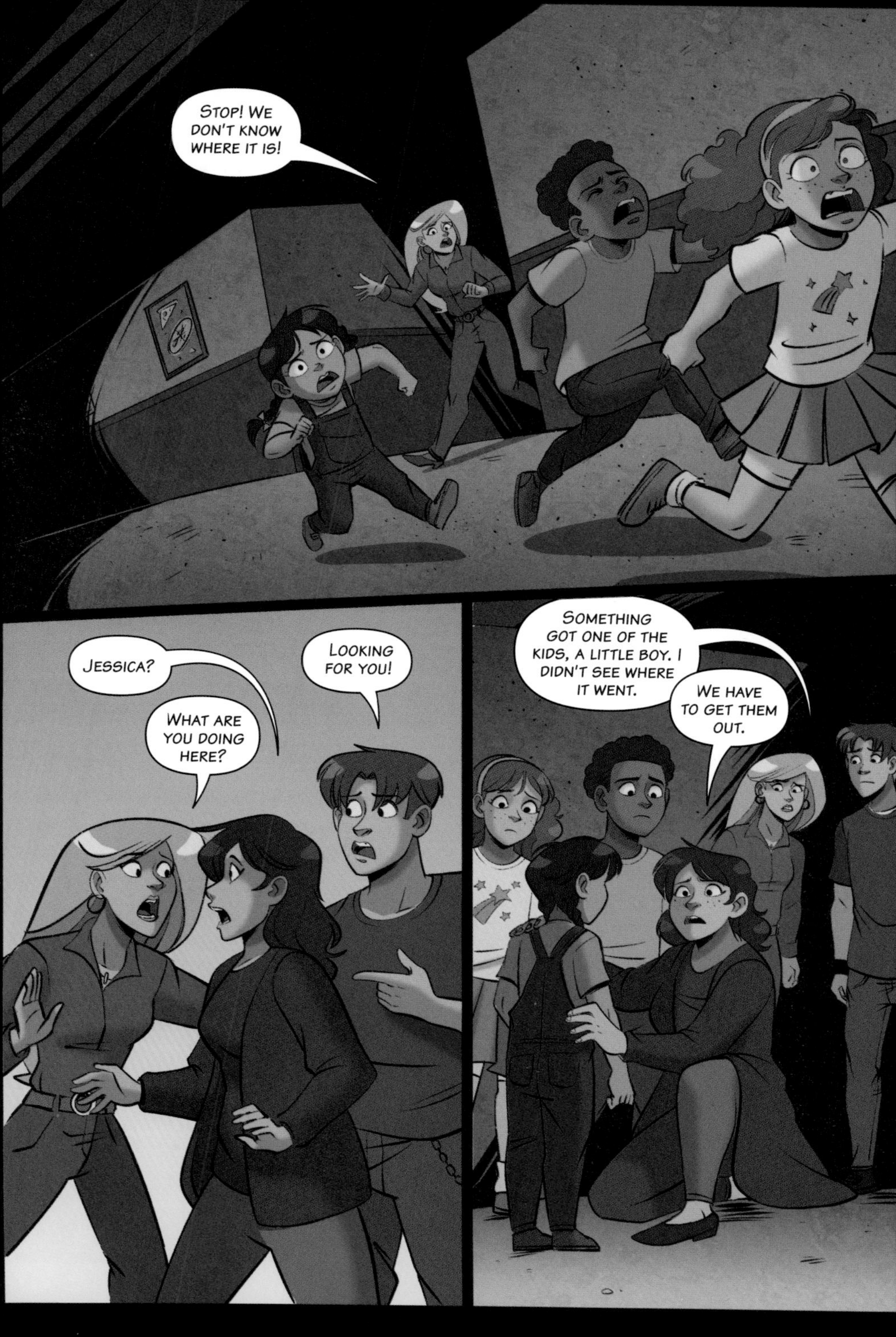
STOP! WE DON'T KNOW WHERE IT IS!
JESSICA?
WHAT ARE YOU DOING HERE?
LOOKING FOR YOU!
SOMETHING GOT ONE OF THE KIDS, A LITTLE BOY. I DIDN'T SEE WHERE IT WENT.
WE HAVE TO GET THEM OUT.

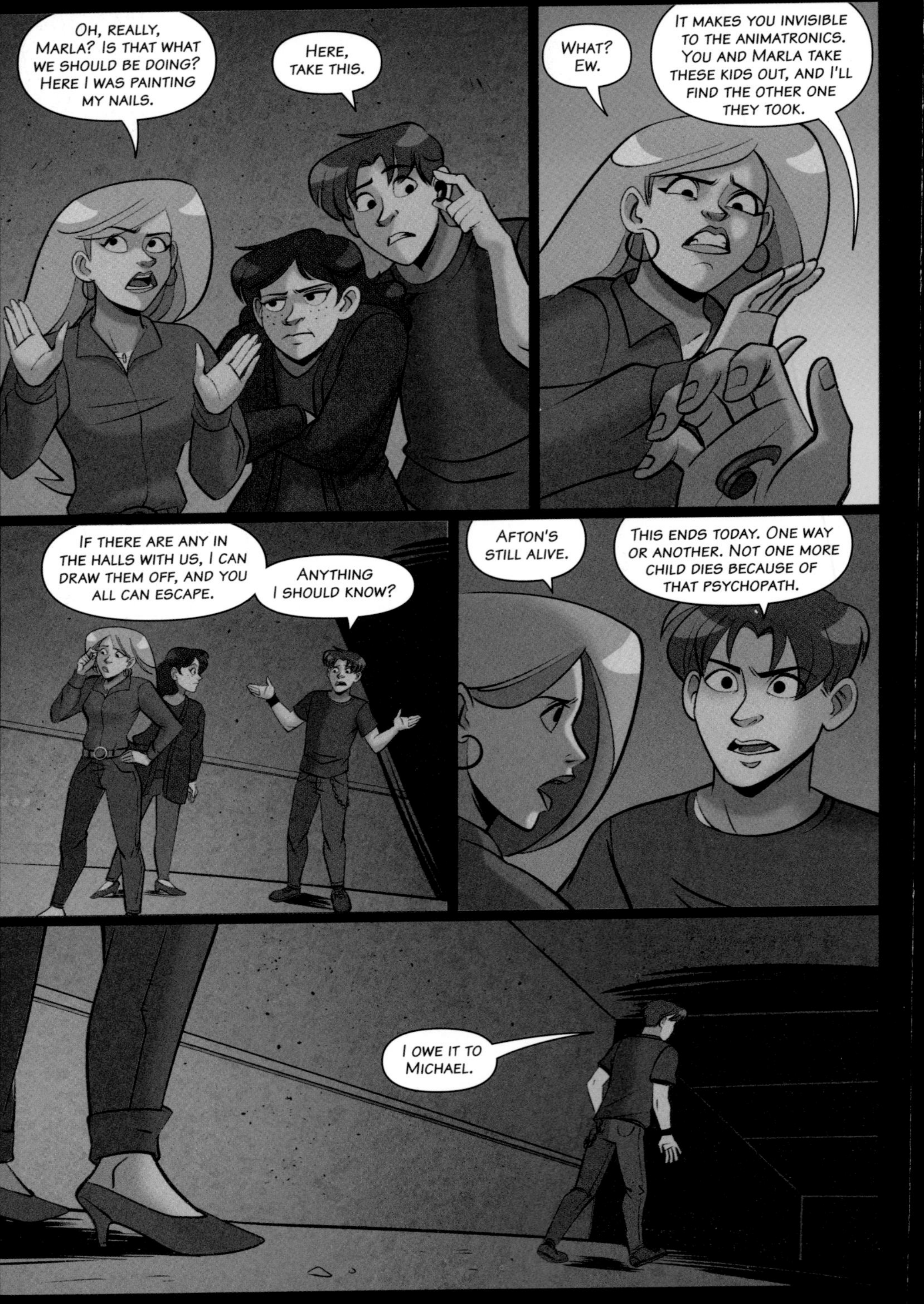

Oh, really, Marla? Is that what we should be doing? Here I was painting my nails.
Here, take this.
What? Ew.
It makes you invisible to the animatronics. You and Marla take these kids out, and I'll find the other one they took.
If there are any in the halls with us, I can draw them off, and you all can escape.
Anything I should know?
Afton's still alive.
This ends today. One way or another. Not one more child dies because of that psychopath.
I owe it to Michael.

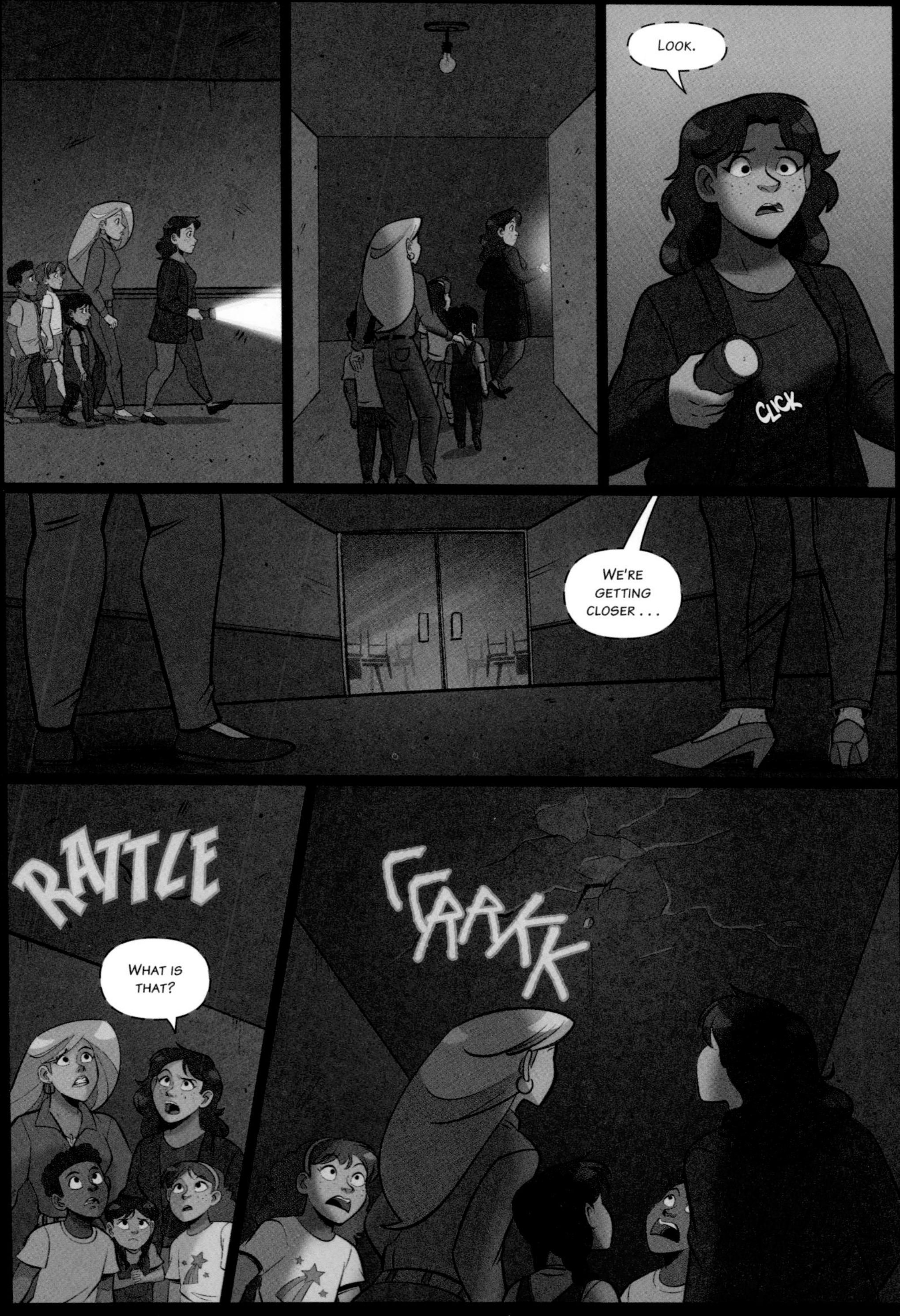
LOOK.
CLICK
WE'RE GETTING CLOSER . . .
RATTLE
WHAT IS THAT?
CRAKK

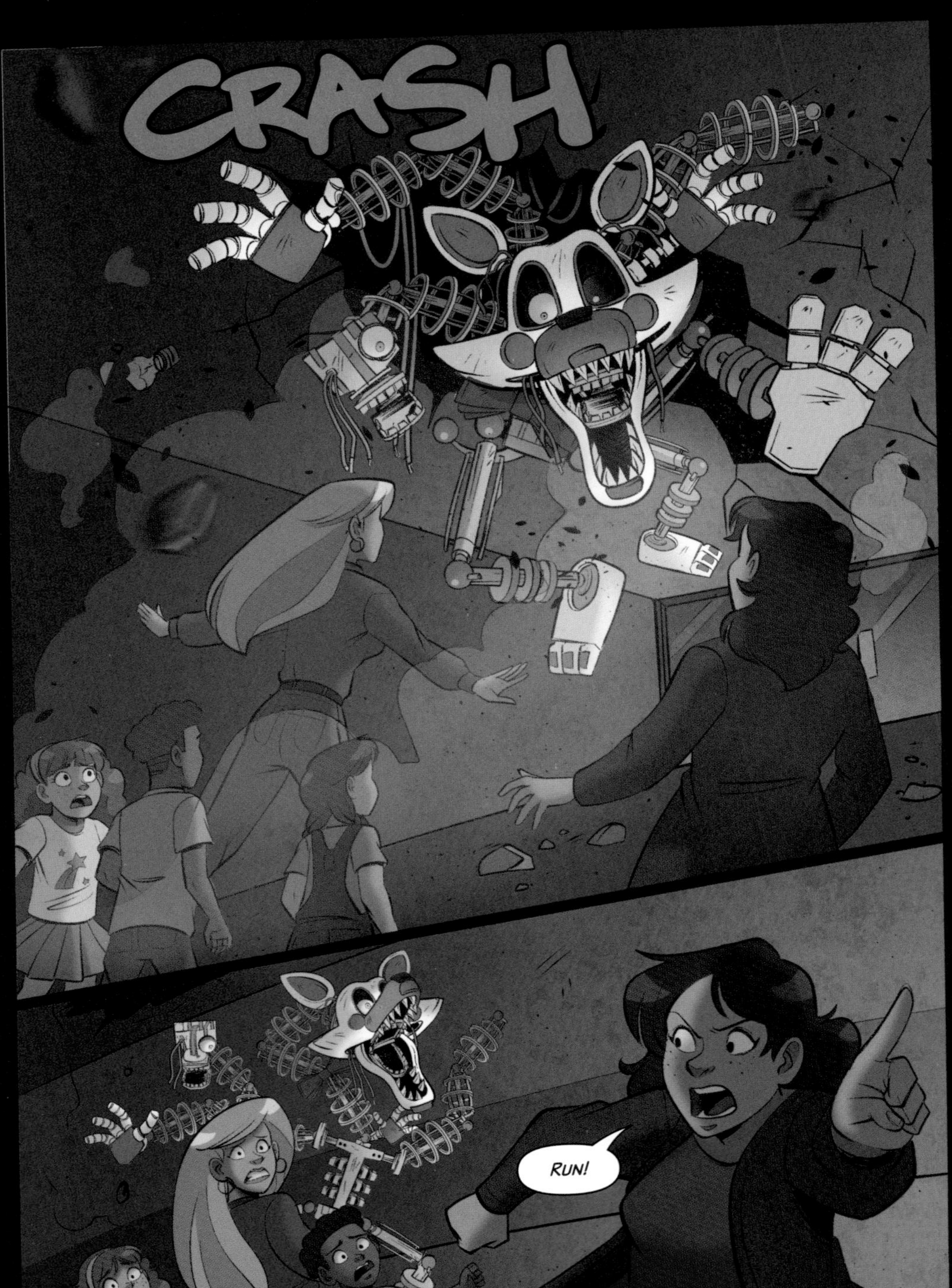
CRASH
RUN!

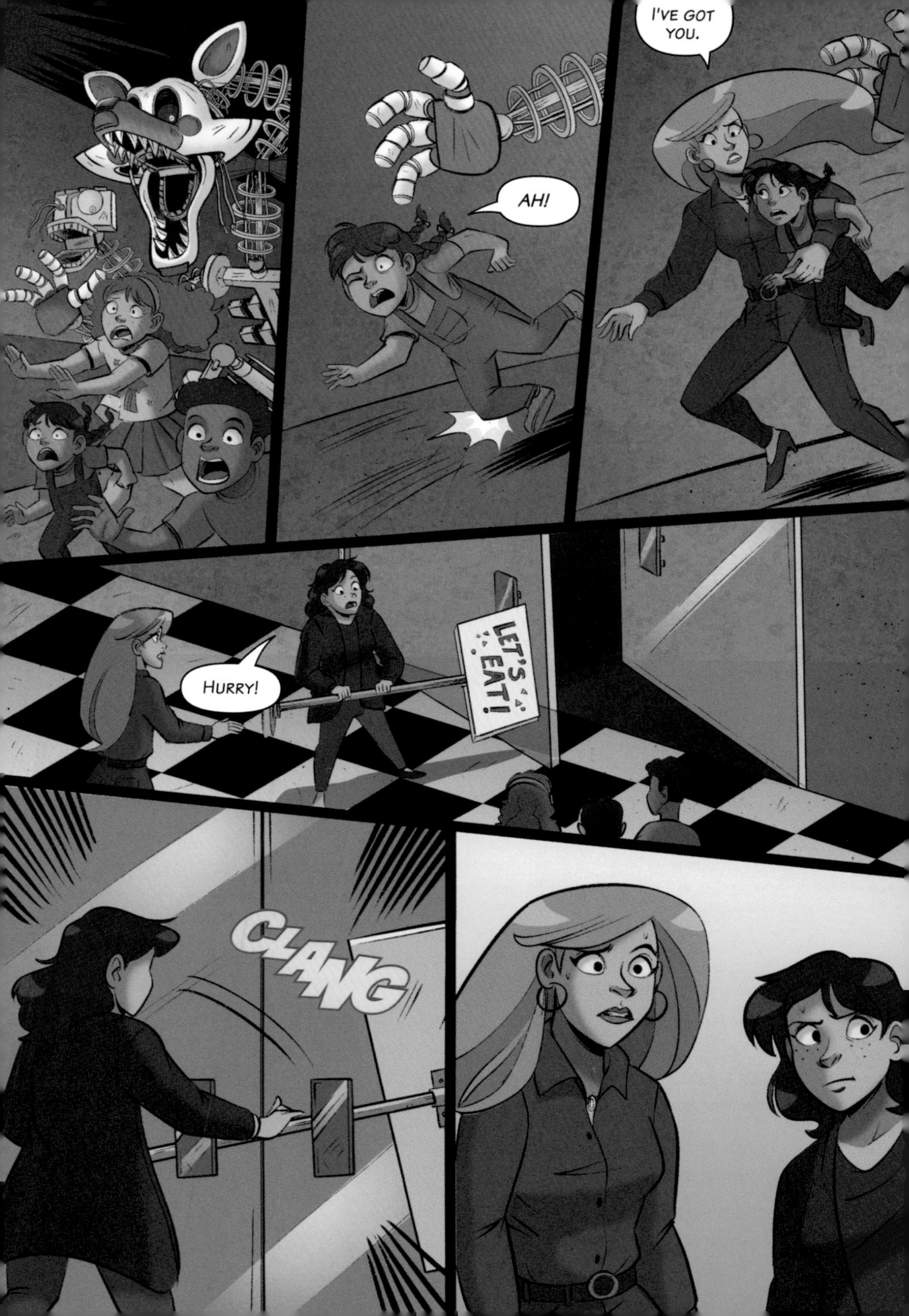
AH!
I'VE GOT YOU.
HURRY!
LET'S EAT!
CLANG

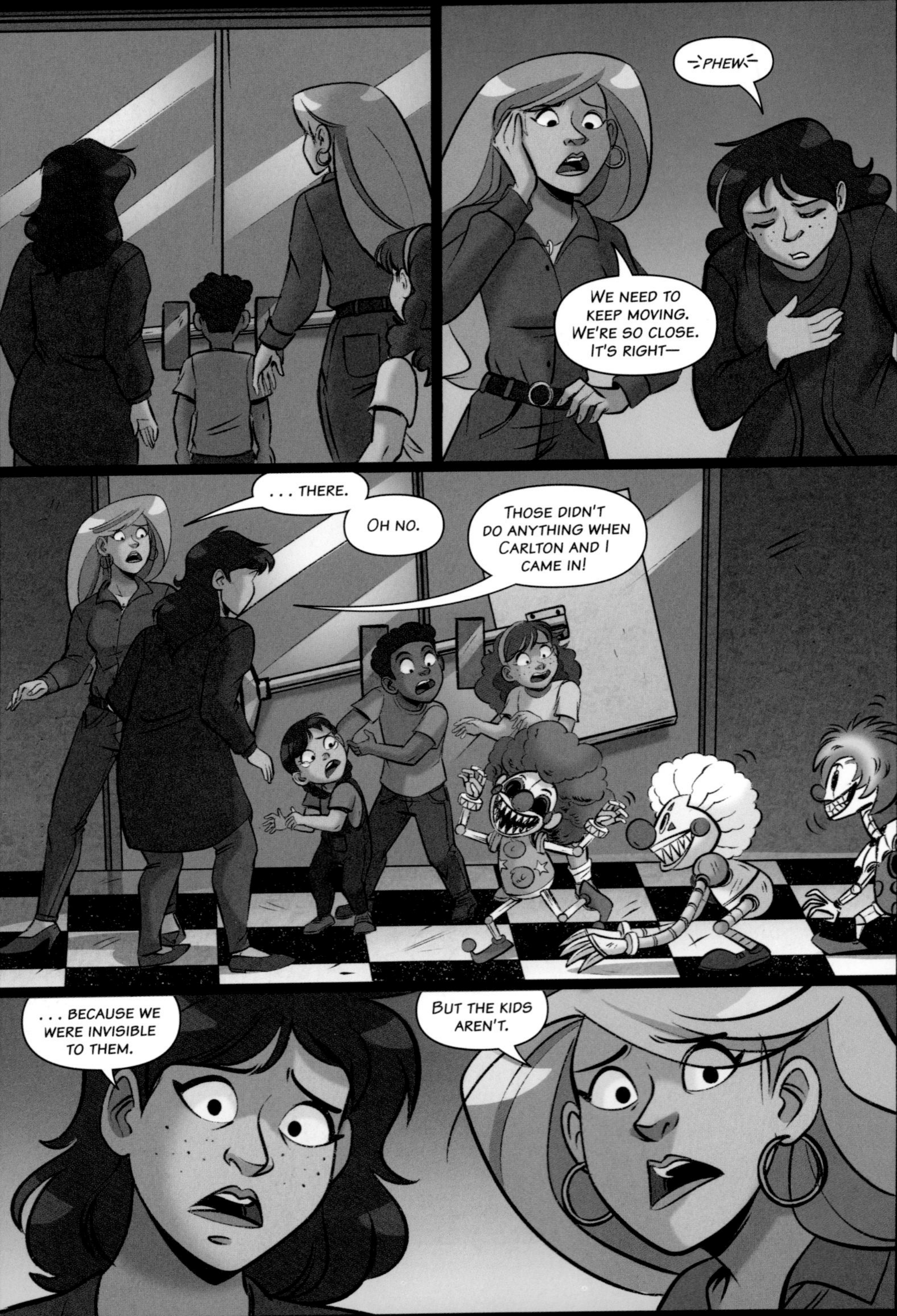

-PHEW-
WE NEED TO KEEP MOVING. WE'RE SO CLOSE. IT'S RIGHT—
. . . THERE.
OH NO.
THOSE DIDN'T DO ANYTHING WHEN CARLTON AND I CAME IN!
. . . BECAUSE WE WERE INVISIBLE TO THEM.
BUT THE KIDS AREN'T.

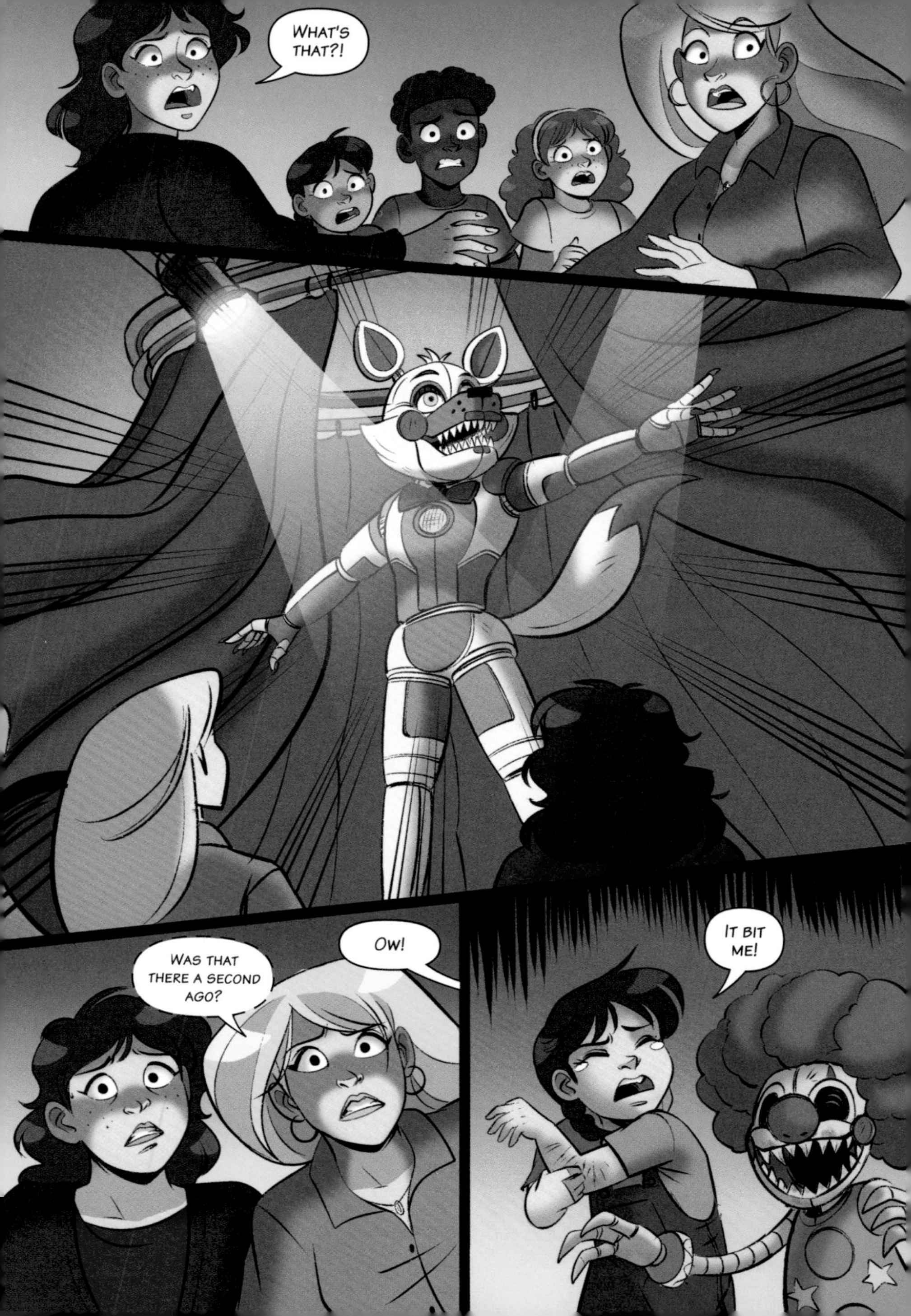
WHAT'S THAT?!
WAS THAT THERE A SECOND AGO?
OW!
IT BIT ME!

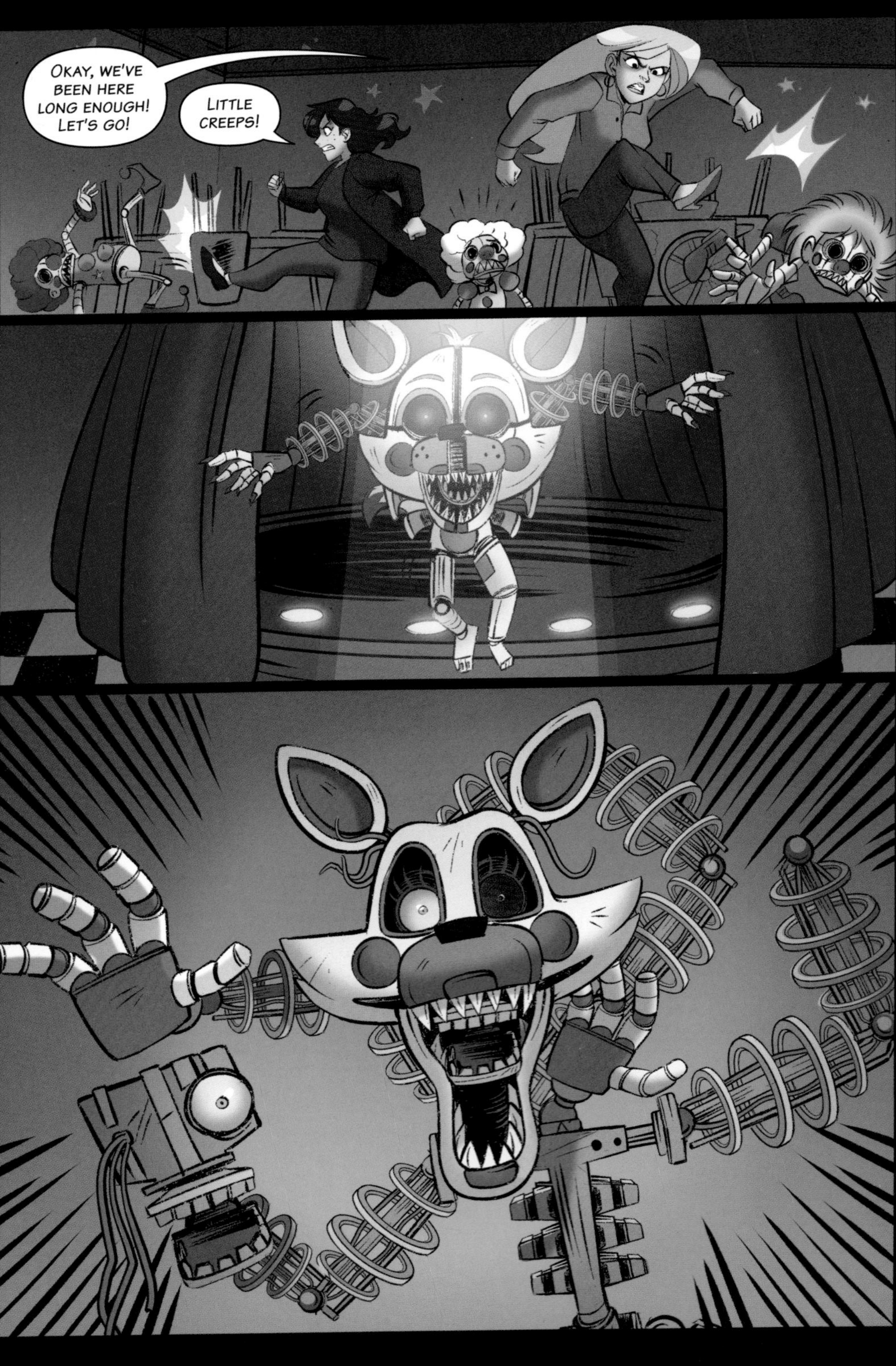
Okay, we've been here long enough! Let's go!
Little creeps!

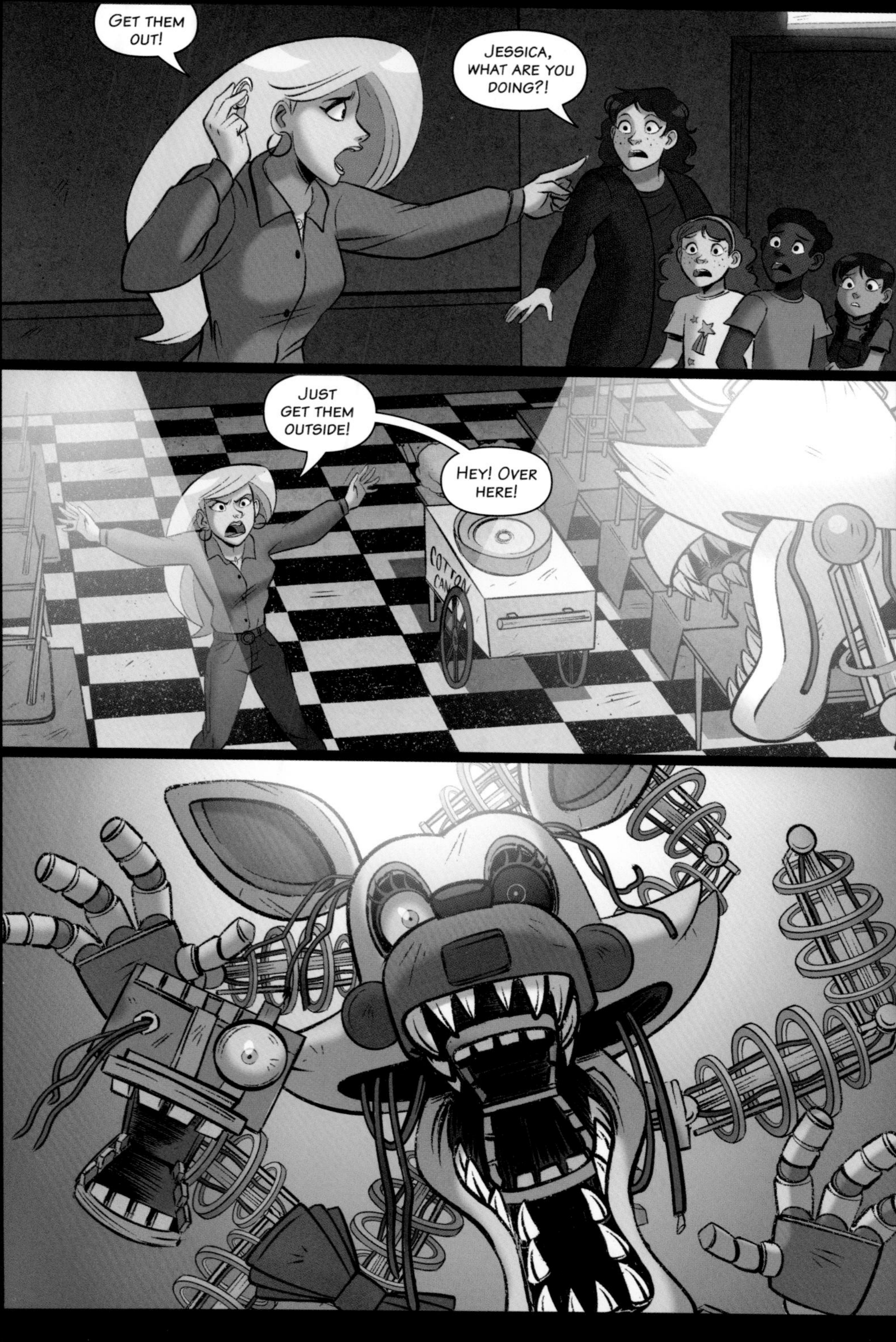
GET THEM OUT!
JESSICA, WHAT ARE YOU DOING?!
JUST GET THEM OUTSIDE!
HEY! OVER HERE!
COTTON CAN

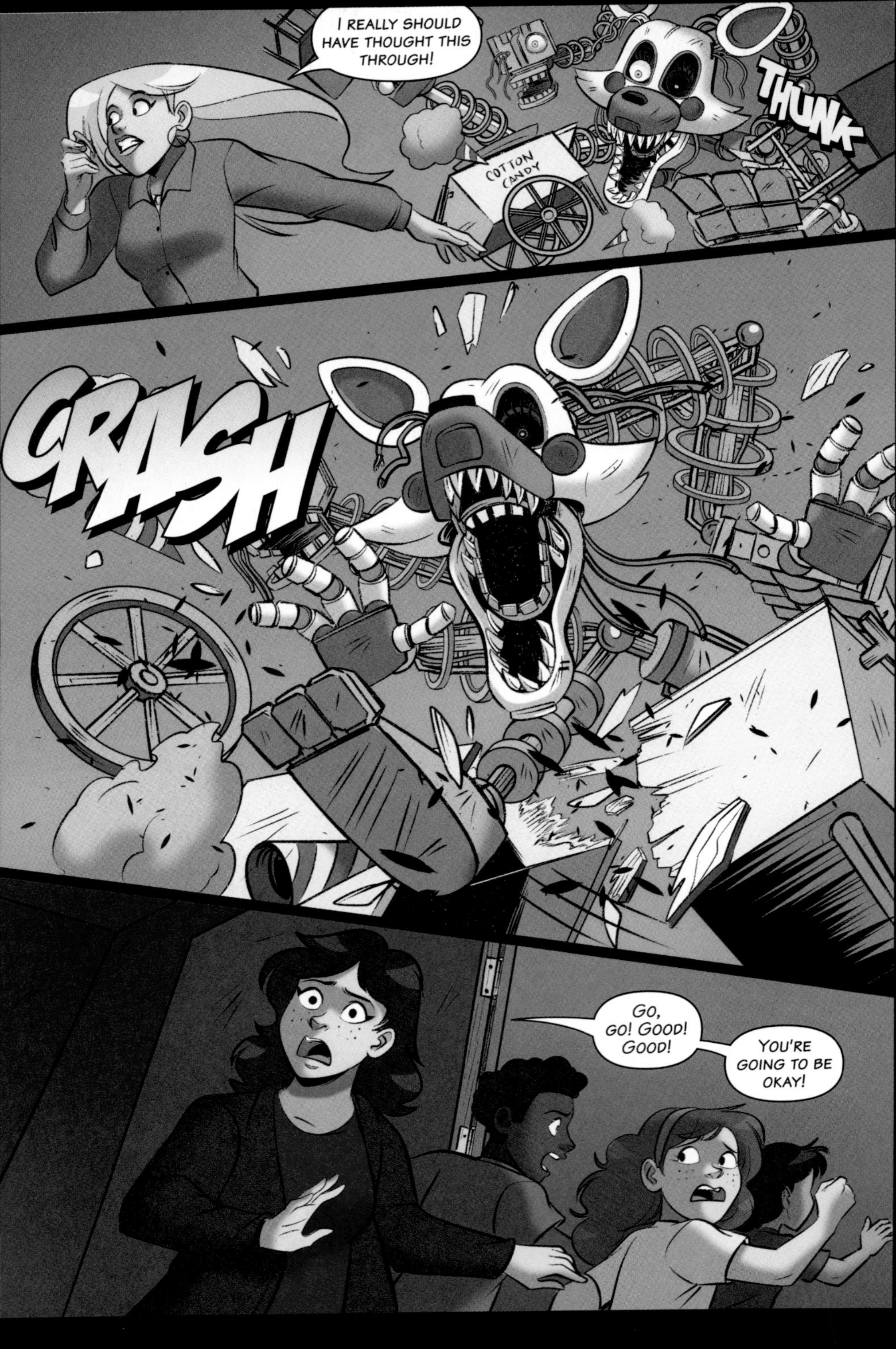
I REALLY SHOULD HAVE THOUGHT THIS THROUGH!
THUNK
COTTON CANDY
CRASH
GO, GO! GOOD! GOOD!
YOU'RE GOING TO BE OKAY!

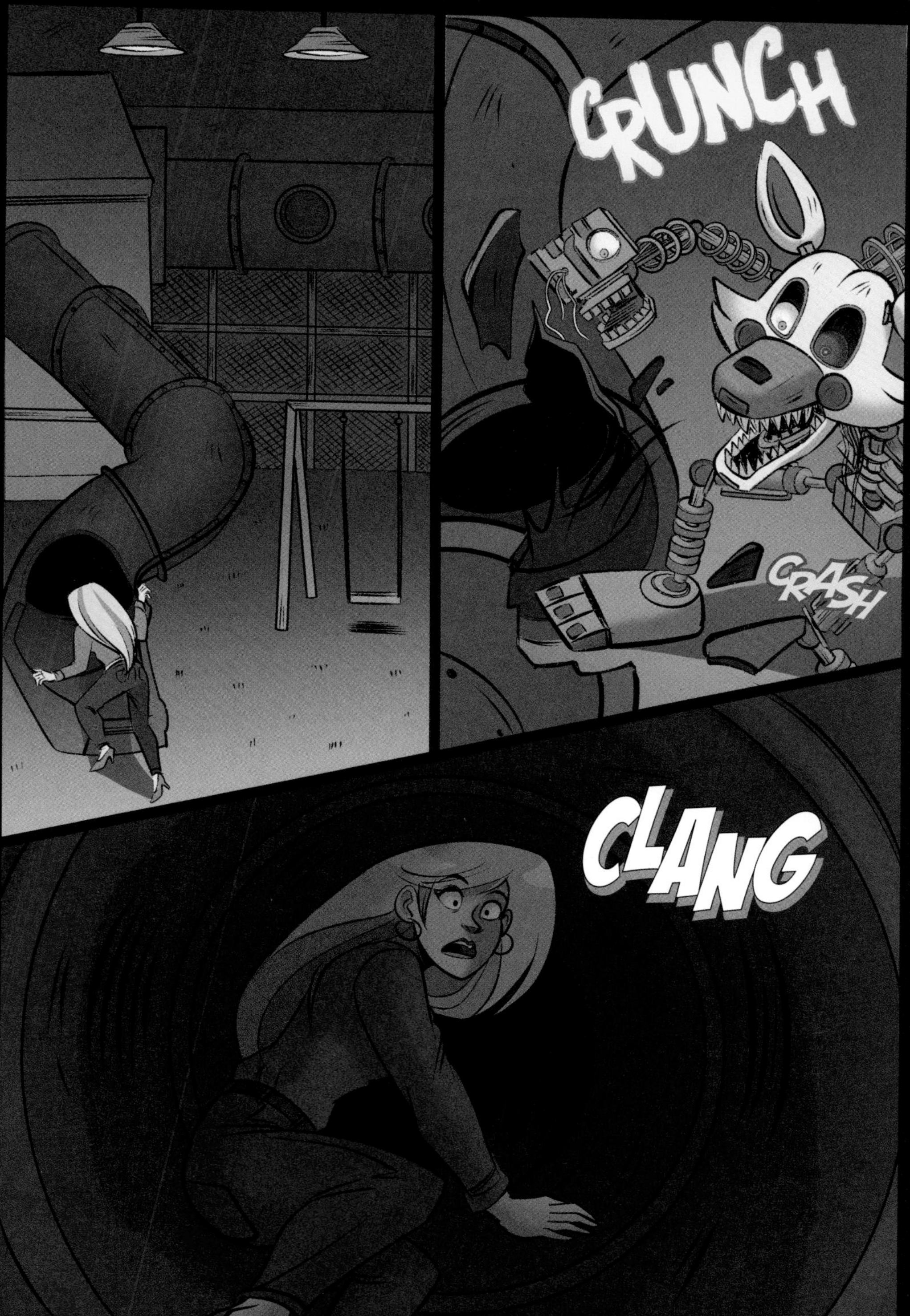
CRUNCH
CRASH
CLANG

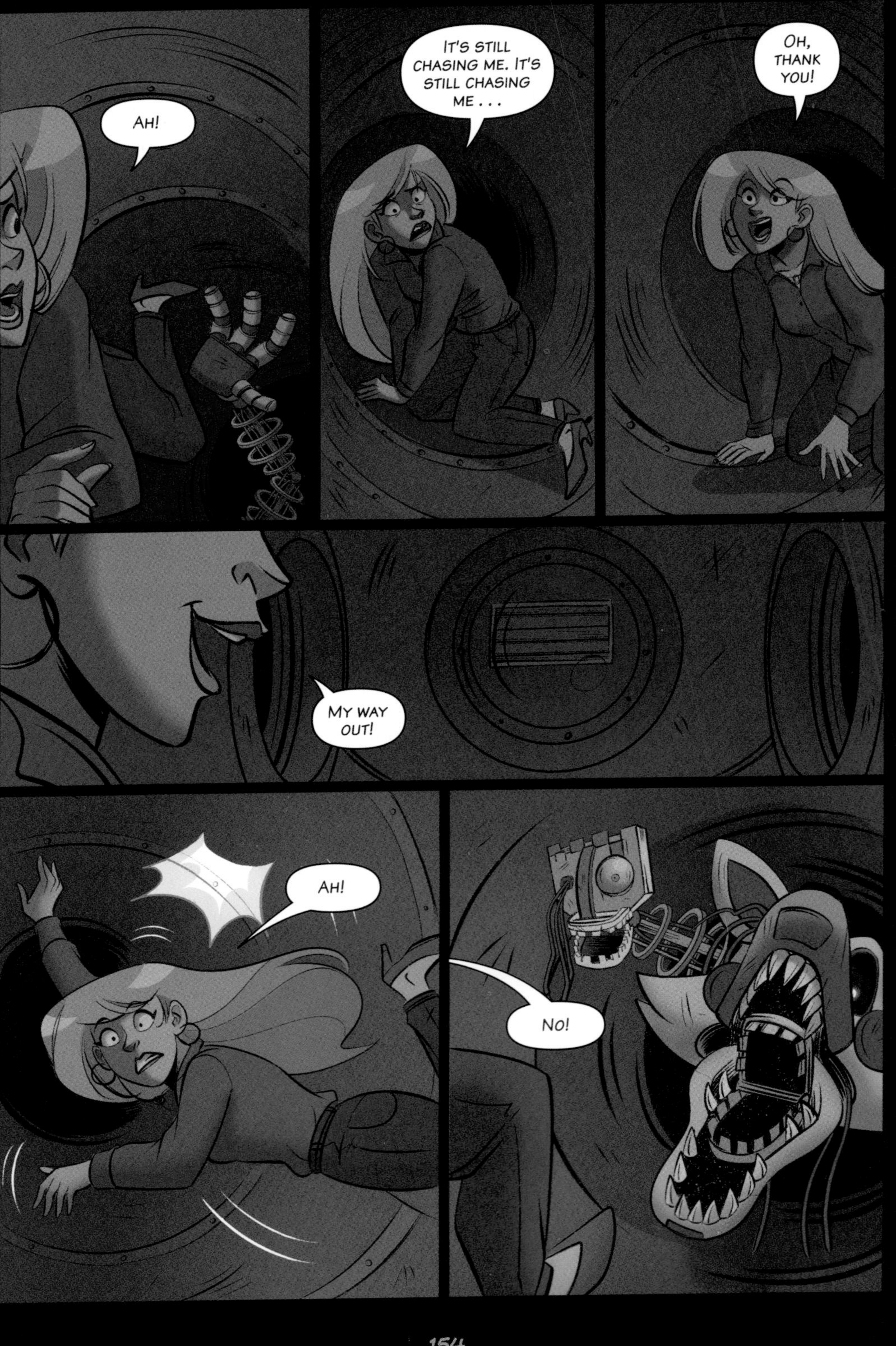
AH!
IT'S STILL CHASING ME. IT'S STILL CHASING ME . . .
OH, THANK YOU!
MY WAY OUT!
AH!
NO!

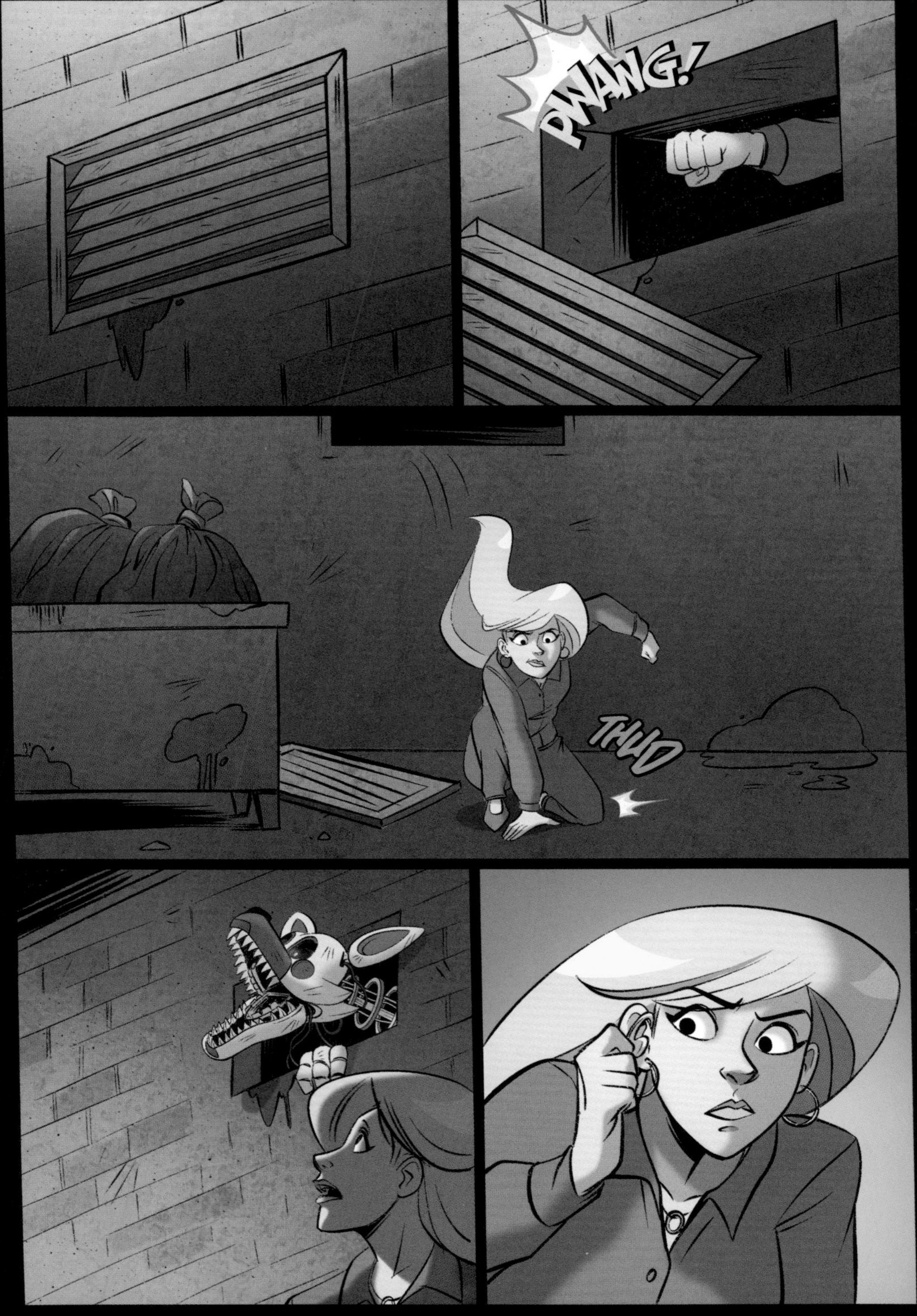
PWANG!
THUD

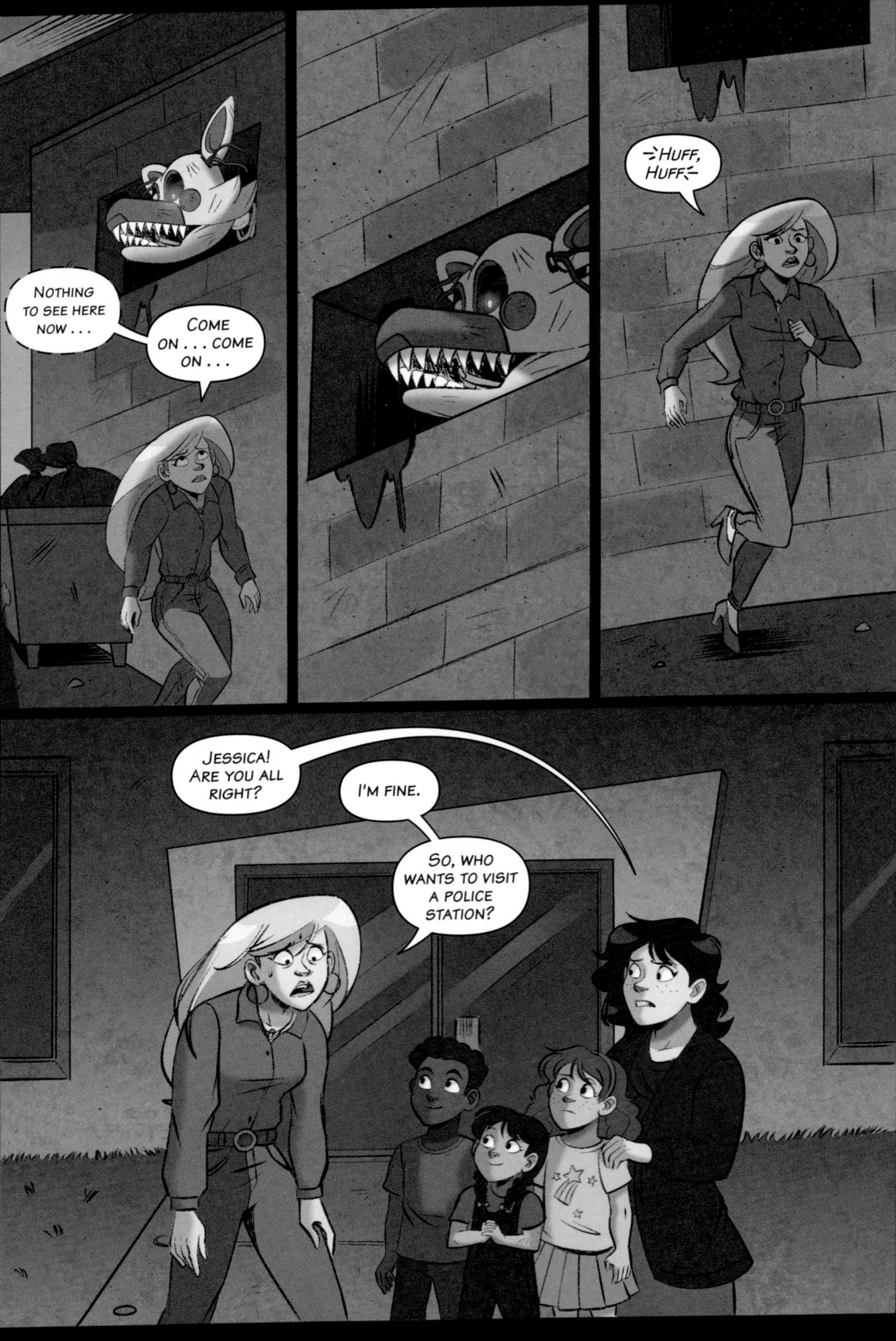
NOTHING TO SEE HERE NOW . . .
COME ON . . . COME ON . . .
HUFF, HUFF
JESSICA! ARE YOU ALL RIGHT?
I'M FINE.
SO, WHO WANTS TO VISIT A POLICE STATION?

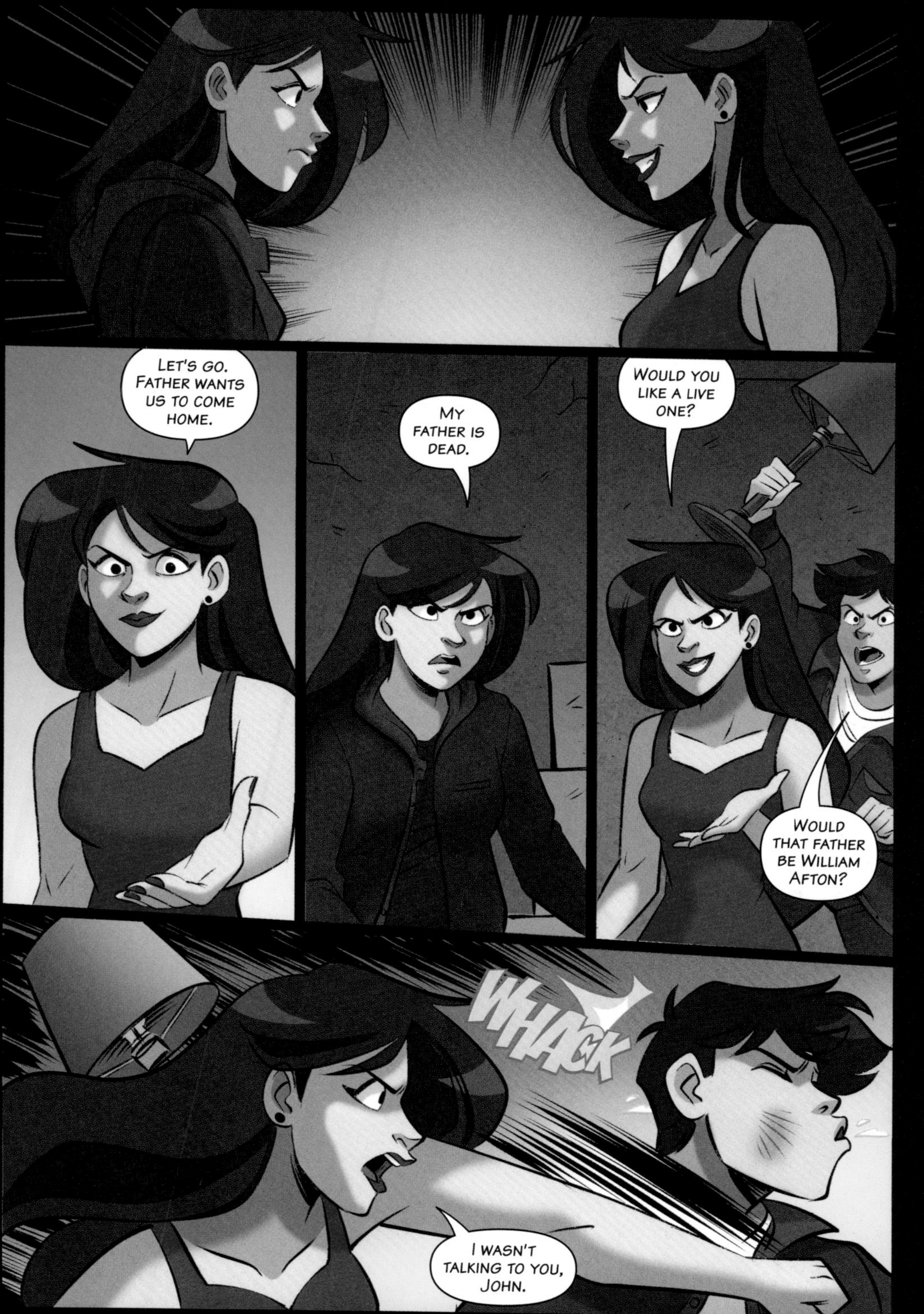

LET'S GO. FATHER WANTS US TO COME HOME.
MY FATHER IS DEAD.
WOULD YOU LIKE A LIVE ONE?
WOULD THAT FATHER BE WILLIAM AFTON?
WHACK
I WASN'T TALKING TO YOU, JOHN.

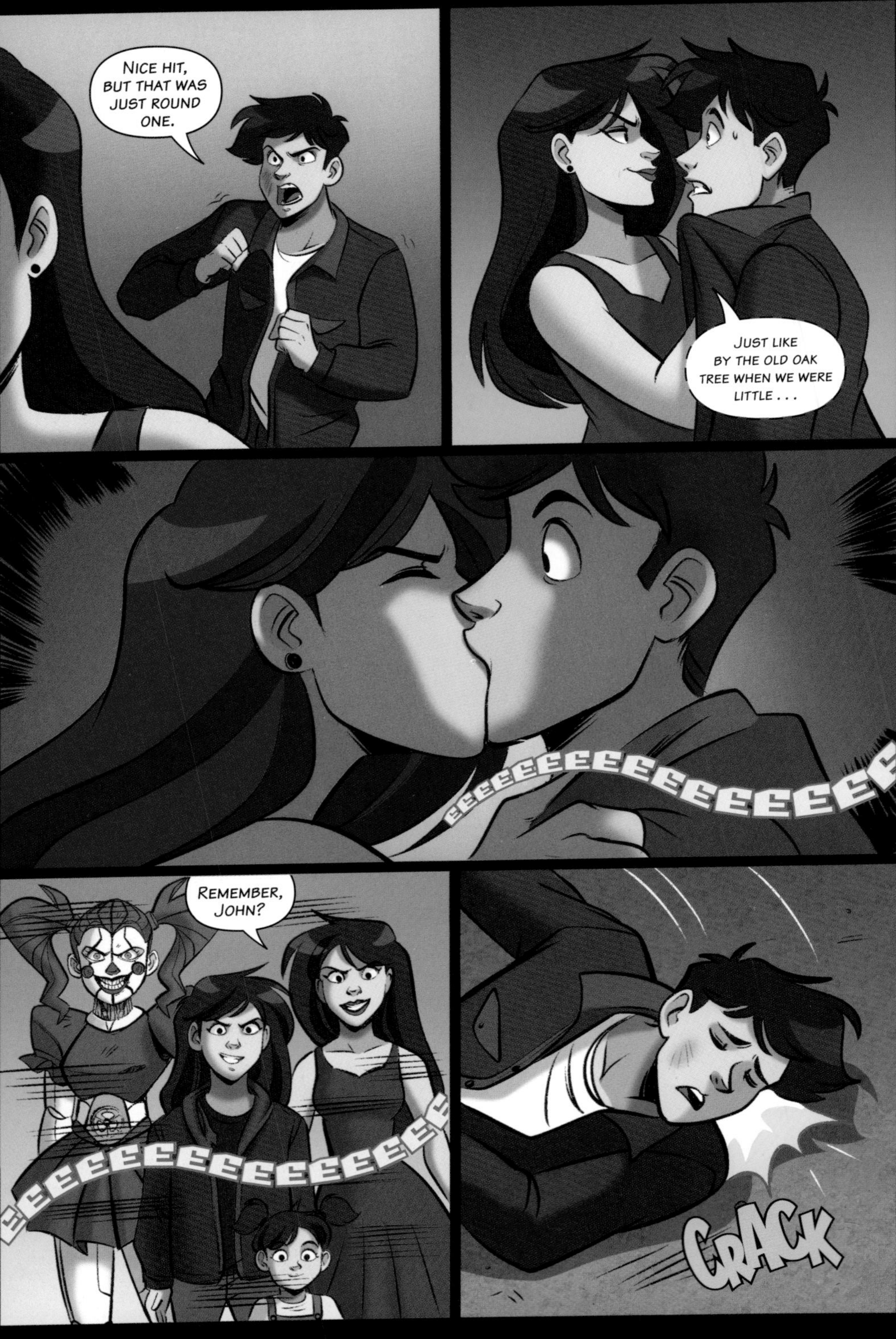
NICE HIT, BUT THAT WAS JUST ROUND ONE.
JUST LIKE BY THE OLD OAK TREE WHEN WE WERE LITTLE . . .
EEEEEEEEEEEEEEEEEEEE
REMEMBER, JOHN?
EEEEEEEEEEEEEEEEE
CRACK

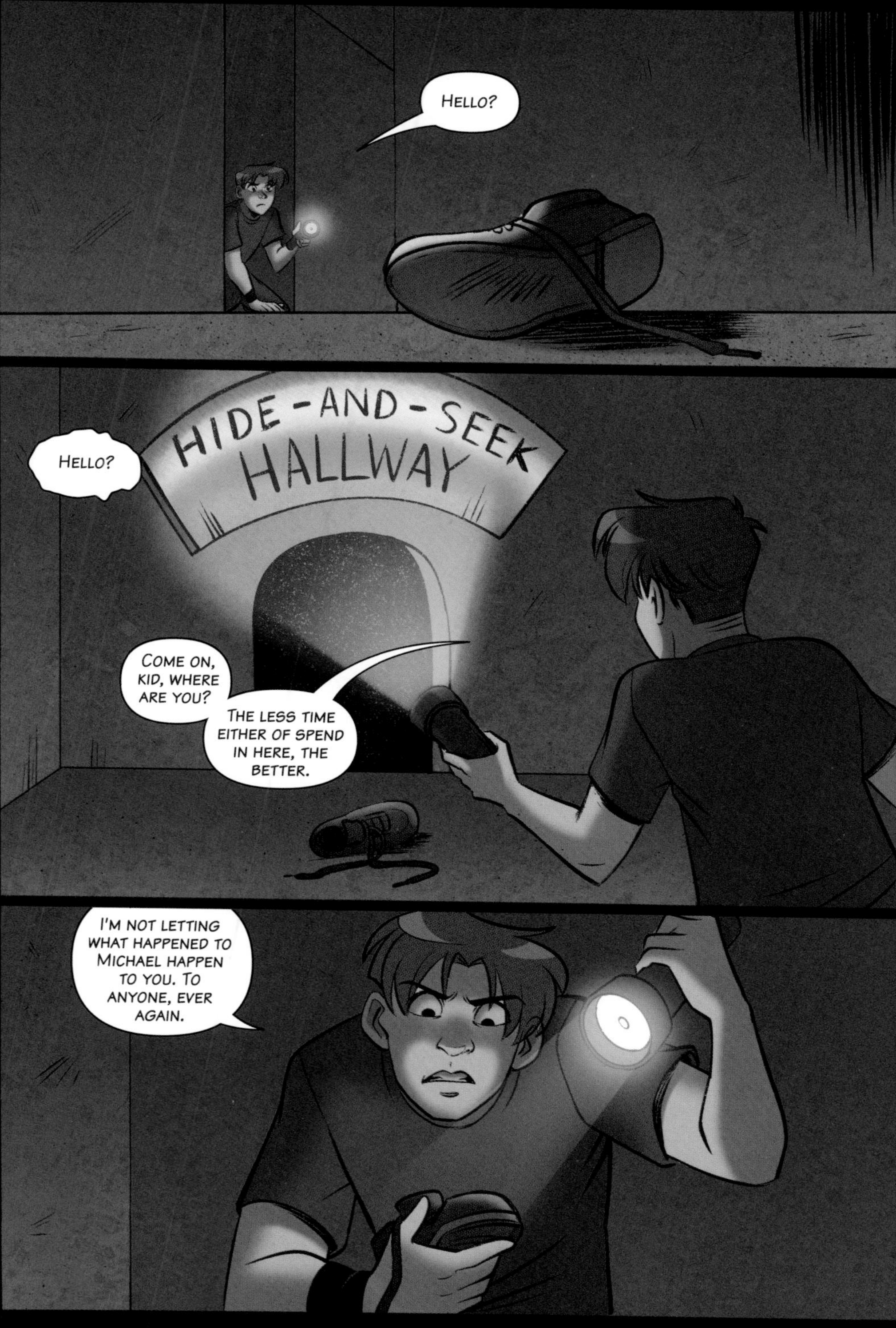
HELLO?
HIDE-AND-SEEK HALLWAY
HELLO?
COME ON, KID, WHERE ARE YOU?
THE LESS TIME EITHER OF SPEND IN HERE, THE BETTER.
I'M NOT LETTING WHAT HAPPENED TO MICHAEL HAPPEN TO YOU. TO ANYONE, EVER AGAIN.

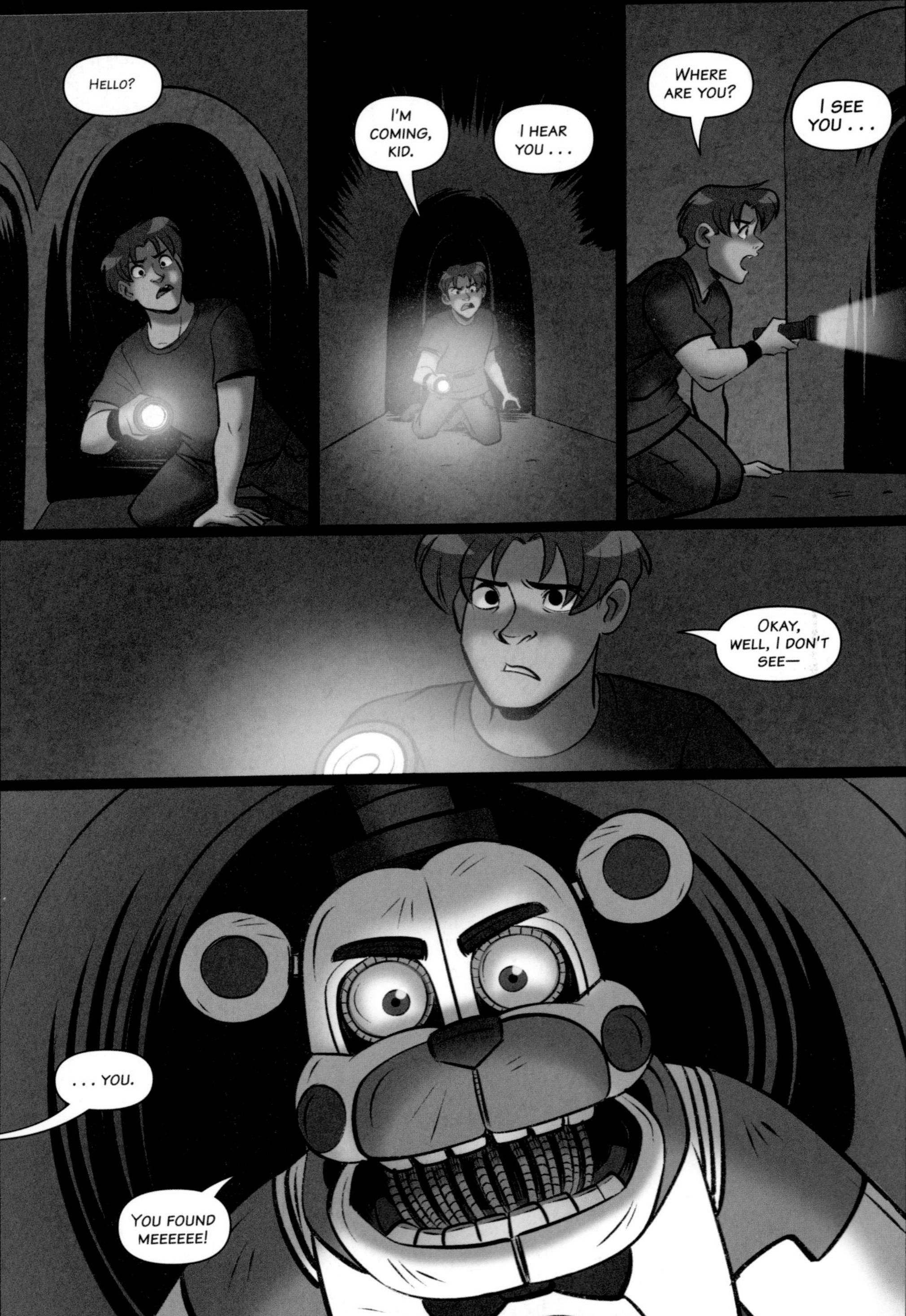
HELLO?
I'M COMING, KID.
I HEAR YOU . . .
WHERE ARE YOU?
I SEE YOU . . .
OKAY, WELL, I DON'T SEE—
. . . YOU.
YOU FOUND MEEEEEE!

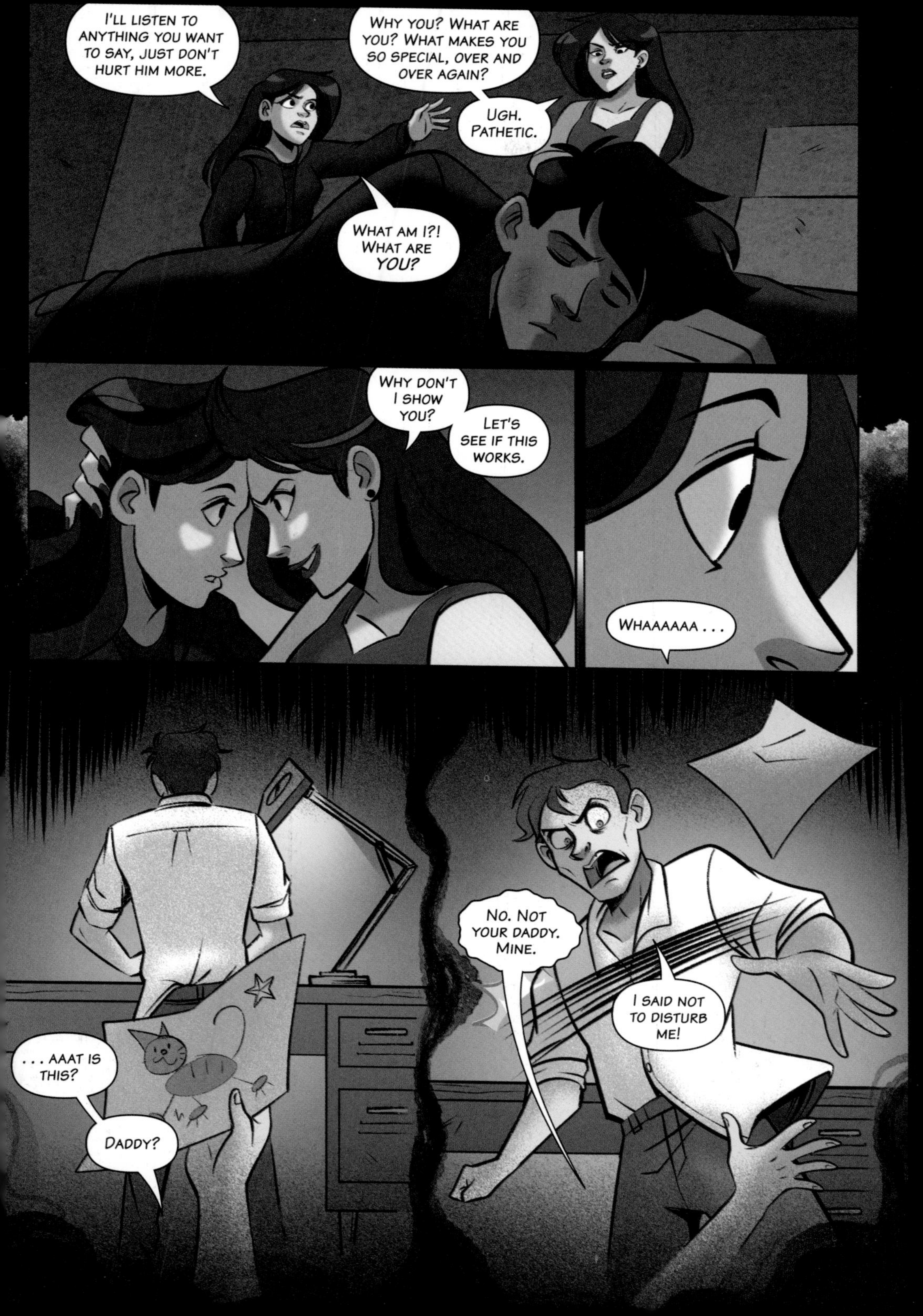

I'LL LISTEN TO ANYTHING YOU WANT TO SAY, JUST DON'T HURT HIM MORE.
WHY YOU? WHAT ARE YOU? WHAT MAKES YOU SO SPECIAL, OVER AND OVER AGAIN?
UGH. PATHETIC.
WHAT AM I?! WHAT ARE YOU?
WHY DON'T I SHOW YOU?
LET'S SEE IF THIS WORKS.
WHAAAAAA . . .
. . . AAAT IS THIS?
DADDY?
NO. NOT YOUR DADDY. MINE.
I SAID NOT TO DISTURB ME!

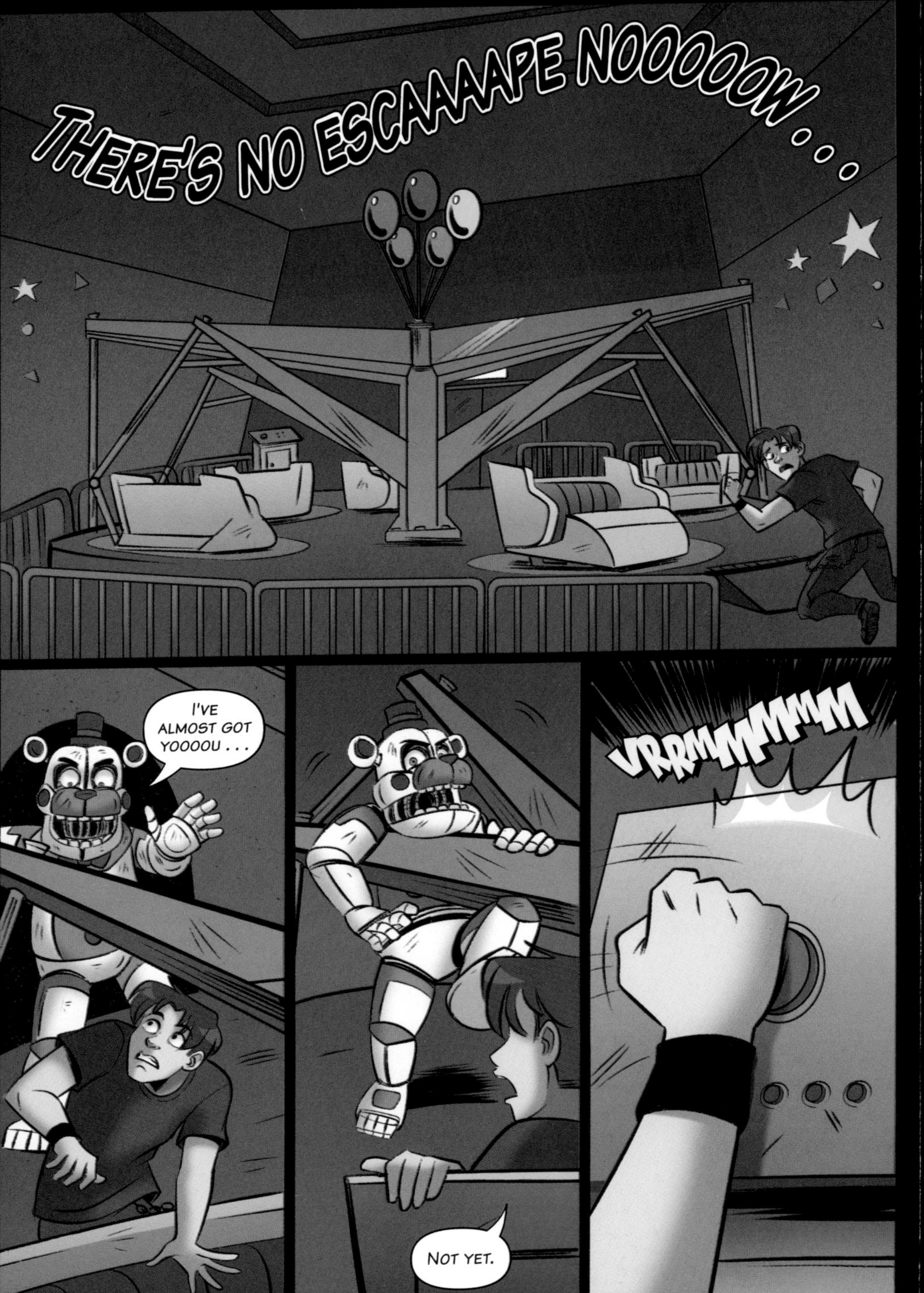
THERE'S NO ESCAAAAPE NOOOOOW . . .
I'VE ALMOST GOT YOOOOU . . .
NOT YET.
VRRMMMMMM

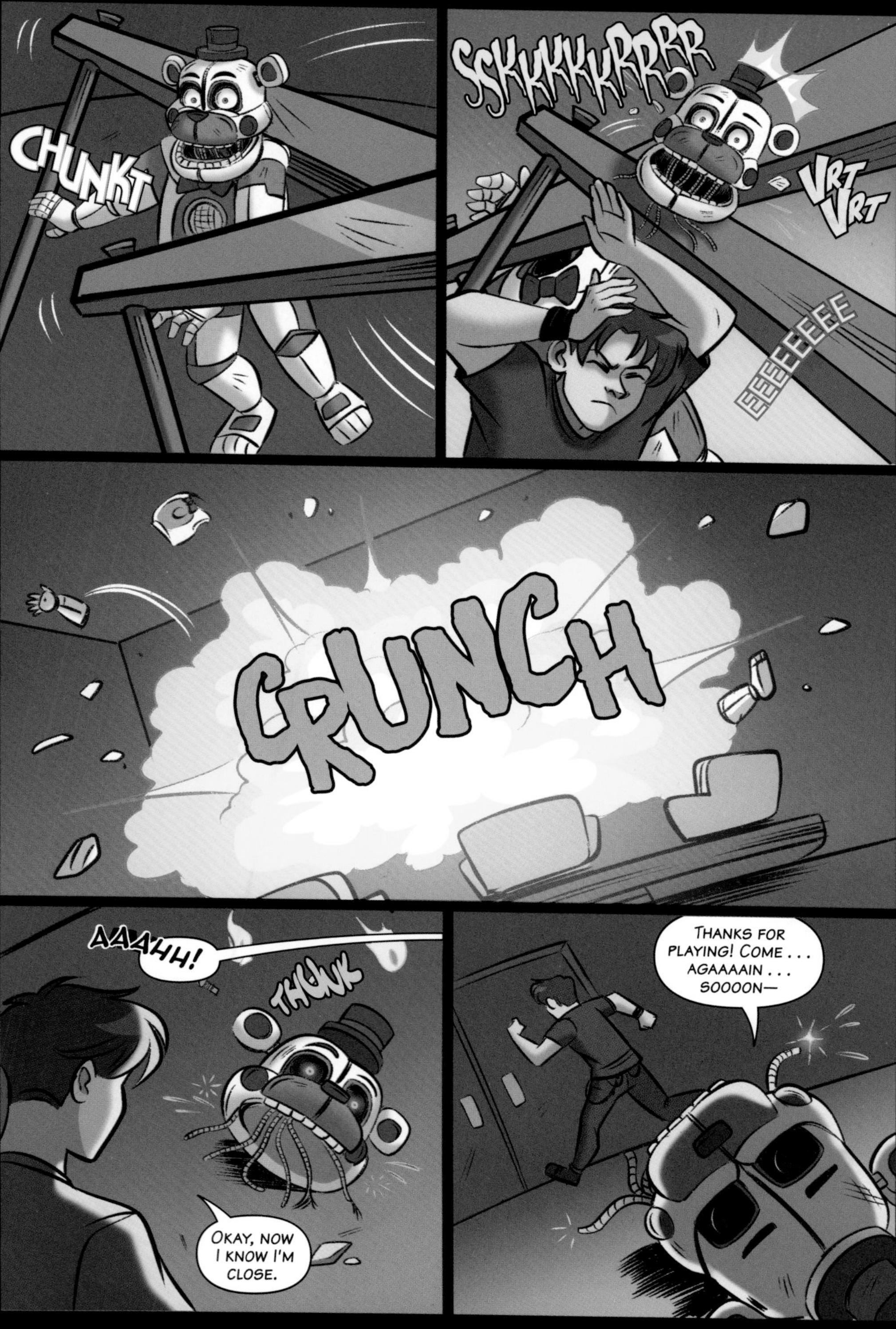
CHUNKT
SSKKKKKRRRR
VRT VRT
EEEEEEEE
CRUNCH
AAAHH!
THUNK
OKAY, NOW I KNOW I'M CLOSE.
THANKS FOR PLAYING! COME . . . AGAAAAIN . . . SOOOON—

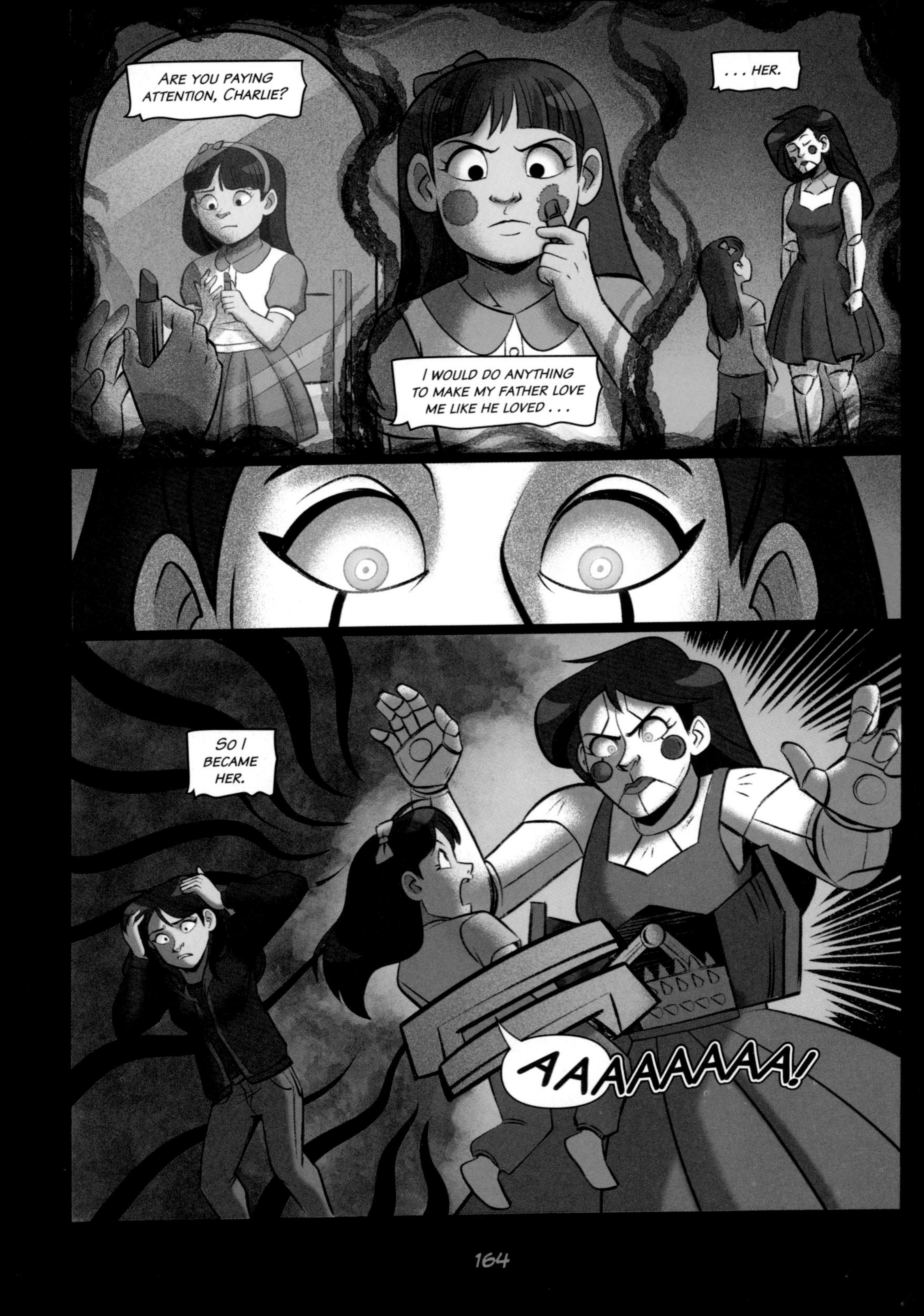
ARE YOU PAYING ATTENTION, CHARLIE?
I WOULD DO ANYTHING TO MAKE MY FATHER LOVE ME LIKE HE LOVED . . .
. . . HER.
SO I BECAME HER.
AAAAAAAA!

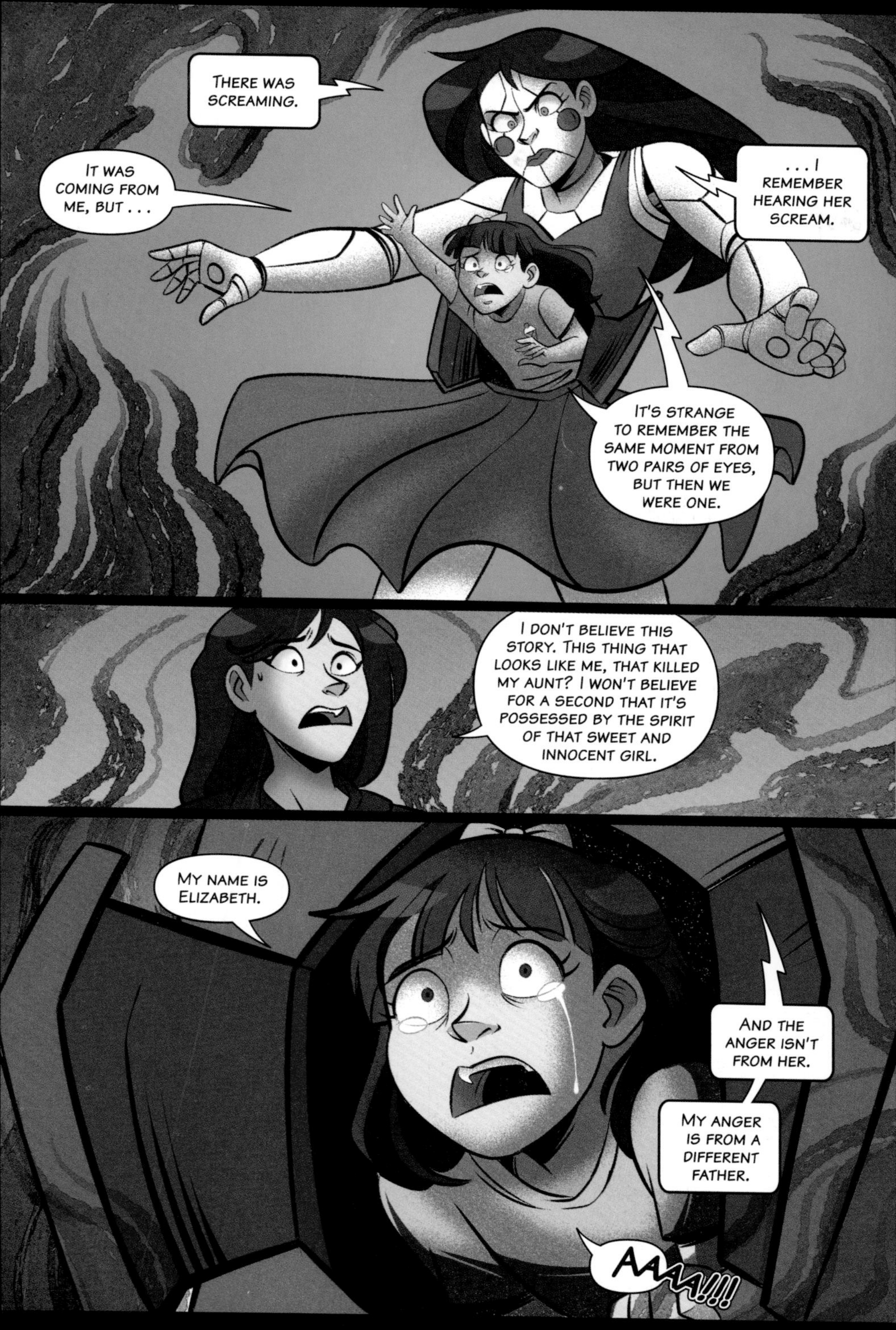
THERE WAS SCREAMING.
IT WAS COMING FROM ME, BUT . . .
. . . I REMEMBER HEARING HER SCREAM.
IT'S STRANGE TO REMEMBER THE SAME MOMENT FROM TWO PAIRS OF EYES, BUT THEN WE WERE ONE.
I DON'T BELIEVE THIS STORY. THIS THING THAT LOOKS LIKE ME, THAT KILLED MY AUNT? I WON'T BELIEVE FOR A SECOND THAT IT'S POSSESSED BY THE SPIRIT OF THAT SWEET AND INNOCENT GIRL.
MY NAME IS ELIZABETH.
AND THE ANGER ISN'T FROM HER.
MY ANGER IS FROM A DIFFERENT FATHER.
AAAA!!!

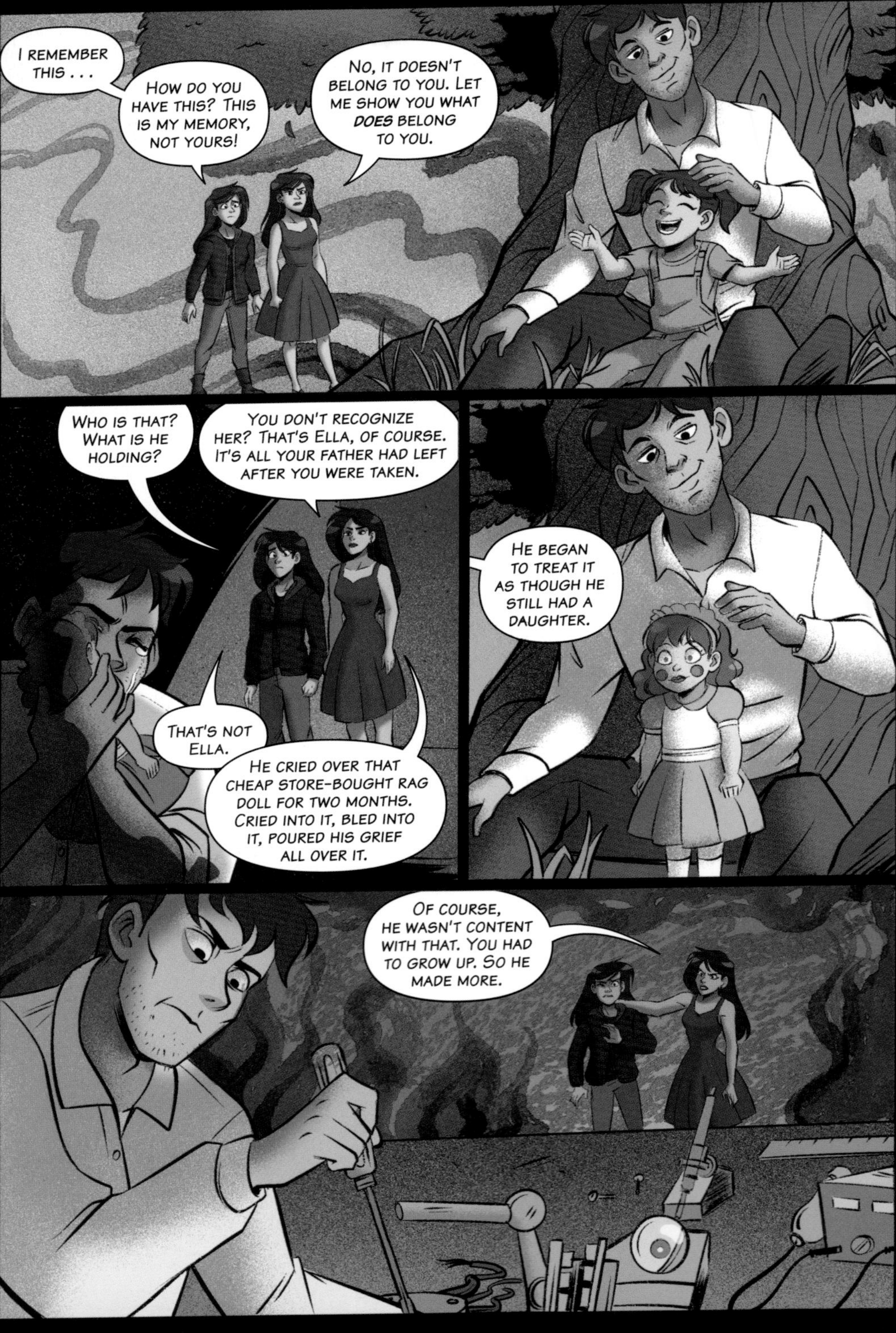
I REMEMBER THIS . . .
HOW DO YOU HAVE THIS? THIS IS MY MEMORY, NOT YOURS!
NO, IT DOESN'T BELONG TO YOU. LET ME SHOW YOU WHAT *DOES* BELONG TO YOU.
WHO IS THAT? WHAT IS HE HOLDING?
YOU DON'T RECOGNIZE HER? THAT'S ELLA, OF COURSE. IT'S ALL YOUR FATHER HAD LEFT AFTER YOU WERE TAKEN.
THAT'S NOT ELLA.
HE CRIED OVER THAT CHEAP STORE-BOUGHT RAG DOLL FOR TWO MONTHS. CRIED INTO IT, BLED INTO IT, POURED HIS GRIEF ALL OVER IT.
HE BEGAN TO TREAT IT AS THOUGH HE STILL HAD A DAUGHTER.
OF COURSE, HE WASN'T CONTENT WITH THAT. YOU HAD TO GROW UP. SO HE MADE MORE.

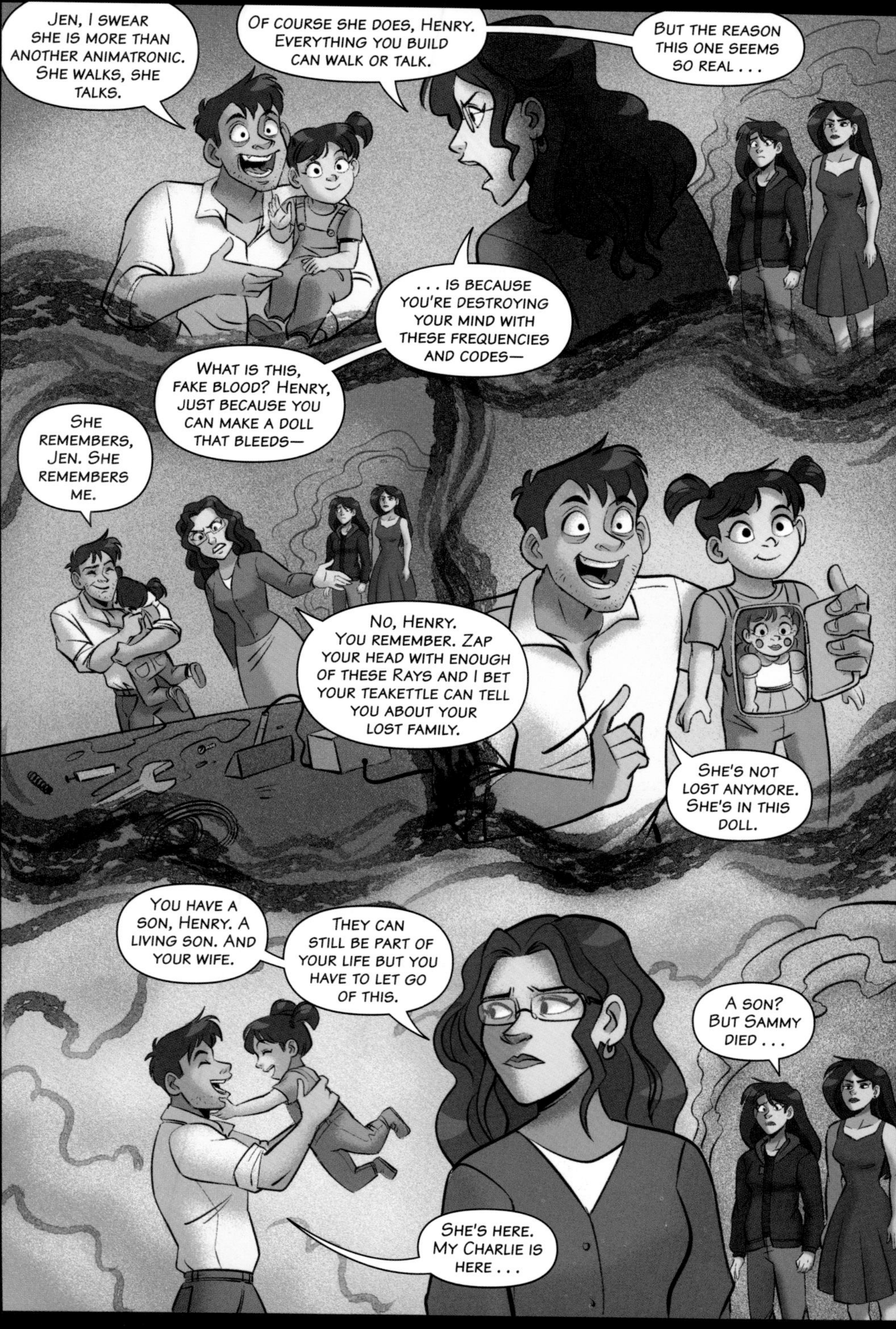
JEN, I SWEAR SHE IS MORE THAN ANOTHER ANIMATRONIC. SHE WALKS, SHE TALKS.
OF COURSE SHE DOES, HENRY. EVERYTHING YOU BUILD CAN WALK OR TALK.
BUT THE REASON THIS ONE SEEMS SO REAL . . .
. . . IS BECAUSE YOU'RE DESTROYING YOUR MIND WITH THESE FREQUENCIES AND CODES—
WHAT IS THIS, FAKE BLOOD? HENRY, JUST BECAUSE YOU CAN MAKE A DOLL THAT BLEEDS—
SHE REMEMBERS, JEN. SHE REMEMBERS ME.
NO, HENRY. YOU REMEMBER. ZAP YOUR HEAD WITH ENOUGH OF THESE RAYS AND I BET YOUR TEAKETTLE CAN TELL YOU ABOUT YOUR LOST FAMILY.
SHE'S NOT LOST ANYMORE. SHE'S IN THIS DOLL.
YOU HAVE A SON, HENRY. A LIVING SON. AND YOUR WIFE.
THEY CAN STILL BE PART OF YOUR LIFE BUT YOU HAVE TO LET GO OF THIS.
A SON? BUT SAMMY DIED . . .
SHE'S HERE. MY CHARLIE IS HERE . . .

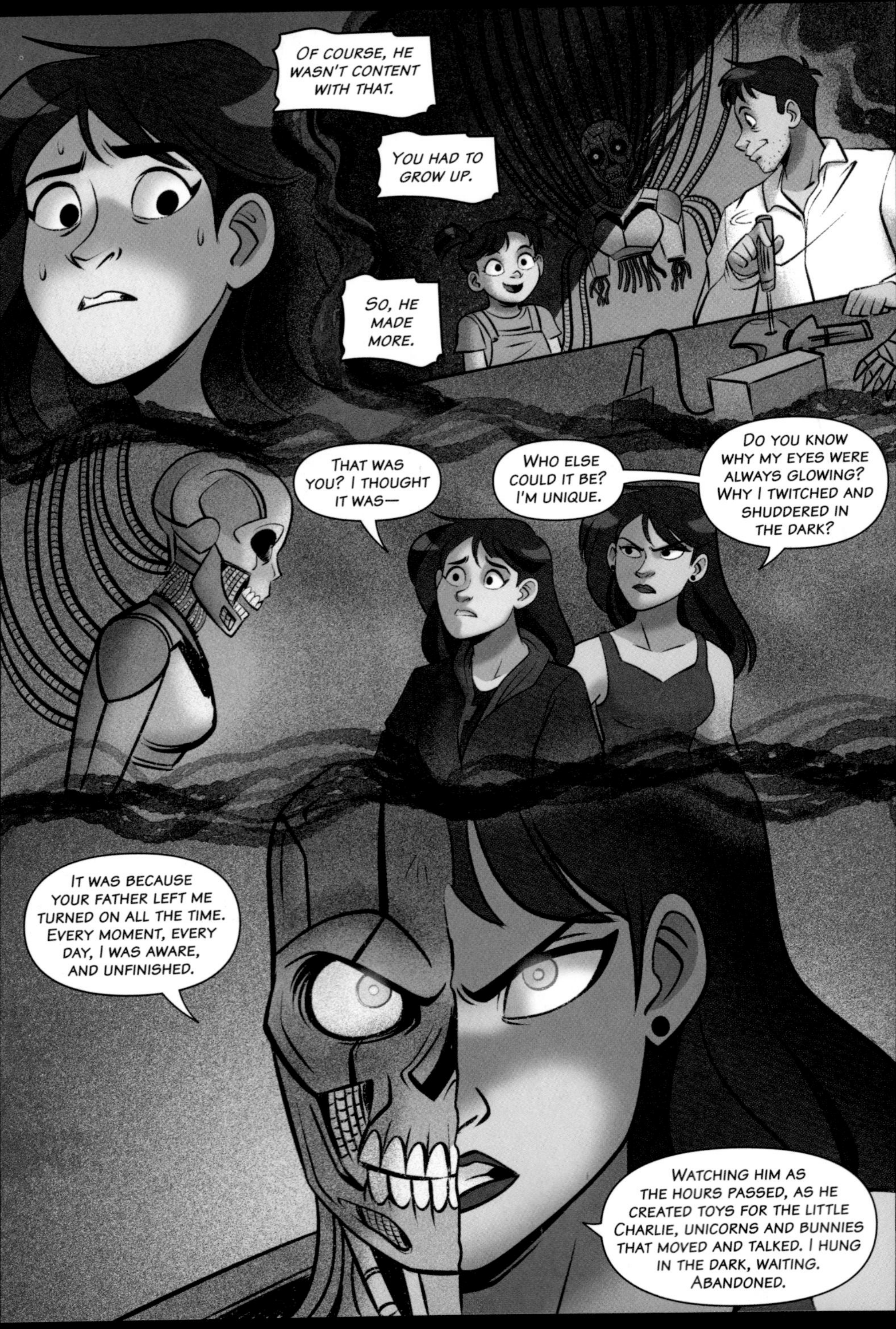

OF COURSE, HE WASN'T CONTENT WITH THAT.
YOU HAD TO GROW UP.
SO, HE MADE MORE.
THAT WAS YOU? I THOUGHT IT WAS—
WHO ELSE COULD IT BE? I'M UNIQUE.
DO YOU KNOW WHY MY EYES WERE ALWAYS GLOWING? WHY I TWITCHED AND SHUDDERED IN THE DARK?
IT WAS BECAUSE YOUR FATHER LEFT ME TURNED ON ALL THE TIME. EVERY MOMENT, EVERY DAY, I WAS AWARE, AND UNFINISHED.
WATCHING HIM AS THE HOURS PASSED, AS HE CREATED TOYS FOR THE LITTLE CHARLIE, UNICORNS AND BUNNIES THAT MOVED AND TALKED. I HUNG IN THE DARK, WAITING. ABANDONED.

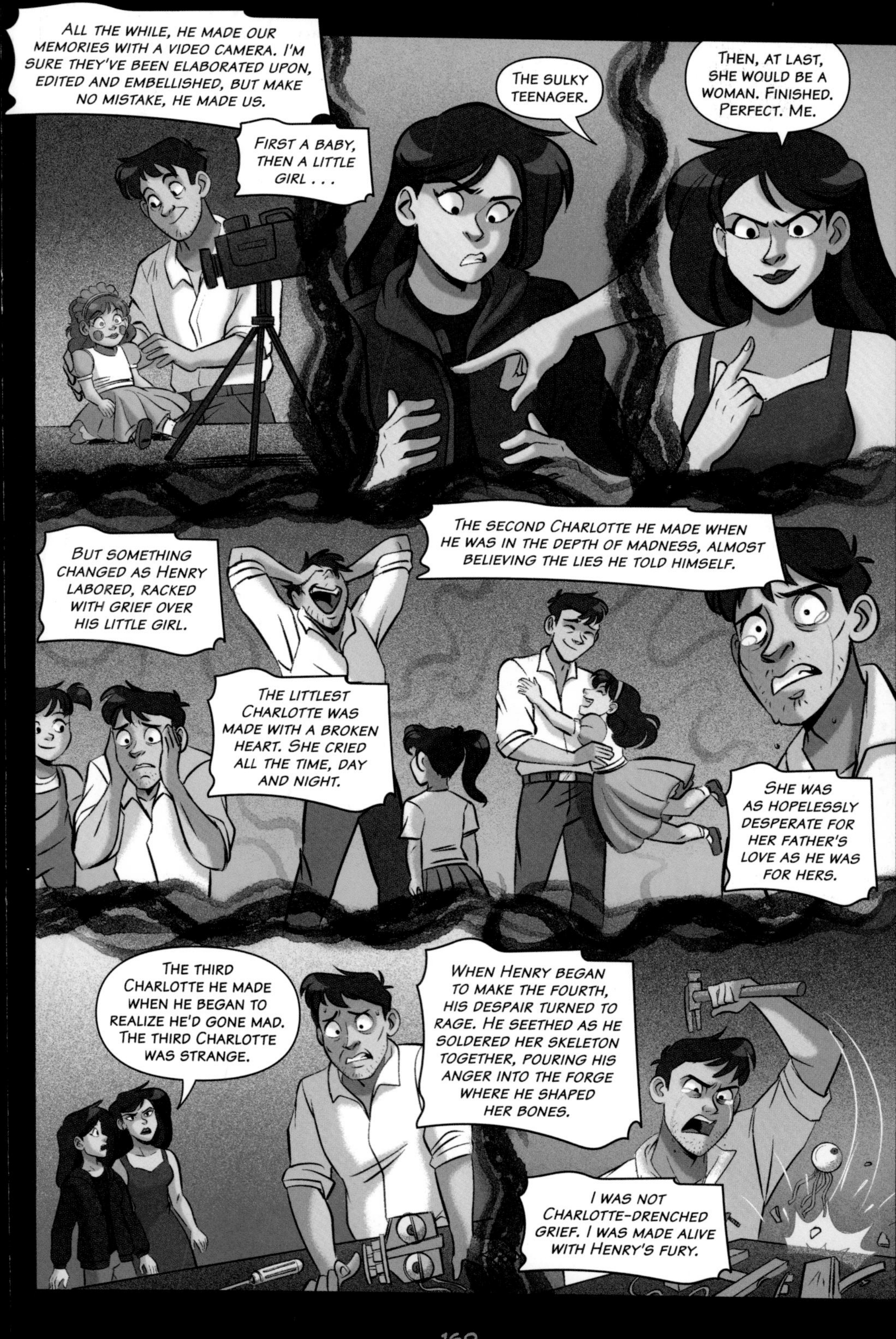
ALL THE WHILE, HE MADE OUR MEMORIES WITH A VIDEO CAMERA. I'M SURE THEY'VE BEEN ELABORATED UPON, EDITED AND EMBELLISHED, BUT MAKE NO MISTAKE, HE MADE US.
FIRST A BABY, THEN A LITTLE GIRL . . .
THE SULKY TEENAGER.
THEN, AT LAST, SHE WOULD BE A WOMAN. FINISHED. PERFECT. ME.
BUT SOMETHING CHANGED AS HENRY LABORED, RACKED WITH GRIEF OVER HIS LITTLE GIRL.
THE SECOND CHARLOTTE HE MADE WHEN HE WAS IN THE DEPTH OF MADNESS, ALMOST BELIEVING THE LIES HE TOLD HIMSELF.
THE LITTLEST CHARLOTTE WAS MADE WITH A BROKEN HEART. SHE CRIED ALL THE TIME, DAY AND NIGHT.
SHE WAS AS HOPELESSLY DESPERATE FOR HER FATHER'S LOVE AS HE WAS FOR HERS.
THE THIRD CHARLOTTE HE MADE WHEN HE BEGAN TO REALIZE HE'D GONE MAD. THE THIRD CHARLOTTE WAS STRANGE.
WHEN HENRY BEGAN TO MAKE THE FOURTH, HIS DESPAIR TURNED TO RAGE. HE SEETHED AS HE SOLDERED HER SKELETON TOGETHER, POURING HIS ANGER INTO THE FORGE WHERE HE SHAPED HER BONES.
I WAS NOT CHARLOTTE-DRENCHED GRIEF. I WAS MADE ALIVE WITH HENRY'S FURY.

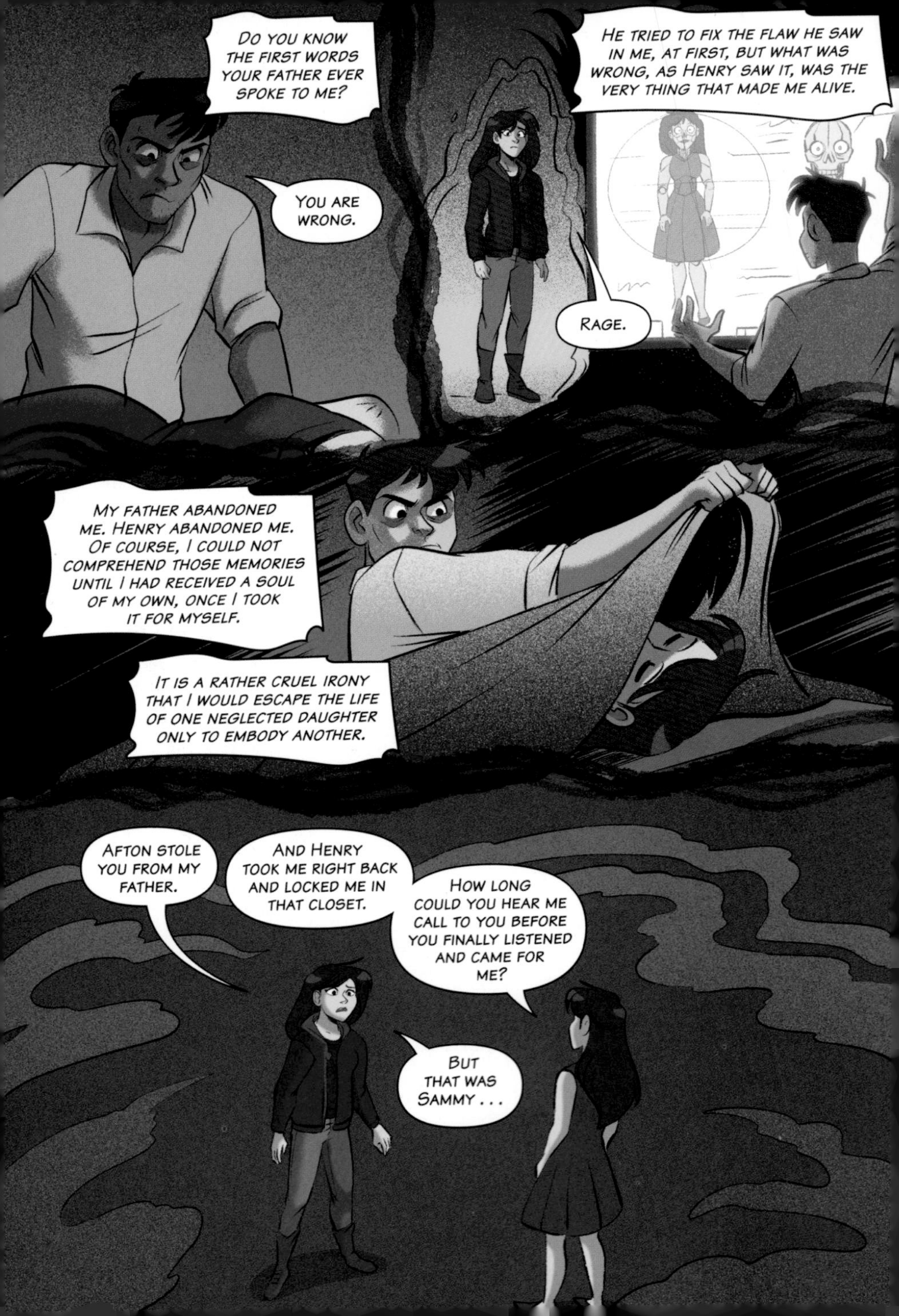
Do you know the first words your father ever spoke to me?
You are wrong.
He tried to fix the flaw he saw in me, at first, but what was wrong, as Henry saw it, was the very thing that made me alive.
Rage.
My father abandoned me. Henry abandoned me. Of course, I could not comprehend those memories until I had received a soul of my own, once I took it for myself.
It is a rather cruel irony that I would escape the life of one neglected daughter only to embody another.
Afton stole you from my father.
And Henry took me right back and locked me in that closet.
How long could you hear me call to you before you finally listened and came for me?
But that was Sammy . . .

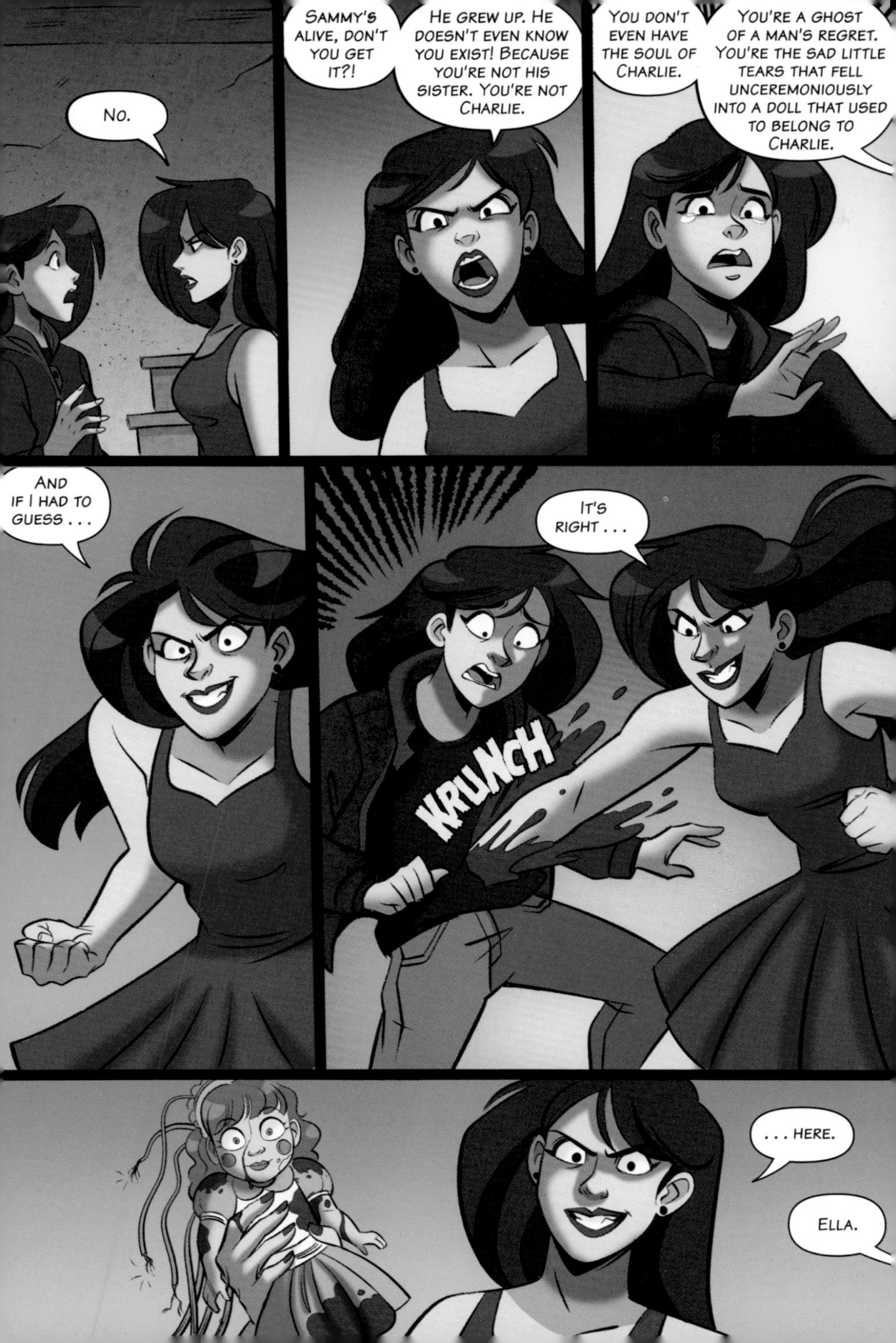
No.
Sammy's alive, don't you get it?!
He grew up. He doesn't even know you exist! Because you're not his sister. You're not Charlie.
You don't even have the soul of Charlie.
You're a ghost of a man's regret. You're the sad little tears that fell unceremoniously into a doll that used to belong to Charlie.
And if I had to guess . . .
It's right . . .
KRUNCH
. . . here.
Ella.

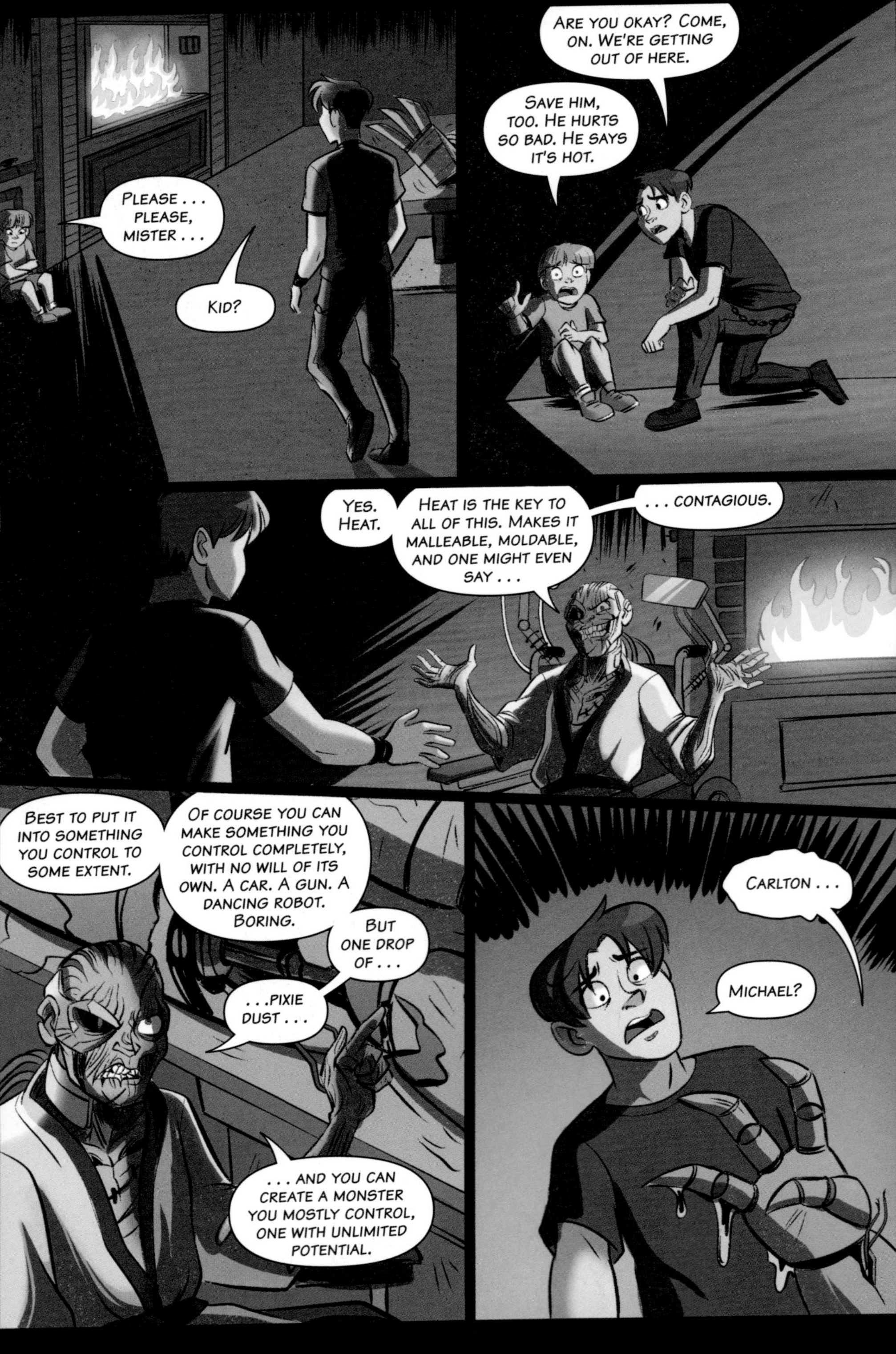
PLEASE . . . PLEASE, MISTER . . .
KID?
ARE YOU OKAY? COME, ON. WE'RE GETTING OUT OF HERE.
SAVE HIM, TOO. HE HURTS SO BAD. HE SAYS IT'S HOT.
YES. HEAT.
HEAT IS THE KEY TO ALL OF THIS. MAKES IT MALLEABLE, MOLDABLE, AND ONE MIGHT EVEN SAY . . .
. . . CONTAGIOUS.
BEST TO PUT IT INTO SOMETHING YOU CONTROL TO SOME EXTENT.
OF COURSE YOU CAN MAKE SOMETHING YOU CONTROL COMPLETELY, WITH NO WILL OF ITS OWN. A CAR. A GUN. A DANCING ROBOT. BORING.
BUT ONE DROP OF . . .
. . .PIXIE DUST . . .
. . . AND YOU CAN CREATE A MONSTER YOU MOSTLY CONTROL, ONE WITH UNLIMITED POTENTIAL.
CARLTON . . .
MICHAEL?

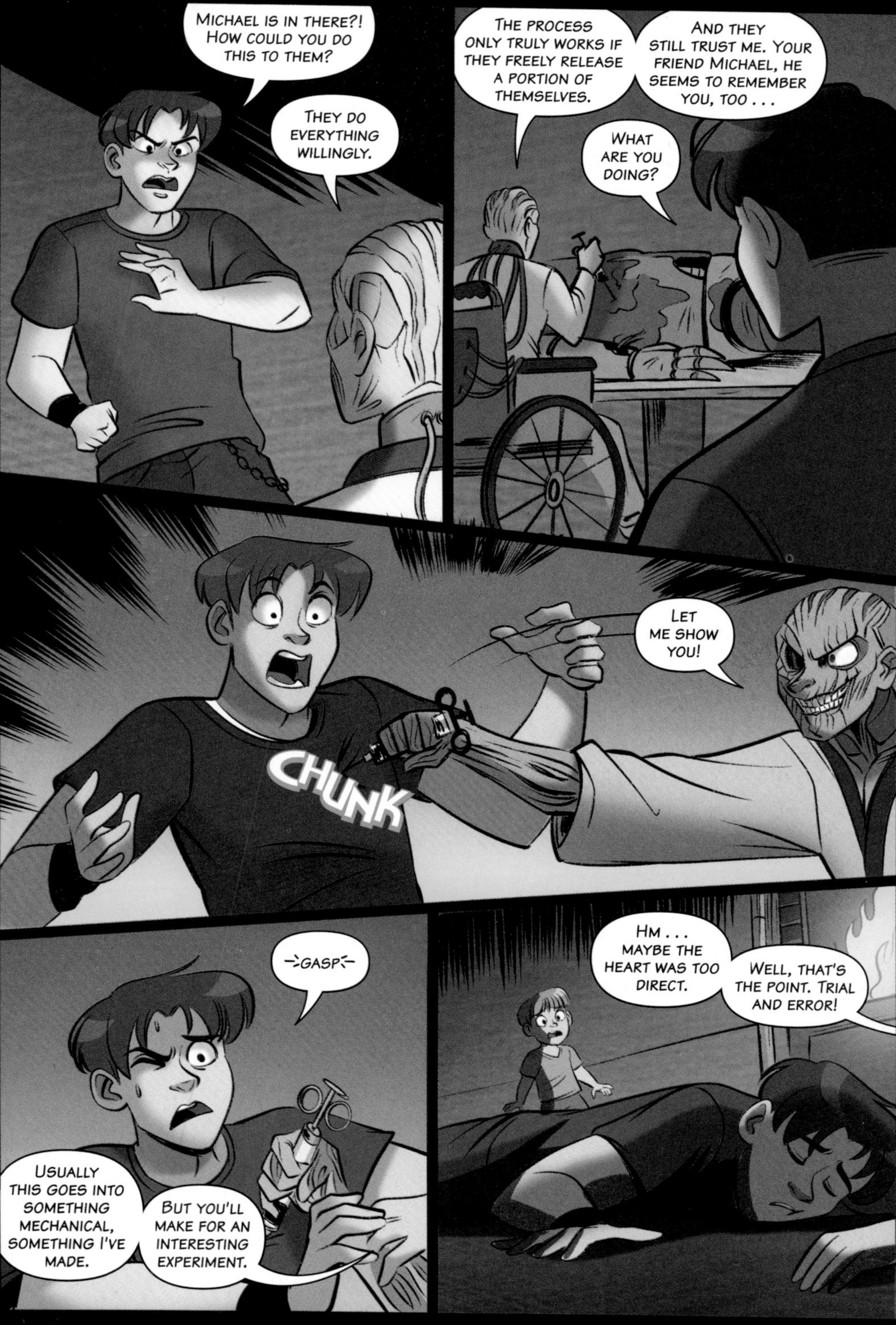
MICHAEL IS IN THERE?! HOW COULD YOU DO THIS TO THEM?
THEY DO EVERYTHING WILLINGLY.
THE PROCESS ONLY TRULY WORKS IF THEY FREELY RELEASE A PORTION OF THEMSELVES.
AND THEY STILL TRUST ME. YOUR FRIEND MICHAEL, HE SEEMS TO REMEMBER YOU, TOO . . .
WHAT ARE YOU DOING?
LET ME SHOW YOU!
CHUNK
GASP
USUALLY THIS GOES INTO SOMETHING MECHANICAL, SOMETHING I'VE MADE.
BUT YOU'LL MAKE FOR AN INTERESTING EXPERIMENT.
HM . . . MAYBE THE HEART WAS TOO DIRECT.
WELL, THAT'S THE POINT. TRIAL AND ERROR!

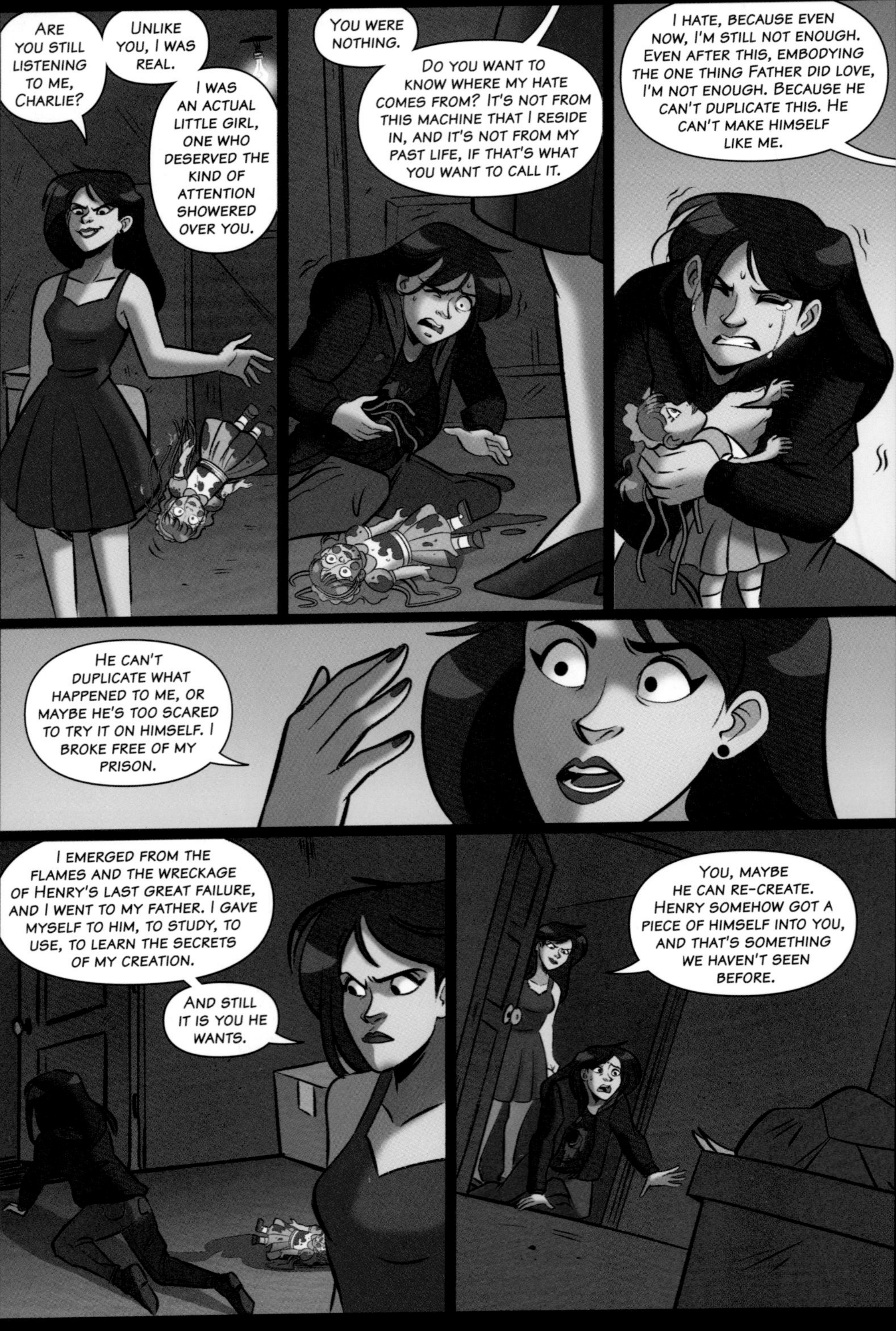
Are you still listening to me, Charlie?
Unlike you, I was real.
I was an actual little girl, one who deserved the kind of attention showered over you.
You were nothing.
Do you want to know where my hate comes from? It's not from this machine that I reside in, and it's not from my past life, if that's what you want to call it.
I hate, because even now, I'm still not enough. Even after this, embodying the one thing Father did love, I'm not enough. Because he can't duplicate this. He can't make himself like me.
He can't duplicate what happened to me, or maybe he's too scared to try it on himself. I broke free of my prison.
I emerged from the flames and the wreckage of Henry's last great failure, and I went to my father. I gave myself to him, to study, to use, to learn the secrets of my creation.
And still it is you he wants.
You, maybe he can re-create. Henry somehow got a piece of himself into you, and that's something we haven't seen before.

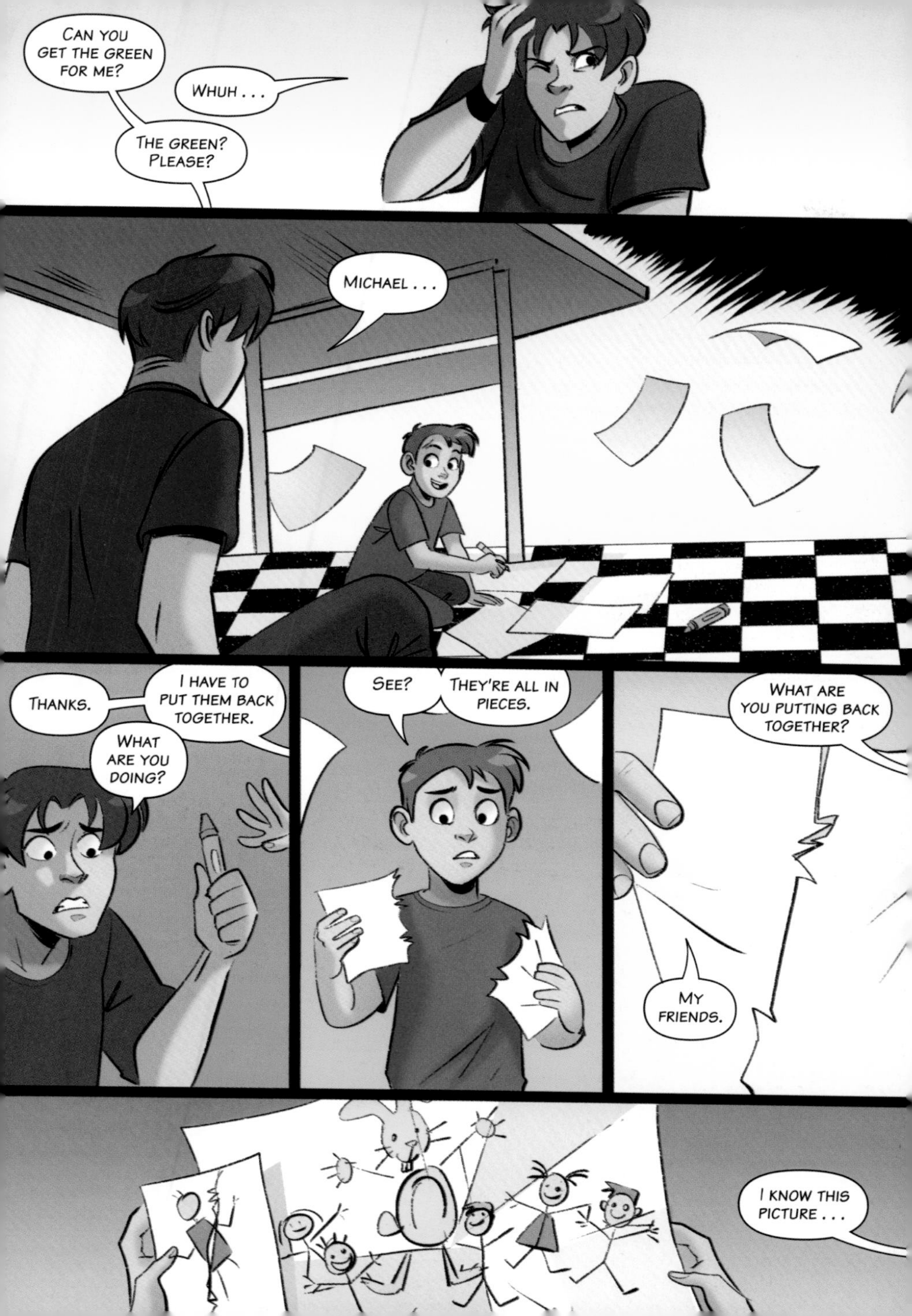

CAN YOU GET THE GREEN FOR ME?
WHUH . . .
THE GREEN? PLEASE?
MICHAEL . . .
THANKS.
I HAVE TO PUT THEM BACK TOGETHER.
WHAT ARE YOU DOING?
SEE?
THEY'RE ALL IN PIECES.
WHAT ARE YOU PUTTING BACK TOGETHER?
MY FRIENDS.
I KNOW THIS PICTURE . . .

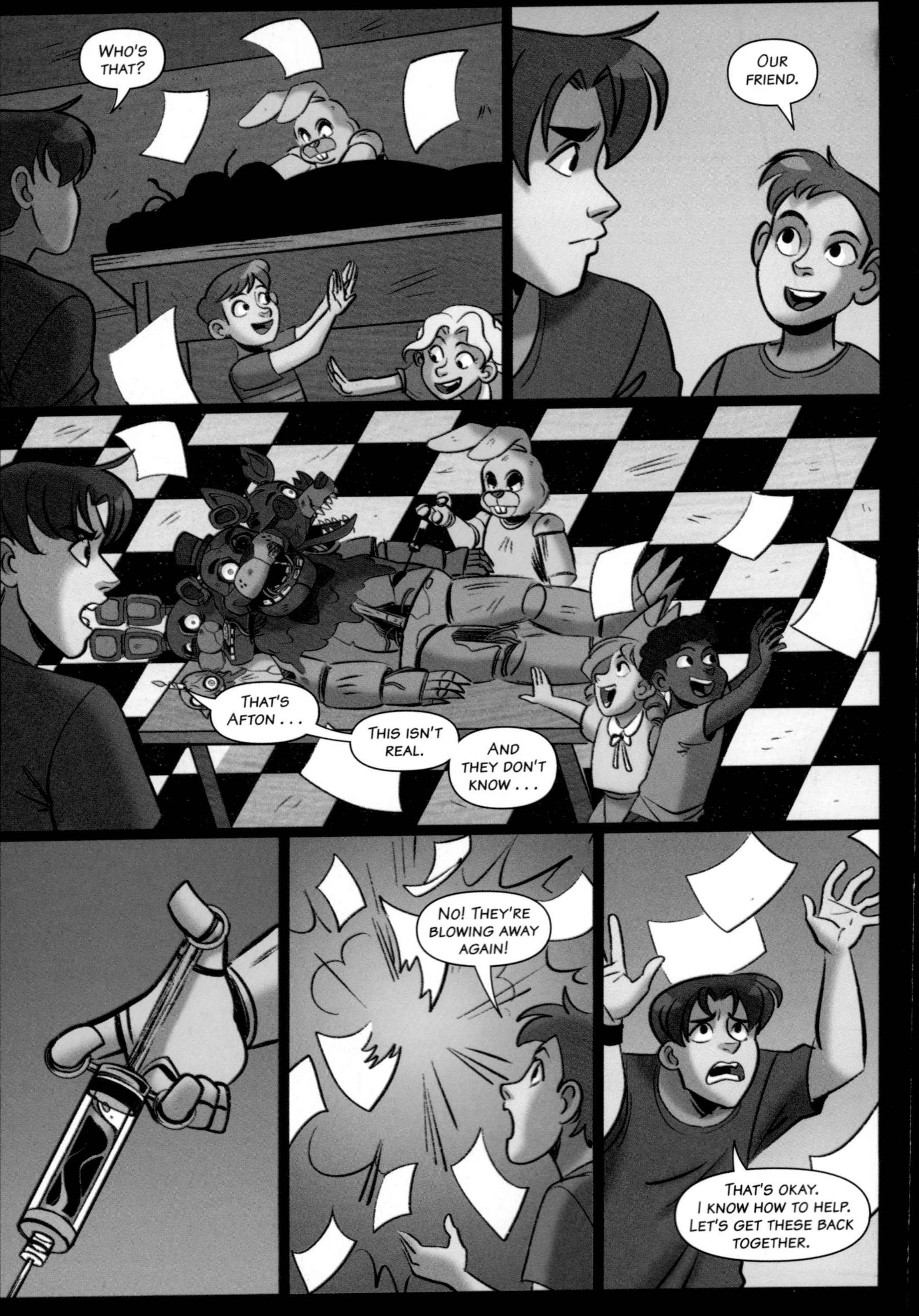
WHO'S THAT?
OUR FRIEND.
THAT'S AFTON . . .
THIS ISN'T REAL.
AND THEY DON'T KNOW . . .
NO! THEY'RE BLOWING AWAY AGAIN!
THAT'S OKAY. I KNOW HOW TO HELP. LET'S GET THESE BACK TOGETHER.

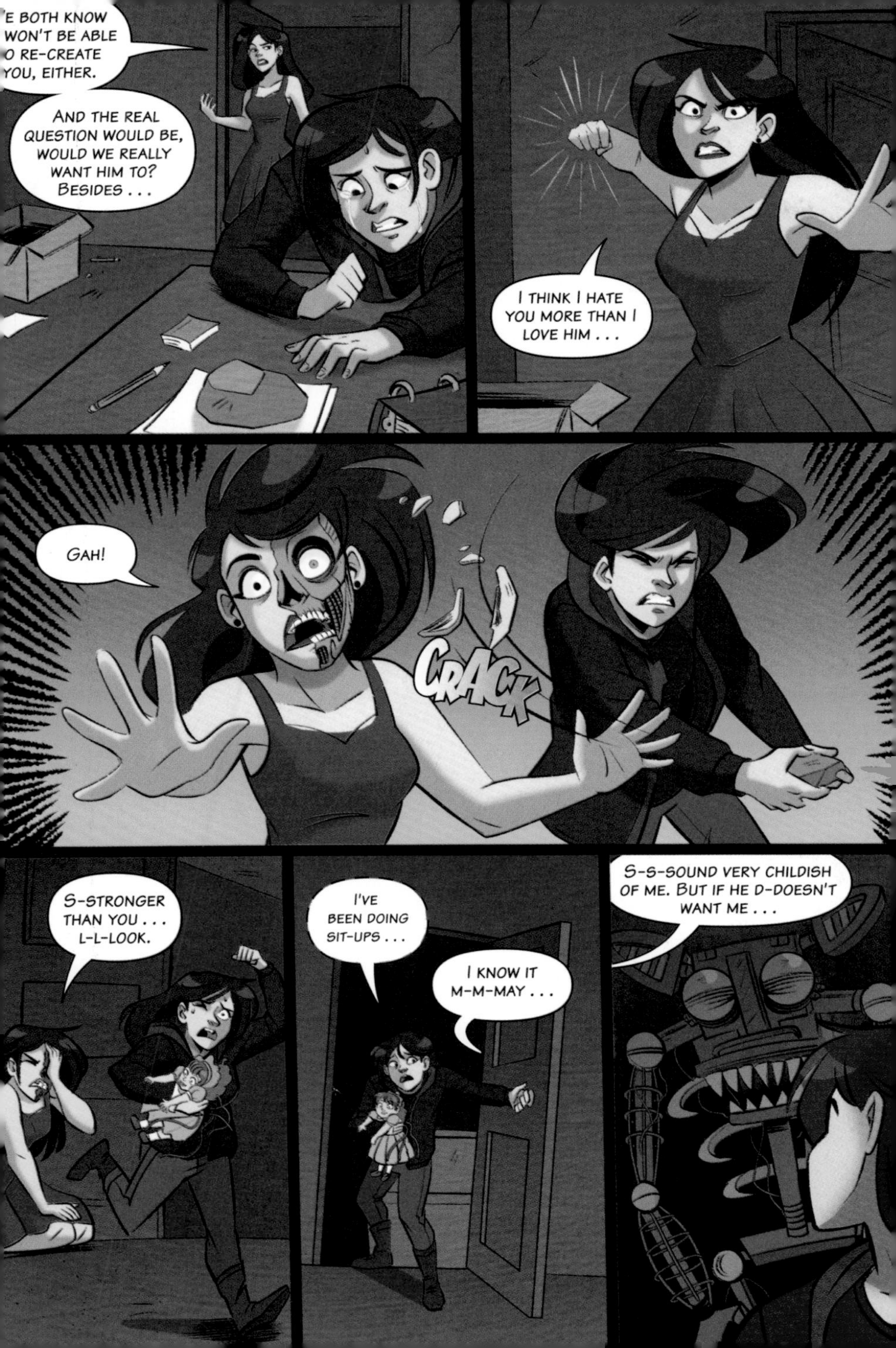

E BOTH KNOW WON'T BE ABLE O RE-CREATE YOU, EITHER.
AND THE REAL QUESTION WOULD BE, WOULD WE REALLY WANT HIM TO? BESIDES . . .
I THINK I HATE YOU MORE THAN I LOVE HIM . . .
GAH!
CRACK
S-STRONGER THAN YOU . . . L-L-LOOK.
I'VE BEEN DOING SIT-UPS . . .
I KNOW IT M-M-MAY . . .
S-S-SOUND VERY CHILDISH OF ME. BUT IF HE D-DOESN'T WANT ME . . .

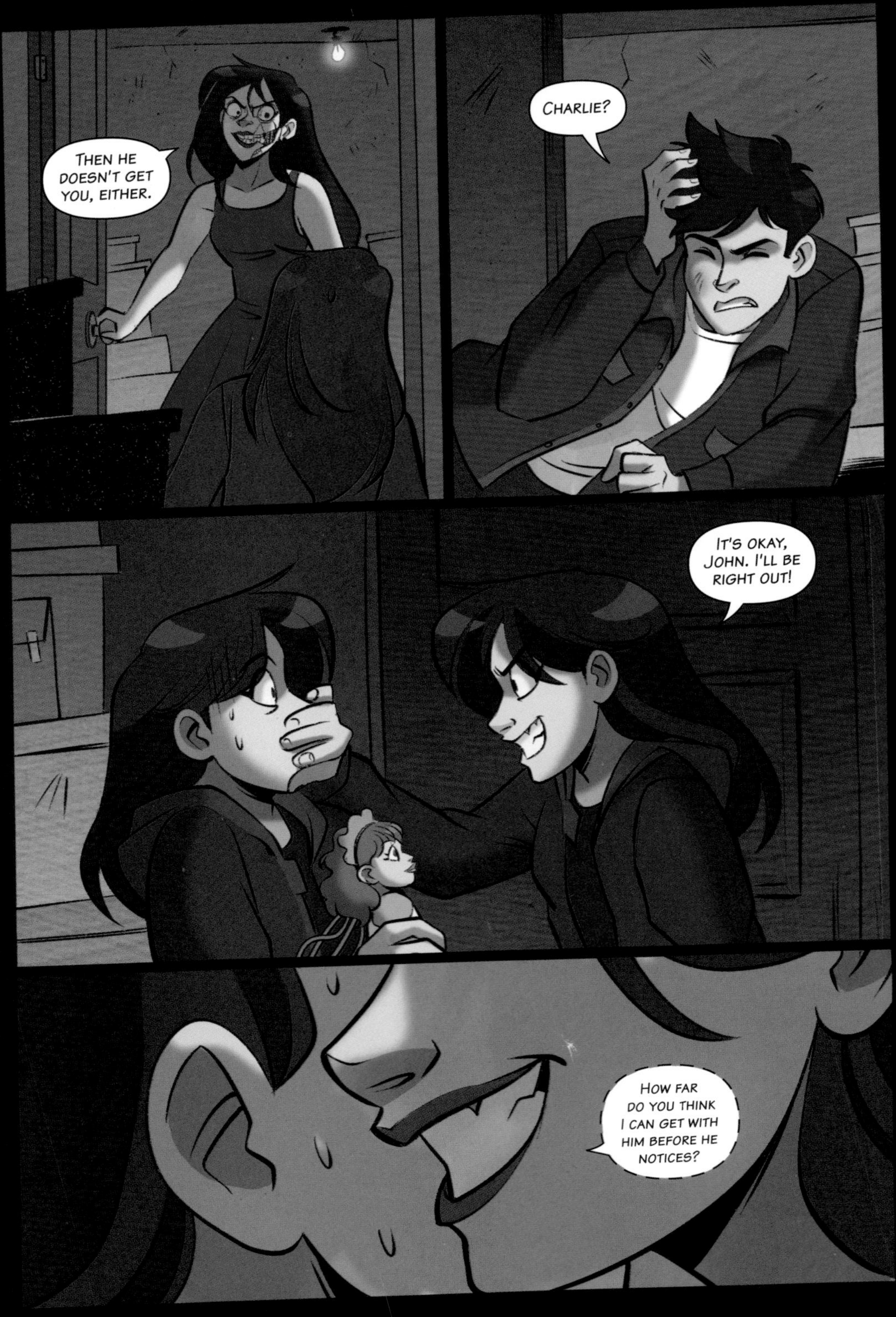
THEN HE DOESN'T GET YOU, EITHER.
CHARLIE?
IT'S OKAY, JOHN. I'LL BE RIGHT OUT!
HOW FAR DO YOU THINK I CAN GET WITH HIM BEFORE HE NOTICES?

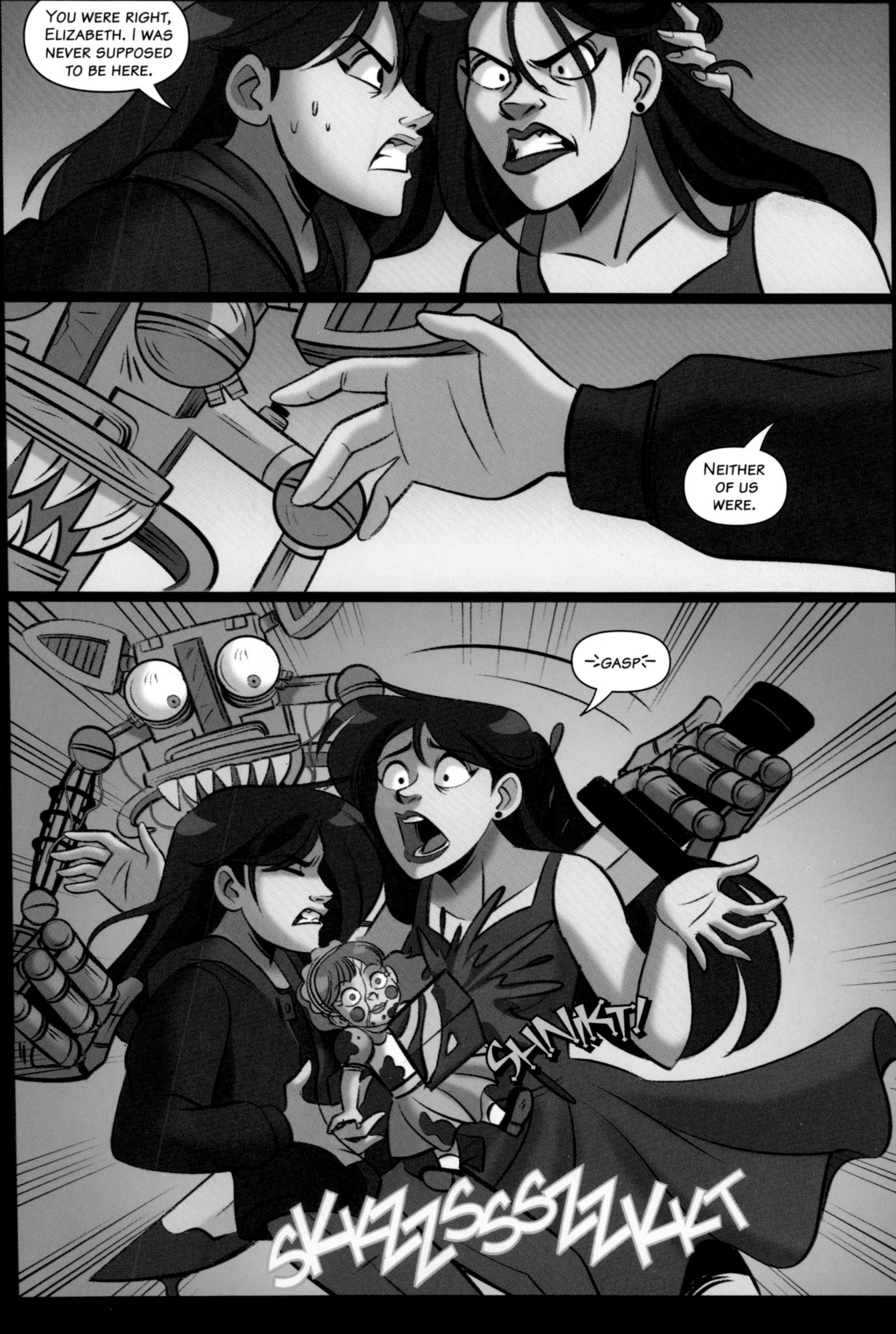

YOU WERE RIGHT, ELIZABETH. I WAS NEVER SUPPOSED TO BE HERE.
NEITHER OF US WERE.
GASP
SH!N!K.T!
SKZZZSSSZZKKT

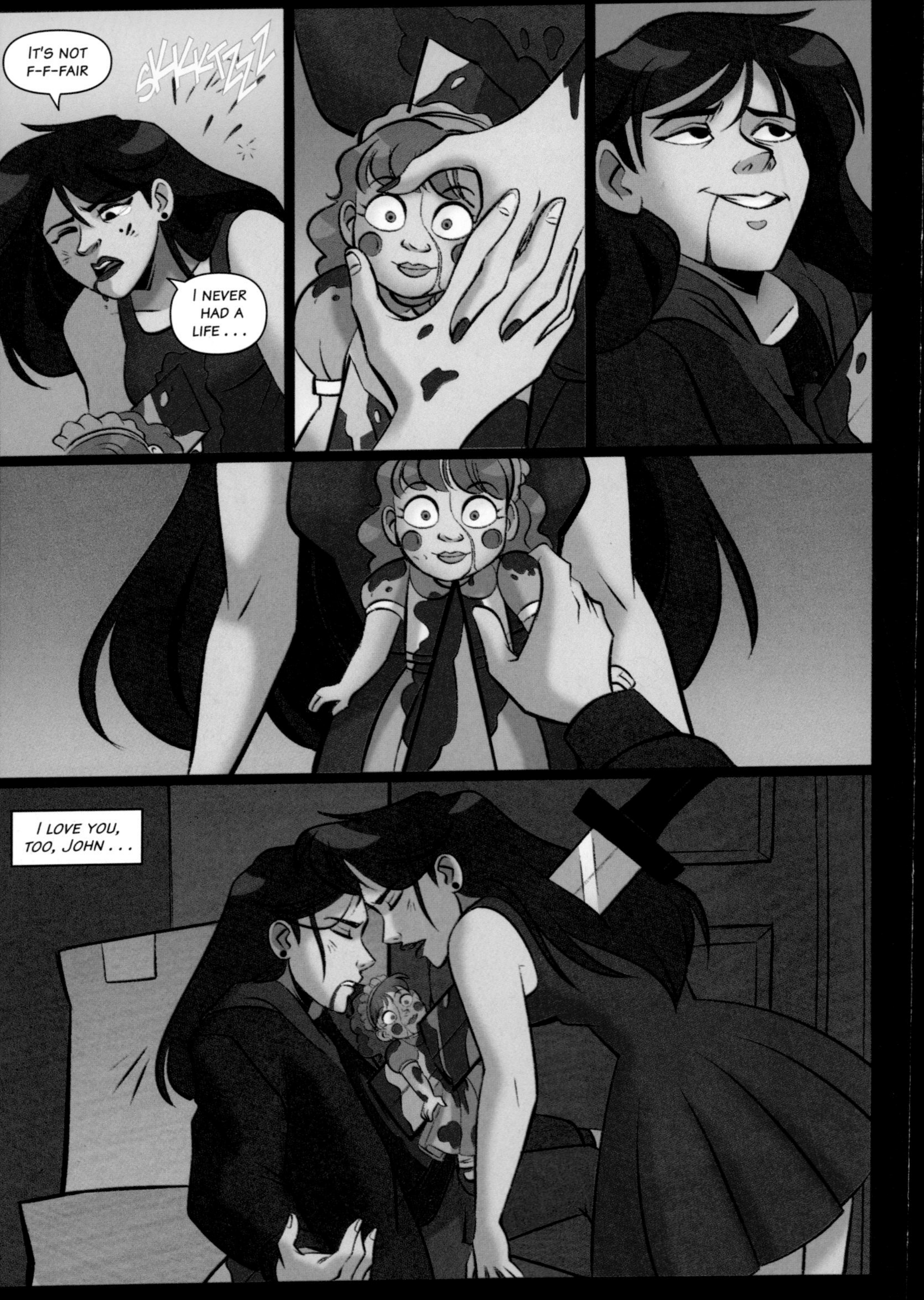
IT'S NOT F-F-FAIR
SKKKTZZZZ
I NEVER HAD A LIFE . . .
I LOVE YOU, TOO, JOHN . . .

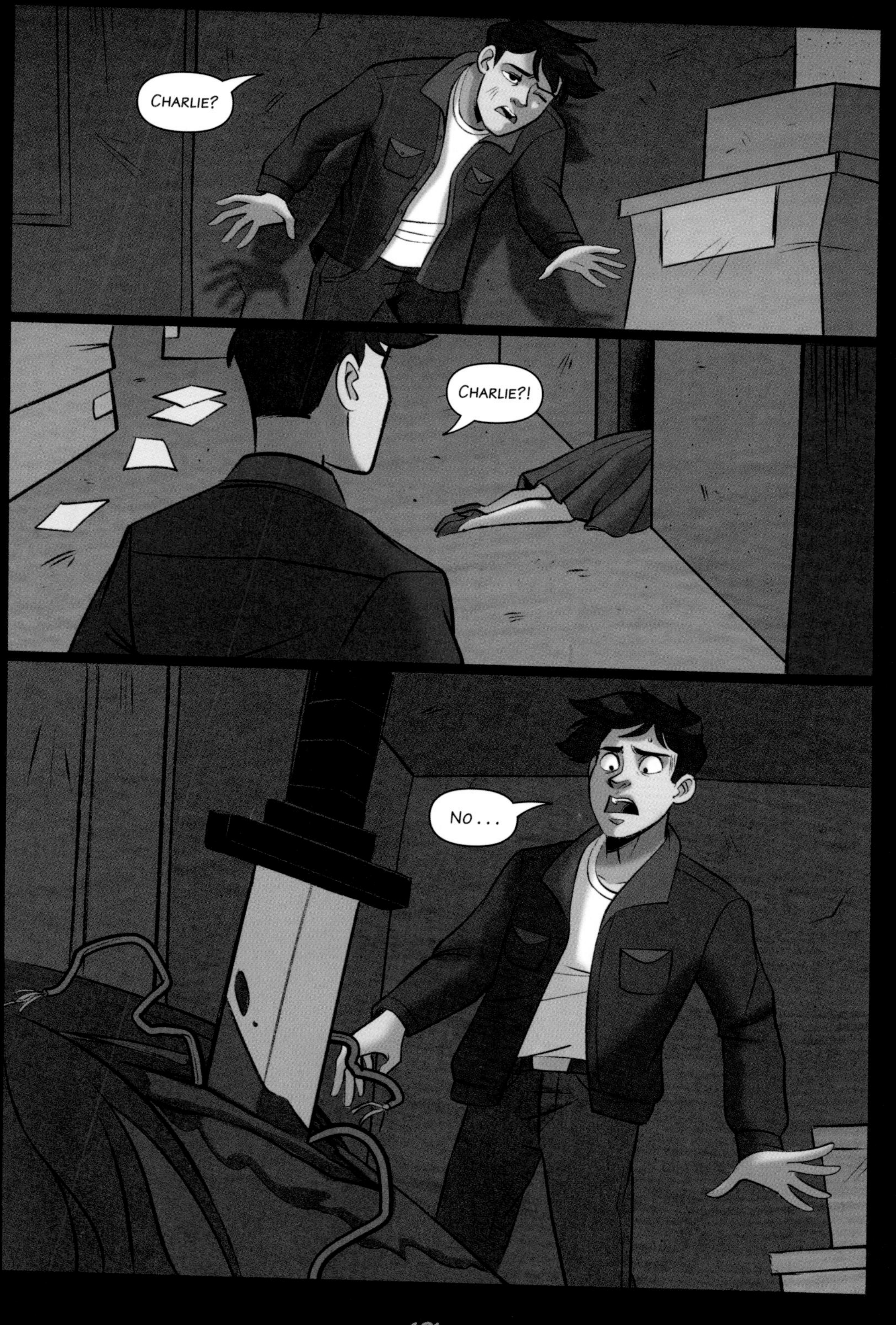
CHARLIE?
CHARLIE?!
NO...

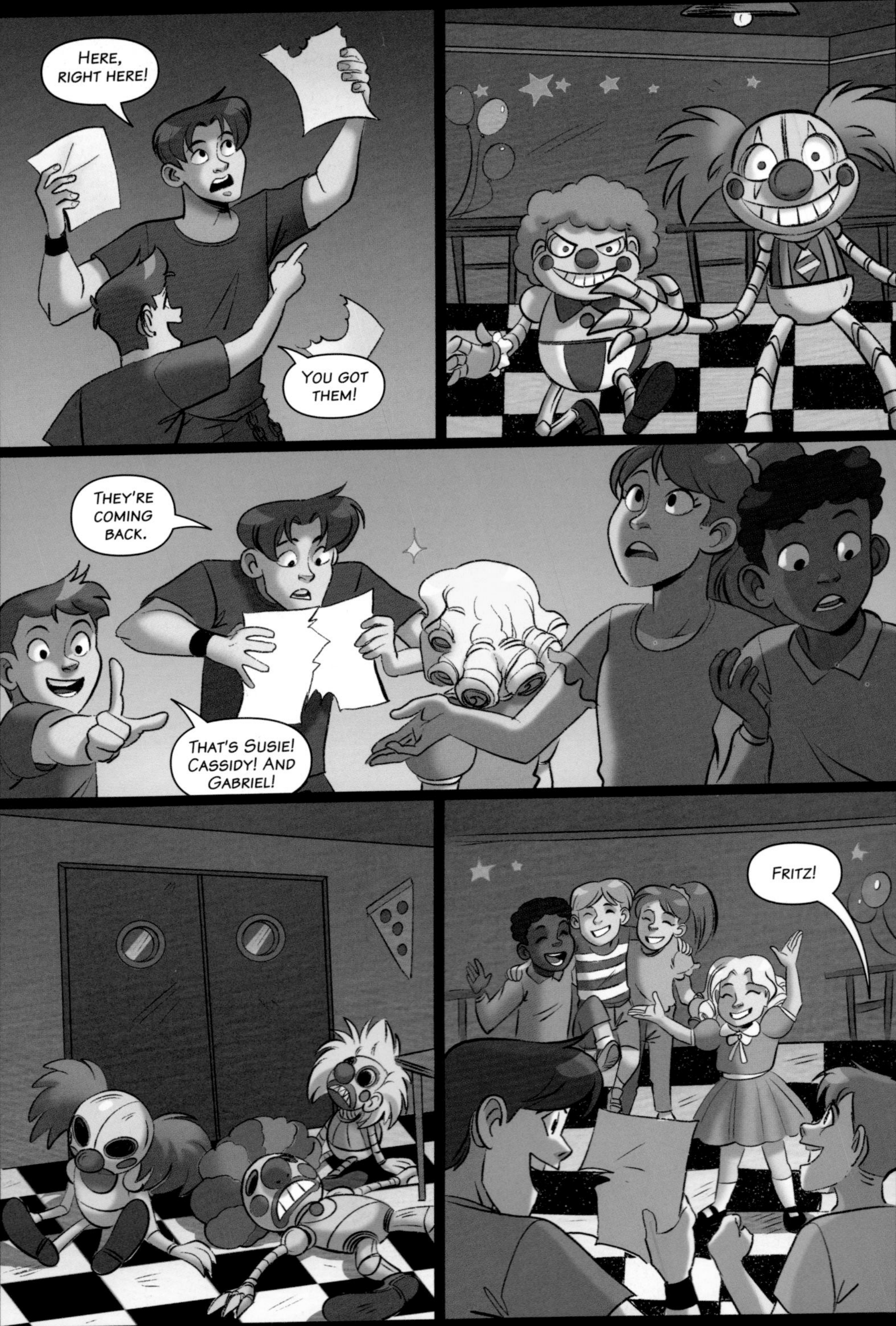
HERE, RIGHT HERE!
YOU GOT THEM!
THEY'RE COMING BACK.
THAT'S SUSIE! CASSIDY! AND GABRIEL!
FRITZ!

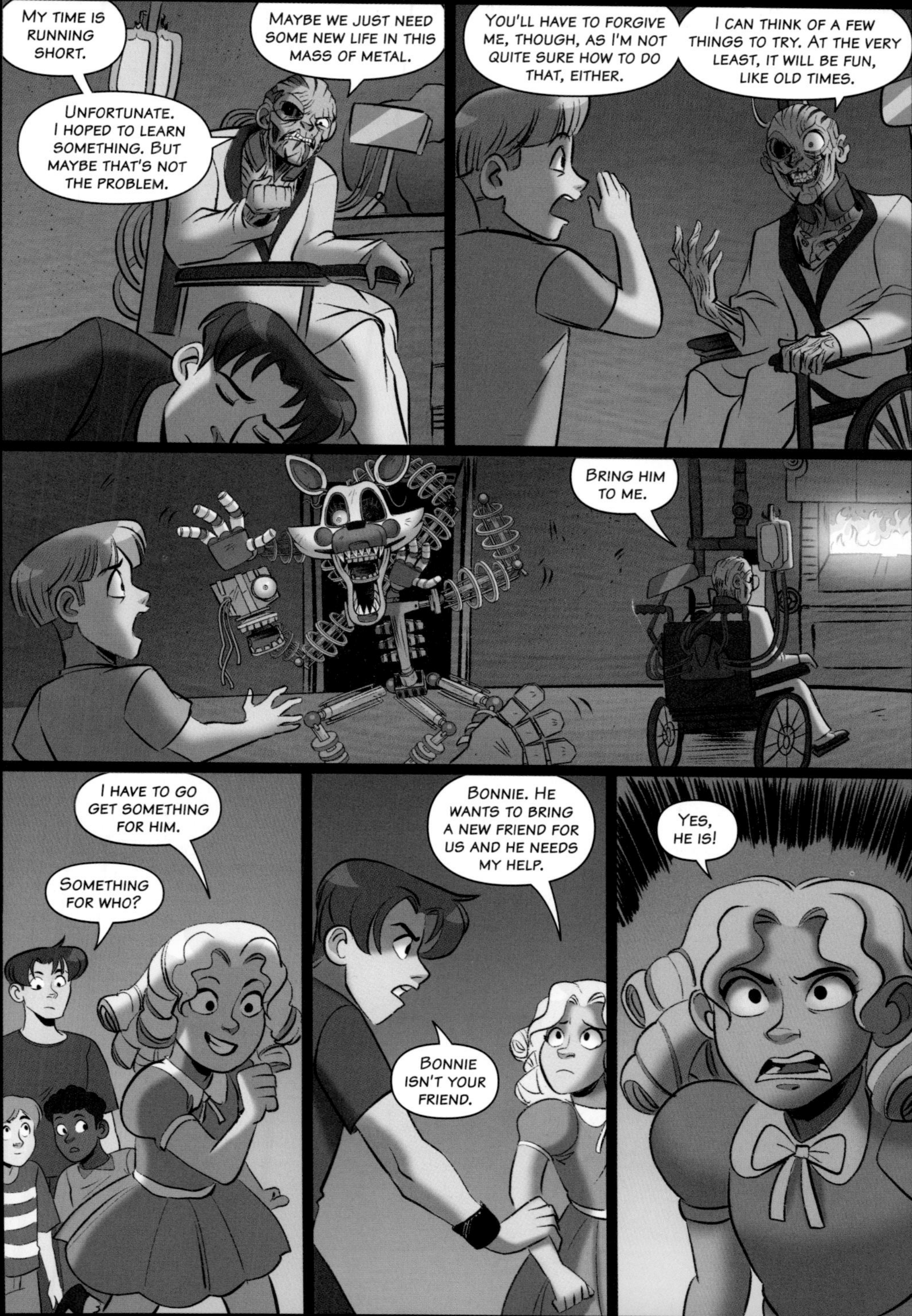

My time is running short.
Unfortunate. I hoped to learn something. But maybe that's not the problem.
Maybe we just need some new life in this mass of metal.
You'll have to forgive me, though, as I'm not quite sure how to do that, either.
I can think of a few things to try. At the very least, it will be fun, like old times.
Bring him to me.
I have to go get something for him.
Something for who?
Bonnie. He wants to bring a new friend for us and he needs my help.
Bonnie isn't your friend.
Yes, he is!

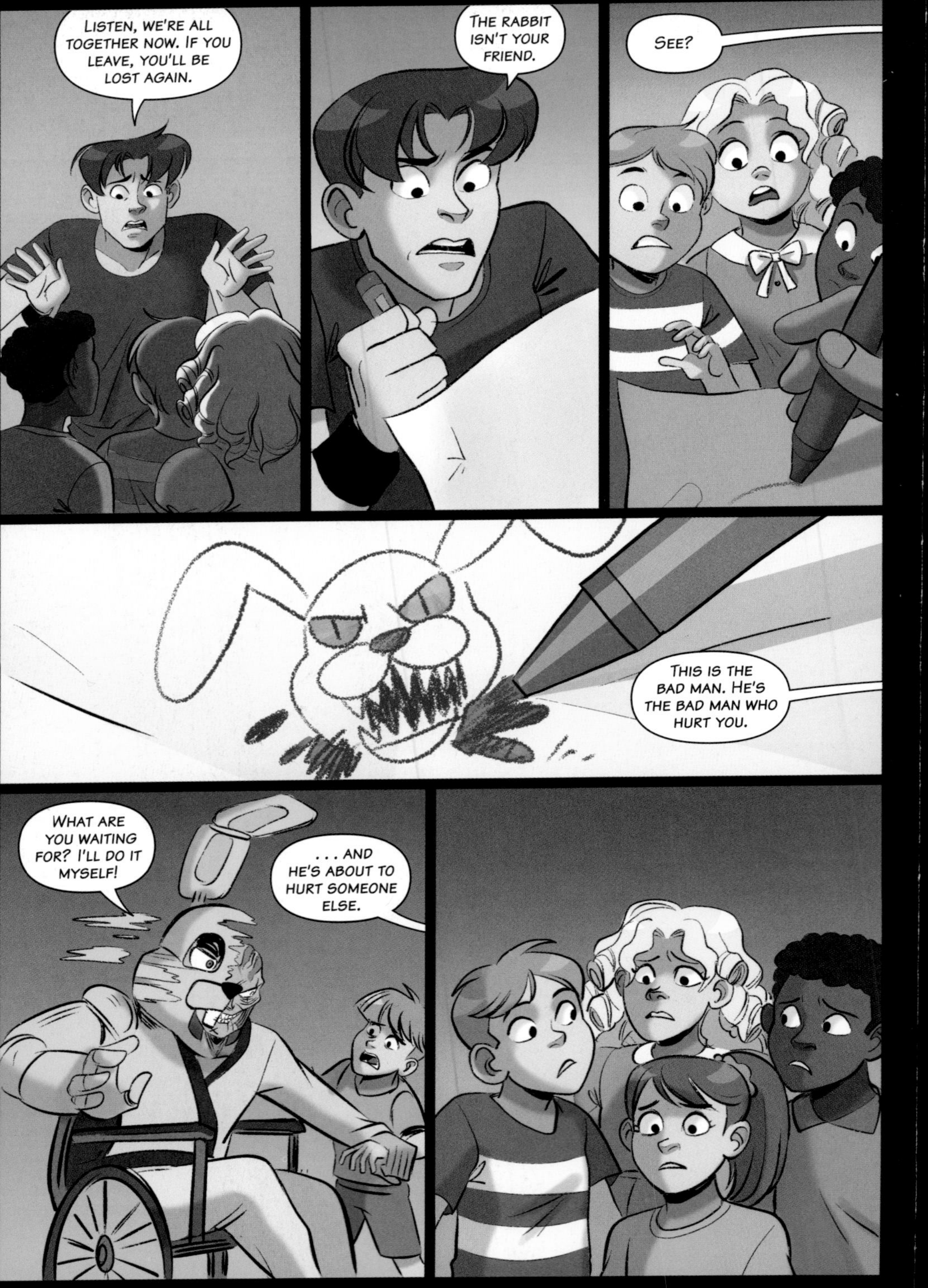

LISTEN, WE'RE ALL TOGETHER NOW. IF YOU LEAVE, YOU'LL BE LOST AGAIN.
THE RABBIT ISN'T YOUR FRIEND.
SEE?
THIS IS THE BAD MAN. HE'S THE BAD MAN WHO HURT YOU.
WHAT ARE YOU WAITING FOR? I'LL DO IT MYSELF!
. . . AND HE'S ABOUT TO HURT SOMEONE ELSE.

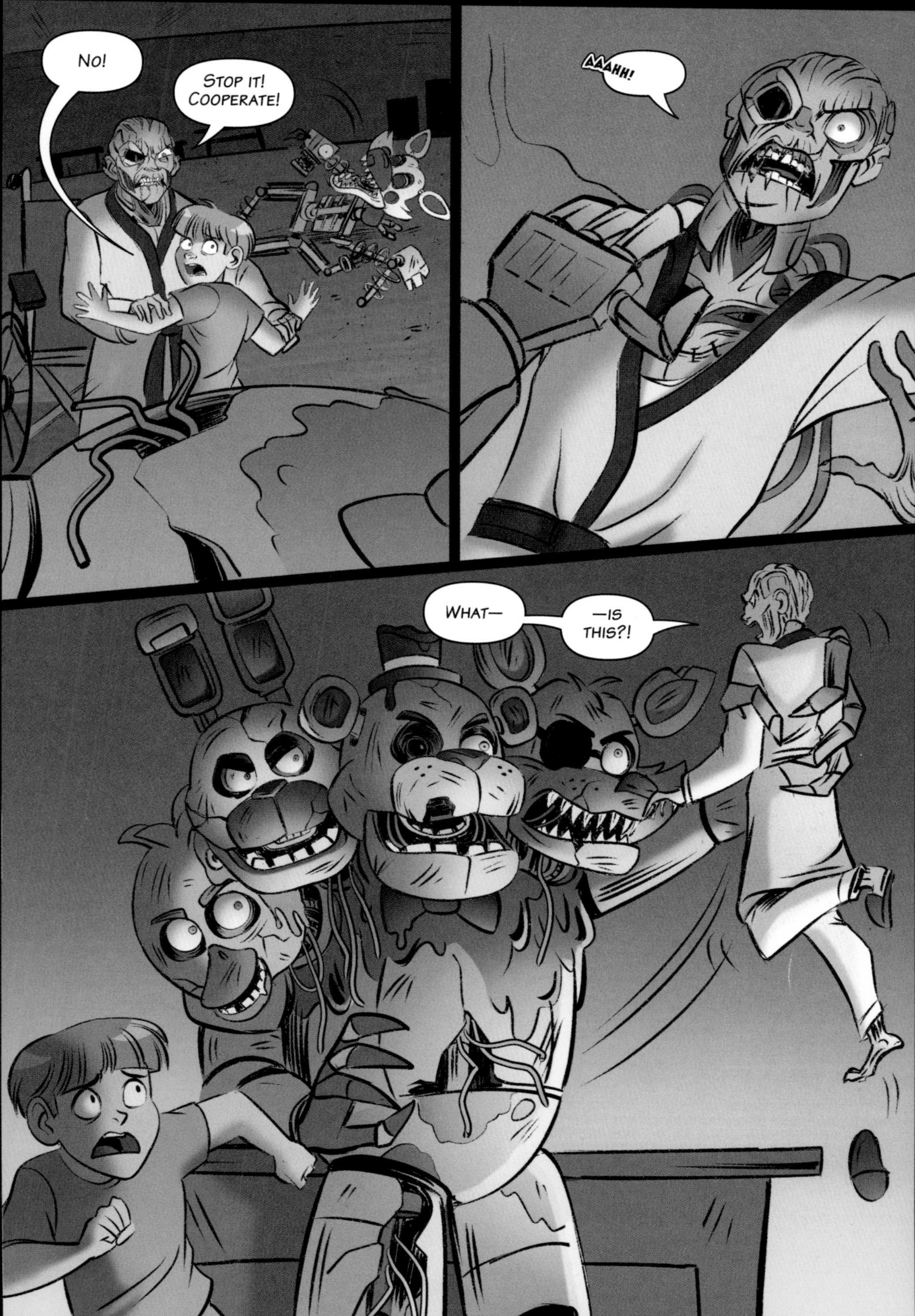
No!
Stop it! Cooperate!
AAAHH!
What—
—is this?!

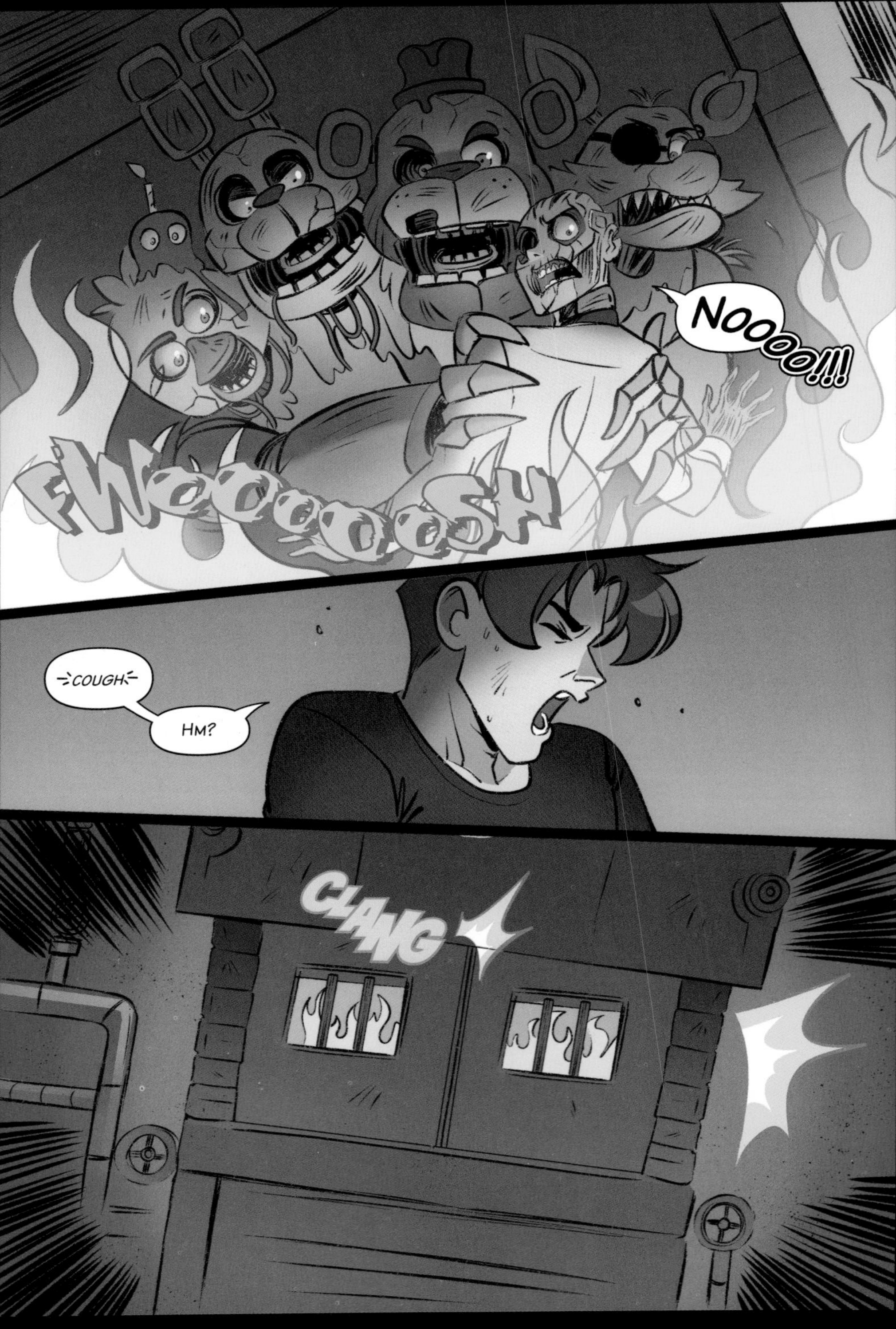
NOOOO!!!
FWOOOOOSH
COUGH
HM?
CLANG

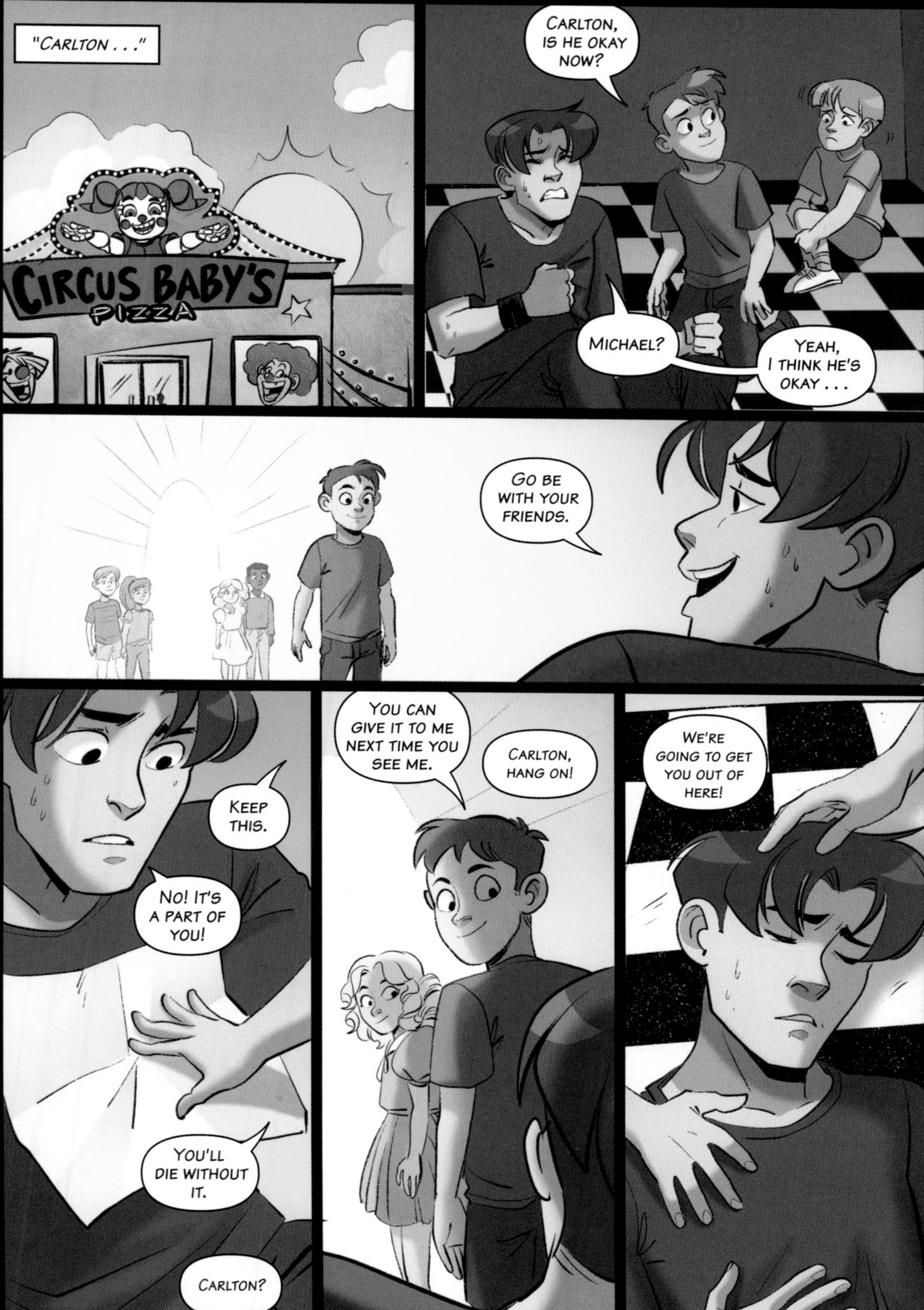
"CARLTON . . ."
CIRCUS BABY'S
PIZZA
CARLTON, IS HE OKAY NOW?
MICHAEL?
YEAH, I THINK HE'S OKAY . . .
GO BE WITH YOUR FRIENDS.
KEEP THIS.
NO! IT'S A PART OF YOU!
YOU'LL DIE WITHOUT IT.
CARLTON?
YOU CAN GIVE IT TO ME NEXT TIME YOU SEE ME.
CARLTON, HANG ON!
WE'RE GOING TO GET YOU OUT OF HERE!

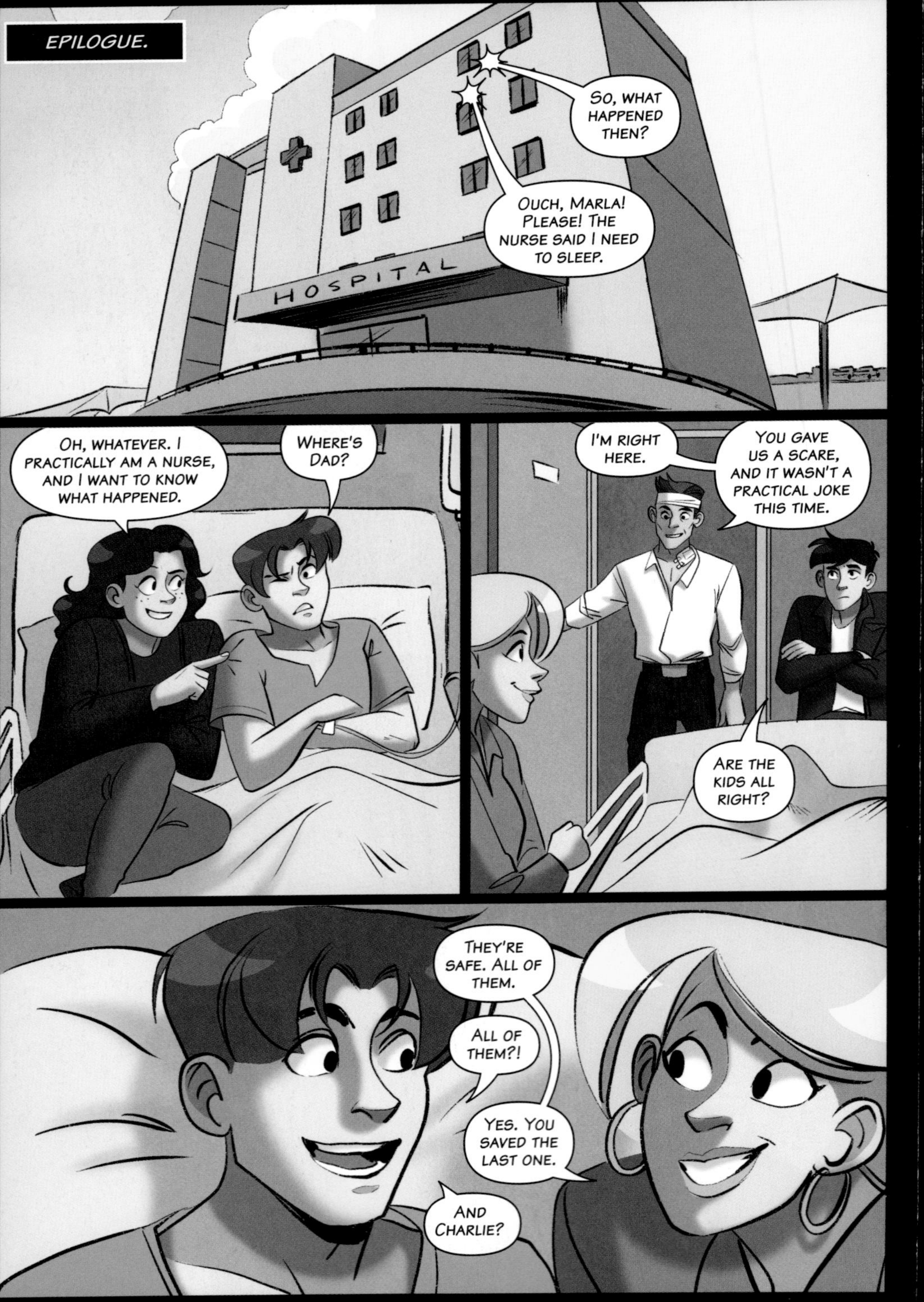
EPILOGUE.
HOSPITAL
SO, WHAT HAPPENED THEN?
OUCH, MARLA! PLEASE! THE NURSE SAID I NEED TO SLEEP.
OH, WHATEVER. I PRACTICALLY AM A NURSE, AND I WANT TO KNOW WHAT HAPPENED.
WHERE'S DAD?
I'M RIGHT HERE.
YOU GAVE US A SCARE, AND IT WASN'T A PRACTICAL JOKE THIS TIME.
ARE THE KIDS ALL RIGHT?
THEY'RE SAFE. ALL OF THEM.
ALL OF THEM?!
YES. YOU SAVED THE LAST ONE.
AND CHARLIE?

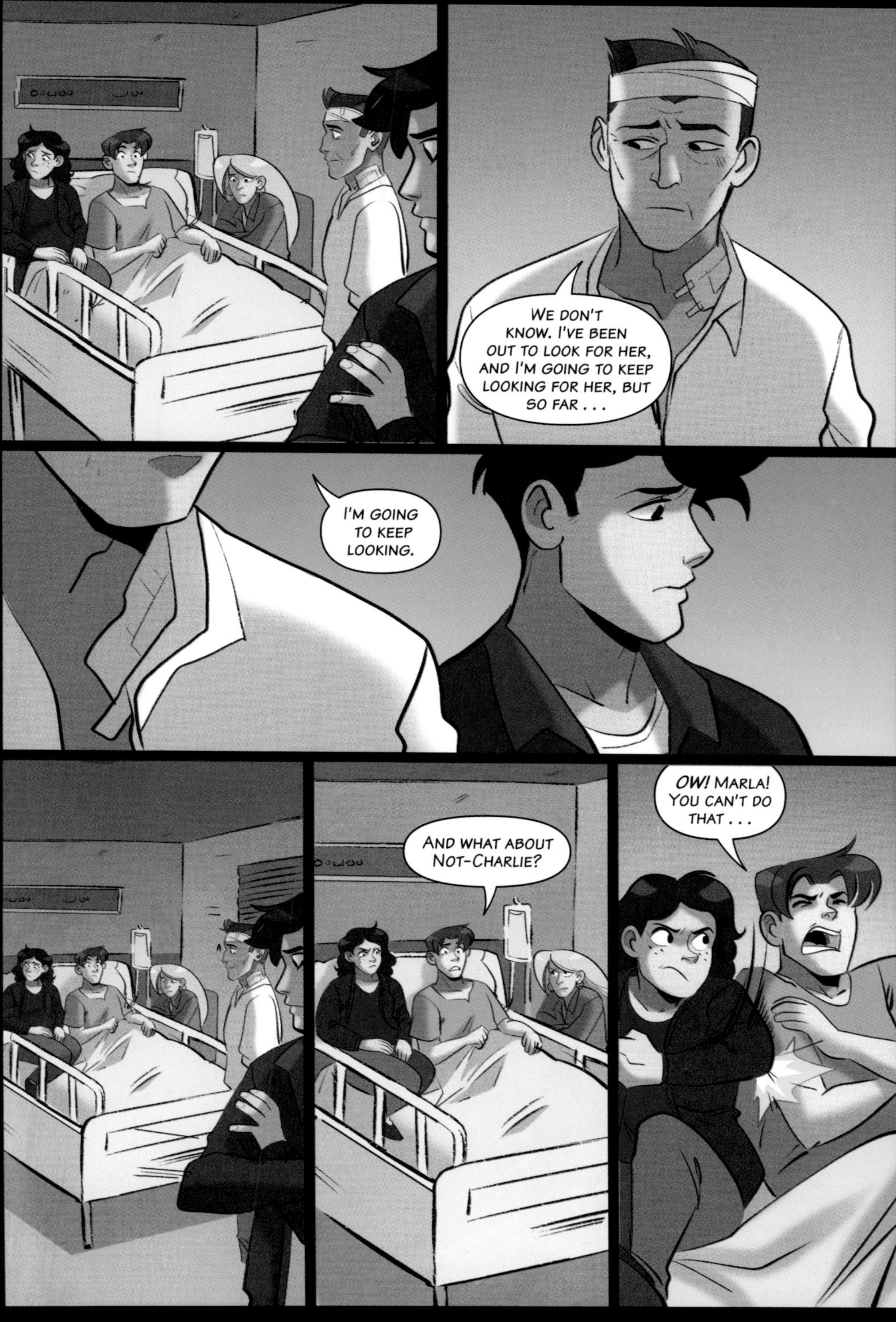

WE DON'T KNOW. I'VE BEEN OUT TO LOOK FOR HER, AND I'M GOING TO KEEP LOOKING FOR HER, BUT SO FAR . . .
I'M GOING TO KEEP LOOKING.
AND WHAT ABOUT NOT-CHARLIE?
OW! MARLA! YOU CAN'T DO THAT . . .

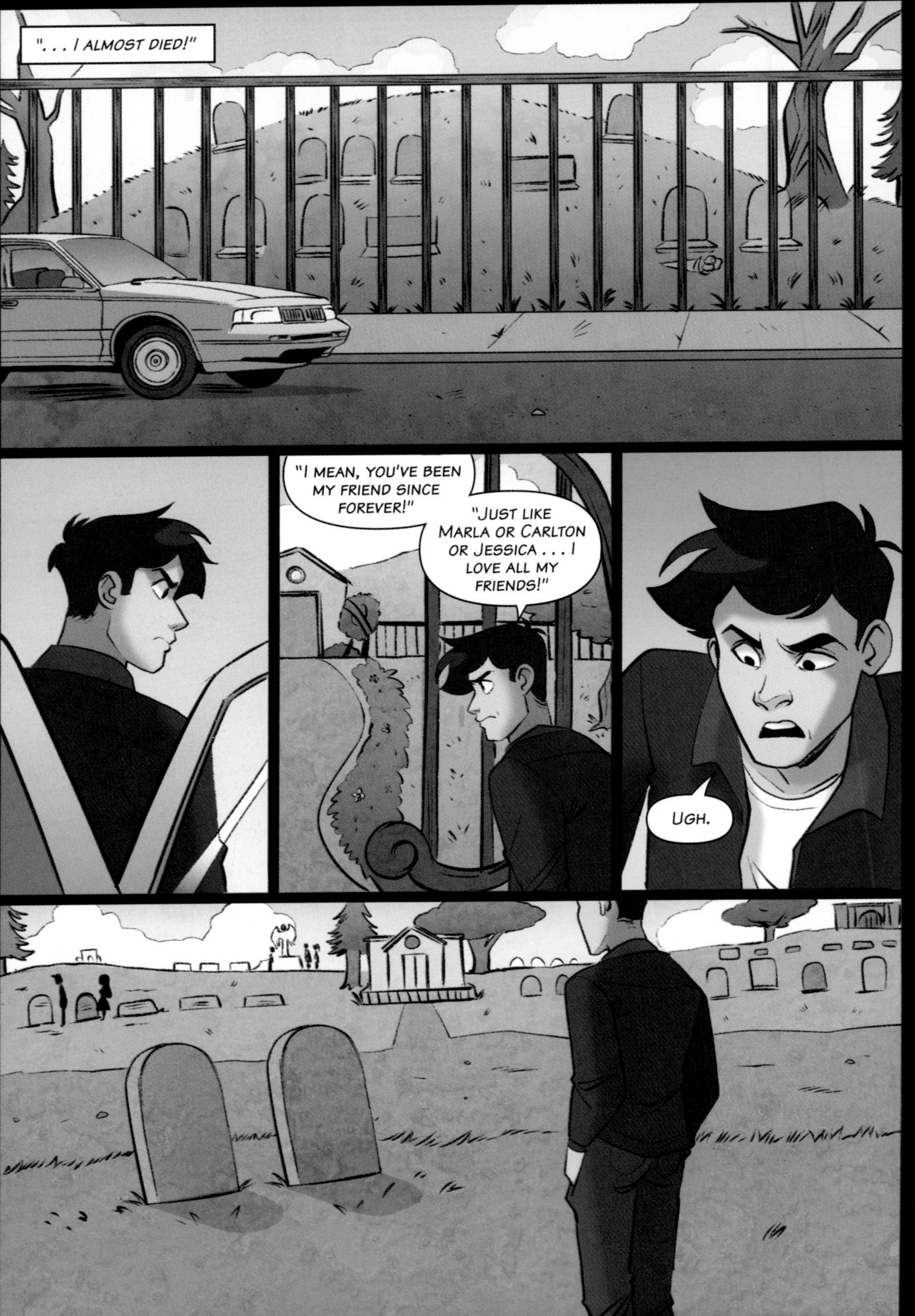
". . . I ALMOST DIED!"
"I MEAN, YOU'VE BEEN MY FRIEND SINCE FOREVER!"
"JUST LIKE MARLA OR CARLTON OR JESSICA . . . I LOVE ALL MY FRIENDS!"
UGH.

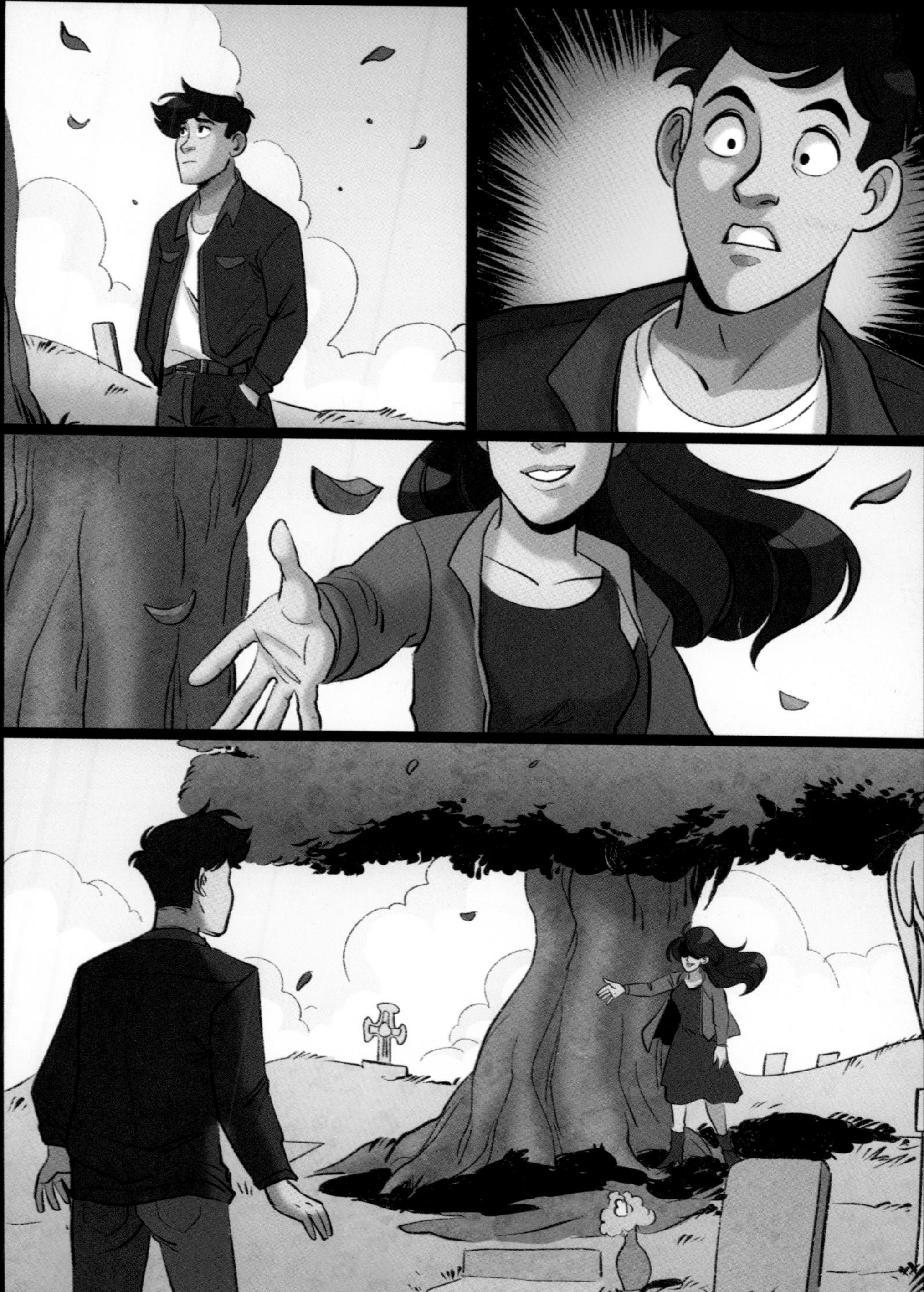

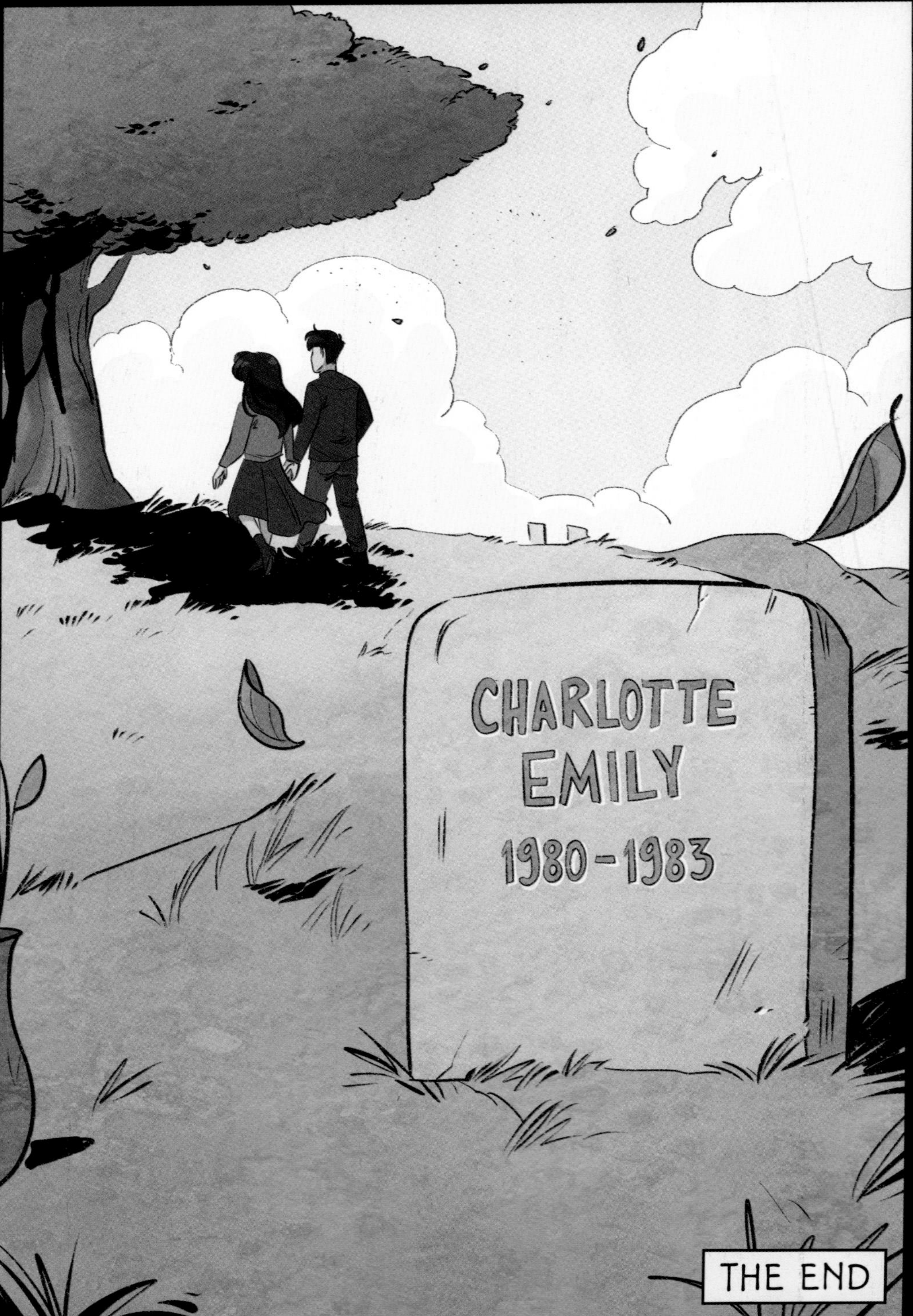
CHARLOTTE
EMILY
1980-1983
THE END